THE SEAL OF SULAYMAN

The Fires of Qaf: Book Two

Kyro Dean & Laya V Smith

Eight Moons Publishing

Published in the United States by Eight Moons Publishing, LLC.

Paperback ISBN: 978-1-957475-04-2

EBook ISBN: 978-1-957475-03-5

Printed in the United States of America.

www.eightmoonspublishing.com

CONTENTS

For my son, my rambunctious little Bakr. May no darkness ever dim the brilliant light of your smile.
And for my daughter. You are strong, funny, beautiful, and so very smart. Whether you end up a princess or a dragon slayer, or both, your mommy will always be right behind you cheering you on.
-Laya V Smith

This book's dedication is for my daughters. I want you to know you can be strong and smart and independent and still make mistakes and downright dumb decisions. You will always shine like Ard's sun in my eyes and nothing will ever change that.
And for my son. Don't ever let shame take you, especially for things others do to you. You are valiant, strong, and have a smile as bright as Bakr's. Your worth is innate, inherent, and unchangeable.
I love you more than Allah does both his worlds. Blasphemy or not.
-Kyro Dean

MAP OF QAF

BAHAMUT SEA
SHAMAAL SEA
Kurijun Muhaniad
JASRAIB
AHMAR
The City of Pearls
Al Madini
MUTHALATH SEA
Muthalath Al'Ard
SHIHALA
ORKESH
VESPAR
Jurdam
SHARQ SEA
IZRAK
Gerih
Ashkuh
The Glass Plains
GHALUMA
GHARB SEA
ELMARAN SEA
Karazan
Kufah
ZABRIYA
FYRE
Wardi
EASTERN ELM
WESTERN ELM
Bahamut
Shamaal
Gharb
Sharq
Janu'ub
Bone Island
JANU'UB SEA
The Nine Kingdoms of Qaf

The Royal House of Shihala

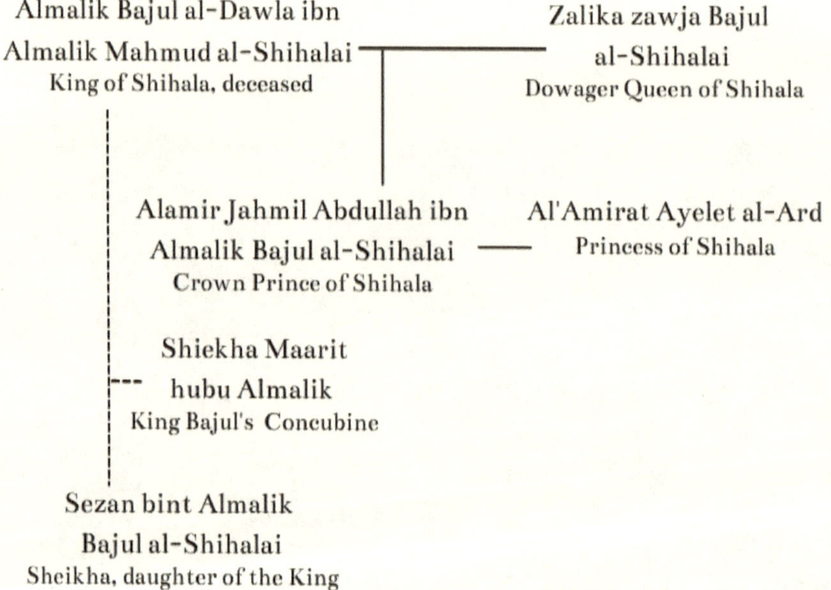

CHAPTER ONE

Bakr

Bakr struggled into his pants as quietly as possible. He was still dizzy from drink and so tired, but he couldn't afford to sleep. Not here. Not like this.

He knew that's what Queen Qadira was hoping would happen, that he would pass out cold and miss Jahmil's wedding, leaving a black spot on an otherwise perfect day. She was looking for some small revenge against her ex-fiancé. A sort of backhanded *I don't want you anymore, and by the way, look at what I did with your friend.* She was a mean-spirited, petty pain in the neck, and Jahmil really had made her look like a fool.

Actually, it was Ayelet, Jahmil's new fiancée, who finally succeeded in upending the Queen of Ahmar's carefully laid plans and turning her into a laughingstock. Allah knows, the love-potion-wielding queen deserved every bit of condescension she got.

But Jahmil, being Jahmil, couldn't let it go. He was so obsessed with the idea that his old flame would find a way to ruin his wedding that he was incapable of enjoying what should have been the happiest day of his life. And Jahmil, still being Jahmil, hadn't wanted a stag party, so Bakr figured the best gift he could give his friend was to make doubly sure Qadira wasn't coming.

He knew it was dangerous going to see her. The queen's temper was almost as legendary as her cruelty. But the way Jahmil spoke of her, always comparing her to a constrictor readying for the kill, made Bakr wonder just how talented a snake charmer he could be.

Pretty talented, it turned out. At least so far.

Somebody needed to make an effort to smooth out relations with Ahmar. The country had always been Shihala's most important trading partner, never mind that should the bitter queen decide to exact revenge on Prince Jahmil for not only leaving her at the altar but smashing the altar to smithereens, there was no telling the damage she might inflict.

Bakr was no diplomat, but he knew how to put a smile on a woman's face, at least for a night. And she wasn't such poor company when she wasn't talking.

Qadira moaned and rolled over in the silken folds of her massive bed, her hand reaching into the warm space where he used to be. Bakr froze in mid-step, his leg hanging stupidly in the air. Why did floors never seem to squeak except when you were trying to sneak away from a light sleeper? Not for the first time, he wished he could apparate like every other djinn in existence, but the half of his blood that was human held him fast in place.

"You dare try to sneak away from a queen?" Qadira moaned, rolling onto her back. The sheet slipped from her chest, revealing all that taut, sparkly skin the shade of springtime lavender.

Smiling, he lowered himself onto the edge of the cloudlike mattress and traced his fingers over her flat stomach until she giggled. She was pretty, in a cold and difficult-to-believe sort of way. Like the twists of a dead tree standing its ground over a vibrant horizon. Her fiery passion had left him with claw marks all over his back and bite marks on his shoulders, all covered in a fine dusting of silver glitter.

"I didn't want to wake you," he said, giving an exhausted little laugh.

"General Bakr, I order you to get back into this bed."

"You really don't want me to do that. I snore. Loudly. A queen needs her beauty sleep, after all."

She pushed her thick lips into a pout. "I think you're lying."

"I'll stay if you really want me to." He laid back on the bed beside her and put his hands behind his neck. "But you will not get any sleep. I don't just snore, I hack. Like there's a sock stuffed in my throat." He opened his mouth wide and made a horrible scraping noise. Then he snorted loudly, making sure there was a good amount of snot in it.

"Stop it!" She slapped his chest. "That's disgusting."

"It's worse even than that. I burble and wheeze. I mean, I nearly die ten times a night." She rolled her eyes.

"This is the problem." He patted the scar on his throat. Upraised pink tissue about two fingers thick ran from the lobe of his left ear diagonally across his Adam's apple, and down his chest to end in a twist just above his right nipple. "It messed up my trachea."

"It is disgusting," Qadira conceded, walking two fingers down its length. "Where did you get that?"

"Karzusan." His lips twitched with memories of the battle that always hid just below the surface. He forced them down with a smile. "Where else?"

She rolled onto her side and ran a finger over his chest. "I'll have a room made up for you."

"You think I won't come back?" He looked at her askance.

"I know you won't, you filthy Shihalan mongrel."

He grinned at the insult. "Are you a gambler?"

Scoffing, her eyes tipped to the ceiling. "What are you talking about?"

"What do you want to bet that I won't come back?"

She smirked coldly. "You have absolutely nothing that I would want."

"Now, that just isn't true. My best friend is the Prince Regent of Shihala. I bet you…" He ran his tongue over his teeth. "I bet you the island of Biddafa that I will come back before the next Moonless Night."

She drew her brows together. "Are you allowed to gamble with Shihalan lands?"

"Allowed by whom?" he scoffed, then rolled to a seat and snatched a bottle of Ahmaran red wine from the pearl-encrusted table beside the bed. He took three long gulps and wiped his mouth on his sleeve. Then he burped and looked back at the queen with a rakish grin. "In for an opal in for a dinar as far as sin is concerned. Jahmil gave me the island. It's mine to do with as I like."

"He'd be angry if he found out you gave me an island in Shihala."

"He would be fuming!" Bakr looked deeply into her candy green eyes. "But I'm not offering to *give* you anything. Jahmil will never know because I will be back."

Qadira smirked and turned away. "What do you want for it?"

He stroked his rough, stubbly chin. "How about a vineyard? The best wine in Qaf is right here in Ahmar."

"That's true."

"Then it's a deal." He snatched her twiggy hand and shook before she had a chance to respond, then rolled out of bed and pulled on his shirt.

"The island of Biddafa…" She laughed and rolled onto her back. "Now I hope you don't come back."

"We both know that isn't true." He growled playfully, then yanked on his boots and threaded his steel sword into the leather frog at his hip. Qadira flinched just looking at the weapon, as all pure-blooded djinn did. A single touch of the blade would have left her with third-degree burns, but he was immune to the effect. It was the only real advantage of being half-human, and he exploited it as much as possible.

"You'll be seeing me again very soon, whether you like it or not," he said and swept out the door. He quickened through the glowing, mirrored halls of Ahmar palace, his boots leaving dusty prints on the carpet, even as a fleet of servants scrubbed at the ones he'd left when he'd come in.

His mount waited for him in the stables, a baby drakonte straight from the kingdom of Fyre in Zabriya. She'd come with some complex, unpronounceable Fyrish name, but Bakr called her Bubbles because of her effervescent personality. She was only about twenty feet long—mostly silver with little blue spots, huge bug eyes, and a cute pout to her lips. By the end of the year, she'd be a hundred-foot-long monster, but for now, she was still his baby. She rushed him excitedly and wrapped him in her coils, as warm as any cold-blooded hug can be. Bakr climbed onto her back and, without so much as a whistle, she beat the white feathers of her massive wings and lurched into the sky. Young drakonte were faster than full-grown adults; she'd have him in Karzusan in twenty degrees flat. He'd only be a little late for the wedding.

As the wind rushed through his hair, he vaguely hoped it would lick the smell of Qadira from his clothes, the florals and honey and mint. Though there was little he could do about the glitter. He'd be sparkling for days.

He had to laugh at the whole thing. He didn't own any islands, but that didn't matter. He was out of the palace and what was Qadira going to do about it? Invade Shihala over a clandestine wager made between the sheets while her lips were still flushed with blood? Either way, he'd be leaving Qaf tomorrow morning. And he had no intention of ever coming back.

He arrived at Karzusan as the First Moon limped to its zenith, bathing the land below in ruddy light. It was always just a little dark in Qaf. The spray of brilliant, multicolored churning stars and galaxies helped some, but after spending three years in the land of the djinn without a single visit back to Ard, Bakr was sick of it. Sick of all Eight Moons, sick of the shivering nebulae, sick of darkness and cold and night. Sick of djinn and their inconstant eyes. He missed sunlight, the heat of the desert, and the smell of dust and camels. Ard and Qaf were both his home, and neither of them was. Which was why he had to keep moving. The year he'd spent in Orkeshi, spending every waking moment trying to make life as difficult for the Vespars as possible, had left him with a desperate need for the sun, and the open vastness of the Arabian desert.

Jahmil had asked him to stay in Shihala and be his grand vizier, which was insane, though Bakr hadn't the heart to tell him that. Instead, he'd just smiled. After the wedding, he was going to tell his old friend the truth. Hopefully, Jahmil would be too giddy with love and joy to be disappointed. Bakr would rather take a shot to the kidney than endure the pain in Jahmil's disappointed eyes.

Six months had passed since the last of the Vespars were driven from Shihala and resettled in their own lands. Jahmil's mother, Queen Zalika, was there now, overseeing the reconstruction of the country's government, which meant her son and future daughter-in-law were effectively the rulers of Shihala until she returned. Jahmil lamented this, saying all he had wanted was time and space to be alone with the newfound love of his life, but Bakr knew better. Government was a part of Jahmil and as much as he groused, he could never fully separate himself from it.

The reconstruction of Karzusan was well underway. The builders had made tremendous progress with the palace and surrounding city, but there were still decades of hard labor ahead. A thousand scintillating columns of marble to carve, a thousand frescos to paint. Ten thousand flowers to plant. He did not envy the bureaucrat that would have to supervise the labor; it sure as hell would not be him.

A crowd had gathered around the entrance of the palace. Hundreds of carriages from all over Qaf containing silk-draped courtiers and bejeweled princes. The peasants were holding their own festival in the streets. On Ayelet's advice, Jahmil had given them a day off from work and provided them with all the wine they could drink and all the bread they could eat. Unlike virtually every other member of the court, the new princess knew what it was like to be hungry and to work her fingers to the bone. It was one of many reasons Bakr liked her so much. They were cut from the same cloth: born and raised on Ard in poverty and hunger, then elevated to the highest echelons of djinn society by the same diamond-eyed, midnight blue prince.

"Get me closer, bubbly baby!"

Bakr rose to his feet on Bubbles' back as the drakonte angled her wings and swept close to the ground. When she was about thirty feet away, he leaped off and did a triple jackknife dive before landing on his feet in the middle of the crowd. If he'd done that move in the town square, the peasants would have gone absolutely mental. Screaming, cheering. The lot. Especially considering virtually everybody in the kingdom still thought he was dead. But the scandalized courtiers couldn't even muster a smattering of applause. They gasped and whispered, pointing at him and holding their robes to their chests like they were frightened he was going to bite them.

They had always hated him. For his brown, human skin. For his dull, human eyes. For his steel sword. Most of all, they hated him because Jahmil Amir hung on his every word.

Bakr bared his teeth in a wide, threatening smile. He wanted to bite them.

Shrugging it off, he sawed through the crowd towards the palace. As he passed by the large reflecting pool out front, he couldn't help that his gaze lifted to it. It had been over two years since that night—the Festival of the Eight Moons. But every time he saw the sky of Qaf reflected in still water, he thought about it. About her and her eyes of sunshine, her hair like starlight. The feeling of her laughter shivering over his skin as they floated away from the world to a place that was soft.

Would she be returning today along with all the other exiled courtiers?

His breath became short thinking of the horrible night when he'd been forced to leave her without saying goodbye. And then dying—or being in a state of being almost death for nearly a quarter pass of an Ardish sun before finding himself trapped behind enemy lines in Shihala. No doubt she'd thought him dead, and for two years he didn't write to say anything to the contrary.

Why, when he may die at any moment?

Bakr looked down at his hands and sighed. If she did return, best she did not see him covered in Qadira's silver glitter. Even if she would never want him back, the shame of it would be too much to bear. He'd have to kill himself.

A carriage pulled up in front of him and a grating, nasally voice called, "Well, paint me pink and call me a Gurlak. That can't be General Bakr."

The familiar voice crept over his skin like maggots, tearing away all gentle thoughts and replacing them with putrid loathing, as ever it had.

"Of all the people not to die in the war," Bakr cursed under his breath.

The carriage door swung open and a barrel of a man wiggled free. He stood a full foot shorter than Bakr, but thicker. Rounder. A bald head with furry black eyebrows. He had that royal Shihalan blue skin and may have passed for handsome if it weren't for the sweaty fat packed onto every inch of his frame and the cruelty in his eyes. The late king's younger brother, Jahmil's uncle, and the most powerful person in the kingdom behind only Queen Zalika and Jahmil. He wasn't a dog, or a rat, or a weasel. Bakr couldn't think of a single animal in either of Allah's worlds lowly enough to compare him to. Maybe a hagfish with an array of skin diseases.

"I thought you were still in Orkeshi fighting the good fight," the wart said.

Bakr laughed, throwing his whole body into the sound just to ease his own discomfort. "The good fight is over. Peace prevails. *Alhamdulillah!*"

"So they say." Rahik took out his snuff-box and sucked a little black corn up his nose with a dry snort. "I'm surprised to see you here. I thought a man with such tremendous unpaid debts would keep a lower profile. Or have you forgotten?"

Bakr sucked in a harsh breath. Of course, he had not forgotten. If he lived a thousand years, he would never forget the night Rahik kidnapped and held for ransom everything he cared about, leaving him no choice but to sell himself into servitude.

"Still gnawing on that bone, huh?" said Bakr, forcing his voice to remain even and casual. "You can't say I'm in default when two million Vespars stood between me and your contract." He spat at his feet. "*Eaqduk allaein.*"

"Do you believe for a moment that the King of Eastern Elm would be swayed by your argument?" Rahik cocked his head, and the flesh around his neck squelched. "Or would you prefer we brought this matter before the prince regent?"

Bakr's smile tightened. "Do not bring Jahmil into this, or I'll be forced to explain why we have a contract in the first place."

"Ah, ah, ah..." Rahik shook his finger in the air. As he waddled closer, the powerful stench of cardamom and anise assaulted Bakr. "The first stipulation of the contract is that you must not speak of the contract."

"I can mime it," he replied through clenched teeth.

"The poor, abandoned sheikha. Has your affection for her grown so cold you no longer worry how your actions might affect the purity of her blood?"

Bakr's hand tightened around the hilt of his sword. Though Rahik had not said her name, hearing him speak of her was enough to set Bakr's blood to boil. Every instinct told him to lash out and strike the little goblin down. Send straight to Jahannam where he belonged. But he couldn't. The years had done nothing to fade the ink on that infernal contract. Rahik still had him in chains.

"After the festivities," the goblin rasped. "You know where to meet me."

"Try to brush your teeth before then." Bakr wrinkled his nose, then took a step back and laughed loudly. "So good to see you, your grace."

"You have no idea." Rahik looked him up and down before turning and walking through the entrance to the palace.

Bakr stole a moment to compose himself by sneaking away from the crowd towards the back entrance, assuming the builders had deigned to put in the back entrance. The only good thing that had come out of the war with Vespar was he got a respite from the hideous web of Shihalan politics. But now they were back with a vengeance. Rahik was back and he hadn't forgotten anything.

CHAPTER TWO

Sezan

Sezan leaned out from the carriage window, reaching for the passing purple and pink leaves that shimmered with morning dew. Even burnt, ravaged, and stripped entirely bare, her homeland was perfect. Every rounded dome of the palace had managed to remain upright despite the battles, each spire a sharp call to the heavens. There were a few shattered windows and black tarry streams down the sides of the cream-colored ramparts, but even now, dutiful citizens hurried to make them new. The war with Vespar had ended. She could return home at last. They all could.

"Sezan?" her servant, Lila, chided, poking a finger into her shoulder. "You should not show yourself so brashly through the window. It is unbecoming."

Sezan scrunched her nose, took one last delicious inhale of alyasmin and lavender, clementine and olive, and then pulled herself back inside the carriage. "We are not in Eastern Elm anymore, my dear Lila. A woman is allowed to breathe."

The last two years she had spent with her extended family had been nothing short of lavish torture. She was one baklava away from not fitting into even her loosest pair of salwar, and her vibrant turquoise skin had lost a shade of shimmer under the cloudy skies that drowned the country in constant rain. But no longer. The moons shone brightly over Karzusan and the grand palace of Shihala. She bit her bottom lip and grinned up at the crystal clear skies.

Lila shook her head. "You don't know who or what we've come home to. War and time do not sweep through a country without leaving change."

"Oh pish," Sezan waved her fingers dismissively. "As long as time moves, Shihala will welcome all with open arms. Look how the moons shine."

Lila let out a raspy sigh of disapproval. Her light blue skin was the color of the ring of light around the Third Moon. Her eyes shone with copper, and her blonde hair hung in thick braids that curled wildly at the ends. Sezan had more than once encouraged her to flatten those out as she did her own, but Lila only cared about making sure courtiers looked their part. The hypocrisy was maddening.

Sezan ran a hand over her own shimmering hair, tucking it under her purple hijab, and puckered her lips to the side. The Elmaran double-headed goats clopped their way into the grand square in front of the palace, while her giddiness threatened to manifest itself through trembling fingers. She closed her fist to keep the shaking at bay.

Lila looked up through furrowed brows. "You're getting your hopes up."

"I am not."

"Yes, you are. You only get that look on your face when you're thinking about one thing."

Sezan soured her smiling lips into a pout and narrowed her eyes. "Better?"

Lila sighed and leaned back against the velvet seats of the carriage. "My dear Sezan, these lands have been through a terrible war. Shihala still weeps for the fallen. Perhaps you should, too."

It took all of Sezan's restraint not to stiffen at her words. "I'm very aware of the death that lingers here. I am not so foolish to pretend otherwise."

"Yet, you hope."

"I hope? Of course, I hope. I did not leave the prospect of joining the King of Elm's harem to come here and fail. I shall be emissary to the royal throne and traverse the lands, striking deals of peace."

"That is not the hope to which I referred."

"And why shouldn't I be emissary?" Sezan stepped over Lila's words. "If my merits aren't enough, my blood should be. Jahmil is my brother and someday he will be King."

"Half."

"Half-king or half-brother?"

"Both." Lila leaned back against the seat in a tell-tell sign of condescension, the ivory chain over her forehead clacking lightly with the bumps in the road. "Jahmil only rules as regent while his mother supervises the restoration and rehabilitation of the Vespar lands, and you only share a father."

"Blood is blood," Sezan said. "And I'm technically the highest-ranking sheikha, not that it affords me more than Jahmil's unwanted marriage contracts. And what was my future worth to him? A few more troops on the front." She bristled. "That sack of silver knew what I had just been through. Knew about..." She bit off the name lingering on her tongue and huffed.

Lila reached out to pat her knee. "Jahmil Amir didn't follow through in the end."

"How could he after the disgraceful failure of his own arranged marriage? Either way, he owes me a favor."

Lila chuckled dryly. "Good luck telling him that." Then she fell quiet. "Or are you planning to get what you want through your shared soft spot?"

"What soft spot?" Sezan quipped, pulling her shoulder blades together.

"Bakr."

Sezan's eyes widened before she turned her head with a fake, dainty sneeze.

"May you live many years," Lila obliged with a smirk and eyes that shimmered with too much knowing. "I know how you felt about him, but, *eaziziun,* he was at the front lines at Karzusan. Only the amir and Queen Zalika made it out of there alive with Takisha Alqayid."

"I'm aware who made it out, thank you. The tales of the Shihalan prince and his magic-sucking sorceress are well known." Bitterness seeped into Sezan's words despite herself.

"Sezan." Lila snapped. "I refuse to chase the moons with you. You must accept that Bakr is dead."

"It has not been confirmed."

"Ten thousand soldiers piled in ditches outside Karzusan should be proof enough! Should we have driven in from the sharq so the stench could convince you? And if not, then how about Bakr's silence? I've watched you these past years, waiting for anything to come from him. Watched as all the other soldiers sent word of their well-being and eventually returned home while he sent you nothing. So if he isn't dead, I should think you'd want to kill him, not see him alive. Especially considering the circumstances of his leaving." Lila finished with a harrumph.

Lila was wrong about Bakr's death. Sezan had paid dearly to ensure that. But the second half of Lila's accusation rolled around her stomach like a marble in a ceramic bowl.

She pressed her back hard against the cushions behind her, restraining her fire so it did not erupt on her fingertips like Jahmil's always did when he lost his temper. "Perhaps the circumstances surrounding his departure are why he didn't write. Maybe he assumed *I* was dead this entire time. I was dying when he left, after all."

Lila scoffed, an auditory wound on her aching heart.

"But enough of this useless talk," Sezan snapped as the hollowness of her words filled her belly.

Unbidden, her eyes flashed a shimmer of soft yellow across the small carriage. *Like the morning sun*, Bakr used to tell her and always when she was angriest. He always had a way of making her smile when she least wanted to. She squeezed her eyes shut to put him out of her mind and straightened once more with an air of importance. "What matters now is looking forward, not looking back."

The carriage came to a halt with the *bleat* of the goats. Sezan peeked out behind the thick curtains. Dozens of courtiers milled about the grounds, silk tunics and kaftans flashing bright colors in honor of the royal nuptials. Under any other circumstance, Sezan was certain the court would be in a tizzy over a mere human marrying the crown prince, but relief that the war was over swept everything else out of sight. Well, that and the fact that the human princess could drain their very life from their bones.

The door to the carriage opened, letting light from Shihala's moons stream into the carriage. Sezan inhaled, slow and steady, to calm her nerves. Petty courtiers she could handle, but the thought that *he* might be here nipped at her no matter how much she shushed it. She slid a flowered slipper with yellow jewels out onto the step and pulled herself free. Her plum robes draped elegantly about her beaded waist and overly-full salwar pants. She held her head high. Time to play nice with the court so she could get what she needed before time ran out.

Back straight. Neck high. Coy smile. Chin upturned just so. She was ready. Sezan moved through the crowd of bustling servants, all tending to trailing robes or luggage or whatever their masters barked at them. A gaggle of women across the foyer met her eyes and waved her over. She turned to join them when sandy brown skin and a tussle of dark hair caught her eye. She whipped around, but a behemoth of a man with a crate on his back blocked her view.

"*Naqli!*" she snipped. The man bowed an apology and tried to move out of the way, bumping into her twice more as they each vied in the same direction. "Bah! May ghouls feed on your impropriety!" she snapped before finally pushing her way around him. The tan skin was gone.

Sezan forced her fingers open and relaxed at her sides. She probably imagined it anyway. But just as she turned away, a smooth hand of gray with nails as sharp as splinters beckoned her from behind a pillar. A chill rippled down her spine despite her protests. With an apologetic gesture toward the women and their impatiently tapping feet, she slipped toward the far end of the courtyard. The gray hand had vanished, but she knew what lay in wait behind the pillar.

She swooped around the side and forced her hands to stay at her side. "Lilith," she said in as cordial a tone as she could muster.

"Djinn," the lilith said back.

The light of Shihala's moons danced lightly on the lilith's skin; a lake of silver. Her brown and gold hair hung in blunt strips around her face, and her light pink lips smirked in a way that looked both entirely innocent and completely evil. In contrast, Sezan's turquoise hue looked ridiculously bright. The demon's copper horns parted her hair neatly and gleamed with a menacing hint of moonlight, and the strips of animal fur that made her dress dipped scandalously low. Everything about the demon was haram. She looked no older than Sezan but had been alive thousands of years. Sezan hated the creature as much for the deal they had made together as for her flawless, never-aging beauty.

"You shouldn't be here," Sezan said, mustering a humorously false sense of authority. "If the other djinn saw you they'd—"

"They'd what?" the lilith purred in her husky voice. "You think you're the only djinn desperate enough to make a deal with me?"

"Our deal concludes on my twenty-fifth birthday. You are nearly a month too soon."

"Who says I'm here for you?"

Sezan suppressed an eye roll. "You beckoned me like a common dog."

"Then why did you come?" the lilith smirked.

"Because I didn't want you making a scene." Sezan's eye twitched. Why was she letting this monster get the best of her? "If you're not here for me, then who could you possibly owe a visit?"

The lilith tilted her head to and fro, a night owl assessing its prey. Then she pointed a finger past Sezan's shoulder.

Sezan turned to follow and nearly choked. Bakr stood a carriage away, speaking with the Marqiz Rahik, his thick hair shining and his smile flashing. The check-mark scar on his cheek only accented his strong cheekbones and light-green eyes. He was nothing less than healthy, joking, and completely unconcerned with whether or not she existed. That son of a...

She shook her head and stepped back, making sure to conceal herself completely behind the pillar even as her heart ached to see more.

"Delivered alive as promised." The lilith smirked.

Sezan pressed her shoulders into the rough stone to keep from shivering. "How do I know that's thanks to you? Maybe he survived on his own."

"Don't tempt my rage, mortal." The lilith cocked her head. "Just look at the scar on his neck. You think something that cuts from his jaw down his entire chest would heal on its own?"

"It's a valid question," Sezan said, tilting her chin up to hide her dismay. There was no lie in the lilith's voice. And the tip of a scar did peek out of Bakr's jacket; a wound she hadn't yet noticed, so distracted she had been by his jade eyes. What exactly had she managed to save him from?

"Mmm," the lilith sighed deep in her chest. "I have to thank you for sending me to him. He's tasty."

"*Tasty*?" Sezan's eyes flashed, a streak of sun across the lilith's moon-silver skin.

"Tut, tut, sheikha. You can't blame me for indulging in something you have enjoyed yourself on occasion. I've spent countless days and nights wrapped in those arms, tracing the scar on his chest. Just the other night we—"

"Lies." Sezan squeezed her fist, not wanting to hear another word.

"What?" The demon shimmied her shoulders. "He slept with you. His best friend's prudish little sis. You don't think your lecherous lover boy would sleep with a piece like me after that? In his mind, we're the same thing, only I'm better."

Sezan's nails nipped at her palm, and she pressed them in harder. Bakr would absolutely sleep with a demon. Or any woman. Anything that moved frankly. "Enough," she snapped, a mixture of hatred and revulsion shaking in her chest. "What you and I do with Bakr will never be the same thing."

"Sleeping with anyone outside of marriage is haram in Allah's eyes," the demon purred with a pouty smile. "That sounds the same enough to me."

Sezan bit her tongue until tears dusted the corner of her eyes. How long had she struggled with the fate of her soul, only to justify it by telling herself they'd marry someday? What a fool she had been. She swallowed despite the dry desperation in her throat. "The deal was my magic for his life, not for you to *bed* him. I am your debtor, not him. So leave him alone."

"And what about when he calls for me in the night? You expect me to leave him cold and trembling? Cruel."

"Then our contract is void."

"Please." The lilith giggled. "A deal is a deal. He lives because of me. It's not my fault he also lives *for* me. There was nothing in the contract that said he couldn't fall madly in love with me."

"Bakr can't love you."

"Why?" The lilith asked, pushing her pink lips out. "Because that means he doesn't love you?"

Sezan's temper flared. She grabbed at the monster, but in a puff of air that sounded like a gasp, the lilith vanished. Instead, Sezan punched the column in a pathetic display of emotion and winced at the pain.

Everything she had done with Bakr, everything she had already given him weighed her soul towards Jahannam. But even worse than sinning against herself was being a traitor to her country. There was no more egregious trespass she could commit against Shihala than to give her birth magic to a demon on her twenty-fifth birthday, the very day she would be old enough to pledge it in the service of her land. But that is exactly what she had done. And now, no one could find out. No one would if she could control herself and become an emissary. Royal diplomats honored Shihala through the magic in their official seals instead of the magic in their hands. One brief ceremony that mixed her magic with Jahmil's, and that was it. The seal only had to be filled once. If she could do so before her birthday, she could fool everyone and keep her status. It was her only salvation.

At least for this mortal life. She headed for Jahannam in the one after because of Bakr, anyway. Her stomach twisted, and she rested her forehead against the cool marble of the pillar, the jewel of her headband pressing into her skin. To become an ambassador, she first needed to speak to Jahmil. And to do that, she'd have to stop hiding behind the column. And to do *that* she'd have to swallow her pride, the ache tearing apart her chest, and the rage steaming her blood over what the lilith had dared speak to her.

She counted by threes to regain her composure, then peeked around the corner at Bakr, letting her heart ache just enough to acknowledge the pain. How many times had he buoyed her spirits with a laugh? A kiss? How many times had he let her rest her head upon his shoulders, arms wrapped around one another long into the cold hour between the moonsets just to be? She sighed. Not half so many as the number of days that had passed since he'd left her dying on the cold floor without so much as a goodbye, or nine hundred twelve days, to be more precise. Logic told her he must have had a reason, but her heart could see no way around it. She had loved him with all she was, and he had not loved her.

She allowed a dainty snort. Her mother had been right: she was a stupid woman.

Gathering the folds of her harem pants, she squared her shoulders, stepped out from behind the pillar, and marched in the opposite direction.

CHAPTER THREE

Bakr

Bakr paused outside of Jahmil's chambers, closed his eyes, and took a long slow breath. His run-in with the Marqiz had left a sour taste in his mouth and the throb of a hangover was growing slowly in the back of his brain, but he was determined to be happy. For Jahmil. For Ayelet. For the love they shared and the happiness they so desperately deserved. The last thing either of them needed was to waste his wedding day worrying about anything, especially him.

Gnawing on the inside of his cheek, Bakr pushed open the door.

The massive chamber buzzed with activity. A hundred servants and eunuchs, all puttering from one task to the next, and dozens of groomsmen, all dressed in their finest, dripping with gems and topped with absurdly fluffy feathers. Most of them were Jahmil's cousins, distant or otherwise. Djinn which Bakr either barely knew or didn't know at all. He wasn't a fan of these stuck-up rich boys on the best of days, but seeing them as Jahmil's wedding party was unexpectedly painful. They weren't supposed to be there. Dhikrullah should have been there instead, dancing on the tables and spouting his utterly pointless, yet infernally hilarious, poetry. Ajda should have been at Jahmil's side pestering him about his hair, clothes, jewelry, and all that nonsense that had always meant so much to him. And Yusuf and Chadli were supposed to be groaning in a corner, so hungover that Bakr looked a teetotaler by comparison.

But all of those men were all dead. Of the old clique, only the prince and his cousin, Zamir, had survived for Bakr to come home to. So instead of being surrounded by his friends on his wedding day, Jahmil had to make do with this load of peacocking princelings.

As Bakr looked around, soaking up the Evil Eye being thrown his way from all angles, he felt more and more out of place. The sooner he got out of Shihala, the better. The last thing Jahmil needed was a half-human lowlife slouching around and ruining his reputation.

But the Marqiz's deal was scratching at the back of his brain, reminding him there was still one more price to pay before his life could be his own.

He made his way through the chamber to the back where a large, bejeweled screen had been set up to shelter the prince from the rest of the goings-on. Bakr stepped around the side and slapped his hand across Jahmil's back. "So, you got cold feet yet?"

Jahmil started and turned, then sighed when he saw his face. "You're late."

Bakr shrugged and propped his butt on the dressing table. "Ayelet and I agreed that so long as I got here before the actual ceremony started, we'd call me early."

Jahmil let out a mirthless laugh, his diamond eyes shifting with a dozen colors.

"What's wrong?" Bakr asked, smiling even brighter to make up for his friend's worry. "You can't seriously have cold feet."

"Of course, I don't," he snapped, then his face softened and he rubbed a hand absently over his forearm "Ayelet and I are already married as far as I'm concerned. Today is just a formality."

"So...?"

His eyes focused with intense fractals of pink and brown. "I can't shake the feeling that Qadira is already here. That she'll find a way to..."

"She's not here." Bakr sighed and leaned back, crossing an ankle over his knee. "I guarantee it."

Jahmil's eyes darkened and his face pinched. "What did you do?"

"I had a talk with her."

"Is that where you were last night?" Jahmil ran a finger over the back of Bakr's hand, then glared at it. "Is that glitter?"

"Don't look at me like that." Bakr laughed uncomfortably. "You can't take two steps in Ahmar without getting doused in the stuff."

"Bakr, why?" He sighed heavily and pressed two fingers into his eyes. "Please tell me you didn't..."

"Don't be ridiculous. I just went there to talk to her." Laughing, Bakr rubbed his palm over the back of his neck. "And you can believe me when I say she doesn't want to come within a thousand parasangs of you. Ayelet terrifies her."

Jahmil nodded, yet somehow his expression managed to darken still further.

Bakr clenched his teeth in a tight smile. "What is it *now*?"

"Nothing." He shook his head.

"It's never nothing with you, *akhi*. Spit it out."

"I'm worried about Ayelet. She's agreed to stay in Qaf, but she's still human. And you know better than anyone how prejudiced djinn can be against humans."

"She'll be fine." Bakr waved his hand dismissively. "She's a tough cookie. Triple baked."

Jahmil nodded slowly, his gaze fixed on the ground. "I'm just glad you're here. You're basically the only other human in ten thousand miles, besides Serap. You can help both of them navigate all of this."

Bakr bit his bottom lip. It flashed through him to tell Jahmil right then and there that he was leaving after the wedding, but the words wouldn't form in his mouth.

"Promise me you'll help Ayelet get settled into her new role." Jahmil smiled weakly and looked up, his eyes filling with blue. Hope. "I know what some of the courtiers put you through and I can't bear thinking of the same thing happening to her."

"You're the prince regent, dummy. Just order them to respect her."

"I will. I have. But I can't be there all the time. And don't tell anybody else this, but..." Jahmil waved off the servants and leaned in closer. "Ever since the magic of Vespar settled, Ayelet can't call the wisps the way she used to."

Bakr narrowed his eyes at that. Saying that Ayelet could no longer call the wisps was like saying a drakonte could no longer fly. He didn't pretend to understand Ayelet's unique powers—something about Köle Amir of Vespar torturing his childhood to transform into a powerful instrument of destruction—but the little puffs of pure magic called wisps had always responded to her call like loyal dogs. It was the reason every djinn in Shihala, if not every djinn in Qaf, was frightened of her.

"What are you saying?" Bakr said. "She's lost her powers?"

"No, not completely. There just isn't nearly as much free magic as there used to be, so summoning has become harder for her. There are fewer wisps to respond to her call."

Bakr opened his mouth to reply, but the thunderous knell of one hundred wedding chimes called the official *nikah* to service. The servants and groomsmen swarmed, and Bakr slunk to the back of the crowd to watch as Jahmil was given a final polish, then escorted through the door, the gaggle of noblemen bustling after him like baby ducks in a line.

Alone in the chamber, Bakr stripped and crouched at the basin of a *hinfia* in one corner where warm water ran free and clear. He cleaned his teeth and scrubbed his skin, focusing on his face and hands in an attempt to rid himself of the damning evidence of glitter. He refused to put on all the fluff the rest of the men in the wedding party were wearing, though such an outfit had been provided—all diamonds and sumptuous, jewel-toned fabrics. His dull skin and scars looked ridiculous draped in all that regalia. Like at every other official occasion Jahmil had ever forced him to attend, his uniform would have to suffice. Gray pants, tall boots, a heavy jacket of green leather that fell to his knees. He strapped his worn sword onto the thick, ceremonial belt and tied a black keffiyeh over his head, then made his way into the great hall.

The officiating sheik had taken his position on the podium, an old Elmaran djinn with a puffy white beard and even puffier hat. Glass chairs filled the space and on each chair was an overdressed, ostentatious royal bottom. The sunny-skinned king and queen of Zabriya had come out for the occasion, as had the magnate of Ghaluma, and the so-called 'Bloody Queen', Mapenuk of Izrak. Jahmil's mother, Queen Zalika, had returned from Vespar for the occasion and had the best seat in the house. She looked down her long nose at the proceedings with palpable displeasure if not disgust. To say she disapproved of her son's choice in a wife was putting things rather mildly, but she had little choice. Jahmil had threatened to disown his crown if Ayelet was not allowed to become his queen.

Conspicuously absent from the ceremony was the King of Eastern Elm, which was a shame. Bakr would very much have liked to spit in his eye and tell him what he thought of his unbreakable seal and enslaving contracts. It was his seal that held Bakr fast to Rahik's hideous contract. After one signed a contract sealed by the King of Elm, to break it meant fast, but excruciating, death. No matter where the person happened to be, whether at the very center of Watali or off in the far backwaters of Ard. The seal imprinted itself on the signer's soul and forced compliance.

As Bakr jogged down the aisle towards the altar to take his place beside Jahmil, gasps went up through the crowd, followed by conspiratorial whispers. Bakr decided it was better they all found out he wasn't dead at once, then perhaps he could stop having the same tedious conversation about it.

Ayelet stood opposite the podium from Jahmil, the wedding contract laid between them and penned in beautiful golden calligraphy. Ayelet shined still brighter in her vibrant red dress and bejeweled hijab, but it was her smile that filled the room with earthy sunshine. If she was nervous, she didn't show it. And now that Jahmil was standing before her, holding her hands and gazing into her eyes the way he always did, he didn't look nervous anymore either. They looked natural together. Like they belonged exactly at that spot at exactly that moment.

Bakr twitched at an old familiar sting in his chest, then let it go with a heavy sigh.

Jahmil leaned close to Ayelet and whispered something in her ear. She stifled a laugh and shook her head. Bakr smiled and patted his friend's back. If anybody deserved to be happy, it was the two of them.

He caught the eye of Ayelet's attending maid over her shoulder. Little Serap was already crying, the happiest, most genuine smile on her face he thought he had ever seen. A laugh filled his throat just looking at the street urchin turned princess. She was the perfect combination of jaded and innocent, a foul mouth in a poofy dress.

The old sheik performing the ceremony raised his hands, and a hush filled the room. As he began to speak, laying out the terms of the marriage, Bakr turned his gaze to the crowd.

It seemed the prince's nikah was the great homecoming of the scattered Shihalan nobility. As he scanned their faces, he realized he hadn't seen most of these people in almost two years. Naturally, the courtiers had fled first when Vespar invaded, leaving the military and peasants to sort matters out. And now that the dust had settled, they were coming back to rule over the lands they had so readily abandoned.

Spineless hypocrites, the lot of them.

He was about to turn back to the ceremony when a familiar shade of turquoise caught his eye and he narrowed his gaze. The woman was sitting behind Alqayid Abd Manaf, a great behemoth of a man with shoulders like a battering ram. Bakr took a discrete step away from the podium, turning his head to the side to peer around the massive shoulders, and caught a glimmer of black hair that shined and sparkled like stars in the night sky, hidden under a fashionable, yet oh-so-conservative, hijab of lilac satin. Another step and he could see one half of her face. Her eyes shined in tones of amber and gold, as bright and warm as the Arabian sun, and her perfectly painted red lips were pressed into a neutral frown.

Blood rushed in his ears, a thrill of panic and joy. Lightning prickled his senses. Sezan's eyes twitched and met his, so bright they stilled his breath. The smile that filled his face felt as warm as her eyes looked. He took a deep breath, then winked at her. She shifted and looked away.

Folding his arms, Bakr walked back to the podium as Ayelet and Jahmil finished putting their marks to the magic paper, binding them forever in the eyes of Allah, Shihala, and eternity. The sheik lifted the contract and the crowd rose in a standing ovation. Fireworks crackled in the dome of the chamber and music began to play. In the ancient tradition of Shihala, the ceremony had lasted only twenty minutes, but festivities would go on until the Fourth Moon was fading over the horizon of janu'ub.

Jahmil and Ayelet left through a door behind the altar. They were entitled to a little time alone before making an official appearance at the after-party. The guests and wedding party filed from the chamber towards the atrium, where the ball would take place. Bakr kept his place for a moment, his gaze sweeping the crowd for a flash of turquoise skin, but the color was swallowed up in a swarm of flashy djinn.

As light as he felt seeing Sezan again, and looking so well, a tightness was growing in his heart. She hadn't smiled back. Did she hate him? Would she be disappointed to have learned he wasn't dead?

He needed to talk to her, but the very idea left him with a stomach ache.

Wine first, talking after. A good plan, yet here he was trapped at a royal wedding. In Shihala, where there would be no wine. He'd have to bribe a kitchen boy.

He hopped down from the altar and started making his way through the river of people, but could barely take a step in any direction without someone whose name he didn't know and whose face he couldn't remember coming up to him to express the fact that they thought he was dead. The strangers all asked the same questions. What happened to you after the capital was lost? Is it true you led the guerillas in Orkeshi? Did you ever come up against the Spider of Karzusan? How did you *ever* survive?

Many of them were effusive with their praise and the word *hero* kept cropping up in conversation. It felt weird and slimy. These people hated him, or at least they always had. Had so much changed just because he wasn't dead? Because he'd spent a year living like a feral dog in the mountains hunting down stray Vespars?

He didn't trust it. And he certainly was in no mood to tell any of his stories. He never was.

Some war hero.

When Bakr finally made it into the atrium, the ball was in full swing. Strings of incandescent pearls lit the sky. Ayelet's wisps played in the air like earthbound comets, bouncing up against the more traditional balls of multi-colored djinn fire. A large group of men was dancing together in concentric circles for the amusement of the entire party, balancing things on their heads, flipping one another in the air, and juggling each other's fire. Tables as long as city streets sprawled down the center of the space, piled with every delicacy Qaf and Earth had to offer. His stomach growled and dragged him towards steaming dolma, kofta, fluffy pita, and bitter tea. More people approached, some he recognized and many he did not. He let them talk while he filled his belly, nodding and smiling along. His head was still pounding from the night before. He found a kitchen boy and obtained an unmarked waterskin. Soon a new tipsy tingle was glowing in his cheeks.

It seemed hours had passed before he caught a glimmer of unmistakably vibrant skin across the room. She was standing on her own, her hands clasped tightly in front of her and her shimmering eyes scanning the dancefloor like a cautious lioness. His chest tightened even as a rock dropped in his stomach. He couldn't stop the memories from welling in his brain, a torrent of rain to bring a flash flood and sweep the desert. Sezan wrapped in white sheets, her brow glistening with sweat. He felt the tremendous softness of her skin, the sweep of her dramatic curves. Her makeup wiped clean and her impeccable hair in tangles. He remembered her smile, her laughter, her biting wit that cut into him even as she quivered beneath his touch. And an ache in his bones. Something unnamable and terrifying and wonderful.

Bakr cleared his throat and looked away. How many nights trapped in the horrors of Orkeshi had he thought of her, wishing he could speak to her? To let her know... what?

Nothing he said now could matter anymore, not after what he'd done. Still, he had to speak to her, if only to confirm how much she hated him.

He took a few deep breaths, then turned to cut through the crowd towards her. Her gaze lifted and met his briefly before sweeping away. He leaned against the wall at her side, crossed his arms, and kicked back one heel. "Funny seeing you here."

Her eyes stayed locked on the dancers in the center of the room, but her hands pressed against her dress. "Especially considering the entire kingdom thought you were dead until you ran up to the front of the king's own wedding, late as always."

"I get that all the time." He smiled and bumped his shoulder against hers.

She flicked a disapproving glance his way, then moved a step away from him. "All the more a mark against you that you haven't learned better. However did you manage to survive Karzusan with an attitude like that?"

"Just lucky, I guess." He raised his eyebrows, his gaze devouring her. Her hair was longer, her makeup darker, and her scowl deeper, but otherwise she looked exactly the same. The tightness in his chest began to warm.

"You look good," he said.

"And who gave you permission to look?"

He laughed and shook his finger at her. "Are you mad at me for not being dead?"

The smallest flicker of amber light flitted across her eyes. "How can I blame *you* for that?"

"Oh, you're very talented. I'm sure you'll find a way."

"I daresay you came back from war even glibber. How is that possible?"

"Go on. Admit it. You missed me just a tiny bit."

"Oh, yes. I missed you so much I committed haram by drinking away the nights and making deals with demons for the promise of seeing your pretty face just one last time," she said dryly.

"You cut me deep, Zan. Really deep." He smiled even wider and took a step closer. "So, I hear you've been hanging out in Elm? How was that? Laugh a minute, I bet."

"If you call being asked to join the King of Elm's harem a hundred times a day at Jahmil's behest a laugh, I suppose so. The air there is as thick as honey. I couldn't breathe just living. It is good to be back. Even if people who I thought were dead come to talk to me at a party as if two wretched years haven't passed at all."

His abs tightened painfully. Jahmil had told him she was in Elm; he'd never said a word about her joining the king's harem. He couldn't imagine Zalika or Jahmil had intended her to marry that ancient green bastard. Surely the king had simply seen her beauty and become possessed of the idea. But should they not have predicted that when they sent her away to live in his court? Jahmil often spoke of the importance of Elm as an ally in the war against Vespar. Strengthening that allegiance would have been at the forefront of his mind. But he wouldn't have sold his sister into that. Not knowing what the King of Elm was like. And especially not knowing what she meant to him.

Would he?

Thinking about it twisted his guts in knots. He would reserve his judgment for now, but once the haze of wedded bliss had run its course, Bakr had some very serious questions for Jahmil.

Bakr forced himself to smile, refocusing on Sezan. "I'll take that as a thank you for my service."

"And what thanks shall I get for mine?" she asked, her lips tightening slightly.

"Have I ever been unappreciative?"

"Ha!" she let out a bitter laugh. "I hardly say that counts. You'd be appreciative of any woman's attentions. Human, djinn, succubus. Everyone knows you don't have a type."

"You say that like it's a bad thing." He chuckled, his eyes sweeping over her again. Try as he might, he couldn't shake the image of the King of Elm with his green tentacles all over her. Everybody knew what he looked like, though few ever actually saw him. His image was printed on the Elmaran dinar, paper money legitimized by the seal and used for debts public and private all over Qaf. A youthful feminine face, despite his indescribably long years, large black horns twisting up from his head like a ram. He was no ordinary djinn—a freak of nature. Not that Bakr could easily tolerate the thought of any man touching Sezan.

"Tell me more about Elm," he said, hoping to needle more information out of her. "I've never made it to the Lower Continent."

She hesitated before answering, her glittering eyes taking in the room before glancing his way. "I'd prefer not to reduce myself by talking gossip. If you have something substantive to say, I'm all ears, but I'm not some trite woman to be entertained by petty harem talk."

"Excuse me." He ran his tongue over his teeth. "It's been so long, I almost forgot how uptight you are."

The tiniest twitch passed over her cheek. Then she smiled. "Did you need something? I was perfectly happy watching the room when you walked up and started talking to me like some fellow soldier on a piss break."

"Piss break?" He laughed so hard he bowed over himself. "It sounds so vulgar when you say it."

Again a glint of yellow streaked through her eyes—disgust, as he might have expected. She pulled back her shoulders and nodded toward him. "It's a good thing this kingdom no longer rests its fate on your shoulders. If you'll excuse me." She lifted her silks and turned to leave.

He caught her wrist. Her head whipped back to look at him, and at last her eyes focused on his. Just as quickly, she looked away.

"Where are you going in such a hurry?" he asked.

"I shouldn't think that concerns you. I'm sure you have a trough of women waiting to flirt with the war hero."

"You know me and my trough." He smirked and took a slow step closer. "I'd be happy to move you to the top, though."

"Your hold on me crosses a line," she said, pushing him away. "And you just want to hear more about the King of Elm."

"What would you prefer we talk about?" He knew he should step back but suddenly was possessed by the need to smell her perfume. "Politics? Religion? Art?"

Her pull against his grip softened. "Since when did you have an appetite for any of those?"

"What do you know about my appetites? Or should I ask, what do you remember?"

The veins in her slender neck tightened. "I would slap you here and now if it wouldn't cause a scene."

"We can step outside."

She opened her mouth, then snapped it shut. "I'm not naïve enough to be caught alone with you, not after the last time." After a breath, she continued, "But I do wish to discuss a bit of politics."

"I am your servant, sheikha."

"Don't patronize me," she said stiffly.

He laid his other hand on top of hers, stealing the smallest caress of her silken skin. For a while, he said nothing, just smiling down at her and watching the golden light play in her eyes. It made him feel homesick, and he almost wanted to tell her that. Instead, he chewed on the inside of his cheek.

"You haven't changed at all," Sezan said suddenly. "You still bite your cheek when you're keeping things from me."

The skin of one eye twitched. He released his cheek. "And you still over-analyze every-thing."

"Not everyone can afford to glide through life without a worry in the world because they're best friends with Jahmil Amir."

"Indeed. My life is a bucket of roses." He sniffed and shook his head. "So. Politics?"

"I want to be Shihala's royal emissary."

"That sounds like a personal problem."

Her hands tightened under his. "I want you to speak to Jahmil on my behalf."

"Me?" he chuckled. "The unappreciative, gossiping, common soldier on a piss break? I'm surprised at you."

"If you're surprised, then you know me even less than I thought. Though that doesn't surprise me at all." She looked up at him through her lashes, her eyes shining. "Would you be more willing to oblige if I pouted? Pleaded? Took your hand and pulled you to my bedroom with promises of a sordid night of quid pro quo?"

"That you even have to ask…" He flattened his chin in thought. "Perhaps you don't know much about me either."

She sighed. With a quick glance at her feet, she lifted her gaze upon him once more. "Please?"

"Now who's the one making a scene?" He tightened his grip on her hand. "Why do you want to be Shihala's emissary?"

A slight blush purpled her cheeks. "Forget it," she said, pushing against his hold. "I don't know why I thought you'd be capable of being serious about anything."

"I'm serious. See?" He frowned hard. "Look how serious I am. If I'm supposed to make a case to Jahmil, I'll need to know your motives and qualifications."

Her golden eyes narrowed. "So if I humor you and tell you why, you'll talk to Jahmil?"

"I don't see any reason why not."

Her eyes widened. "No." She shook her head and abruptly pulled away, ripping her hand from his grasp. "I've heard those exact words before. They were the last ones you spoke to me before…" Her head shaking increased before coming to an immediate halt. "Never again."

She turned and walked away.

"Sezan," he called, causing nearby courtiers to pause and take notice. She didn't stop. If anything, her pace quickened. His feet twitched to follow her. Instead, he sighed and shook his head before walking in the opposite direction. He could hardly remember a time they had parted company without her storming off, except perhaps the last time. He wanted to brush it off, just Sezan being exactly the person she had always been.

Married off to the King of Elm… the words twisted through his brain, screeching and clawing like summer bats.

A scowl lingered on his lips as he made his way out of the palace. The party was dead anyway.

CHAPTER FOUR

SEZAN

SEZAN COULD NOT WALK fast enough in her tiny jeweled slippers to get away from Bakr and his mocking smile. She would have taken them off but worried it would draw unwanted attention. Hurrying up a long flight of winding stairs, she made it to her quarters and slipped inside, shutting the door gently behind her when she wished to slam it. She had only spent a moment in the room to freshen up before the wedding, but Lila had everything in order. Her perfumes and jewelry lay sparkling in the bright white fires overhead, and her dresses hung crisply in the armoire. All of Lila's potion and remedy plants hung in moonlit corners and glistening bottles of tinctures lined a tray by her mirror. Normally, the feeling of order would help her calm Sezan's nerves. But not today. Not after Bakr.

She stomped over to the bed and grabbed a furry pillow. Squeezing it tight, she wished to rip it in half. But then what would the maids say? She growled.

Sezan threw the pillow back on the opulent, ruched sheets and paced the room. How dare he show up back in Shihala and talk to her so casually? How dare he take her hand after he had left it empty all those years ago? Was that how he was going to play this? Stupid? Or was she the stupid one? Letting her heart wobble at the sight of him after he abandoned her. She would not so easily forget he had left her the very night they had decided to elope and he'd promised he'd stay with her always—because *he didn't see any reason why not to*. No, she could never forget that he had gone away from her and off to war without nary a goodbye or acknowledgment that she lived, even after she had become suddenly and violently ill,

But he clearly thought she could. How else could he just pop up, smiling and alluding to their past like she was another one of the women he coaxed so casually to his bed? How dare he pretend it meant nothing when it meant everything to her? He knew he was the only man she had ever been willing to give her soul for.

And what a waste that had been.

She collapsed on the bed and lay her face in her hands. Why? Why in Qaf had she chosen Bakr? And why had she made that terrible deal? Stupid Eastern Elm and its harem and fountains of wine. Even after everything he put her through, part of her—the part that trusted him explicitly and lived for his warm breath against her neck—couldn't give him up and made excuses for why he left. Or defended why his writing her a single letter over two years was too much to ask of him. Because how could that cold, uncaring person be her Bakr? The man whose arms she had fallen asleep in countless times feeling like the luckiest woman in the world? She had not fallen in love with a monster. Had she?

She sighed so deeply it pulled at her ribs. It didn't matter now, anyway. She'd made the deal with the lilith of her own volition, and whether or not he helped her with Jahmil, she couldn't change that. She had given him one final chance to prove right that annoying, loyal piece of her heart, and he had failed. Forget him.

After a few steadying breaths, Sezan sat up straight. It was done. The time to moan and complain—at least outwardly—was over. Now she needed a plan.

Since Bakr refused to talk to Jahmil on her behalf, she would have to try on her own. She grimaced. Jahmil had always given her the cold shoulder at awkward family dinners, in the palace gardens, whenever they were forced to receive nobles from neighboring kingdoms, and anytime he had seen her in the hallways as he walked by with his friends. Some of the animosity was to be expected: any male child she had would be next in line to the throne if Jahmil died before having his own, but he was also just a prickly person who looked upon the members of his court as pawns to be shipped around and married off whenever there was a need. A kingly way of looking down on people. The only time she'd seen him with any sort of softness was around...

The door clicked open and Sezan stood, knocking the abused pillow to the floor. Lila's head poked in, and Sezan sighed in relief.

"I came as soon as I heard," she said, rushing over to Sezan's side.

"Heard what?" Sezan asked, but her stomach already sank like the moons beyond the horizon.

"That Bakr is alive and made a scene with you at the ball."

"A scene!" She had to force each finger loose from her clenched fist. "There was no scene. There was Bakr being his usual self—"

"An insolent fool?" Lila offered helpfully.

"Exactly," Sezan said with a huff. "He won't help."

Lila's brows scrunched together in her usual look of pity. "I'm sorry," she whispered.

"I even said please, *ealayk allaena!*"

Lila patted her shoulder and sat her back down on the bed. "So, what do we do now?"

Sezan released the tension in her shoulders and collapsed back onto the sheets. The feathery down sunk slowly beneath her, and the ruby and ivory chain that dipped across her forehead slid coolly across her skin. "We have to go to Jahmil ourselves and hope Ayelet Amira has softened him."

"Ich." Lila's lips dipped down, a cringe hidden in a smile.

"Agreed," Sezan said as her future dimmed before her eyes. "Ich."

While not cruel or even unkind, her eldest brother had a reputation for being... precise, critical, and a stickler for protocol. She highly doubted his recent lapse in political strategy had softened him. If anything, it probably made him worse as he tried to make up relations between the surrounding kingdoms.

"What if you just tried talking to Ayelet Amira?"

Sezan raised a finger to her lip and tapped it gently. "Jahmil would smell my intentions from a mile away. How many other courtiers do you think are coming up to the new princess trying to gain favors? I saw the way he looked at her at the wedding, like she was the only star in the sky and he was lost at sea. She'll be impossible to get to without him hovering nearby."

Lila sat up and looked at her with a glint of mischief in her copper eyes. "I know who could get close to her without suspicion."

Sezan furrowed her brow, then bolted upright and shook her head. "I just told you Bakr wouldn't help. And frankly, I'd rather die than ask again." He certainly didn't look at *her* the same way Jahmil looked at Ayelet.

"The princess doesn't have to know Bakr isn't willing. You could just say you two are together. It's true a third of the time."

Sezan tilted her head to the side and considered Lila's proposition. "Alright. We shall give it a try." The worst the princess could do would be to suck her dry of magic, and if Sezan failed, that was going to happen in a couple of weeks anyway.

She gathered up a basket of fruit and trinkets from Elm to bring to the princess's private rooms and stepped into the hallway. She slipped between shadows and curtains, trying not to draw attention to herself so that she could approach the princess alone when she retired for the night. As she passed through the large atrium in the middle of the palace, a group of men strolled through, booming with laughter.

She pulled her hijab further over her hair and tucked herself behind a particularly leafy qawiun tree with bright pink fruit that smelled of hibiscus and orange. It was a gift from Izrak, a rare message congratulating peace from the Bloody Queen herself. Sezan pushed the flowers slowly until she could see the room. She recognized a few of the men. A couple of generals from Shihala's lower ranks. An advisor to Ahmar. And her uncle, the Marqiz Rahik, freshly returned from the Jasraib Isles to the bahamut with a moonburn that turned the royal blue skin of his cheeks a splotchy purple. She bit her thumb and prayed they wouldn't see her. Rahik was not an understanding soul when it came to women being anywhere without a man, and she didn't have the patience to hold her tongue at the moment.

Even worse, he was an utter embarrassment to the holiness of the Shihalan royal family. Forget drinking as haram, Rahik constantly ranted and raved about the superiority of men and boasted of his growing power in the pagan cult of the Cybelian Court; a group of wild religious devotees she had only heard about from Lila. He also held a grudge against her and Jahmil because the amir had decreed he would never take the throne, instead giving her future sons the rights should anything happen to Jahmil. No, nothing good could come from her running into her uncle. Sezan bit her lip and let the blooms fall back in place. She had a mind to transform into a butterfly and escape, but the prickly metamorphosis would leave her clothes abandoned and bring her no closer to visiting the princess.

Then their jovial slander caught her ear.

"Can you believe that mongrel Bakr dared show his face here?" Rahik bellowed. "Two years in debt to me in a deal sealed by the King of Elm and he thinks I'll overlook it?"

Sezan leaned closer through the smooth leaves. It did not surprise her one wit Bakr was in debt—he paid for everything with hot air, whether that be affection or food—but in debt to her cruel uncle came as a surprise.

"Walking around like some war hero. Pah!" one of the generals snarled. "He didn't win the war. He just kept a bunch of penniless peasants alive that we now have to feed."

Yes, thought Sezan dryly. *How dare he help the less fortunate?* Insolent swine. For all Bakr's inability to care for her, she knew he'd starve himself before he let anyone else do so. She growled silently at the thought, not wanting to lose her anger over all the terrible things he did to her because of the nice ones he did for everyone else.

"Did you see how those fools groveled to him?" snapped another. "As if they have forgotten what he truly is."

Rahik hiccuped, his fluffy black brows quivering and his belly shaking from the force. "Don't worry. After tonight, we won't have to look at his disgusting human face for very much longer."

Sezan pulled back, moving her pursed lips side to side. Bakr may have dug a hole too deep this time. But she was feeling supremely petty, and if he wouldn't help her, why should she help him? Though... if she could discover some dirt on Rahik, maybe she could force Bakr, or even Jahmil, to trade her a favor in exchange. She set down her basket and hunched her shoulders submissively. Enough deliberating. Growing up in the harem, she'd been training for just such subversive political games her whole life. She scurried out from behind the qawiun tree and looked at the men in fake surprise.

Bowing over and over, she apologized effusively for stepping in the way of such noble and magnanimous men.

"Why you clumsy little..." Rahik's ruddy cheeks cooled a shade as his temper switched to a grating condescension. "I know you." He stroked his flabby chin as if he were trying to solve world hunger. "You're Maarit's daughter."

"Your niece," she bowed her head again. "Sheikha Sezan, daughter of Sheikha Maarit hubu Almalik."

"Your mother was a vixen." He chomped his teeth at her with a growl, and she had to shove her nails into her palms to keep from recoiling.

"I will make sure to tell her of your admiration next I see her," she said, knitting her brows in a look of solemn respect. "But first, you must take care of yourself, uncle."

Rahik grumbled and patted his wide stomach. "What do you speak of, woman? I've fought wars drunker than this."

Sezan smiled through the bitter taste in her mouth. How many times had Bakr railed about how Rahik had never set foot on a battlefield and sent everyone else to die in his place? Four hundred, at least. "It is not the enemy I worry about, but the stairs."

He barked out a drunken laugh and swayed a little.

"Shall I help you to your chambers?" she asked, sweetening her smile with doe eyes.

While she normally would go to great lengths to avoid being alone with the man, he looked a drop of wine away from a blackout. Where he even got the wine in Jahmil's sober palace was a wonder. But it could work to her advantage. Maybe alone she could find out more about what exactly Bakr owed and use it as leverage.

His beady eyes rolled over her, each flick of the washed-out gems like the scrape of beetle legs across her skin. Then he gargled a sigh. "Not tonight, child. I have important things to do that a simple woman like you wouldn't understand."

"But uncle—"

"Don't make me repeat myself," he growled, raising a hand.

Sezan dropped her gaze to the floor and cowered so low the ends of her hijab brushed the floor. Her mind raced desperately for something to say to avoid being hit. And even though she regretted the next thought that came into her mind, she spoke it anyway. "My apologies, uncle. I did not want to be alone. A man has made inappropriate comments toward me, and I feel in need of a familial protector."

"What fool would dare insult my niece?" Rahik sneered. He staggered closer to her, reached up, and grabbed the fabric of her hijab. He looked directly at her face as he rubbed the silky fabric absently between his sweaty fingers. "Tell me the mongrel's name and I will cut him down."

She licked her lip and fought her revulsion at his caraway-laced breath. It wouldn't be a lie. Not really. He *had* made inappropriate comments... She bit back her worries. He didn't care about her anyway, she told herself, and the name slipped from her tongue. "General Bakr."

Rahik smiled cruelly. He stole one more glance at her face and one more feel of her fabric before turning away. "As you wish, my little usurper."

He stormed down the hall laughing and cursing Bakr's name. Sezan felt the pinch of guilt where her anger at Bakr had formerly resided. Maybe she should intervene... It would be an awful waste if she lost her magic to save the idiot only to get him killed now. But his insolence from earlier crept in, washing the burn with cool indifference. He never suffered any consequences for his perpetual, fast-talking dismissiveness. And her uncle wouldn't kill him if he still owed him something, anyway. Dead men don't pay debts. She just prayed her uncle wouldn't remember her name when he found Bakr.

Muttering reassurances to herself, she slipped back behind the tree and picked up her basket. Then cringed. The gifts inside looked vapid. Just the thing a heartless courtesan looking to get ahead would bring. She picked up a bejeweled drakonte statue and turned it slowly in her hand. The princess would not have an easy time in Shihala, not if Bakr's run at court was any indication. Vermin and human were used interchangeably here. Sezan sighed. She didn't have the heart to play the politics game with someone who wasn't playing it themselves. She would find a different way to become emissary, to stop her deal and keep her magic.

Slipping the trinkets into her pockets, she passed through an open side door into the gardens. There, she plucked a few alyasmin and tied them together with a small piece of twine she pulled from a nearby rope that held a glowing sconce.

With a hopeless shrug, she headed to the princess's chambers. After laying the alyasmin and fruit outside the princess's door, she stood to leave.

"Hello."

Sezan straightened, smoothed her face, then turned. "Al'amirat Ayelet," she said hastily, dropping into a bow. The human was far more beautiful than the rumors said, and despite her deal with the lilith, Sezan couldn't help but touch a hand to her chest as if it would help keep her magic in. After all, Ayelet Amira, though pretty and simple-looking enough, was the sole being who could control the wisps of pure magic that floated between both worlds. Such ability to harness the raw pieces of mysterious magic and bend them to her will made her the singular most terrifying woman Sezan had ever before been in the presence of. With the exception, perhaps, of the demonic lilith who pulled her strings.

"Oh, please, no more bowing." Ayelet waved her hand with a sigh. "I'm beginning to think Shihalans would rather look at the floor than me."

Sezan smiled and shifted to a curtsy. "I know what you mean. You'd think with all the time we spend honoring each other we'd make the floors in a prettier design."

Ayelet grinned. "Finally, someone who talks to me to like a…"

"Person?" Sezan offered.

"Yes. Let's call it that." Ayelet's eyes fell on the basket by the door and lit up. Genuine joy. Sezan picked up the flowers and held them out to the princess. "You are fond of Shihala's flower?"

A smile made of secrets crossed the princess's lips. "I am," she said and took them, cradling them in the crook of her elbow like a child. "Come, let's talk inside my room. I worry if we linger here too long the other nobles will catch my scent and hunt me down."

"As you wish, *amirti*."

"Please," the princess groaned. "Call me Ayelet."

"Of course," Sezan bowed, then caught herself and brushed a finger along the cracks in the floor. "We really must get better tiles. Something bright like Ard's sun, I should think."

Ayelet giggled. "Would most Shihalans even know what that looked like?"

"No," Sezan shook her head with knit brows. "Most djinn are too frightened to cross into the human world."

"I suppose they could just look at your eyes," Ayelet said thoughtfully, leaning in closer. "They're remarkably like earth's sun at dawn."

Sezan smiled sweetly, hoping the corners of her lips didn't twitch, Bakr's useless, intoxicating words on her mind. She cleared her throat in a delicate *eh hem.* "Are you sure I won't be imposing? I know you've had a long day."

"Oh no," Ayelet said, pushing Sezan through the doors in an unexpected show of forcefulness. "General Bakr will be by shortly with Jahmil anyway, or so he has promised."

"I would believe a promise from Jahmil far more than from Bakr," Sezan snipped as her heart seized. She smiled guiltily and stifled a groan at her own impropriety. She could not be caught in this room with Bakr. Not after what happened at the party and then with Rahik. "But if you have company coming, *amirti—*"

"Nonsense," Ayelet cut her off. "It sounds like you know two out of my three favorite people. I insist you stay."

Sezan's chest tightened as she watched the door to her escape shut with a bang.

"And I insist you call me Ayelet."

CHAPTER FIVE

Bakr

Bakr changed into civilian clothes and made his way across the city. It had been almost seven hundred degrees—two full days—since the last time he slept, but he was still able to put one foot in front of the other and form semi-coherent thoughts. One of the side-effects of spending so much time being hunted by an army a hundred times the size of your own is you get very good at functioning on little or no sleep, particularly when that army was headed by magic users who can cut your very soul out of your body. Bakr had seen some incredible and horrific things in his life, especially since the fall of Karzusan, but there was no horror that compared to watching a Vesparian Spider rake razor-sharp lines of pure magic through his troops, decapitating and slaughtering hundreds with little more than a flick of a thin, shock-white wrist.

As he dodged through the sprawling construction site that was Karzusan, Bakr couldn't help flinching at every noise. A rat scurrying from one rubbish pile to another, the call of an Ankha bird, or *la samah Allah*, footsteps. Each sound sent a thrill of panic up his spine that fought against all logic. The buildings twisted in the darkness to look like trees, and he thought he heard the screech of bial'dabaye in the distance.

He knew now, of course, how the creatures were made—innocents made to suffer at the hands of Köle Amir, the enemy of Shihala and leader of Vespar's bloodthirsty forces. Human children were captured and enslaved, then twisted with magic to become snarling monsters. Half-man, half-hyena. As strong as a beast and as intelligent as any of Allah's three races. In that state, the children lost all control of their faculties and attacked without thought or mercy. Even sweet Sheikha Serap had nearly perished of such a fate and certainly would have had Ayelet and Jahmil not found a way to save her and release the magic that imprisoned all the others back into Qaf.

During his time in Orkeshi, Bakr had killed hundreds, if not thousands, of bial'dabaye, but he refused to torture himself about it. Their blood was on Köle's hands, not his. He hadn't known what they were, and it wasn't he who transformed them into monsters. Even if he had known, he still would have had to kill them to protect the innocent people to whom he had sworn his loyalty and his life in Orkeshi. He killed the beasts because of what they were in the moment — horrific, evil, blood thirsty. And how can anything be judged on any criteria other than what it is at the moment?

There was no such thing as innocence. Not really. Only the difference between sins of the past, present, and future.

The poor areas of Karzusan had not been rebuilt yet, though the effort was underway. It would take years to remake all the apartment buildings, to fix the sewage system, to re-establish bread lines, public baths, and hospitals. It sounded like the sort of work a grand vizier might be responsible for.

Bakr groaned and let his head hang. He could hardly think of anything more horrible. He wasn't from Shihala. Like every other miserable corner of Qaf, the magic of the place had never done him any favors. Yet, he had given so much blood and sweat and time fighting for it.

No, not for Shihala. For Jahmil. And for the common people trapped behind enemy lines with no other options.

He came to a small square building, little more than a pile of scorched bricks that would have seemed like all the others to someone who didn't know what they were looking for. It had been years, but Bakr had come and gone from this place so many times, often blasted out of his skull on hash or mushrooms or alcohol. He could've found it in a dream. He ran his fingers over the stones, searching for out-of-place smoothness. When he found the stone he was after, he pushed it in and a small door swung open. A quick glance over his shoulder at the empty street and he slipped inside.

He made his way down the winding, narrow stairs as he had a thousand times before. The music filtered up to him, rude and biting. It couldn't have been more different from the cultured tones that shivered over his skin earlier that evening. At Jahmil's perfect wedding to his perfect bride, where once again, against all odds and all expectations, he had found himself alone with Sezan. And once again, with frustrating predictability, he had let her slip through his fingers.

He forced himself not to think about her. That was a bottomless pit and where he stood was dark enough.

At the foot of the stairs, a seven-foot-tall Ghaluman with cherry-red skin and a bald head stood guard in front of the wooden door, the same as ever. The sound of drunken laughter and the sweet smell of hookah smoke brushed up against him in warm waves. The djinn looked him up and down and smiled. "Bakr? Is that you?"

"What's up, Mahmud?" Bakr said, slapping his outstretched hand.

"I thought you were dead, *habibi*."

"Not completely."

He smiled and popped open the door. "Good to see you."

Bakr gave Mahmud a friendly tap on the shoulder and slipped past him inside. Light flickered from hundreds of tiny fires floating about the ceiling like fish in a tank. Some two hundred people were crammed into the tiny space. They lay on divans in the corners, fading into nothing as poppy wax ate away their brains. They played with their own fire in front of their faces. Others were dancing, though that too was nothing like what courtiers did. One woman was pressed against the wall, her skirt up around her navel and a man held her thighs around his hips. They both groaned in pleasure as others looked on.

Bakr paused and watched for a moment, a lazy grin slumping on his face. Just another night at the Izamub.

He made his way to the bar, his eyes scanning the crowd for the sweaty, royal blue figure of Rahik. Nothing. The entitled bastard was going to make him wait.

He ordered a foamy cup of rash wine—thick black liquid that tasted a bit like straw—and found a tiny table in the corner to sit and nurse it. He wished he could say all this business with Rahik had taken his mind off Sezan, but all it did was shine a spotlight on a whirlpool of memories that he did not want to sink into. The night he'd lost her, or the night she'd lost him. Her pale face pressed against the floor, throat swelling as she gasped for air. And Rahik at the doorway, looking down his lumpy nose at the scene. The son of a snake had been smiling.

Rage bubbled through his blood exactly the same as it had that night, and just like then there was no way to dispel it. Rahik had gotten everything he wanted that night; the night Bakr stopped hoping that anything would ever really get better.

Cheers to the status quo, he thought caustically, then glugged down his wine and ordered another. Music pounded around him, and his tired head yearned towards the table until it was cradled in his folded arms. His eyes burned, desperate to close.

A few degrees wouldn't hurt...

A hard jab on the shoulder and Bakr looked up through a blur. He hadn't realized he'd fallen asleep and did not know how much time had passed. The club had cleared a bit. As his vision focused, the hideous face he'd been waiting to see became clearer.

"Are you high?" asked Rahik.

Bakr wiped some spittle from his chin and shook his head. "What took you so long?"

"You're not the only one who knows how to be fashionably late, halfbreed."

Bakr chuckled at the cliche insult and shook his head, driving away the fog of sleep with sheer force of will. "So, tell me, Rahik. What have you been doing with yourself this last year while all the real men of Shihala were off fighting the war?"

Rahik smiled coldly. "Who do you think arranged Jahmil's marriage to the Queen of Ahmar?"

"I should've known you had your hand in that catastrophe."

"No one can predict fate," he snapped. "Speaking of unpredictable, I saw you pushing yourself on Sheikha Sezan at the wedding tonight. I even ran into her on my way over here. She said she was afraid of you. That you had made inappropriate comments to her. She asked me to cut you down."

The words stung like a bite of a *zinbur*. Had Sezan really said that? He knew she felt a lot of very negative things about him, but afraid?

Bakr inhaled through his nostrils, letting it out slowly. "Leave her out of this."

"That was the agreement, wasn't it?" Rahik took out his snuff box and inhaled a big pile of black flakes. His eyes watered, and he sniffed like he was in pain. "She's a little old for my tastes, but still quite the beauty. Refined, cultured. Far too good for the likes of you."

Bakr forced another laugh and tipped his wine towards Rahik. "You'll get no argument from me."

"I hear Jahmil plans to disband the harem, so I suppose she'll be looking for a new place to live soon. She's my niece, but still... maybe I'll take her as my concubine."

"Jahmil is dismissing the courtesans, not evicting his family." Bakr turned his lips up in a snarl. "And Sezan would rather die."

"And she will, if you don't hold up your end of the bargain."

His mouth filled with bile at the threat, and his fingers twitched to snap that fat neck. It would be so easy. But he couldn't. Far from clearing his debt, killing Rahik would put him in immediate default, the consequences of which were unfathomable.

Bakr bit down on the back of his jaw and bared his teeth in a predatory smile. "You have to give a man an opportunity to pay his debt before you punish him for reneging."

"Give a man an opportunity?" Rahik's face furled with irritation. "You've been ducking me for two years!"

"Yes, how crafty of me to have the Vespars take the motherland just so I could avoid your debt." Bakr cocked an eyebrow. "If that were true, the Seal of Elm would have melted the flesh from my bones by now."

"What do you know about the Seal of Elm, half-breed?"

Again, he tried to laugh it off, but the insult which had haunted him all his life slid off Bakr's back like dirty oil, leaving behind a sticky sheen. "You never stipulated what you wanted in return." Bakr tried for another sip of wine, but the glass was empty. He scoffed, turned the glass upside down, and put it on top of his head. "So, just tell me what in the name of Iblis you want and stop wasting my time."

"Is it true what they say about you?"

"Probably."

"Oh, Bakr. How I've missed our little tête-à-têtes." Rahik's skin shook with that hideous, condescending laugh. "They say that once upon a time before you joined the army and somehow succeeded in bewitching Jahmil Amir, back when you were just another worthless, thieving mongrel living on the streets, you somehow managed to find and even ride the Rukh bird. Is that true?"

"You think I got where I am today by being just another worthless thieving mongrel?" He scoffed and shook his head. "I was *the* worthless, thieving mongrel, thank you very much."

"Did you ride the Rukh or didn't you?"

Bakr's lips curved as the vibrant memory of riding on the back of the magnificent bird glowed in his mind. The legendary Rukh—the rare and immortal, the wise and divine. Forged in fire and born of purity, she should have refused to have anything to do with him.

When he stumbled upon the elephant-sized egg while evading capture in an isolated and unforgiving section of the forest, the golden shell had warmed and cracked under his touch. The chick that was born—more fire than feathers—had bonded with him instantly as if he were her mother. And he had loved her in return with no pretense.

He'd named her Fajar, after the dawn, because to look at her glowing plumage of flames and embers had filled his soul with hope and the serenity of sunshine.

He stayed with her until she was full grown, hiding her in the darkness of the forest. She grew and grew until a single talon was large enough for him to lie on. He had helped her learn to fly, sitting on her neck, encouraging her higher and faster. Pure and inimitable freedom. With Fajar at his side, he had let himself imagine a life where he wasn't alone. That she would lift the halfbreed orphan from Arabia on her divine back, elevating him to the level of the stars. But it wasn't to be.

The day he'd had to drive her from his side to keep her safe from the djinn that would try to cage her or kill her for her magic feathers had been one of the saddest days of his life. Even thinking of it now, his heart ached with the stab of sharp ice.

Bakr refocused his eyes on Rahik. "Why?"

"Because if it is, I have a mission for you. And if you complete it, I'll hold your debt fulfilled."

He took the cup off of his head and set it on the table. To hear Rahik speaking about the Rukh was almost as unpleasant as hearing him say Sezan's name. Rahik never spoke of anything unless he wanted to control it or destroy it, and Bakr was not about to let that happen again.

"I will never harm the Rukh," he said.

Rahik lifted his brow, obviously registering the passion in his voice. Bakr's skin crawled at the anxious possibilities, but thankfully Rahik shook his head. "That isn't what I want."

"Then I'll do it."

"You don't even know what *it* is," Rahik scoffed.

"Does it matter? I have to complete a task of your choosing, isn't that the deal? Isn't that what the King of stinking Elm demands?" He let out a dry chuckle. "One thing, though. Keep your disgusting fingers off of Sezan."

"I agreed to spare her life. I never said I'd keep my fingers off of her." Growling, Rahik reached into his robes and took out a small scroll. When he unrolled it on the table, the bright green light from the King of Elm's seal struck Bakr's eyes. Rahik pointed to the paper. "See? It says I will not *harm* her, not that I will not *touch* her."

"Oh, this has nothing to do with the contract." He pushed the paper aside to look at the lamprey's face. "I'm just telling you that if you go anywhere near Sezan, I *will* find out. And then I *will* snap your thigh bone."

"If you hurt me, the contract is void and Sezan will die."

"Ah, ah, ah." Bakr shook a finger. "The contract says that I won't *kill* you, not that I won't *hurt* you."

Rahik's eyes flashed with white-hot anger, but the black mist of fear curled through the green irises. He was a lump of man, soft from luxurious living whereas Bakr was the Terror of Vespar. If it weren't for his *sakhif* contract, Rahik would have been shaking just to look at him. As it used to be in the good old days.

"How dare you threaten a senior member of the Court of Shihala?" Rahik stumbled.

"I'm a senior member of the Court of Shihala, fat head." Bakr cocked a brow, tightening his smile. "So, yes. I dare. Stay away from Sezan, or I will break your legs."

Rahik twitched his chin from side to side, then leaned back with a superior smirk. "If you take this mission, you won't be around to break anybody's legs."

"One advantage of being a general, I have loyal eyes all over the palace. Do you really want to flinch every time you pass a palace guard wondering if he might be one of my guys?"

The disgusting hagfish bristled. "Have it your way."

Bakr flashed a predatory smile—his teeth white and very shiny—then scratched the scar on his eyebrow with the edge of his thumbnail. "Alright, freak. I'm listening."

Rahik took a seat and laid out his plan in exhausting detail. Bakr struggled to keep up, the ghost of sleep whispering in his ear, calling away his attention. The litigious goblin updated the official contract to reflect the terms. It seemed simple enough. All he had to do was find Fajar and have her take him to retrieve an artifact called *Khātam Sulaymān*, whatever that was, and bring it back before the fall of the next Moonless Night.

But nothing Rahik ever did was straightforward. If it were, Rahik would have just hired assassins to kill him rather than getting him tangled in this mess with Sezan. Then again, if Bakr turned up murdered, Jahmil would be upset. It was likely he'd launch a full investigation and not stop until the perpetrator had been found and brought to justice. Maybe this was just Rahik's way around that. If Bakr got himself killed trying to complete an impossible suicide mission, no one would be the wiser.

He comforted himself knowing that if he were to die while the contract still stood in good faith, the default counter clause would kick in. So long as he accepted the mission and sought to fulfill it with *genuine and unerring conviction* (so it was written), Sezan would be safe. And if he faltered in his mission in any way or for any reason other than his death, the Seal of Elm would make certain he collapsed into a hissing puddle of his own liquefied entrails, and the terrible fate from which Sezan had been spared would return to finish her off.

He couldn't allow that. She hated him now because he couldn't allow it. She didn't know why she had fallen so ill that night. Or why he'd had no choice but to leave her like that, to walk away and abandon her to her pain. Proving himself to be the monster that everyone he had ever known believed him to be. Everyone, except Sezan. But now she believed it. After what he had done, how could she not?

He could never tell her the truth. It wasn't the contract that kept him quiet, but he'd decided long ago he would rather have her hate him forever than have to know the truth of the dark curse that coursed through her veins. The curse that Rahik had put there simply because Bakr had loved her.

She deserved freedom; a happy life unencumbered by such fears. He would have done anything to protect her from that.

When all was said and done, the revised contract signed and sealed, Bakr stumbled back to his house. Upon first returning to Karzusan, he'd been amazed to find the ugly wooden structure still standing. It was situated a few blocks from the palace where he kept his bed and his one servant, Ana, an elderly Ahmaran woman whom he'd known since his bandit days. She kept the place nice, purchasing little bits of art and bric-à-brac, rugs and furniture, and kept the kitchen stocked. If it weren't for her, the house would have echoed with emptiness, and he probably would have lived on a diet of horse bread.

Bakr dragged his feet up the stairs and collapsed face down on his mattress. His feet hurt, but he was too tired to kick off his boots. And his shoulders were cold, but he didn't have the energy to wrap himself in the blanket. He closed his eyes and began to drift when the bedroom door banged open.

"Go away," he moaned.

Ana marched across the room and smacked his butt hard. "Get up. The prince has summoned you."

Bakr rolled his head to one side. "On his wedding night?" He groaned and pressed his face into the pillow. "I already told him, I can't help with that."

"Phew. You stink. What have you been rolling in?"

"Leave. Me. Alone."

"I'll get a bath ready." She slapped his butt again. Harder. "Get up!"

"I hate you," he growled and shoved a pillow over his head. "I hate everyone."

CHAPTER SIX

SEZAN

BAKR, OF COURSE, HAD yet to show. Sezan fretting in the first place was ridiculous.

As relief washed over her, Sezan couldn't help but pity Ayelet. Though she kept her spirits up with an impeccably mastered smile, the sadness in her human eyes grew the longer the moons passed through the sky. He was one of her only friends here in the kingdom, Ayelet Amira had lamented, and she wished for a boost to her spirits. But even the prince regent of Shihala couldn't rein Bakr in.

Which was why, Ayelet had reasoned aloud, Jahmil himself was late. He was chasing down the last of his dearest friends because he knew what was best. The princess did not say it bitterly, though. There was no hint of jealousy or frustration. Ayelet simply believed in and trusted Jahmil, and that was that. What a different world they lived in for a woman to trust a man so implicitly. Even as the princess sat alone with a stranger in a vacuous palace with ugly floors.

Sezan scooped up a handful of stones and began dropping them in a line to the right with little glass-like *tinks*. She hadn't played Mangala since she was a child and felt very certain she was losing.

"Oh, no," Ayelet tucked in her lips and shook her head, trying to suppress a smile. "Are you sure you wish to start there?"

Sezan frowned, looking between the stones in her hand and the princess. Then she let slip a grin. "I made a rather large miscalculation, didn't I?"

"That depends on if you were trying to win or lose."

Sezan's smile sharpened. "Always win."

The door to the room burst open, and a harried Jahmil rushed up to Ayelet. Pulling her from her seat, he scooped the princess up in his arms and kissed her as if he hadn't seen her in... oh, two years or so.

Sezan studied the curtains in the corner of the room.

When at last he detached himself from Ayelet, Jahmil turned and looked at Sezan as if he'd just noticed she existed in this world at all. Nothing out of the usual.

"Hello, Sezan," he said, offering her a quirked brow. "You're looking well. I assume you've come to offer my beautiful wife and I well-wishes."

Jahmil's shoulders were tight, arms itching to cross. He kept a hand protectively on Ayelet's shoulder despite her easy stance and even easier smile. Just as Sezan predicted, he had decided her an agent of the Evil Eye before she had even spoken.

"No guard dog duty today, Jahmil," Ayelet said with a laugh. "Sezan and I were just playing Mangala and chatting while we waited for Bakr."

"Is that a fact?" Jahmil's upper lip curled at Sezan. Then his attack eyes shifted to a softness she had not seen in him before as he turned his gaze to his wife. He took her palms in his. "I am sorry. I was certain I could find him. I can't imagine where he's gone." He bent down and kissed the top of her hands.

Did he check the bed of every courtesan? Of the servants? Of the gray-skinned lilith whom he apparently called for in the night? Sezan kept her face smooth and her tongue quiet.

"If you'll excuse us," Jahmil said, pulling his shoulders back to full height. The classic gesture men used to show they would not be argued with. "I would like to be alone with my wife on our wedding night."

Sezan looked between his serious face and Ayelet's apologetic smile. She should definitely go.

"I understand," she said and curtsied dramatically, chin lifted high so she looked to the ceiling instead of the tiles on the floor. Jahmil raised a brow and Ayelet giggled.

The door slapped open, and a large servant bowed before stepping inside, dragging a wooden trunk behind him. As he deposited his burden in the middle of the floor, Bakr swaggered in after. Sezan rolled her suddenly tight shoulders. He looked like he'd just had a bath and a shave, though the shadow of his beard was already coming in and dark circles clung to his under eyes. At first, he didn't notice her, his gaze on Ayelet and Jahmil.

"A gift for the bride." He kicked open the chest. Inside was a pile of at least a thousand *nazaar* charms against the Evil Eye, bright blue eyes of glass staring up at Princess Ayelet, who showed Bakr an indulgent smile.

"You're going to need every last one," he said gruffly, then swept his hand towards the chest. At last, his eyes fell on Sezan. His lip twitched slightly, and the skin under his bright jade eyes wrinkled. His tongue twitched behind his teeth as if he were looking for something to say. He bit his cheek, which meant he was once again hiding something. Sezan stifled an eye roll.

"I didn't realize I was coming to a party," he said, breaking out one of his larger-than-life smiles as he turned back to Jahmil and Ayelet.

"If you had, would you have come sooner?" Ayelet asked, grinning. "It is lucky Sezan was here to keep me company or I would have had my wisps out looking for you, instead."

"I would have come sooner if your ape of a husband had mentioned I was expected."

"I should think knowing you're expected would make you disappear," Sezan couldn't help but mutter under her breath.

"You two are at it again, hmm?" Jahmil's tired eyes flinched to her, then to Bakr. An ember of pink gleamed at their centers. "That's just wonderful."

Sezan's toes curled in her slippers. This would almost certainly end poorly. Bakr was a wild cannon and Jahmil far too keen and cold to let this pass quietly.

"We are not *at* anything." Bakr smiled tightly at Jahmil. "Our paths may have crossed once or twice."

Ayelet grinned. "We shared a story or two while we were waiting. I think twice might be an understatement."

"Is that so?" His voice went up a little as he turned back to Ayelet. Then he shrugged and waved his hand dismissively. "Well, you know me. I don't like to bore people with... things."

Sezan slipped her hand into her pocket and gripped the drakonte statue so hard it stung. A thing? She was now a *thing?* She took a deep breath that hurt more than getting her hair pinned up. "I was just telling Ayelet Amira of the time you climbed up one of the ramparts to save that mewling little namur kitten and then slid down it to show off and nearly broke your neck. You know, usual tales of your... heroics."

"How very kind of you," he said tightly.

"Would you rather I tell them a different set of stories?" She tilted her head just enough to keep from biting her tongue.

Ayelet looked between her and Bakr. "Uh oh."

"I don't know what is going on with you two," said Jahmil, "but just like old times, it is making me uncomfortable. I'm going to get some tea." He turned to Ayelet. "Would you like some tea, *aşkım*?"

"I would love some. And even more so, I would love to join you." She flashed a smile over her shoulder and wriggled her eyebrows at Sezan before following Jahmil to the table on the other side of the room.

"Now, look what you've done," Sezan whispered.

"What *I* did?" He took an uneasy seat in the chair across from her. "What are you doing here?"

"I was bringing Ayelet flowers if you must know."

"How generous of you. And there wouldn't be any ulterior motive?"

Sezan moved slowly behind him so as not to cause a stir and leaned down by his ear. He smelled of spicy agarwood and fig soap. She took smaller breaths to suffocate old memories. "None whatsoever. I spent all my political sleaziness on dealing with you."

"Don't sell yourself short, Zan." He turned to look at her, so near she could smell the mint on his breath. "I'm sure there's plenty more where that came from."

"Why can't you just play nice for once?"

"Because I'd miss watching that beautiful blue vein twitch in your temple."

She snapped back up, wishing he wasn't right about how angry he was making her.

"Black tea or green?" Ayelet asked from the corner.

Sezan turned to Ayelet. "Green, thank you." She curtsied once more, then flipped back to Bakr. "Why do you enjoy punishing me?" she asked in a hushed growl. "And don't say it's because of my temple or my veins or the cute little scrunch I get in my nose like you always do. What have I done that is so horrible to you?"

"Black," he called, not looking away from her eyes. "With lots of honey."

Then in a low voice, he said, "My apologies, *sheikha*. I wouldn't want you enlisting anyone else to cut me down again."

The coldness in his eyes brushed down her spine, and she looked away. "I did not ask him to cut anyone down, I simply reported facts. Maybe if you had been more obliging, I wouldn't have been in that circumstance to begin with. It is not my fault you caused a scene at the party."

"You call that a scene?" he asked too loudly. "Because I can show you a scene, if that's what you're after."

"Don't you dare," she gripped his shoulders and pressed him down into the seat.

He looked at her hand on his shoulder, then swept his gaze back up to her eyes. "Any excuse to touch me."

She removed her hand and pulled his ear hard. Holding it down by his shoulders, she leaned in and whispered, "Don't test me, Bakr. Not right now."

"Ow," he said flatly. "You're in a fighting spirit tonight. And to think I almost didn't come."

She moved to his front, still holding his ear. She wanted to tell him she was doomed in a matter of weeks. That she had given everything for him so why in Jahannam would he not just help her this once? But she couldn't tell him any of that. Not without looking a fool. So she went with the other truth that had driven her actions since she was a small girl: independence.

"As a man you may have the luxury of doing whatever you wish, but as a full-fledged, unmarried woman of the court, my time is almost done. Do you understand?" She scoffed without giving him a chance to answer. "I swear if you mess this up for me..." She trailed off and stood abruptly, taking the teacup from a waiting Ayelet. Sezan's cheeks stung at being caught in such an unbecoming way. She smiled awkwardly and moved back.

"I think the sphinx will leave its perch eventually, Sezan. We may as well tell them now," said Bakr loudly enough for Jahmil to hear from where he stood at the other end of the room. "I asked Sezan to come here tonight. There is something very important I want to discuss with both of you regarding her future."

Sezan couldn't stop her eyes from widening. She crushed them down into suspicious slits. Was he trying to undo the good will she had been fortuitous enough to build with Ayelet, or was he genuinely trying to help?

"Really, *amirti*," Bakr continued, his soft gaze finding Ayelet. "You are the one I wanted to talk to about this. I'm sure you've noticed that the Kingdom of Shihala, for all its beauty and all its virtue, can be a tad... let us say chauvinistic."

Ayelet smiled good-naturedly. "If the tile choices are any indication, I would believe that whole-heartedly." She shot a glance at Sezan who smiled weakly.

Bakr's eyes darted between them. Then he shrugged. "The truth is, Sezan is wasted in the harem. She is a very talented and intelligent woman who knows more about the goings-on in Qaf than virtually anybody alive. I think it would be wise to give her some manner of official appointment. Given her knowledge of culture..." He stole a glance at Sezan, the pale green of his eyes sparkling. "She would make an excellent royal emissary."

Sezan blinked stupidly. What had just happened?

Ayelet nodded and puckered her lips. "I know little about that, but I do like Sezan." Her kind eyes looked to her, and Sezan blushed. "Jahmil, what do you think about all that? Praise from Bakr about more than how a woman looks is high praise, indeed."

Jahmil took long slow strides towards the conversation, his serious eyes fixed on Bakr. Silence stretched on into eternity as he slowly sipped from his tiny, glass teacup. "What are you up to?"

Bakr smiled, but not one of those overly bright, irritating, show-off smiles. He almost looked genuine. Almost. "I simply believe Sezan would be ideal for the job."

"I already have emissaries in every kingdom in Qaf," said Jahmil with a shrug.

Bakr lifted an eyebrow. "Not all."

"You can't mean…" Jahmil scoffed, a look of disgust filling his eyes. "What is the matter with you? You think I'd send my own sister into that?"

"Why not?" Sezan asked. "You already tried to barter me off to the King of Elm."

Bakr narrowed his eyes at Jahmil and cracked a knuckle. "About that, *habibi…*"

"It was my mother's decision." Jahmil shook his head quickly. "And we were simply trying to get her away from the violence."

"He sent me there to be a part of the harem," Sezan snipped.

"So it's true?" Bakr growled lightly in his throat, the smile on his face taking on the quality of a lion about to pounce.

"During the invasion of the Vespars, it was imperative to draw ourselves closer to our allies," said Jahmil quickly.

"Why you slippery son of a blind drakonte…"

"Bakr, please," Jahmil said, taking the tiniest step back. He may as well have retreated to hide behind his bed. His eyes were flashing with brilliant colors, as they so often did, but with stronger tones of orange, pink, and purple than usual. Humiliation, anxiety, and sorrow.

Sezan glanced between the two, uncertain what she had started between such normally familial friends. "There is nothing to defend now on either of your counts. I saved myself from the situation and would like to move on to present matters. That is, if you two can stop slinging flames for two degrees."

"We will discuss this later and in private," Bakr said to Jahmil in a deep voice, then he forced a tight smile onto his face. "Like I was saying, it is high time we re-established diplomatic contact with the glittering kingdom."

Ayelet smiled and walked her eyes around the room. "Where...?"

"Why, Ahmar, of course." Bakr stole another glance at Sezan, and she blinked back a flinch. "I think we all know why sending a man would be a bad idea. And Sezan and Queen Qadira actually have a fair bit in common. I think she might be just the person to repair that tremendous, gaping rift you caused."

Ayelet scowled. "I should think I like Sezan far too much to send her there. We don't need Ahmar, do we Jahmil?"

He didn't answer, eyes still pouring over Bakr.

Sezan held her breath. This whole conversation was getting away from her, and she still didn't know what to say. Ahmar would be a disaster. There wasn't a more contentious hotbed of rage in all of Qaf. One slip-up would mean war. And war would mean at the very least a loss of status and much more likely catastrophic death and carnage. And then even a harem would be too good for her. She'd have nothing. No influence, no sway. But if sending both countries into a terrible war wasn't enough to ruin her life and everyone else's, the lilith's deal would. Ahmar was the one kingdom close enough to Shihala that would render her excused absence from court for a fealty ceremony moot should ever Jahmil decide to bestow royalty status on anyone. No, she could not go to Ahmar.

"Hear me out," said Bakr, taking a sip of tea. "We cannot afford another war. Shihala barely has the resources to rebuild our infrastructure, and what little standing force we have is needed in Vespar to contend with the rebels there. And even if we could spare the men, you and I both know, Jahmil, that Qadira could cause a tremendous amount of damage, even with all of Ayelet's tricks. I mean, look at what the Vespars were able to do even after the magic was drained from their land. We can't repeat that mistake ever again."

"Of course not," snapped Jahmil.

"And don't we owe it to our people to try to maintain the peace that the two of you sacrificed so much to give to them?" He stepped behind Sezan and laid his hand on her shoulder. She bristled. "Queen Qadira is not the horrible constrictor you have made her out to be. She's just your typical spoiled royal brat. Sezan could be a tremendously calming influence on her. There is hardly a more mature and refined woman in all the Nine Kingdoms. Maybe she could guide the petulant queen towards some of the serenity her parents never succeeded in instilling in her."

The way Bakr was talking, so smooth and lacking in barbs, something had to be off. A game he was playing. An angle of some sort. Then it clicked. "You slept with her," Sezan whispered harshly and turned her hard eyes on him. "Didn't you? You son of a snake."

She shook her head and forced a smile, raising her voice for the room. "I'm not a babysitter for women you've thrown to the side, Bakr. That would be a full-time job on its own."

"Jahmil's the one who threw her aside. In truly epic fashion, I might add." Bakr smirked. "Besides, all emissaries are essentially babysitters."

"It's not a completely terrible idea," said Jahmil, stroking his beard.

Of course, Jahmil hadn't heard a word she'd said. "No," Sezan flashed her eyes to her brother. "Your Highness, brother, not this way. What about Elm?" She nearly gagged suggesting it. "The king fancies me greatly, as you well know. The emissary you have there is an old, stodgy man who can barely put two words together, and I've made great inroads with the courtiers there."

"He still fancies you even after your outright refusal to join his court?" Jahmil asked, cocking an eyebrow. Then he shrugged and looked away. "Shihala and Elm already have excellent relations. The king and I exchange letters on a monthly basis. I don't need another emissary there."

"You blame me for delicately handling an unfair marriage arrangement while you obliterated yours and nearly sent two countries to war?" She could hardly hold in her growl but managed it with a deep swallow. "Ayelet?" Sezan turned the most charming smile she could muster under the weight of Bakr's horrid idiocy. "Ayelet. Maybe I could stay here and be an emissary between you and the ladies of the court. They can be a handful."

Ayelet twiddled her fingers. Sezan held in a sigh. The princess was getting uncomfortable. No doubt if she upset Ayelet, Jahmil would banish her to Ahmar, instead.

"You are all welcome to ignore me, of course," said Bakr, stepping away from the group to add more honey to his cup. "One way or the other, we have to send an emissary to Ahmar soon. I would just prefer we send somebody who might actually be able to make an impact, help avert a war, and reestablish trade. Up until six months ago, Ahmar had always been our most important trading partner. We cannot survive without them in the long run. And especially not when Queen Zalika and Queen Qadira have to work together to put Vespar back together. It would be a shame for our poor relations to extend into that kingdom, especially after Ayelet worked so hard to rescue it. If nothing else, we'll have a war by proxy on our hands." He flicked his eyes to Jahmil. "Your mother will be displeased."

Sezan took to her usual method of counting. She could already tell by the way Jahmil leaned into Bakr's words and pulled back from hers that she had lost this cause. Poor

Ayelet didn't know enough to be of help, and she couldn't blame her for that. It was time Sezan accept her fate and get ahead of it.

She flashed her eyes brightly and honeyed her tone. "I see you know so much about Ahmar, Bakr. It is truly amazing. And I will need a guide to get there and make acquaintances I do not yet have. If it wouldn't be a disservice to my princess—" Sezan curtsied to Ayelet, "—could Bakr accompany me on my diplomatic journey? Just long enough to help me settle before he comes back?" She shot a glance at Bakr. If she was going to suffer, she would make him suffer, too. She reveled in his tightened lips. She was certain he had slept with that stupid queen.

"I would never dream of sending you there without sufficient protection," said Jahmil, turning his gaze towards Ayelet.

"I think it's a grand idea. I can forgo Bakr's company for a few weeks if it will put Sezan at ease." Ayelet shot Sezan an apologetic look. "Though I still feel terrible sending you there."

Bakr choked on his tea and stepped closer. "Let me stop you all for a moment..."

"It is a tremendously difficult situation to thrust a green diplomat into," Jahmil cut him off, his gaze fixed on Sezan. "Sheikha, are you certain you would be prepared to take on such an assignment?"

Sezan forced a coolness through her limbs. Like she had a choice. It was either a diplomat for Ahmar or a concubine for some sweaty old man. Or death... And all that for a mere three weeks when everyone would learn her secret and she'd be ruined anyway. She pushed those thoughts away with a sigh. "Of course I am, Your Highness. Shihala means everything to me. And with Bakr at my side, I'm sure we will find success."

"I can give you eight reasons why my going to Ahmar is a bad idea," said Bakr quickly. "Number one—"

"Just promise me you won't let him talk too much," Jahmil muttered, gripping the bridge of his nose.

Sezan couldn't help but smirk. Finally, a statement she could agree with.

CHAPTER SEVEN

Bakr

When Bakr got back to his house, he punched a hole in the wall.

"This is what you get when you try to help people. They throw you under the wagon like a rabid weasel." He punched it again, splitting his knuckle.

"Bad meeting?" asked Ana from the top of the stairs.

"I just won a vineyard," he sneered.

She narrowed her eyes, taking slow steps closer. "Is it an evil vineyard?"

"No." He pressed his back against the brick wall and slid down to a seat. "It's just a very prissy, holier-than-thou, prudish, puritanical, stick shoved so far up her backside you can't see the end of it..." He growled and rolled his shoulders. "It's that kind of vineyard."

"Ah." She groaned as she pulled a wooden chair across the room and took a seat near him. "You've been talking to Sezan."

He pressed his forehead into his palm and massaged his temples slowly. "I also think Jahmil has turned into a real prick since he got married."

"You mean, since yesterday?"

"Yeah. He's a prick now."

"What happened?"

"I need you to pack some bags for me."

"Sure." Ana yawned. "You told Jahmil about Ard?"

He shook his head hard. "It didn't come up."

She narrowed her eyes. "Then where are you going?"

"That's the question, isn't it?" He pulled himself to a stand so he could pace. His body was drawn up with energy, his fist throbbing from punching the wall. He glared at his bloody knuckles. It made him sick that he had let himself get so worked up. Getting angry never helped anything, it just made him stupider. He took a few long slow breaths, then laughed at the absurdity of what had just happened.

"Never do anyone a favor, Ana."

"You're preaching to the prophet, kid." The old cutthroat shrugged. "But who did you do a favor for? The vineyard?"

Fire hurried up his spine. He pushed it down. "She practically begged me to put in a good word for her with Jahmil, and that was all I did. She said she wanted to be a royal emissary and now she is. Why can't she ever just be happy? What is wrong with her brain?"

"That's all you did?" asked Ana, incredulous. "You did her a favor?"

A weird sing-song groan bubbled up his throat. "It's not my fault that Ahmar is the only kingdom in need of an emissary."

"Ah."

"Like I have control over what is happening in the world. Like I'm supposed to magic up a position for her that doesn't even exist. She's such a sheltered little pain in the—"

"She asked for your help, though. That's... strangely vulnerable."

"Just shut up and go pack my bags."

Ana chuckled and slapped her thighs as she stood. "Did you apologize?"

"For what?" he snapped, that irritating high pitch trying to sneak back into his voice.

"For leaving without saying goodbye and letting her think you were dead for so long. She must have been obsessing about it."

"She doesn't give two dry turds what happens to me. She hates me. I'm sure she spent the last two years just getting more efficient at it."

"If you say so," said Ana, then she drifted upstairs to pack.

"I'll only be gone a couple of weeks," he called after her. "You don't need to pack the sink, okay?"

She didn't answer.

It wasn't just that he didn't want to go to Ahmar. That would have been enough, but it wasn't even a quarter of the reason he was upset. He was under contract, and he only had until the next Moonless Night, or about a fortnight, to find Fajar and compel her to take him where he needed to go to get Rahik's stupid trinket. Whatever it was. And if he failed to do that, Qadira would be the least of Sezan's worries.

He needed to sleep; there was no way around that. But the moment he woke up he had to be ready to leave. An emissary couldn't just show up on the back of a drakonte. They would have to bring soldiers, a caravan of offerings, and a small cadre of entertainers. The lot. And the Queen of Ahmar cared even more about pageantry than your average spoiled, royal brat.

He hoped Sezan knew what she was doing, but he couldn't help wondering about her sudden interest in leaving Shihala. She loved her homeland, and he knew she must have missed it these last few years, even if she hadn't missed him. Was she just trying to avoid the King of Elm's harem?

He was going to break Jahmil's nose for that. He'd already made up his mind.

It flashed through him to wonder if, given how taken the King of Eastern Elm was with her, Sezan might convince him to nullify Rahik's contract. He'd done exactly as she had asked and more, practically given her the emissary job on a silver platter. She owed him.

Of course, she wouldn't see it that way. She hadn't gotten *exactly* what she wanted, so instead of being grateful she would only be belligerent. He couldn't even expect a thank you, let alone a favor in return. She only cared about herself, about what she could get out of him. What advantage she could squeeze from their relationship.

It would be a waste of time to ask for her help. Trying to think about this nonsense now was a waste of time, too. Whatever he really wanted didn't matter. It never had. It was best to focus on goals he could actually achieve, like getting a good night's sleep. There was nothing to be done about Sezan, anyway.

Yawning, he dragged himself upstairs, pulled off his shoes, untied his sword, and flopped down into bed. But as he drew the blanket over his chest, he noticed somebody was already lying under it.

He leapt out of bed and snatched up his sword, leveling it at the neck of the person before the face even came into focus. Her feathery golden-brown hair hung over her slight shoulders, perfectly parted by two twisted coppery horns. Her gray skin was barely concealed by a low-cut dress made of fur. Her pink lips twitched looking at the sword and slowly curved into a smile.

"Hello there, lover-boy."

"Shaytana," he breathed, his gaze fixed on her shimmering pink and black eyes. The lilith never blinked, never even breathed, at least not how djinn and humans do. If she did take a breath, it was only for emphasis. "What are you doing here?"

"I just happened to be in Karzusan," she said, but that meant nothing. She could go wherever she wanted in Qaf or on Earth with nothing more than a thought.

She rolled onto her stomach and propped her chin upon her palms, then kicked her bare feet up behind her and rubbed them together absently. "You didn't think I'd miss the long-awaited nuptials of the prince and his magic-sucking lyre."

He dropped his sword to the ground with a loud *clank*. It was no use against her, anyway. No weapon was. Shaytana was already at least thousand years old. No metal or stone could cut her, no fire could burn her. She did not age. And she was so strong and fast she could easily snap his back before he even knew what was happening. With a single kiss, she could walk inside of the dreams of a man and transform them into paradises or night terrors.

"You don't look pleased to see me," she said, her sultry voice at once paralyzing and invigorating.

"You startled me, that's all." He laughed and shook his head. His heart was pounding, the blood rushing in his ears. A sharp ache grew in his stomach, like an iron belt slowly being tightened, threatening to rend him in two. "If I'd known you were here..."

"Come over here, tomcat." She patted the bed.

He smiled and sat down, determined to ignore the tightness in his lungs, the dryness in his mouth. He folded his hands together and set them on his lap. A month had passed since he'd seen her last, another time he came home to find her waiting in his bed. Her interest in him tended to come in waves. Months of nothing, followed by months when he would see her practically every day. There was no predicting it. No controlling it.

"What can I do for you?"

"You're lucky I don't cut off your ears."

He swallowed hard but forced himself to keep smiling. "I suppose that could be said about anybody."

"Don't I even warrant an invitation?"

He licked his lips and gazed at the wall over her shoulder. He couldn't bear to look directly at the lie that was her flawless beauty. Arguing with Shaytana, even good-naturedly, was a recipe for pain. But he also couldn't charm her with silly platitudes. He kept his mouth shut, and eventually, she smiled.

Moments ago, all he had wanted in the world was to fall into bed and pass out, to sleep off the myriad irritations of the day. Now that Shaytana was in his bed, smiling up at him with those perfectly arched lips, he didn't feel tired at all. In fact, he was certain he had another two or three sleepless days left in him.

"You never did repay me for all my kindness," she said, fiddling with the hem of his shirt. She pouted and gazed up at him from under thick lashes. "Did you ever tell anybody about me? About what I did for you?"

His jaw twitched. "One person."

"Jahmil?" she asked, her voice sweeter than honey.

He nodded.

"Anyone else?"

"No."

"Not even a special woman?"

"No."

"Have you told anyone my name?"

"You told me not to."

"Good boy." She ran her long, sharp fingernails gently over her decolletage, her gaze fixed on his face as she licked her bottom lip. "I couldn't help overhearing the deal you made with that great, bulbous sack of blue pimples."

He chuckled. "You couldn't help it?"

"He's so cruel to you," she pouted, bringing out a raspy, babyish voice. "Would you like me to flay all his skin off?"

He was tempted to say yes but decided he would sooner cut off his own testicles than place any part of Sezan's fate in Shaytana's hands. Besides, owing her a favor would have been a thousand times worse than anything Rahik could ever throw at him.

Another favor, Bakr thought, walking his fingers over the scar on his neck. He already technically owed her one for scraping him off the field at Karzusan and using her magic to seal the gaping wound.

"That's okay." Bakr clicked his cheek. "So… is there something that you want me to do for you?"

"That depends. Are you off to play bodyguard to some silly little harem girl, or are you going after the Rukh bird to take you to the *Khātam Sulaymān*?"

He leaned closer to her. "Do you know what it is?"

"Are you telling me you don't?" She smirked and cocked her head to one side. "You sure are pretty, but you're not very smart. Haven't you ever read the Recitations?" Giggling, she rolled onto her back. "Oh, that's right. You never learned how to read, did you?"

He swallowed, trying to remove the hard lump at the back of his throat. Nobody knew that about him. But one of many unfortunate side effects of Shaytana spending so much time dancing around in his subconscious was she knew things about him nobody was ever supposed to know.

"It's funny, isn't it?" she said. "Rahik could have written literally anything in that contract of his and you still would have signed it." She gripped her stomach, positively quivering with laughter. "You can barely write your own name."

He coughed and looked away. "Yeah. That is funny."

"Oh, sweetheart. I don't mean to pick on you." She sat up and scooched closer to him on the bed, her dress falling down her shoulders revealing far more than her clavicles. "Tell me you aren't seriously planning on giving the *Khātam Sulaymān* to Rahik?"

"What is it?"

"Why don't you ask your little harem girl what she knows about it? Anybody with a halfway decent education would be able to tell you." She reached out and ran her fingers over his chest, sharp blades that sent tingles racing all over his body. "If you go through all the trouble to find it and then turn around and give it to Rahik, I may have to flay the skin off of *you*." She dug a nail under the collar of his kaftan and ripped it open in one quick motion.

On instinct, he recoiled and sucked in a startled breath.

She pressed her hand against his chest, the heat of her fingers almost scorching. "That would be a shame because this is such nice skin."

She kissed him, filling his senses with a taste of darkness more profound than the blistering cold of the Moonless Night. Her lips were ice, her breath as crisp as the north wind. But he couldn't deny the thrill of excitement that traced through his body. A shock of white lightning threatening to blow him apart.

She pulled away after a few moments, but her lips fluttered against his as she said, "Think about it."

His bottom lip trembled, anticipating what may be coming next. But when he opened his eyes, he was alone again in his bedroom. He covered his face with his hands and took several hard breaths, desperate to calm the trembling in his bones. Hot tears ached to come to his stinging, exhausted eyes, but he pressed them out before they could form and flicked them from the tips of his fingers.

He couldn't stay where he was, trembling in his bed while the scent of Shaytana settled over his skin like stargazer lilies planted in a graveyard. He couldn't go to Ahmar. He couldn't go after the *Khātam Sulaymān*, whatever it was. For a moment, he could barely even breathe.

He peeled himself out of bed and set off from his house in search of the one person who might be able to take his mind off it all. Even if there was a very good chance she had no desire whatsoever to talk to him.

CHAPTER EIGHT

SEZAN

SEZAN SLIPPED HER TIRED body under her silky sheets and stretched out each sore muscle as her mind raced. She had spent the last hour arranging transports and selecting gifts for Queen Qadira. But what could she say that wouldn't damn all of Shihala? Sorry our prince used and then slighted you in front of the Nine Kingdoms by leaving you at the altar?

She would have to make do. Stupid Bakr had been right; being an emissary was just babysitting, except with Ahmar, she had to clean up two royal messes instead of one.

After tossing and turning, she rubbed her eyes and pinched the bridge of her nose. Twice she had almost fallen asleep and twice thoughts of Bakr startled her awake. Thoughts of anger. Of longing. Neither conducive to slumber. She would have to powder her face extra in the morning to hide the dark circles that would rest under her eyes.

Tired of restlessly waiting for sleep, she slid out of bed and walked to her balcony. Maybe a breath of alyasmin would help calm her nerves. She opened the stained glass doors woven in patterns of the moons and stars and stifled a cry.

The shadow of a man leaned on the railing. Broad shoulders, tired eyes, and for once, no smile. She did not need light to know who it was. Bakr had rested many times in that exact spot, waiting for her.

Sezan froze, her heart beating so loud she was certain he could hear it. She wondered why he had come and knew the answer all at the same time. It was the same reason she couldn't sleep. She stepped forward, the cool tiles soothing her toes after a night of squeezing into party slippers. She wanted to yell at him. To slap his chest. To apologize for what she said to Rahik. To ask him why he let her believe he was dead. To ask why he had left her when she could have been...

Instead, she took another step forward so she was close enough to feel his heat and ran a finger down the scar on his neck until it hit the keyhole knick at the top of his kaftan. What was it about this balcony and the moonlight and Bakr—the real Bakr, not the fake one he showed everyone else—that made her ache?

He reached up and lay his hand over hers, then ran his rough palms up her bare arms to the ties at her shoulders. She allowed herself a tiny shiver despite the night's warmth. With a gentle stroke of her throat, Bakr wrapped his other arm around her waist and pulled her closer. Warm fingers slid up the nape of her neck and tangled into her hair. He stood, breathing her in with a sigh as their bodies leaned into each other. The spicy scent of agarwood filled her mind, and she took slow, painful, wonderful breaths, trying to soak it all in. This was a bad idea. An exquisitely terrible one.

She tried to speak his name, to do anything but give in, but the tingles spreading across her skin rendered her tongue useless. He leaned down, and she raised her eyes to his, the warm light of the Seventh Moon shimmering against the pale green.

Her head tilted back, eyes falling closed on their own.

"Do you remember the Festival of the Eighth Moon?" he said, holding her chin in place so when she opened her eyes she was gazing directly into his.

She whispered, "The skies were lit with fireworks and the heat clung to our skin."

"You wore that dress I like. You know the one."

A flush of heat danced across her chest. "You mean the one we left on the side of the reflecting pool?" She could still feel the kiss of cool water against her skin as she slid into the starlit waters, his hand in hers. They had spent hours that night laughing and sighing, living in the world but not of it.

She smiled and cast her gaze aside, then looked back up at him. At his pale eyes full of starlight, exactly as they had been that night.

"You were so beautiful," he said, "and the sky was so full with all the moons, it was almost like day. The water was clear, reflecting everything from above. I felt like we were flying through the heavens, looking down. And from that far away, everything looked… perfect." He ran his thumb gently over her cheek, the curve of her lips. "Do you remember what you said to me that night?"

Warm shivers raced over her. Of course, she remembered. She remembered everything they had both said, promises spoken in the safety of their stolen moment she had meant with all her heart. But her tongue would not move to form words.

He closed his eyes and drew closer until his lips were so near that she could feel their warmth. "What is the light of eight moons if I'm not kissing you?"

She lifted her toes just enough so her lips could brush softly against his. "I meant every word. Life has been so dark without you."

He pressed his mouth over hers and pulled her to his chest with frenetic urgency. A bridge of electricity flickered to life between them. Tiny wings fluttered in her stomach and her mind went blank. One of his hands gripped the nape of her neck, the other clutched at her back, her waist, her shoulder. Trying to seize and cherish every inch of her at once. His breath was heavy and vivid, his voice clinging to each exhalation.

He pressed her back against the doorframe, kissing her with such eagerness. She never wanted him to let go. He pulled back and looked at her—wild heat shining through the constancy of his human eyes—before kissing her again. Each time harder. Each time with more heat. And under it all, his heart thrummed against her breast—furious, and anxious, and filled with more fire than any pureblooded djinn in all of Qaf. It melted the ice from parts of her she hadn't realized were frozen.

He sucked on her lower lip and kissed over her jawline, then down the line of her neck. Her head rolled back, knees weak, every inch of skin yearning for him. He lingered on the sensitive spot just under her ear, then gently nibbled the lobe. The way he always did. The way that gave her chills and set her on fire all at once.

He hugged her tightly to his chest, then pulled back just enough to rest his forehead lightly against hers. With his eyes still closed, and said in a rough, ragged voice. "I never thought I'd see you again."

She touched a hand to his face, rubbing the cut along his brow with her thumb. "I would not let that happen."

Grabbing her cheeks, he kissed her again, slower than before. Deeper, ardent. As if he hadn't seen her in years. It was all she had wanted since the moment he'd left.

"Let me stay," he whispered.

His words plucked at her heart, sending her stomach twisting with the thrill of excitement while pulling her back to reason. She had not forgotten Bakr's appetites; even as he whispered sweet nothings, he was still a man. Which meant it didn't matter how many times he stayed the night, he would just as readily leave the next day without a word and never come back. This path would only bring her pain. Just like last time, and every time. Her soul was not worth the price.

She smiled gently to hide her pain. "Lila would kill you."

He let out a noise somewhere between a laugh and a groan. "I forgot about Lila."

"Well, she certainly hasn't forgotten about you." Sezan tapped his nose with her finger. He grabbed it and put the tip between his lips, sucking gently. She stifled a giggle and swallowed hard, determined not to succumb. "She's fairly enraged at the thought of you entangled with Queen Qadira, which she's convinced of, by the way."

He grunted, still holding her body tightly. "I don't see how that is any concern of hers."

"She worries for me, Bakr." She tilted her head and looked at him through her lashes, more on her tongue that she refused to say.

He pushed back the hair that had fallen into her face. "And I don't?"

"No goodbye and more than two years without a word is a fairly strong argument," Sezan said, trying to keep her voice light and the tremble from her lips. "Especially considering the state of things... of me at the time." She knew she sounded petty. And she knew Bakr hated pathetic women. But he made her so weak, and she was still so raw.

"I had to leave. There was nothing I could do." He let out a sharp exhalation followed by a mirthless laugh. "And as far as sending you word, I knew I might have been dead at any moment. Like everybody else, you'd already heard that I was. Why would I want to put you through that twice?"

"Maybe because what I heard and what I believed were two different things. And maybe because I'd be willing to suffer a thousand times over if it meant you could live one more day."

"Don't be ridiculous." He pulled away completely, his hands dropping to his side. Then he turned from her and gazed at nothing over the edge of the balcony. "I can't be held responsible for what you believe. And if you're stupid enough to give up a single drop of blood for my worthless..." He cut himself off and bit down on the inside of his cheek, but then let go immediately as if hyper-aware of the meaning she attached to it. "I should not have come here."

Sezan felt the burn of hot tears threatening to make her look even more a fool. "Is that why you push me away? Push everyone? I gave up something far more precious than blood to—" She chomped her teeth together with a snap and took a step further away even though she wished never to leave. "Why *did* you come here?"

"What are you talking about, Zan?" He narrowed his eyes. "You gave up what?"

She pressed her teeth together so hard they hurt. She should not have said anything. It would be just another thing he'd brush under the rug and laugh at her for. He had already called her stupid for giving everything to keep him alive without even knowing. "Maybe if you had written a letter every once in a while, you'd know."

He downcast his gaze, rubbing his thumb and forefinger over his eyebrows. "Where do you think I was, *ya amar*? You think I had mail service trapped in the mountains under a firewall with forty thousand blood-thirsty Vespars and bial'dabaye fighting over who got to rip out my entrails? Never mind the Spider of Karzusan tearing apart my troops, burning my food supply, doing everything his sick little mind could think of to drive me mad? I couldn't even get official correspondence out to Jahmil."

"And how many times have you apologized to his royal majesty? Played nicely with his wife since coming back? You didn't arrive in the kingdom just now. And Shihala and Ahmar have a very robust mail system, I assure you. Yet you felt even that wretched queen was worth a visit before me. I am nothing to you but another indulgence for your appetite, at the bottom of your list if I'm on it at all."

His jaw twitched, one side of his lips curling into a sneer. He opened his mouth twice only to shut it without saying a word.

"Bakr without a sarcastic comment? Not even a word? Is it too hard to finally admit that I'm right?"

"You just dropped a giant pile of wet, hot crap in my lap. I don't know which bit of nonsense to argue with first. You..." He pointed at her. "You are impossible."

"Why?" she snapped, anger replacing his warmth with a burning heat. "Because I don't giggle at your stupid jokes and slide naked into your bed?" She let out a bitter laugh. "Poor Bakr. Your life is so hard."

"You wouldn't recognize a hard life if someone smacked you in the face with it." He laughed through clenched teeth, turning his eyes up to the sky. "You are a spoiled, pompous, sheltered little brat."

"And you're a selfish, egotistical, ridiculous man."

"Good!" he shouted. "Maybe now you'll stop looking at me that way."

"What way?" she asked between icy gasps of laughter, waving him away dismissively.

He sucked in an audible breath through his nostrils and let it out with a low hiss. Then he walked closer, his eyes fixed hard upon hers. "You'd be a lot happier if you let yourself laugh every once in a while. I'd be willing to sacrifice my blood for that."

The heat drained from her cheeks, leaving her hollow and cold. She itched to reach for him, to pull herself close. She left her arms at her side. "It is not your blood I want, Bakr. It never has been."

He set his hand gently on her shoulder and ran his palm down her arm. His touch on her skin felt so good it hurt, which only made the ache in her chest yawn wider.

"That's all I have, Zan," he said, meeting her eyes. "I know you want me to be something else. Something... I don't even know what you want me to be. But I'm just an ordinary sack of blood. And tainted blood, at that."

"I have never once cared about your blood, Bakr." She sighed and took his hand in hers. "Jahmil is a lucky man. You've given him far more of yourself than anyone ever deserved. And I don't want you to *be* anything." With a sad little pat, she pushed his hand back towards him. "But you never believe me."

"That's how you look at me."

"What is?"

"Like I'm constantly disappointing you."

"Then stop," she said, clipping the words short.

"I don't know how." He shrugged and turned away, taking a few steps towards the edge of the balcony. He paused and smiled sadly at her over his shoulder. "That's what it boils down to, Zan. I'm just a sack of dirty blood. And you are so much more than that."

"Bakr!" She called after him, already regretting everything she'd said. How was it possible to be so angry at a person and desperately want them to stay? "I... I don't want to be alone."

He climbed over the railing, dropping his foot onto the lattice below. Smiling, he looked up at her. "You think I'm just some sordid hussy that's going to slide naked into your bed for a bit of *muqayada*? Some quid pro quo?" He shook his head and let go of the railing, disappearing down the side of the building as quickly as a rush of water.

She ran to the edge and hit her fist against the cool marble, looking out over the darkness. "You have nothing to *quo*!" She swung around and shoved open her doors, then found the first pillow she could and screamed into it. Pulling it hard and harder, she tore it by the seams, gleeful in the ripping sound it made as she channeled her rage for that awful, glib, beautiful man who had never once left her thoughts since the day she first met him.

When the pillow finally burst in a satisfying puff of feathers that settled around her, she got out Lila's sewing kit and set to work stitching it back together. Everything she did had a consequence. And everything Bakr did had a negative consequence... for her. Why? Why had she forced him to join her for what would be the second most important negotiation she'd ever been a part of? It was already his fault she had so massively destroyed her life with the first. All he did was distract her and fray her nerves. Even now, she could barely sew anything for how her hands shook.

A knock on the door caused her to prick her finger. She sucked it clean, remembering his words and cringing. Don't waste a drop of blood on him? Well, too late for that. She stood and kicked back the ottoman she had sat on, then hastily ripped open the door.

A messenger dressed in the royal garb of Ahmar bowed lowly before her, letter in hand. The ridiculous purple feather in his hat brushed against Sezan so she had to step back and left a noticeable smear of glitter. The upper portions of his sleeves poofed out twice the size of his head while the skirt of his kaftan clung to his hips, a good three hands above the knee. Thick wool pants descended from there, woven with even more sparkles that, Sezan was sure, must leave the poor djinn's skin covered in rashes and utterly on fire.

She smoothed her face and thanked him, certain her eye twitched. With a rattling breath, she shut the door far more gently.

Seven steps took her to the dresser where she pulled out a pearl letter opener. One slit and a garish rose-colored paper slid out in an enormous puff of purple sparkles that coated everything from the door to the bed behind her. She stifled a groan, flakes of oleander-scented glitter smeared across her dress, in her shoes, and in her mouth. *Qadira.* News traveled fast. More evidence that the mail systems in Qaf worked fine.

To Sheikha Sezan Bint Malik Bujul

Shihalan Royal Emissary to Ahmar,

I'm sure you're aware of the great and numerous offenses Shihala has committed against Ahmar and against me personally. (Who wasn't?) Needless to say, I find your prince repugnant (Fair.) *and Shihala a cesspool of corruption.* (Harsh.) *While I would rather drown you in the quicksilver lake that surrounds Ashkult* (Excessive.)*, my cousin and royal advisor, Ajmal Amir, has advised against it and insisted I allow your presence in the capitol.* (Great...)

I will give you one chance. Do me wrong, and I will rip every hair from your head and make a coat out of it, then have you sent to Ashkult to die like the Shihalan pigdog that you are.

Sezan blinked at the last line, then sighed.

Expecting your presence in no less than five turns of the First Moon,

Queen Qadira al-Ahmar, The Astonishing

Sezan was tempted to crumple the floral-scented paper and set it on fire, but that would not do. Not for a *ghabi* harem girl who thought she could run from her troubles by playing royal emissary. Nothing she studied in the libraries of Eastern Elm could prepare her for this mess. If running out of magic would bring her exile and shame in Shihala, what would happen to her if Qadira found out? There would be no greater slight aside from Jahmil's own.

She ran a finger over the paper and pulled it back sparkly with purple. It was impressively vain to sign a royal document in such a brash fashion. Maybe Bakr had been on to something when he went to sleep with the queen instead of coming to her. Impetuous. Selfish. Childish. Condescending. They were cut from the same cloth. Only Qadira had a leg up. She was a woman.

CHAPTER NINE

BAKR

HE WENT STRAIGHT HOME and went to sleep. To Jahannam with everything else. With Sezan and her moonlight and her sophistries. With Rahik and his contract. With Shaytana and her lips and her thinly veiled threats. And even with Jahmil and Ayelet and their stupid, perfect happiness. Into the fire with all of them. These hours belonged to him, and so he slept. And when he awoke, he rolled over and went back to sleep. By Allah's mercy, he dreamt of nothing.

He awoke with moonlight on his brain though, a heaviness in his chest that refused to be pushed aside. He remembered now what he used to know. Everything always went better with Sezan when he didn't say anything. She didn't get mad at him when he was silent, when he simply let his eyes do the talking. She was so much happier drawing conclusions from his gestures, from the urgency of his kiss or the softness of his gaze, than she was actually listening to what he had to say.

It didn't matter. He would not go to her balcony again. He would see her off to Ahmar and then be done with it. Never to write, never to talk, never to ache for her ever again.

That was what he told himself as he dressed, had his syrupy black tea, exchanged meaningless pleasantries with Ana, and fed Bubbles. He told himself that as he walked to the palace and was treated with even more vapid courtiers who were so anxious to remind him he wasn't dead. By the time he arrived at the amir's chambers, he had almost convinced himself it was true.

He needed to talk to Jahmil and clear up all this nonsense. Explain why his going to Qadira's court was an absolutely terrible idea bordering on ridiculousness. And he needed to tell him, once and for all, of the decision he'd taken to recuse himself from the Shihalan court and go back to Ard. Back to sunshine and obscurity, where he had always belonged.

Most importantly, he still needed to break Jahmil's nose for trying to sell Sezan into the King of Elm's harem.

Normally, he would have just walked in, but it only took one instance of barging in on a half-naked Ayelet for him to learn his lesson. He knocked out a little tune and waited.

The door was drawn open, and he found himself looking at the wrong face. All soft smiling lips and playful gray eyes, not the stern blue Adonis he had been hoping for.

"*As-salamu alaykum*," he said, smiling. "Jahmil?"

"Had to attend a council about grain, or grazing... I do not know."

"The morning after your wedding?" he smirked. "For somebody with such a reputation for being romantic, he's not very romantic."

"Three days have passed since the wedding."

"Really? That's crazy." He sighed and let his shoulders slump. "I wanted to speak to you anyway. Before I go off on my diplomatic mission I'm not allowed to talk during. Can I come in?"

She smiled warmly and tugged her robe over her shoulders. "Always."

He stepped inside and helped himself to the tea set out on her table before flopping into a chair. If there was one thing from Ard all djinn seemed to love, it was tea. "Jahmil is worried about you."

"He would not be Jahmil if he were not. Is that what you so urgently needed to discuss with me?" She grinned.

"He asked me to help you get settled, as one semi-human to another. And since I'll be leaving soon, I've been trying to come up with something useful to say."

She sat in the chair across from him, so her nightgown puffed up around her. "Well then, settle away."

"First of all, I know you're going to be just fine."

Ayelet twisted in her seat and kicked her legs over the side of her chair. Then her brows furrowed, and her lips puckered off to the side. "You are not usually this..." She hemmed and hawed. "... bland. What is going on with you?"

"I've had a peculiar couple of days, punctuated by not enough sleep and then too much. Apparently." He shrugged. "It doesn't matter. The point is, don't listen to gossip."

"You are just pulling from old adages, now. Tell me straight, Bakr. One semi-human to another."

"When you're living in the palace, it is really easy to become convinced that everybody and their dog is conspiring to murder you. But it isn't true. Courtiers are just a bunch of hateful, petty, jealous bags of hot air."

"I knew there was a darkness in you." She poked a finger at him in the air. "It's sharper than Jahmil's, though. And not everybody can be as you describe. Jahmil's not. And Sezan is delightful."

"Sure. She's a peach." He sighed and forced himself to smile. "The point is, the decent ones aren't the ones you need to worry about. So there's no point in talking about them. I'm here to give you advice—on royal orders. Take it or leave it. I would just say, your best bet is to focus on the peasantry and the military. You have a much better chance of winning them over, and if you do that, you don't have to care what gossips say."

Her brows knit together while she studied him for a moment. She put her feet back on the ground and tipped a hand to her forehead. "Aye aye, General." Then she paused, and her eyes grew soft. "Now it is my turn to give you advice, on royal orders of my own and as a friend. Maybe, just maybe, the decent ones *are* the ones we should worry about."

He rolled his eyes. People in love were always so annoyingly optimistic, and Ayelet and Jahmil were the worst of them. "Shihala is a dangerous place for people like us. I know you're the chosen one, or whatever, but I don't want to see you get hurt. And I certainly don't want anything to happen to your little shadow, Serap."

Ayelet patted his knee. "Thank you, Bakr. Just promise me you will consider taking care of yourself every once in a while, too. I shall never forgive you if you make a mess of things for Jahmil. I prefer it when he is not sulking."

"He has you now." He smiled, wrinkling the skin around his eyes. "He doesn't need me anymore. So it doesn't matter."

"Ah." She nodded solemnly and bent her finger to beckon him forward. "May I tell you a secret?"

"I'd advise against it in general, but if you insist."

She chuckled, then leaned closer. Locking her gray eyes on his, she flicked him hard on the forehead. "Stop moping. No one in this court thinks less of you than you. I have a strict no-bemoaning policy in my chambers, I will have you know. Go find Sezan if you must lay bare your soul to someone."

There was hardly a soul in Allah's two worlds who would be worse to lay bare his soul to. He pushed down the unpleasantness creeping through his stomach and snarled playfully. "Second piece of advice. Are you ready?"

"Perpetually."

"Don't get so wrapped up in all this nonsense that you forget to go back to Ard from time to time. It gets really depressing not seeing the sun after a while. Humans don't make our own fire; we must soak it up from heaven."

"Done. We shall go together as soon as you return from Ahmar."

"It's a date." He nodded and leaned back in his chair. It wasn't a lie. She and Jahmil would always be welcome to visit him at his new home on Ard once he made it there.

Bakr took a deep breath and licked his chapped lips. Ever since Jahmil had asked him to have a chat with Ayelet, he'd been debating whether to talk to her about Rahik. He'd always handled that situation on his own, but considering he'd be leaving soon and never returning, it only seemed prudent. On the other hand, if he told Ayelet the truth about Jahmil's uncle, her reaction would likely be extreme. If she knew, for instance, that he kept human slaves in his house it was possible, nay likely, that she would lose control and rip his heart out with the aid of the magical wisps that obeyed her every command.

Imagining the scene made Bakr smile, but still, he was wary. If Rahik died because he had told somebody else something that made them want to kill him, did that count as breaking the contract? If he got Ayelet all excited and puffed up and sicked them on him, would Bakr's bones melt out from under him?

Even if the Seal of Elm did recognize the difference between murder and murder by proxy, pitting Ayelet against Rahik would have devastating consequences for Shihala, for Jahmil. Putting aside Queen Zalika and the amir themselves, Rahik was the most powerful man in Shihala. Half the court—the more conservative half, the half who were scandalized that their prince's wife was human, the half who secretly hated Jahmil for ending the war with Vespar with a peace treaty rather than continuing to campaign for their total destruction—would rally behind Rahik. Taking any overt action against him would lead to civil war. Blood would coat the streets of Karzusan once again, and so little of it had yet dried since the last time.

Bakr sighed. He wasn't prepared to risk it, so the best thing he could do was keep his mouth shut as he always had.

"Just keep a watchful eye," he said at last. "There are many courtiers who dislike you. Who would dance in the streets if something were to happen to you. Some of them may try to cause something to happen to you. You need to be vigilant."

Ayelet let out a sigh. "I am still not convinced I need to go around thinking ill of everyone. I know what ulterior motives are, but most people are just trying to get by, not exact doom."

He stifled a laugh and rolled his eyes. "That's true enough when you're dealing with people who have actual problems. People who are worried about freezing in winter and figuring out where their next meal is coming from. Rich people have nothing better to do with their time than play mind games with each other."

"You really are on a rampage today. Who has done what to you? Tell Ayelet Amira and I shall be magnanimous in my gifts," she said regally, unable to keep a straight face.

"I'm not on a rampage," he laughed, sitting back and crossing an ankle over his knee. "I would have preferred to disseminate all this negativity over several conversations. But I have to leave soon."

"To see... Sezan, perhaps?" She fluttered her eyelashes.

"You really want to ask me about it, don't you?"

"I am being painfully obvious."

He rubbed his temples. "Go ahead."

Her teasing eyes fell to the floor before coming up under knit brows. "Why does she look so sad when she speaks of you? And... why do you look so sad when I speak of her?"

He groaned and refilled his teacup. "She looks sad because... because she made a grievous error in judgment. And I look sad because I think she has figured that out."

Ayelet's playful demeanor returned in full force as she leaned over and pinched his cheeks. "Aww, you are so cute when you genuinely like someone." She released his cheeks and put her hands on her hips. "Good news for you, though."

He narrowed his eyes. "What is?"

"That your heart is human."

"You're patronizing me now." He stood, finishing off his tea in one gulp. "I didn't come here to be mocked. I get quite enough of that at home."

"That is good, you quite need it." Ayelet pinched his elbow. "And do not worry. I will not tell Sezan... unless I get drunk. No guarantees then. I think it is all the more motivation for Jahmil to keep a sober palace."

"I don't like Sezan. She's a tremendous pain in my everything."

"Of course. I understand. It is like... she is ruining your life?" A coy smile played on her lips.

"She would love to. I think she stays up nights thinking about it. But it doesn't matter. Once I get her settled in Ahmar, I'll never have to look at her smug, superior face with its twitching veins ever again."

"Done now?" Ayelet smirked. "Or do you need to go make out with her first?"

"Don't make me strangle you, Ayelet. It is technically treason."

She twitched a finger and a wisp brushed against his cheek, cold and a little moist. "I shall do as I please."

He slapped the wisp away. "There's a part of me that wants to ask what stories she told you about me, but I'm not going to. I don't care."

"Okay, good. I was worried you might interrogate me about that mewling namur," Her voice raised in pitch as she mocked him. "Or about how you got the tattoo that apparently wraps around your oh-so-muscular chest."

"I work out." He puckered his lips smugly.

"Or maybe about a certain time you, oh, went skinny dipping?" She bit her lip and took a step back.

"She told you about that?" He shook his head, laughing incredulously. "That is really interesting."

"She told me *you* went skinny dipping," Ayelet's eyes glittered. "But now I think you *both* did."

His smile tightened. "She is... such a... I can't..." He growled and looked down at the ground.

"Jahmil was right," said Ayelet.

"About what?"

"He was certain the only way you would ever shut up was if a woman reached down your throat and grabbed your tongue herself. And Sezan has quite the hold."

"He's an idiot." Bakr straightened his jacket. "I have to go."

"We are still on for Ard, though, right?" She skipped to the door and opened it for him.

"I wouldn't miss it for anything." He pecked her cheek quickly.

"In the meantime, you can bask in the glow of Sezan's sunny eyes."

He slumped his eyes to one side and glared at her, but he couldn't hold it. He laughed and shook his head. "You know what? You're an idiot, too."

Her shoulders shook as she chuckled. "Get out of here, Bakr."

Snarling, he walked out into the hall. He clenched and unclenched his fingers, knuckles stiff from punching the wall. As he turned the corner, he saw Jahmil coming in the other direction.

"Bakr, there you are." Jahmil nodded quickly. "I need to speak with you about Sezan."

"You're an idiot," he said and punched him in the face. Bakr smiled at the crack of bone, as Jahmil's feet went over his head.

"*Al'ama!*" Jahmil cursed. "Why did you do that?"

"That is for trying to sell your sister to the stinking King of stinking Elm, you filthy sack of silver."

Jahmil started to speak, perhaps to justify himself, but Bakr didn't want to hear it. He kept walking, fists clenched hard at his side. Idiots, all of them. Total idiots. And so was he.

CHAPTER TEN

Sezan

Where was Jahmil? Sezan fidgeted in her shoes, slipping the heel off and on again under the puff of her harem pants. He was supposed to arrive with her ambassador's seal before she left for Ahmar. And after days of her brother not showing, the mindless tedium preparing for the trip, and the fog of Bakr eating away at her mind, she was a mess of nerves. The early moons were in the sky, and the air still held a crisp hint of the cold hour.

"Such a scowl," Lila said, appearing at her side and handing her an orange. "Unhappiness will give you wrinkles no matter how much shujai root I put on your face."

"And how am I to be happy about this?" She slit the skin and peeled it open all in one piece.

"I don't understand. You got what you wanted. You're a royal emissary. And didn't you call Qadira fantastic just the other day?"

"I was being facetious." Sezan popped a quarter into her mouth and swallowed the tang.

"You could not have asked for a better assignment," Lila continued. "With Ahmar so close, we'll be able to visit with friends and family, and be home for the Festival of the Four Winds."

"Splendid," she said and crushed a piece of orange between her tongue and the top of her mouth, enjoying a brief moment of pleasure before her life would be ruined.

"And we can visit Al-Madinat. You always say how much you love the culture and art there." Lila nudged her with a tilt of her head.

"It is you who always says that," Sezan said, the temptation of a refined city trip little comfort considering the circumstances.

She still had not told Lila about the deal with the lilith. And what good would it do her now? She was headed into a den of magical paranoia with a rapidly approaching deadline. What would even happen to her with her magic gone? The people of Vespar started dying when their magic disappeared. Queen Qadira lost a shade of purple from her skin from just a moment of Ayelet's touch. What would it mean for the lilith to take hers? Besides being ostracized from society and called a traitor for failing to pledge her magic to Shihala. She shivered. Perhaps she had debased herself groveling to Bakr for a mere three weeks of misery before something far worse happened. Why had she ever thought Bakr worth this?

Lila touched her shoulder. "It won't be that bad. You've been training for this your whole life. And whatever Queen Qadira is like, she's still an important figure in Qaf and someone Shihala needs to work with. An added perk? She won't try to marry you." She nudged Sezan playfully.

Sezan tossed another slice of orange in her mouth and dabbed at the juice that dripped down her lip. "I guess," she said around the pulp. Then she spat the orange out and grabbed Lila's arm, shoving her inside the closest carriage.

"What is going on?" Lila demanded, smoothing out her tunic. She peeked out the window and groaned. "What did you not tell me?"

Sezan studied the curtains on the closed side of the carriage.

"*Eaziziun*," Lila said sharply. "Why is Bakr headed this way, riding gear and luggage in tow?"

"He comes with us to Ahmar," she mumbled, still inspecting the purple brocade.

"Why?" Lila drawled.

"Because... I insisted he do so."

"*Why?*" Lila drew out the word even slower through her clenched teeth.

Sezan abandoned the curtain and looked to her servant. "Because! Because... he makes me so mad, and I wanted to punish him."

"For giving you exactly what you asked of him? You punish only yourself."

"No," she scowled, crossing her arms in an obvious display of irritation she told herself she'd never do. Bakr brought out the worst in everything. She suppressed the memory of his touch upon her skin and squeezed her arms tight before forcing herself to relinquish their strangely comforting hold on her stomach. "I wanted him to suffer for being Bakr. That's enough."

Lila harrumphed. "That makes about as much sense as a lilith marrying, oh, I don't know, something ridiculous, like a human. You just can't let him out of your sights, can you?"

Sezan leaned over to glance out the window, willfully ignoring every one of Lila's words. Bakr was wearing a dark green kaftan that brought out his eyes, the moons of Shihala accenting his strong jaw and tempting sandy-brown skin. Initially, she hated the scar he acquired on his brow while away on one of his first war ventures, but eventually it became as much a part of him as his easy smile and broad chest. Even now it lifted lightly as Bakr laughed about nothing. It was good she had sent him away the other night. Had repelled his meaningless advances. It was good. It was good.

"The most merciful person..." Lila looked at her pointedly.

"I know the phrase," Sezan snapped. "But I've already taken my revenge. The best we can do now is avoid the consequences."

"You can't just hide in here all morning. You're in charge of this entire mission."

"Then you go tell people what to do." Sezan scrunched into the corner of her cushioned seat. "I daresay it's what you do best."

"And what's the point of telling people what to do if they don't listen?" Lila tossed a cushion at her. "Besides, Jahmil won't just hand the sea off to anyone. You kind of need to be there for that."

Sezan snuck another peek out the window, then leaned forward for a better look. Bakr was nowhere to be found. She breathed a sigh of relief. "Fine, I'll do my duties," she said, chin raised to the sky to make up for her recent uncomely display. She pushed open the door and stepped back into the spotless courtyard.

"Sheikha Sezan," an oily voice called to her from behind. "You are a vixen like your mother."

She tensed on instinct before forcing her shoulders to loosen. For good measure, she opened her palms to be more inviting before she turned. Nothing good could come from making enemies now. She turned and bowed twice. "Uncle Rahik. You are looking healthy."

He stepped in much too close, his eyes fixed intently on hers. He took a step closer, then another, coming around from behind. He moved his face forward so his cheeks were a breath away from hers. "Rumor has it you are leaving for Ahmar."

"Yes, uncle," she said, holding stiller than a jerboa in the middle of a drakonte fight. "I am to be an emissary there."

Rahik wheezed out a laugh, covering her cheek in spittle. "A woman doing a man's job. Such ideas of grandeur you have." He looked past her shoulder for a moment and his watery eyes hardened. "And General Bakr goes with you. I thought he frightened you."

She held her breath and took the chance to move away, then nodded. "It is by Jahmil Amir's orders."

Rahik ran a hand down her arm without quite touching her skin, leaving her with ghostly trills of queasiness. He smirked, then pulled his fingers back. "May your trip be fruitful," he sneered before bowing and bumbling away.

Sezan shook off the chills from his slick words and pungent breath, then rubbed furiously at her cheek. He had a merciless, mocking look to his eyes, but she couldn't help shake the thought they weren't meant for her. Sliding a hand down her arm to keep away the shadows, she turned slowly. Bakr marched through the other side of the courtyard, his back to her. As Marqiz Rahik passed by him, Bakr snarled something and shoved an overloaded cart of citrus into his path. Rahik jumped back, barely saving his legs from being crushed by an axle, and was pummeled by huge yellow fruits that broke open and stained his clothes. Rahik began to shout. Bakr laughed, but it was red with anger. Guards in freshly pressed uniforms rushed to the scene, obscuring her view.

She furrowed her brow. It was normal—nay, expected—for Bakr to make a scene, but he rarely ever did so in rage. She had always been the one to storm out of their arguments, infuriated when nothing ruffled him. Was he that mad she had made him come? Was he still stewing about the other night? The thought that he might regret leaving her standing on the balcony even a little emboldened her in a pinching sort of way. For once she got the upper hand. It had just come at a price.

A hoard of servants rushed into the courtyard, and Jahmil Amir followed at a clip. He had finally decided to show up to give her the seal. She wanted to chide him for his lack of punctuality and take the win. On the other hand, what Rahik had said about Bakr's debt the other night had been nagging at her. About him not being around much longer. About the overturned cart full of oranges and lemons. If something was up, Jahmil should know... And if he already did know, then maybe she could find out more. She sighed and put up a smile, then nearly choked.

Jahmil Amir's normally blue and straight nose was as purple and crooked as an Ahmaran king's. Dried blood dusted the edges of his nostrils, and bruises shone under his eyes.

"Your Highness," she bowed deeper than necessary, trying not to stare.

"Marhabaan." He glanced at her quickly and showed a controlled smile, but his eyes were still sweeping the scene with Rahik and the broken fruit.

What happened to Jahmil that he would not speak of? Who would dare harm an amir? And why had he not healed it with a potion? Knowing the martyr prince, he probably felt he deserved it, and she had no doubt he did. But for what it was inflicted, she was in the dark.

She straightened and cleared her throat. "Looking for someone?"

He snorted, then winced, before tilting his head towards her. "Are you feeling sufficiently prepared for your departure?"

"Your Highness has been generous. I have everything I need." She almost left it at that, but a flash of Bakr's serious eyes pushed her further. "Except…"

"What is it? Ahmar is going to be a difficult enough mission without leaving home under-prepared."

How pragmatic. She kept her smile soft, his broken nose soothing the natural spite she held toward her elder brother. "I just wondered what Marqiz Rahik knows of the venture," she continued. "He seems… unusually invested."

"I think you'll find the entire council is deeply invested in your success. And while I do not share the opinion, the fact that so much responsibility has been placed on the shoulders of an untested woman has many of them more than usually concerned."

She swallowed the sting left by his words. "It is not that which concerns me, Highness. I know the expectations placed upon my shoulders and am confident I will bring Shihala and Ahmar to a peaceful union. I just wondered if perhaps you had assigned General Bakr to the mission before I had requested it?"

He flattened his chin and shook his head. "Absolutely not. I would prefer he stay here. I fear General Bakr and the Queen of Ahmar may have a less than ideal dynamic. But it is more important that you feel safe enough to perform your duties. And given that you received this commission based solely on his recommendation, it seems appropriate he should see the venture through."

Sezan resisted the urge to tap her fingers against her pants, ignoring the excoriating burn left by Jahmil's admission. It took everything she had to not abandon the man who Jahmil credited with her success and storm off. But she held her ground.

"I hope I did not pull General Bakr away from something far more pressing. Something else that may have taken him away from the kingdom?"

"You have pulled him away from many things which are more pressing. Again and again." Jahmil glanced across the cobbled courtyard at Bakr, who was now sitting on a rock by himself with his back to everyone and nursing a bottle of wine. Jahmil's eyes shifted with colors, and he bit his thumb. "Let us speak privately for a moment."

"Of course." She nodded respectfully and followed him to a shaded path that led to the courtyard. The obvious worry on his face made her stomach tighten.

His gaze scanned the shimmering pink and purple leaves of the trees at the edge of the courtyard. With his back still turned, he asked, "What is going on with you and Bakr?"

"Absolutely nothing. He made sure of that when he went off to war and never even—" She bit off the last of her comment.

"I'm assuming you are sleeping together."

Her face burned hotter than Ard's sun, and she was grateful Jahmil's back was turned. "Do you ask as an older brother or the amir?"

He turned and looked at her, his brow raised and his lips dipped in a slight frown. "Both. Either way, it is my right to know the nature of your current relationship."

"You're incorrect, *amiri*. The brother half of you has no business inquiring as to my affairs because he has never once cared before. And to the amir..." She opened her mouth to speak, then closed it. She would not be one of those buffoons who stuttered while she spoke, even if he abused his princely power to force her to talk. "I do not know what we are. Can anyone with Bakr?"

Jahmil sighed and turned his gaze to the ground. "I understand he jilted you, Sezan. Am I to understand you have forgiven him?"

She looked away, heat and spiders and humiliation crawling over her skin. "How can I forgive someone who doesn't think he did anything wrong? I'm certain I'll die a thousand deaths before the thought even crosses his mind."

Jahmil nodded quickly and rolled his shoulders. "I don't want the details. I just need to know if this is going to be a problem. When the two of you get together, whether you love him or you hate him, things have a tendency to get a bit..." He swallowed hard. "... Excessive? Fanatical? It's like he's a flame and you are oil."

"Shihala is my only priority," Sezan said, pressing a single nail into her palm to keep her temper. Why shouldn't she be the fire and Bakr the one that burned? Still, he had a teeny tiny point. "I forgot to whom I was bringing up my reservations. My humblest apologies."

"Do you still want him to accompany you? There are many other skilled soldiers in Shihala, ones whose company might be more... ignorable."

"I—" She looked away from Jahmil. The usual sharpness in his eyes she could handle, but for a moment there had been something else above his puffy, swollen nose. Not a softness... but sympathy, or Allah forbid, humor? It left her feeling altogether unsettled. "I requested Bakr's attendance as a personal favor from Ayelet Amira and have already sent correspondence to Ahmar about who shall be attending. I would not go back on my word."

"It would be I who was going back on your word, and I can't possibly have a worse reputation in Ahmar." He stroked his trim beard, his eyes moving over her face in flashes. "But if you want him to come, then you may have him. However, it did not escape my notice how you two were bickering. I cannot stand for it. Not while you are on official business."

Have him? She stifled a scoff. No one ever had Bakr. But if she pulled him off of the job, he'd know it was her doing and never let her live it down. He'd win. He'd gloat. And she couldn't stand for it. She dug this well, and she would drink the water from it.

She raised her chin to feign confidence. "I admit that his presence may at times create challenges, but I am confident in my ability to handle the official business with aplomb. Besides, he clearly knows Queen Qadira. For whatever that's worth." Her lips twisted over the sour words.

Jahmil made a coarse moan in the back of his throat, acknowledging he knew exactly what she meant. He did not want to talk about it anymore than she. He narrowed his eyes, studying her. Then he sighed and looked away. "Bakr would never have put you forward for this position if he did not think you equal to the task. That much I know."

The spiciness was back in her throat, and she knew what it was this time. Agarwood. The success of her future rested solely on Bakr's recommendation. She had become as dependent on men and the royal court as her mother which was the opposite of all she had worked toward. Lovely.

"How honored Bakr must be that you take his word so highly," she offered. "But I can assure you that I am up to the task. I studied peace accords, negotiations, and the King of Elm's seal during my time away. The same blood as yours runs through my veins. I am highly qualified regardless of... any man's recommendations."

"That has yet to be proven," he said, furling his upper lip before wincing once more. He took a small cloth from his pocket and dabbed at his nose. "Which brings up another, even larger problem. Qadira."

Sezan bristled, as frustrated by his dismissal as she was determined to show her worth. "I received a charming note from her just last night. She anticipates my arrival with eagerness." Just not the good kind.

He laughed, but it transformed into a gray, little cough. "No amount of studying can fully prepare you for what you are about to walk into. She is..." He shivered. Reaching into his jacket pocket, he took out a small box made of mother-of-pearl and held it out to her.

She offered a small bow and accepted the gift. "What's this?"

"Your official seal. And a little something from Ayelet in case you find yourself in desperate circumstances."

Even with the threat of Qadira, the lilith, and Bakr's stupidly charming smile, she couldn't help but heft the box proudly. *Her* seal. It was official.

"Thank you, Your Highness. I won't disappoint Shihala." She licked her lips, suddenly determined to figure out the Rahik situation and everything else on her own. No more relying on others, especially men.

"You are not a mere sheikha anymore, Sayidat Ambassador. And I need you to be frank with me in all things otherwise your appointment will not last."

The weight of his words felt heavier than she expected. She inspected his face. Eyes on hers, head tilted just to the left, body leaning slightly forward. He might actually listen to her from now on. At least a little. She took a breath and looked Jahmil in the eye. "Please, thank Ayelet for me. She is lovely."

"She is. And I will." He smiled, his eyes filling with soft light. "*Adhhab mae Allah,* Sayidat Ambassador."

"*Adhhab mae Allah,*" Sezan said and bowed once more before hurrying back to the carriage.

She clutched the box with her seal close to her chest. The seal of *Ambassador* Sezan bint Malik Bajul. She would add her magic to the ember of Jahmil's right then if she could, but the binding of the seal required an official contract to work. She ran a hand over the smooth finish, and a thought formed in her mind. A thought as cloudy as the change in Bakr's eyes since he had returned.

She had spent all her time in Elm studying the official seals and contracts of the Nine Kingdoms of Qaf. But what if the seal she needed to foil the lilith wasn't one created in this realm? If she could find another, one made to control the fires of Qaf... She popped back up and hurried from the carriage, not caring if Bakr or anyone else saw her run. She needed to find a copy of the Recitations for a little light reading on the way to Ahmar.

CHAPTER ELEVEN

BAKR

IT WAS RIDICULOUS, BUT they had to make their way to the City of Pearls the old-fashioned way. They could have blinked through to Ahmar instantly, but everyone had to see the procession of the new ambassador. The train of gifts. The tremendously beautiful clothing of all the courtiers who had decided to join the retinue. The shiny new buttons on the soldiers' uniforms. It was all so painfully stupid.

He stuck to the back, clinging to Bubbles with his thighs as she slithered and hopped lazily along, almost as irritated by the slow pace as he was. He'd decided to bring along his own retinue, twenty of his best soldiers who had all been with him in Orkeshi. When he left Ahmar, they would stay with Sezan to make sure she was safe. He owed her that much. And it was a relief to have some normal people around to keep him company. He'd spent over a year with these guys in the mountains and trusted each of them with his life, as they did him and each other. It was the only way they had survived.

He also knew they would have followed him into hell if that's where he'd decided to lead them because he had worked for every bit of their respect. They didn't follow him because Jahmil had made him a general, or because of the shining insignia on the official uniform, which he virtually never wore. They followed him because he walked with purpose because he knew how to make decisions. Because he fought harder, stayed up later, and worked more than anybody else. They followed him because he knew how to keep his cool in combat, if not in conversation, to spot the strengths and weaknesses in others and help them make the most of them. Most of all, they followed him because he was the craziest son of a snake in a giant pile of vipers.

Maybe that was his problem. He'd lost his purpose. He wasn't used to just loafing around anymore. He was used to being hunted every moment of his waking life, to playing constant mind games with crafty Vespars. His brain had been left with too much time since leaving Orkeshi and didn't know what to do with itself.

That's all this recent melancholy was. He just needed to remind himself of who he was, who he had always been. Who he was meant to be. But more than anything else, he needed to stop thinking so much.

He'd started drinking before they left Karzusan. He held his liquor like a champion, and by the time they decided to make camp for the night, he'd had three bottles of Ahmar Dark. His cheeks were warm, but the rest of his body was immune to temperature. His vision wasn't exactly blurry, it was just hard to focus on any one object for too long. But he wasn't stumbling. In fact, he'd spread his drinking out so much that he was barely even buzzed. He just had a headache.

As everyone worked to get camp set up — a circle of massive yurts filled with furs, furniture, books, and every other luxury of Shihalan court life — Bakr and a few of his friends made their way over to a lake with a massive waterfall pouring into it. They were in the heart of Shihala now, surrounded by red trees that stretched up so high you'd think they were reaching for Allah himself. The water shone in jewel tones of green and bright blue, cascading into a pool that seemed to have no bottom. Bakr found a spot near the edge and uncorked another bottle of wine with his teeth. He noticed a number of the ladies that had been sent along as Sezan's retinue sitting around a red and white fire, watching the men swim in the water and whispering to each other. And on the other end of camp, Sezan was on her own, sitting stiffly in a wooden chair and reading. Always reading.

He watched her through his periphery for some time, but she never glanced up at him.

He growled.

Turning to the braying laughter of his friends, he watched them swimming in the cool waters. They were taking turns climbing up the rock-face to a short shelf and diving into the water. Showing off with twists and rolls, as well as cannonballs and flesh-stinging belly-flops.

He put the bottle to his lips and sucked down several large gulps of the rich liquid. His eyes wandered up the cliff, far past the high rock currently being used as a diving board. Up a face of jagged, glasslike stone that went at a ninety-degree angle two-hundred cubits or more to the crest of the falls. To look at the top, he had to crane his neck all the way back, and even then, it was a blurry haze.

Bakr pushed off his boots, then stood up and took off his jacket and kaftan. He rolled his pants to the knees, then cracked his neck and swung his arms back and forth to loosen himself up. He dove into the water.

The coolness washed over him, and he stayed under for a while, gazing up at the winking surface above. It was finally quiet. Down here, he could pretend nobody existed, not even himself. Especially not himself. It crossed his mind to just stay. To hold his breath until he couldn't hold it anymore and then breathe in to find equilibrium with the silence.

The fantasy brought serenity to his twitching muscles until his chest began to tighten for lack of air. He kicked to the surface, breaking through a moment before he felt like he might give in.

One of the guys made a sound like a petulant rooster and leapt into the water. Bakr smiled, swimming towards the waterfall, towards the cliff.

Finding the first hold to drag himself up out of the water was difficult, but once he was on the wall, it started to go faster. The rocks were slimy, coated in purple and green moss that he had to keep ripping away before he could get his next hold.

"Bakr!" one of the men shouted from below, but he wasn't calling for him. He was calling him out, calling attention to him. He heard laughter from the guys below, hoots, and more calls of his name. They were behind him again, watching. Waiting to see what he would do next.

He looked down, realizing he'd made it halfway. A rush of adrenaline and vertigo hit him at once. Laughter filled his lungs that he didn't have to force, falling from his lips like a release of pressure. He leaned back, straightening his arms so he could gaze up at the stars. He closed his eyes and sighed, letting one arm fall limp by his side. A wave of calm rushed over him. He took a breath that filled his lungs completely for the first time in months.

Ripping off a chunk of slimy moss, he caught the next handhold and pulled himself up. His body felt reinvigorated, the blur of wine completely forgotten. Like when the sun goes down in the desert and for a single beautiful moment of twilight, the temperature is perfect, neither hot nor cold. As if your skin cannot even sense the temperature because you are totally at peace with it.

"Bakr!" a more distant voice called. The camp was watching now.

His foot slipped, throwing him off balance. He held on with one hand, dangling over the rocks like a drop of heavy dew at the edge of a leaf. His heartbeat thudded as he swung himself back in.

He reached the top of the falls and pulled himself over. He could hear distant cheering, but he didn't look down. He looked out over the horizon—the indescribable beauty of Qaf. This was Shihala, not that stuffy palace. The shimmering purple mist clinging to the tops of bushy trees, the shift of starlight on leaves. Crystal waterfalls. The forest alive with creatures and birds, and the essence of the land that made even the rocks seem to breathe. The embrace of a warm western wind, kissing his naked chest. Welcoming and kind, but always mysterious. Always standoffish with him, never allowing him to get too close.

Shihala always made him chase Her, and he knew She would never fully embrace him. Not the way She did her own children, people who actually belonged in the beautiful place.

He wondered if he fell from such great heights, would Shihala catch him?

A crowd had gathered around the lake at the bottom, gazing and pointing up at him. Anything they shouted came at him like an echo. Sezan was watching him now, standing at the edge of the lake, her impeccable white dress shifting around her in the soft wind.

His smile widened. If he died, at least she'd be free. It all felt worthwhile.

He pointed both his arms at the sky and let loose a loud, high-pitched ululation, then he leaped over the falls.

For a moment there was nothing but the wind and his hot, rushing blood. He screamed and laughed all at once, straightening himself into a line and pointing his arms as he barreled towards the water.

When he hit, he slipped into the stillness like thread through the eye of the needle. It hurt just enough to make him feel alive. His blood was pumping, skin on fire. He opened his eyes underwater, and every bubble twinkled in slow motion as sharp as crystal. He kicked to the surface.

His men were already screaming for him. The ladies were gasping, holding their chests, laughing with relief. One woman looked like she had fainted. Sezan was there, many yards away at the edge of the crowd, her book limp in her hand, and watching him with a look of... he wasn't sure. But he could almost hear her voice in his ear calling him a fool, or a braggart, or a shameless egotist.

It didn't matter. She was looking at him.

He laughed and leaned back, floating lazily. He didn't want to talk to anybody, so he stayed in the water for a long time. Eventually, the crowd dissipated. He dove under several times just to watch those pretty bubbles, but after a while, even the slosh of cool water began to fight against his serenity.

As the Fourth Moon rose in the heavens, Bakr dragged himself onto dry land and made his way over to the communal fire where his men were entertaining a few of ladies whom they'd invited to join them for the evening. He wished he had his own fire to throw into the mix, but he was only half-djinn. A fireless pile of mud that was simply lucky to be included in such rituals.

Bakr draped a towel around his shoulders and sat down to nurse a small hookah. He listened to them shout poetry at one another over the whoosh of the fire and the clumsy strum of a lyre. Each man was trying to outdo the rest, trying to sound the most profound, the most interesting, the most lyrical. Some women joined in too, their poems less blustery and more contemplative. He listened to the words, trying to make sense of their meaning as much as he tried to soak up the sounds and turn them into colors in his mind so he could understand their meaning. The sweet smoke from the hookah soothed him, lulling him with its silent music. The edges of the world blurred and faded away, multi-colored shimmers filling the periphery.

"Why don't you go, general?" said one of the women, bumping her shoulder up against his.

He looked at her and smiled. She had a soft round face, bright blue skin with deep red lips. A jewel hung at the center of her forehead on an elaborately braided chain of white leather. A red stone shimmered at the center. He wanted to touch it, so he did. Smooth and cool as water.

Turning away, he shook his head. He had no mind for this game on the best of days. His men had long given up asking. And what right did he have to contribute words when he could not contribute fire?

"You've been so quiet all night." She laid a hand on his thigh. "You must have something to add."

He looked down at her hand, tepid and pleasant. A shy, yet emboldened question in her fingertips. And in her red swollen lips a hint of a challenge. He didn't know her name, and when he looked away from her face, he instantly forgot the color of her eyes, but the easy invitation of her touch was all he really needed to understand. As it always was with women; they were interchangeable. All but one.

Bakr leaned in and kissed the corner of her mouth. She let out a shivering sigh and moved closer. Her breath smelled of wine and campfire smoke, not the minty delicate taste he longed for. And just like that, he changed his mind.

He squeezed her hand gently and set it back on her own knee. Then took another drag of his hookah, her words tumbling through his broken brain. Did he have anything to add to the fire?

Rising, he stumbled towards the flames. The last poem had been about the sky, the movement of the moons and constellations like bees to flowers, spreading life as they go from place to place. He'd heard it before, he realized. When there were women at the fire, a lot of the guys had tried and tested bits of *improv* they'd pull out, again and again.

He hated that. It was boring.

When the speaker finished, a beat of silence rushed the flames. Whispers. They all waited patiently for him to speak.

Fear threatened to well up, but the sweet smoke scattered it. He cleared his throat, no plan.

There was never any plan.

> *"Crystal waters, drunk on midnight stars*
> *Sweeter than honey,*
> *Brighter than lightning,*
> *Louder than cannon fire."*

He paused, his gaze boring into the fire. A flash of something rosy and brighter than the rest. He licked his lips.

> *"Pink and dewy,*
> *The flesh of a ripe fig.*
> *So fresh, my gut strains with hunger.*
> *So fresh, my eyes swell with tears*
> *The scent fills my nostrils.*
> *From such heights*
> *I fell."*

They waited for more, but that's all there was. He staggered to bed after that, into the yurt that had been set up for him with far more luxury than he deserved or desired. He crawled into his pile of furs and watched hallucinations explode and shimmer on the ceiling as he finished another bottle of wine. A little voice was in his ear, egging him on. Filling his brain with bad ideas.

Ideas, anyway. Maybe they weren't all bad.

As time passed, his body restless, the voice grew louder and louder until it was all he could hear. He peeled himself out of bed and stumbled out of the tent.

CHAPTER TWELVE

SEZAN

OF ALL THE DANGEROUS antics Sezan had seen Bakr pull off over the years, jumping off the waterfall barely ranked in the top ten. It didn't matter. He wasn't doing it to be dangerous. He was doing it for attention. And the camp more than provided for that even if she had not. And why should she? She had watched him nurse bottles of wine the entire day and knew what would come of it. Still, when he flung himself into the air without a care in the world—for her or anyone else—her heart had leaped into her throat and her legs had shot up from her chair. His back taut, arms stretched free, his face alive with a fire he only found when free of others. She had foolishly thought long ago that she could make him look that free. Make him feel as if he were flying above a crystal lake before plunging into ecstasy. Into peace.

She clenched her fist around the book of Recitations she had almost dropped, digging her foot into the soft mud on the shore of the lake as the shushed lapping of the water pushed her nerves further and further. He charmed her as easily as Shihala Herself and would turn his back on either of them if given the chance. *It's the human in him*, Lila would say, but she knew better.

Bakr's eyes glanced to meet hers once he emerged from the shimmering depths. A wide, reckless smile stretched across his face, and at once she was twenty again, watching him brave a wall of fire that licked up the forests of the Emerald Mountains to prove he had once ridden a Rukh bird without getting burned.

It was the first time he had pulled one of his more life-threatening stunts, and she had spent the rest of the night hiding in her rooms with tears streaming down her face, so frightened she had been of losing him. He had consoled her later, a tender hand on her cheek, a hunger on his lips that drove their passion. It was not the first time they had slept together, but it was the first time she had ached afterward, hoping he would never leave. The antics didn't stop. And each time the tears grew fewer and fewer until her eyes only burned. And still...

She rubbed each eye discreetly with the back of her hand and hurried away from his cavalier smile and open arms and into her yurt. Lila had set up everything in perfect order, furs laid invitingly on the floor, sconces of light glimmering in each corner, and one woven in the pattern of stars hanging from the center. It was perfectly set up for a restful slumber, but that was the last thing on her mind.

Sezan sat upon the furs, the Recitations open before her, and slowly coaxed a smokeless flame from the palm in her left hand: a soft rosy light whose blurry edges twinkled with flecks of gold the same color as her eyes. Her chest tightened just looking at it, and the magic wavered. She pushed back her fear of what may come and held the light over the book, opening the worn pages to where she had left off. The *Khātam Sulaymān*. A myth. A legend. Sacred lore. Something most scholars sneered at. But there were two things she had learned from the vast and ancient libraries of Eastern Elm. First, that the impossible happened often enough to believe in it. And second, that the deals beings made with each other were often absurd. The latter point eased the sting of her stupidity, and the first one gave her hope.

Hope enough to research the Seal of Sulayman. In its basic form, a hexagram of inter-twined metal that would burn her flesh. In its complex form, a talisman of frightening power. For legends said it belonged to wise King Sulayman of Ard, a gift from Allah himself, that had the power to command djinn and demon alike. A demon like the lilith.

She brought the book closer to her nose as the words slipped in and out of focus. She was tired, she told herself. Exhausted from a day's journey. But it wasn't really true. Her mind kept wandering to sandy skin dappled with water and the look of joy on Bakr's face. Her hand fell limp over the pages, and the fire in her palm went out.

Sezan stood abruptly, leaving the warmth of the soft furs. Would he be asleep by now? She frowned. Would he be alone? She bit her lip harder than she intended, frozen as she stared at the door. For all his grandstanding and disregard for his own life, she couldn't shake the depth in his eyes. They nearly always said something different from him, and she constantly found herself drawn in, wanting, yearning for him to tell her the truth. She reached a hand for the flap of her yurt. Clenched her fist. And remained alone in the dark. It was no use talking to him. They couldn't even have a conversation without one of them storming off.

A shadow moved over the fabric of the tent. She held her breath. Clumsy footsteps and an even clumsier song mumbled on smokey breath.

Bakr.

Drunk.

Sezan took a step back, a hand to her chest. Only embarrassment awaited if Bakr discovered she had been leaving to find him.

The shadow shrank as he moved closer to the flap of the door, then he stopped, and his voice went quiet. He stood like that for a long moment, unmoving and silent. She held her breath, half wanting for him to come to see her and more than half not.

He turned his head to one side and cracked his neck loudly, then threw open the flap and stumbled in. Red streaked the whites of his eyes, and he still wasn't wearing a shirt. His chest was half shadow and half muscle, brown skin shifting in the moonlight as he breathed heavily. A black and red tattoo wrapped around his left ribs and back—his beloved Rukh bird, its wings raised and talons bared to strike. The eyes sparkled, the feathers and flames moving in an unseen wind. He was as impressive as ever, but tonight was the first time she had seen all of the massive scar he'd acquired in the war. Thick and twisted, it cut across his neck and down the center of his chest. She wanted to touch it, to slide a cool finger down the white, but refrained. What exactly had the lilith—had she, herself—saved Bakr from? For a moment, the loss of her magic felt worth it.

He smiled when he saw her and approached until he was only a few feet away. "Is Lila here?"

Sezan had a mind to lie. But even drunk he'd figure it out. "No. But why are *you* here?" She tried to sound chastising, but her voice came out breathy and unsure.

"I like looking at you. Do I need another reason?"

"Proper form generally requires one, yes."

"Will you shut up about proper form?" He chuckled, raspy and dull. "Why do you like to pretend so much?"

She held as still as she could manage. This was how these things always went. Bakr in a mood and her engaging him until they were both upset. "It is all I have, Bakr. The pretending. We can't all be as genuine as you, with your aggressively bright smile and cheek biting."

"Yes, you can." He stepped closer, touching her with the radiant heat of his bare skin. "I've seen you be genuine. When you drop all the... princess nonsense and just be. Like a person. You know?"

"You ramble when you're drunk."

"You ramble when I'm drunk."

"You—" She stopped herself, pleading internally not to engage. Why was this so hard? "Well, you've had your look. Be on your way."

"It's not enough." He shook his head lazily and ran his fingers through her hair. His chest heaved with each breath. "I want to kiss you. Every inch of you. I want to see you smile at me. Actually smile. Why won't you smile at me anymore?"

The whisper of an ache spread over her heart and into her lungs like a fire, only the kind with smoke that ate up everything it touched. It hurt. His words. The longing in his eyes. The touch of his finger brushing through her hair and over her skin.

She wanted to tell him so many things but instead turned her head to the side. "It's late. You should sleep."

"I wanted to write to you. You think I never thought of you, that I never think of you, but you're wrong. You're so wrong about so many things." He laid his rough fingers on her elbow.

The stinging in her chest crept up her cheeks, shaking her voice. "It is not so hard to pick up a pen and put it to paper."

He laid his other hand on her cheek, drawing her gaze to his. "I wasn't sure you'd want to hear from me. I don't like disappointing you. And you have this whole... I don't know... life planned out for yourself. And I don't fit into it. So, I thought, just let it die. But then I saw you again...."

"How—" She cast her gaze away from the softness in his eyes. "How could you give up on me like that? I never once... I always thought...."

"Look at me. Please. Why won't you look at me?" His voice sounded desperate, almost frantic, though it remained so soft.

Slowly, against all reasoning, she lifted her gaze, trailing it along his scar, across his battle-hardened shoulders, and up to his light-green eyes: jade that had not yet lived long enough to soak up all its color. In them, she saw what she always did. Something sad and honest that he would never share with her. Since the Vespar war, it had grown much darker.

"You really should go," she whispered.

"It would have been better if I had died. Just faded into nothing after Karzusan. That's what was supposed to happen." His hand went to his own neck, rubbing the flesh roughly. "For your sake."

His words nipped at her, chasing away her desire to be wrapped in his arms and replacing it with pain that coiled tight around her heart. "It doesn't matter how many times I tell you otherwise, you never believe me. So why should I say it again?"

His face pinched with pain, and he stepped away from her, casting his eyes aside.

She reached for him on instinct, her body betraying her. But as soon as her fingers slid over his warm, familiar skin, she savored it. And she knew then that she had to say it, the words she said the night before he disappeared, and she lost everything. So he'd know her words were real and not desperation. Genuine.

"I would gladly change my life for you," Sezan said in a haunted whisper. She stared up into his eyes as he had wished, and so she knew he was listening. "I would leave with you this very moment. And I would give myself to you with everything I have and try desperately to make up for all that I lack. I'd lay with you as the moons passed by the heavens. I'd smile when we kissed and laugh as we left the whole world behind us. I'd even give up my magic and follow you to Ard. I would do these things for you, Bakr, but you never let me." She exhaled in a shaky breath, afraid to continue but aching for an answer. "Will you let me now?"

His shoulders shook, and he exhaled as sharply as if she had knocked the air out of his lungs. He glanced up at her, his eyes red and watery. His lips parted and hardened. His tongue moved behind his teeth, but the only sound that left his mouth was heavy breath.

Bakr shook his head and fled the tent. Just as he always did when she tried to be serious. Whenever she tried to tell him how much he meant to her, how he lingered in her thoughts, how she already had given up so much just to watch him throw himself off cliffs for a moment of freedom. And that's how she knew, despite his tender words and urgent kisses, that he did not love her. Not truly.

That internal, smokey fire greedily ate up all the tinder. She would soon be a scorched forest; the shadow of trees and bits of charred leaves floating aimlessly in the acrid breeze. Empty. Dead.

She stood there, shivering in the dark and welcoming inky shadows as the gnawing sound of crickets overtook the night. The smell of agarwood lingered in her tent. And she couldn't help but think he might be right. She would be better off if she forgot him, though that was an impossible task made worse by her deal with the lilith. How could she forget the man she had given everything for? Obtaining the seal from Jahmil only delayed the inevitable. Soon, her magic would evaporate, and she would not be able to swear her loyalty to Shihala as required by law and tradition. She would be summoned home as soon as Jahmil felt benevolent enough to bestow a royal position and called for a fealty ceremony. And what was she to do then? She'd march up to the Book of Life and have only a hand bare of magic to place upon it, and then even Shihala would know what she had done. She'd be lost forever, and not even Bakr would stay with her because he never would have anyway.

Her hands hung limp at her side as she allowed herself to wallow, briefly, in a pool of misery. Then she balled them into fists so gold flashed in her tent. If the flesh-burning seal of Sulayman was the only way to get rid of the lilith, to restore her powers and relieve the pain in her heart, she would stop at nothing to find it.

CHAPTER THIRTEEN

BAKR

THE NEXT SEVERAL DAYS passed in a blur. Every night he drank and smoked until he couldn't stand. While the First Moon was up, he stumbled along with the procession, cocooning himself in the raucous, pointless revelry of his friends. And under the Fourth Moon, he sat by the fire but didn't hear a word anyone said. From time to time he'd let out a hollow laugh, or stumble in a stupor with a faceless woman on his arm. But he couldn't feel the sensation of touch any more than he could taste the wine. He even forgot to eat until one of his men brought him a slab of bread. He took two bites that turned to ash in his mouth.

His friends were worried. None of them ever said so, but they kept bringing him things—more bottles of wine, different herbs for him to stuff in his hookah. Enabling him, which he supposed was the friendly thing to do. They told him jokes, sang songs, and brought women to dance for him. And he smiled at all their efforts. He was pretty sure he was smiling.

No matter what substance he put into his blood, Sezan's words kept going around in his head like a song. Not only what she had said in the tent, but so much she had said over the years. Her beautiful, painful words had flowed so easily in the beginning, before she had learned not to trust him.

He needed to stay away from her. He knew that. He'd known it for so long. What Sezan needed, what she deserved, was space to forget about him. It was the only noble course of action.

But he couldn't stand it. And when he thought about it, he raked his nails on his arm until tiny, stinging rivulets of blood appeared.

Nobody had ever said such things to him. Nothing that could hold a dead candle to the sweet and sincere devotion that flowed from Sezan. More importantly, nobody had ever shown him how to give it back. His mother had despised him. He'd been worthy of nothing less.

She was born a Bedouin, a member of the nomadic al-Rubia tribe that traveled the Arabian desert, keeping all the oldest traditions of their people alive. One night when she was sixteen an invisible djinn sneaked into her tent and took what he wanted from her. She told her father what had happened, but he didn't believe her. Nobody did, until nine months later when she bore a child, forged in the unholy union.

She was ostracized from the tribe after that, forced to live at the fringes of their society without a protector, with no one to help feed her, and with all prospects of finding a good husband destroyed.

The only reason his mother had refrained from exposing him to the elements as an infant was her fear that the djinn who was his father might punish her. But she had wanted to. She'd said so many times. She made some effort to provide him with food and shelter, though they were always hungry—frying in the merciless sun during the day or shivering in the dead of night. She never held him, never kissed him. She moved through life like a specter, barely speaking a word. And because she had told everyone in the tribe that his father was a djinn, none of them ever even looked him in the eye. Instead, they spat on him and muttered the *Bismallah* as they rushed by.

She had named him after the caliph, Abu Bakr, in hopes that it would help cleanse the evil from his soul, but she never called him that. She only ever called him *musikh*. Monster.

Even if he knew how to return to Sezan what she had always offered so freely, everything inside of him was broken and tainted. A filthy sack of blood with no soul.

He couldn't even find the nobility to leave her alone, which was proof of how monstrous he really was. He knew how much it hurt her. Still, he longed to soak up her fidelity like sunshine. To selfishly use it as a respite from the moonless night that had relentlessly followed him since the moment he was conceived.

They arrived on the shores of Buhayra Ruwarin, and the party moved across the five-mile-long floating bridge that led to the glorious City of Pearls at the center. Say what you may about Ahmar, it was an impeccably beautiful kingdom, littered with reflective lakes that filled the landscape with starlight. Massive sea turtles with diamonds and emeralds growing on their shells swam in the waters. The first time he'd seen them, Bakr had wondered if the jewels were natural to them—like the famed healing stone of the deep-water Tabib—or if Queen Qadira had had them affixed to the shells for the sake of aesthetics. He still didn't know for certain. Scintillating waterfalls cascaded all through the city, as clean and lovely as dawn. And the palace itself, the largest he had ever seen. White marble capped with huge domes of blue glass that shimmered with the crowded stars of Qaf.

Bakr drank six cups of coffee as thick as mud to prepare himself for appearing in polite society, sober for the first time in days and twitching. He shaved and put on his uniform—jacket, gloves, proper insignia. All that nonsense. Sezan was at the middle of the procession, riding in a massive, bejeweled carriage drawn by eight winged horses. He flew above on Bubbles' back, making slow circles over the lake, the cool wind cleansing his skin.

He needed to get out of his funk. Smile, he told himself. So, he practiced, biting back all the thoughts, burying them deep. It didn't matter anymore today than it had a week ago. A year ago. Eight years ago when he had first seen Sezan sitting in the garden as Karzusan, reading one of her books. When he closed his eyes, he could still see the way her starlight hair had scattered around her shoulders. He'd leapt the wall and sat down in the grass beside her, then told her stupid jokes until finally she smiled and told him her name.

From his drakonte-eye view, Bakr watched some ceremonial nonsense take place at the gate before it was drawn open and the procession was allowed inside. He circled a few more times, then brought Bubbles into land beside Sezan's carriage. He was her official escort and had to be at her side when she met Qadira.

A little hook caught in his lungs when he thought about Sezan and Qadira being in the same room together. Hopefully they'd be too busy thinking about politics to worry about him. Maybe it wasn't such a bad thing that he wasn't allowed to speak.

He patted Bubbles' nose and leaned in close to her ear. "Be ready to dart at any moment," he whispered and every scale on her body wound tighter. "Qadira is bound to have firewalls all around the island. If things go south, you take Sezan and get out. Don't worry about me."

She snorted so smoke came from her nostrils, then leaned back on her coils and stuck her chin up in the air.

Bakr snatched her bridle and yanked her ear back towards his mouth. "Fine, worry about me. But get Sezan first."

She tilted her head to one side, her snake eyes aimed levelly at his.

"And I'll get you a cow after. Two. Two cows. Deal?"

A quiver of delight licked through her body. She leaned back on her coils and stretched her fifty-cubit wings.

"There's my bubbly baby." Bakr smiled, then turned from her and walked to the carriage. When he drew open the door, he'd never seen Sezan look so stiff, her dress sharply starched, her hijab tied so it covered all of her hair. Her back was straight, lips a flattened scowl. Lila sat at her side, staring daggers at him as he offered his hand to help Sezan out of the carriage.

Without a single glance at him, she took his hand and stepped out, letting go immediately when both her feet were on the ground. Then she strode past him and curtsied to the Ahmaran bureaucrat who'd come out to meet her. He couldn't hear what they were saying but supposed it didn't matter. What did he care about Shihalan and Ahmaran relations anymore? Once he'd completed his mission for Rahik, he was going back to Ard never to return to the land of djinn as long as he lived. He hoped that wouldn't be very long.

They were led inside, through the glimmering halls of the pearl-encrusted palace, and into the throne room. Purple-skinned courtiers lined the aisle, all of them glaring at Sezan like she was carrying the plague. There was no fanfare, no music. Only animosity and suspicion. Up on a high podium, the queen reclined on her throne. She looked particularly sparkly today, so much makeup and glitter applied to her lavender skin that she shone like silver. She wore the crown jewels on her head, a turban of diamonds and pearls the size of fists that looked almost bigger than she was. Her head rested on a pile of silk pillows, perhaps to compensate for the weight. The air sparkled with her lime green fire, her eyes glowing brown—malice, disdain, utter confidence. Her legs sprawled over her sofa-like throne, an elbow rested casually on her knee.

When Qadira saw him, her fire quivered and she lifted an eyebrow. But she quickly resettled into her casual condescension.

Sezan curtsied low until she was practically on the floor, a gesture of ultimate respect reserved for only the most formal occasions. Bakr brought up his voice and called out, "Your Astonishingness, may I present Sheikha Sezan bint Malik Bajul, Ambassador for the Kingdom of Shihala."

The queen pursed her birdlike lips and narrowed her eyes of fury but said nothing. The tension in the air was thick and chewy. They were in Qadira's world now, contained within her fire barrier so even full-blooded djinn could not steal a quick escape via apparation. If she decided she did not want to negotiate, it would have been nothing to have their entire party surrounded and put to death without delay, a declaration of war on Shihala.

Bakr rested a hand on the pommel of his sword as his eyes swept the room. The exits, possible fodder, the shape of the gathered crowd. He would never be able to get everybody out alive, but if worse came to worst, he was standing close enough to Sezan to protect her and drag her out the way they came. Bubbles was ready to make a break for it at any moment.

He was ready.

Without rising from her curtsy, Sezan looked up at the queen and said, "Your Astonishingness, I'm honored to be in the presence of the mightiest queen in all of Qaf. The tales of your majesty and kingdom are known far beyond the courts of Eastern Elm."

Silence.

"Shihala acknowledges with utmost gratitude their greatest ally in the fight against Vespar and your magnanimous hospitality and charity during Shihala's darkest hour. We are ever in your debt."

Sezan managed to bow even deeper, her eyes still on the queen, but Qadira's lips only pursed tighter. No doubt Sezan was analyzing every twitch and spasm in that sharp face to decide how to proceed.

Sezan opened her mouth the tiniest bit before closing it and taking a breath. "With all due respect, and if the courts will allow me a brief moment to speak candidly, our honorable amir and regent behaved with incredible and unacceptable disdain for your hospitality. In short, he acted as a spoiled brat. But we should not allow the fickle whims of men to stop us from our own goals. Ahmar is grand, its walls sparkle and shimmer even through cloudy skies. You have built and maintained a tremendous empire, and Shihala can be a valuable ally in ensuring it remains so. I promise, on my honor as a humble diplomat and a woman weary of the condescension of men in the various courts around Qaf, that I will attempt to persuade you only when the matters at hand are as beneficial to Ahmar as they are to Shihala. No lies. No tricks. Only honesty."

Qadira lifted her brow and her lips pursed. She stayed like that a moment, her bright green eyes sweeping over Sezan, though the dull brackish lights within were unchanged. The skin around her eyes tightened and a small wrinkle formed at the corner of one lip. "I see," she said, her voice tight and throaty. "A new force of chicanery has emerged from the thicket of thieves and blustering fools that is Shihala. You would try to trick me with sincerity?" She laughed cruelly and shook her head as well as she could in that massive, heavy crown. "To admit that your so-called prince is a spoiled brat is to say the Moonless Night is a bit chilly."

Bakr kept absolutely still, deftly filling the role of physically imposing and silent bodyguard. But his attention was all on Sezan, ears aching for her next words. He had known she would be good at this. Heaven knew he could never win an argument with her except by distracting her tongue with other activities.

"Would you prefer I be duplicitous, Your Astonishingness? It is not my first choice, but I can oblige." Sezan raised her chin higher. "But let me say first that forgoing the Shihalan trade routes necessary to reach Zabriya and both Western and Eastern Elm would be like tossing a haul of uptka fish onto moon-bleached sand. He would have a monopoly on all that comes through from the south. It would be a detrimental declaration to all of Qaf that Jahmil Amir won your dignity *and* your trade." She paused and pinched her brows together in a thoughtful look. "What an awful and humiliating waste that would be, no?"

Qadira cocked her head harder to one side, though if that was a reaction to what Sezan had said or merely her avian bones crumbling under the weight of the jewels was debatable. She snapped her fingers and a man in princely robes rushed to her side far more readily than any dog. She said something quietly to him. He bowed and rushed away.

"Very well, Ambassador. I will suffer your presence in my court." Qadira stroked her chin with long, tapering fingers. "You and your household may stay in what was once your disgusting amir's apartments. My chamberlain will show you."

With a wave, Qadira dismissed the entire party. Sezan dipped her body in appreciation. Bakr turned to follow, but the biting royal voice cut into him from behind. "Not you, General. You stay."

He flinched, and Sezan shot him the most subtle look of utter disgust he had ever endured, the first time she'd deigned to look at him since the tent. Then she and everyone else followed the chamberlain out of the throne room, leaving him alone with the queen and her retinue.

Turning to Qadira, he smiled brightly. "*Malikati.*"

"Approach," said Qadira. There was none of the playful lust on her face that he had seen the other night. Her expression was stony, lime-green eyes bubbling like tar pits.

He laid a hand on the pommel of his sword and stepped closer, pausing a few feet from the first stair that led up to the throne. She beckoned him closer with a finger, the fire dancing around her like a kaleidoscope. He did as he was bade, moving closer and closer until he stood mere inches from her throne. Even then, she beckoned him nearer. He leaned down.

Qadira snatched the collar of his shirt between the lapels of his leather jacket and yanked him to her face. "Is this your doing, you disgusting mongrel?" White lightning flashed in her eyes, momentarily blinding him. "Have you been spying on me?"

"No." His smile shrank, but not so much as to appear contrite. "This is Jahmil Amir's doing…"

White spittle foamed at the corners of her silver-painted lips. "The next person to speak the name of that human-loving, blue-assed, malingering cheat is going to get his manhood crushed between two red-hot stones."

"Then that person will not be me." He pressed his lips together hard to keep his smile. "Your Astonishingness, I was not spying on you. My intentions may not have been pure, but they were straightforward."

She narrowed her eyes, gaze sweeping his face and hunting for his giveaway. Djinn were used to being able to read each other's emotions in their flashing eyes. The white-hot fire in Qadira's gaze said she was very angry, the dark-green sparkles in her naturally light-green eyes hinted at feelings of jealousy and resentment—no doubt left over for Jahmil. Flecks of pink spoke of anxiety and suspicion. And buried deep in the facets was the soft yellow mist of disgust.

Bakr's pale green eyes always remained the same no matter how he felt. Some djinn found it irritating, others mysterious. And some, like Qadira, took it as a challenge.

"You're a liar," she said flatly. "All Shihalans are. Furthermore, I think you must have used an enchantment on me to trick your way into my bed."

Bakr tried to pop his neck, but Qadira just tightened her grip on his shirt. The angle was less than comfortable, as was the intense floral smell assaulting his nostrils. "That's your move, not mine."

"The only reason I slept with you, you lying son of a khanaziri pig-dog, is because I was curious what it would be like with a human." She flicked her gaze down and then back up. "Unimpressive."

"Right…" He smirked, jutting out his lower lip. "So unimpressive you offered me a vineyard to come back and do it again."

"I ought to have you skinned alive in the public square for your insolence." Her grip tightened on his shirt until the fabric squeaked. "That would show your ambassador what happens when someone tries to double-cross me."

Bakr lowered his brow. It was the second time someone had threatened to skin him that week. He wondered if there was something peculiar about his face that made women want to remove it.

"That's an option..." He cast his gaze askance. "I can't help thinking there must be another way."

A golden light dawned in Qadira's eyes and a most unpleasant smile overcame her lips. Playfulness had returned to her expression, but that was not reassuring. "Yes, I think there is another way." She let go of his shirt and sat back on her throne. "It's a good thing you're a gambler, general."

CHAPTER FOURTEEN

Sezan

Sezan followed the chamberlain through spacious hallways of crystal-streaked marble. The ceiling overhead revealed the heavens of Qaf, its galaxies as beautiful in Ahmar as they were in Shihala. She tried to take comfort in their twinkling light, but her hands still shook no matter how hard she clasped them.

The first phase of her mission, getting Qadira to let her stay instead of cutting her head off right then and there, had been a success. But the queen was far more open with her cruelty than Sezan had expected. Qadira was not an utter fool, though, and that would make Sezan's job easier. Duplicity, politics, and back-stabbing were all things she expected from Qadira and had the skills to deal with. It was sheer stupidity that left her with no ground to work with.

The chamberlain escorted her to a grand room with shining curtains and a view of the lake that caught her breath. It reflected the sky so perfectly, the fish that broke its serene surface seemed to swim into heaven. And for a moment, she was in the water, too, hair streaming around her bare shoulders as Bakr brushed a loose strand from her skin and chased away the chill with kisses. He had left for the war shortly after that, and she had not gone swimming since.

"Sezan!"

She touched a hand to the clear pane that separated her from her dreams, then sighed and turned.

Lila trundled into her room with a stream of servants behind her, ready to make the quarters livable. She pinched Sezan's elbow and offered a wide smile. "You did it!"

"I have quite a long journey ahead of me before I can celebrate." Or perhaps just two weeks.

"You must take the victories as they come."

Sezan sighed when a knock sounded on the frame of the open door behind them. It would be too soon for Qadira to call for her unless she had broken Bakr's face in and needed someone to smooth the situation over. Justice never tasted so bitter. Sezan covered up a frown and turned.

An immaculately dressed man in creamy straight-legged pants and a matching kaftan embroidered with fig leaves stood politely at the door. He was only a little taller than she, his hair thick dark brown and his beard trimmed with soft curves around his mouth. His skin was a shade of purple similar to Qadira's, only softer, like lavender, and without all the garish sparkles. His ice-blue eyes were gentle, unassuming, his smile almost apologetic. He leaned against the door, one hand with a large onyx ring by his side and the other tucked behind him, a charming blend of regal formality and affability.

"Ambassador Sezan bint Malik Bajul?"

She put on a soft smile to match his own. "I am." She offered a perfunctory bow. "And you are?"

His smile widened, a shadow of what Bakr's would be. "Ajmal Amir."

She bowed a little lower this time and ran through her memory to find his name. There weren't many to go through. The Ahmaran's rituals for who ascends the throne included the court-sanctioned murder of siblings and family until only one victor prevailed. That there was even one amir as old as Qadira still living while she sat on the throne was a peculiar novelty often subject to rumors.

"Ah yes," Sezan smiled. "Qadira's only living *eben khaltee* and royal advisor."

"Don't remind me," he said with a chuckle and ran a hand through his hair. "I do not choose my cousins."

Sezan nodded, as neutral a gesture as she could make it. She would not put it past Qadira to send a spy to trick her, but his eyes were clear as the lake outside. Perhaps he was just a prince bored with palace life and come to see the new arrivals.

"I would be honored if you'd join me for a tour of the palace," the amir asked in a tone as formal as his kaftan. "Though I'd hate to impose on the time of such an important official."

She opened her mouth and paused, an awkward puff of air escaping. She had been about to sass back, so used she had become to Bakr's condescending quips over the last few days.

He smiled again. "It is okay. I do not mean to push. I simply wished to enjoy the company of our newest member of the court. It only hurts that your hair sparkles from across the palace. I shall have nothing else to do but watch as some other lucky man escorts you around."

The corners of her lips twitched up unbidden. "As ambassador for Shihala it is my sworn duty to foster good relations between the members of the court. I would be remiss to turn down such a generous offer, Ajmal Amir."

"Please, just Ajmal."

He bent over in a bow, his back straight, and swooped his right hand to the side. Lila caught her eye and clapped her hands together in a sign of teasing victory. Sezan ignored her and obliged, gliding past his outstretched arm close enough that the puff of her pants brushed against his legs.

They strolled casually throughout the castle, no physical destination in mind. For a tour guide, Ajmal was terrible; he cared as little for the construction of the palace as he did for most of the rooms that lay within it. It was the art of conversation he excelled in. She had found only a few scholars in Eastern Elm who would so readily discuss with a woman their opinions on politics, religion, and art. And while his insights weren't fantastically keen or revelatory, they were solid and knowledgeable.

Ajmal stepped aside so she could lead into the next hallway filled with oil paintings of djinn and war and views of the heavens. "If I had known I would find myself in the beautiful company of someone so well-read, I would have shown you our library first. Though after a stay in Eastern Elm, I'm afraid it will pale in comparison."

"That would be grand," Sezan said. "I have some research I need to attend to while I'm here. While extensive, Elm's libraries are mostly stuffed full of dreary legalese and copies of every contract ever sealed by the King. While the latter bit can be quite fascinating, it doesn't do much in the way of exploratory reading."

"Oh?" He raised a defined brow. "May I inquire as to what you are trying to find?"

She stopped walking and placed a hand on her cheek. "I think if I told you, you would laugh at me."

"I would never dream of it."

She kept back a Bakr-flavored scoff. "Promise?"

"On the honor of Ahmar and my dignity."

She sighed and looked at him through her lashes. He did not seem like a spy. And a spy would think her answer childish anyway. She let out a puff of air, then answered, "The *Khātam Sulaymān*."

He sucked air in through his teeth, and she winced, waiting for his judgment. Then he let out a soft chuckle.

"You laugh!" She pointed her finger at him as a blush crept into her cheeks.

"No." He raised his hands, still chuckling. "Okay, yes, but only with pleasure. I love the tales of the all-powerful Seal of Sulayman. I used to have my nurses read them to me every night before bed."

"You jest at my expense," she said, pouting just a little.

"I would never do anything at your expense." He bowed low, taking her hand in his and kissing the top. She startled, uneasy at Ahmar's more forward customs. They were not so conservative as Shihala. Not so gendered. She forced her hand to relax within his, not wanting to offend. "Please," he continued, "let me make it up to you. Keep walking with me, and I'll tell you all I know."

Her cheeks stayed warm, but she obliged. He kept his hold on her hand and tucked it over his elbow. It felt unnatural, to be touching any other man than Bakr, but diplomats were obliged to obey the customs of the lands they attended. And Ajmal Amir felt safe and unassuming.

After a few minutes of easy walking, her nerves cooled, and she asked, "Are the tales of Sulayman's Seal just that to you? Or..." She looked at him sideways. "Do you believe it actually exists?"

"And what would life be if we could explain it all away in neat little boxes? I believe there are enough stories to justify its existence."

"A safe answer."

"I do not wish to scare you away."

She smiled and patted his arm with her free hand, enjoying the boldness of her own actions. "If someone were to scare me away from this palace, it would not be you."

"Good." He grinned, his cheekbones mirroring the shape of his beard below it. "Next question?"

She pursed her lips and tapped them with a finger. "I shall try your expertise on the matter with this one."

"I stand at the ready."

"I've read through many of the Recitations and various legends of the Seal, and not one agrees on where it resides. Would you dare make a guess?"

"Ah," he said gruffly, or as gruffly as someone with the voice of a rabbit could. "You are a treasure hunter."

"No," she said, shaking her head thoughtfully. "I am a seal hunter."

He chuckled again, the sound crisp and clean. "I suppose that's to be expected from anyone who stays in Eastern Elm too long." He stroked his beard. "It would have to be on Ard."

His words dropped like a pebble into her stomach. Ard was a dangerous place for djinn, despite Bakr's homesick musings. "You sound so certain."

"It is the only way," he said, flashing his straight teeth. "Such a powerful talisman would have to be protected from djinn, demons, and humans alike."

"So why Ard? Wouldn't that give the humans an unfair advantage?"

"A year ago, I would have said a race with no magic could never have an advantage, for who is anyone without the fire they wield?"

Sezan's heart stopped, sending a jolt from her fingertips to the toes curled inside her slippers. Would she not be one of those lost, fireless souls soon enough?

"But then," he continued, unaware of her discomfort, "Shihala's new queen arrived, and I don't believe anyone would argue with me when I say she proved us all wrong. The magic that creature possesses is..." The skin around his eyes crinkled. "Untenable."

She offered a weak nod, tucking her shaking fingers behind the folds of her tunic. She was not sure which thread to process; that Ajmal looked nearly afraid of Ayelet—if his mild mannerisms could be interpreted at all—or that he clearly had disdain for those who could not wield their own fire.

He smiled awkwardly. "I'm sorry. I've made you uncomfortable. That is all we ever hear about within these walls. And now that I finally get to have a stimulating conversation with a gorgeous woman who isn't obsessed with *Jahnmi Jahmil* and his human wife—" He shook his fist in mock anger. "—I squander it." He pulled at his ear. "Where were we?"

"It is your palace," she said, surprised at how easily the tease came to her lips and how comfortable he had made her feel so quickly.

"Ah-ha, clever woman. I meant in our conversation."

"Ard."

"Ah, yes. To protect the sheer power of the Seal, God kept it safe by requiring a hand from both worlds, Qaf and Ard, knowing neither could convince the other to help."

Sezan scrunched her nose. "So if Ard's piece is the location of the Seal, what is required of Qaf?"

"The means to get there," he said, and this time his smile almost did rival Bakr's. "The grand Rukh bird." He puffed out his chest and pulled his shoulders back. "Legend says only a Rukh and his rider can fly into the sun and find the floating city of Eayima. That is if you believe in such things," he added with a wink.

His burst of energy, so unexpected and warm, almost made her laugh until she realized why. "Why are all men obsessed with that bird?" she muttered.

She scraped her nail across her palm to scatter the memories of light green eyes and to stay in the present. But it was no use. The mention of the Rukh, of Bakr's precious Rukh he had never shown her and spoke of with a tenderness far sweeter than he ever spoke of her, refused to let go of her mind. Was the only way to save her magic to ask for his help? She forced her hand open and inhaled deep within her belly. Of course, it would be.

Still, the information Ajmal had given her was infinitely useful and she thanked Allah for her luck in finding a man with such knowledge hidden away in Ahmar.

Sezan turned to Ajmal and focused on the easy curve of his lips. "You have lived up to your name as an expert on the Seal. I almost forgive you for laughing at me when you said you would not."

He paused, his light blue eyes bright and thoughtful beneath his dark hair.

Not once had his eyes flashed any color. Not once had his mannerisms given away anything but honesty and interest. She didn't know what to think of it and kept preparing for battle when there was none to be fought.

"Will you eat dinner with me?" Ajmal asked.

She breathed out the muted beginnings of a giggle. "I am required at the banquet tonight. You know, emissary duties."

"Of course," he nodded. "My apologies for misstating. Would you allow me to be your plus one at the banquet tonight? I hear the guest list is quite short. Only amirs and dignitaries and that sort of thing. Very droll. Very exclusive."

She bit her lip softly. After a moment it popped out from between her teeth. He seemed almost decidedly on the side of lonely, bored, yet charming prince. And it would not be out of protocol for an emissary to attend such proceedings with a member of the host country's royal court. In fact, it would be seen as a gesture of good faith. Though Bakr would have a conniption. Or not. Despite her sending Lila to remind him repeatedly of his duties while here, there was a good chance he wouldn't even show up tonight. Or care about her one wit if he did. As long as she bribed a servant to water down his wine....

"Sezan?"

She lifted her eyes up to Ajmal, startled by the informality and the fact that she had clearly drifted.

He smiled. "You don't mind if I call you by your given name only, do you? I find it makes everything less stiff."

"No," she said almost as an afterthought. "I don't mind. And yes, I will allow *you* to accompany *me* to the banquet."

"Splendid," he said and grinned. "Unfortunately, as you can see, we have come full circle and arrived back at your rooms."

She let her hand linger on his arm. "You did not show me the library, *amiri*."

"Ajmal," he said, chastising. "Just Ajmal. And you caught me. I wished to see you again tomorrow and hoped the lure of books would drive you to endure my company once more."

She tilted her head, a strand of her sparkling hair slipping loose from her hijab. He reached forward, hesitated, then slid the hair between his fingers and tucked it carefully behind her ear.

"So?" he asked, and for the first time, she saw a tiny flicker in his eyes just a shade bluer than they already were. *Hope.*

She smiled, trying so hard to feel something flutter inside her. "It sounds like we are set for dinner and a date."

"You are gracious," he said and pulled her hand free from his arm, kissing it before letting her go. Then he turned and strode off.

She watched him go, waiting, hoping, and not feeling even the whisper of a stir within her. Then she sighed and slipped into her room to change for dinner.

"Ah-ha, clever woman. I meant in our conversation."

"Ard."

"Ah, yes. To protect the sheer power of the Seal, God kept it safe by requiring a hand from both worlds, Qaf and Ard, knowing neither could convince the other to help."

Sezan scrunched her nose. "So if Ard's piece is the location of the Seal, what is required of Qaf?"

"The means to get there," he said, and this time his smile almost did rival Bakr's. "The grand Rukh bird." He puffed out his chest and pulled his shoulders back. "Legend says only a Rukh and his rider can fly into the sun and find the floating city of Eayima. That is if you believe in such things," he added with a wink.

His burst of energy, so unexpected and warm, almost made her laugh until she realized why. "Why are all men obsessed with that bird?" she muttered.

She scraped her nail across her palm to scatter the memories of light green eyes and to stay in the present. But it was no use. The mention of the Rukh, of Bakr's precious Rukh he had never shown her and spoke of with a tenderness far sweeter than he ever spoke of her, refused to let go of her mind. Was the only way to save her magic to ask for his help? She forced her hand open and inhaled deep within her belly. Of course, it would be.

Still, the information Ajmal had given her was infinitely useful and she thanked Allah for her luck in finding a man with such knowledge hidden away in Ahmar.

Sezan turned to Ajmal and focused on the easy curve of his lips. "You have lived up to your name as an expert on the Seal. I almost forgive you for laughing at me when you said you would not."

He paused, his light blue eyes bright and thoughtful beneath his dark hair.

Not once had his eyes flashed any color. Not once had his mannerisms given away anything but honesty and interest. She didn't know what to think of it and kept preparing for battle when there was none to be fought.

"Will you eat dinner with me?" Ajmal asked.

She breathed out the muted beginnings of a giggle. "I am required at the banquet tonight. You know, emissary duties."

"Of course," he nodded. "My apologies for misstating. Would you allow me to be your plus one at the banquet tonight? I hear the guest list is quite short. Only amirs and dignitaries and that sort of thing. Very droll. Very exclusive."

She bit her lip softly. After a moment it popped out from between her teeth. He seemed almost decidedly on the side of lonely, bored, yet charming prince. And it would not be out of protocol for an emissary to attend such proceedings with a member of the host country's royal court. In fact, it would be seen as a gesture of good faith. Though Bakr would have a conniption. Or not. Despite her sending Lila to remind him repeatedly of his duties while here, there was a good chance he wouldn't even show up tonight. Or care about her one wit if he did. As long as she bribed a servant to water down his wine....

"Sezan?"

She lifted her eyes up to Ajmal, startled by the informality and the fact that she had clearly drifted.

He smiled. "You don't mind if I call you by your given name only, do you? I find it makes everything less stiff."

"No," she said almost as an afterthought. "I don't mind. And yes, I will allow *you* to accompany *me* to the banquet."

"Splendid," he said and grinned. "Unfortunately, as you can see, we have come full circle and arrived back at your rooms."

She let her hand linger on his arm. "You did not show me the library, *amiri*."

"Ajmal," he said, chastising. "Just Ajmal. And you caught me. I wished to see you again tomorrow and hoped the lure of books would drive you to endure my company once more."

She tilted her head, a strand of her sparkling hair slipping loose from her hijab. He reached forward, hesitated, then slid the hair between his fingers and tucked it carefully behind her ear.

"So?" he asked, and for the first time, she saw a tiny flicker in his eyes just a shade bluer than they already were. *Hope.*

She smiled, trying so hard to feel something flutter inside her. "It sounds like we are set for dinner and a date."

"You are gracious," he said and pulled her hand free from his arm, kissing it before letting her go. Then he turned and strode off.

She watched him go, waiting, hoping, and not feeling even the whisper of a stir within her. Then she sighed and slipped into her room to change for dinner.

CHAPTER FIFTEEN

Bakr

He was strangely calm as Qadira's men took him from the throne room, cast a haze of black fire over his head, so he could not sense where he was being taken, and led him through a series of twisty hallways. And then down. Down. Descending ten or more flights of stairs into the cold and dank.

When the obscuring haze was lifted, it took his eyes a moment to adjust in the dark. He heard the drip of water, but no other movement. A few sparkles of starlight came through long channels in the ceiling. He stood on a small ledge, before him a cavernous cistern. Columns of perfectly smooth white stone rose from the waters, holding up the ceiling some hundred cubits from the surface. It was quiet and echoic and seemed to stretch on for miles to the front and sides. He glanced behind him and saw the door through which he had entered. Iron and gold—physical and magical barriers for the average djinn, though they held him in place just as well.

Qadira had offered no explanation other than she was giving him an opportunity to prove himself. Was he supposed to prove that he hadn't been spying on her? That he wasn't responsible for some elaborate circuitous plan?

He laughed just thinking about it. If that was what she suspected, she knew even less about him than he would have assumed.

Bakr narrowed his eyes at the two guards who had brought him, now standing at his back. They could have been twins for how similar they looked. Deep purple skin, long yellow beards, each nearly seven feet tall and built like fortresses.

"Alright, boys," he said, folding his arms across his chest and tossing a smile over each shoulder at each of the guards. "What exactly am I looking at here?"

"Cetus," said the one.

"What now?"

"Cetus," said the other.

Bakr narrowed his eyes. "That helps a lot. Thanks."

"The underwater King of Buhayra Ruwarin," said the one.

"The rulers of Ahmar must feed it or be fed to it," said the other.

He laughed nervously. "What was that last bit?"

"It eats criminals," said the one. "Infidels, murderers, thieves. And liars."

"Hmm." He flattened his chin. "So basically, it eats everybody."

"Only the guilty." The one shook his head. "Queen Qadira has decided that your soul will be weighed by Cetus. If you are found wanting, it will devour you, bones and all."

Bakr had a strong suspicion of what the verdict of this particular trial was going to be.

A low-pitched, horrific screech cut through the air and reverberated all around. He guessed the echo of the massive chamber added a few cubits to his estimation of how large the creature was, but it was bigger than Bubbles at the very least. Thirty cubits, maybe? Forty?

Both the guards' pink eyes turned black with fear.

Bakr gripped the pommel of his steel sword and shifted his weight onto one foot. "So, Qadira has sentenced me to death."

The other guard shook his head quickly. "If you are innocent, you will be spared."

"Death it is." Bakr rolled his shoulders. Ahmar was as good a place to die as any, he supposed. Why he had ever slept with the queen of glitter made no sense to him now. Of all the people, of all the places, in all the worlds, why Qadira? Why?

He really was a glutton for punishment.

Thoughts of Sezan flashed through him followed by a quick rush of dread. He knew the contract contained a clause that prevented him from committing suicide, but what happened if he simply was killed? Would the contract become void? And if the contract was voided, did that mean the poison Rahik had given her—the poison which even now flowed through her veins—would simply reemerge to kill her?

The screech came again. Louder and much closer. It rattled the chamber, echoing like thunder. The guards fell over themselves to escape through the door. Bakr tried to follow, but one of the guards shot a blast of yellow fire at his face. He threw up a hand to protect his eyes, hesitating just long enough for them to slam the door shut. He heard a series of chains and locks being done up.

Bakr drew his sword and flipped it over in his hand by the grip. It was nothing special, a steel crusader's blade he had picked up in Jerusalem long ago. Single-handed, straight, about a yard long, and a bit thin from so many years of dutiful sharpening.

The water was bizarrely still, rippling gently from the impact of the creature's scream. He watched it closely as silence crept back in. Then he noticed a gentle ripple in the darkness, like a massive fish swimming close to the surface. Spikes as long as his sword broke through the water—needlelike points of midnight blue that ran in a line, shifting and changing, rising and falling.

His muscles tightened and his breath quickened, mouth bone dry.

Another screech exploded, loud enough to sting his ears. In a sudden rush of water, the creature reared up. A triangular head filled with teeth like daggers and covered in scales. Whiskers like tentacles hung from its face, its eyes blobs of wet sulfur that glowed faintly yellow in a crocodilian snout. Its chest was vaguely human, with massive arms twice as long as Bakr's own body and three-fingered hands at each end, with claws as big as battering rams. Its body was vaguely snake-like, then split at the bottom into dozens of long, wormlike tentacles. The spikes he had seen ran over its neck and down its back, shivering with iridescence as it screamed.

He had no idea what in Jahannam it was. Half snake, half-octopus, half-man, half-crocodile. He'd never been good at math.

He watched in horror as flickers of blue lightning gathered in its yawning, screeching maw into a ball of energy.

Bakr dove hard to one side a moment before the blast hit. The crash broke the stone he was standing on, shattering it into razor-sharp shards that glanced off the thick leather of his uniform jacket.

Thank Allah he'd been wearing it.

The creature swiped for him with its pincer-like hand. He rolled aside. It grabbed with the other hand. He dodged again, then rolled off the platform into the murky water.

Plunged under, Bakr kept his grip on his sword and swam for the surface. The salty, acrid water stung at his eyes as he struggled to get his bearings. When he looked up, he saw the creature had moved back and was gathering another massive ball of lightning in its mouth.

Lightning. In water.

There was no time to reach the platform. In desperation, he lunged for the creature. His hand found purchase on the armor-plated scales, and he yanked himself free from the water moments before the second blast of electricity struck the surface. It crackled and arced, pure energy spreading in every direction.

The monster snatched at him with its three-fingered hand. He brought up his sword and stuck it into the palm. It screamed so furiously Bakr nearly lost his grip. The beast reeled back, and he faltered, dropping him into the water again. A wave rushed into his windpipe, and he came up hacking. He swam with all his might, pushing towards movement, even as more light gathered in front of him.

He caught hold of one of the creature's slimy tentacles, which waved and waggled in the water, lifting him up from the murky cistern.

Another blast of lightning crackled across the water's surface. He looked to the back of the sword-like spines, gauging the movement of the free-swinging tentacle. When it came close, he leaped for the back. He caught himself on one point, narrowly avoiding impaling himself on others. When he had a foothold on the scales, he brought up his sword and swung down at the creature's back. It was like he'd struck a diamond boulder. The sword clanged and his body trembled with the reverberations.

The great beast whipped back and then forward with such speed that he was thrown. His body shot through the air and hit a wall, knocking the breath from him. Back on the rock platform, the gold and iron door at his back, Bakr rolled to his knees.

He tried to get to his feet, but the beast lunged at him, snapping with its crocodilian mouth. He rolled aside, but it came back. Snap, retreat, snap, retreat. He was reaching the end of the line of stone when he recognized his chance. Bakr tossed his sword up and caught it by the middle, his leather gloves protecting him from being cut. When the creature came in for the next snap, Bakr leapt towards it and jammed his sword lengthwise into its jaws, locking them open.

Orange blood dripped from the mouth where the tip of the blade dug into the hard palate, the pommel caught between two rows of lower teeth. The beast screamed and snapped its head from side to side. It tried to gather lightning in its throat, but the metal sword acted to collect it and push it back into the monster's mouth. It choked and sputtered, trying again and again to use its electric breath.

Bakr backed up as far as he could, let out a loud ululation, and ran towards the ledge. He kicked off, leaping across the space between him and the monster, and caught himself by its whiskers. It screeched and grabbed at him with its snapping hands. Its snout swung side to side, rocking him like a pendulum.

He planted a foot on its face and pushed off, then leveraged his weight to swing around to the back of the creature's neck. It smacked its neck against the ceiling. Bakr tried to move in time, but his left arm was caught between the stone and the hard scales. It bruised and smarted. He growled in pain and drew back, cradling it to his chest. Was it broken?

Tears blurred his vision. By feeling alone, he skidded on his feet down the back of the monster until he was bracing himself against one of the long, sword-like spines on its back. He dropped to his backside, and holding onto scales with his one hand, he kicked the first spine he came to. The surrounding scales cracked after the third kick. One more and the spine was loose. Bakr caught it in his good hand as it fell towards the water.

Heavy claws snapped his injured arm. Like skin pinched by hot tongs, a chunk of his flesh was ripped away. He screamed in pain, blood pouring.

The beast snapped its hand at him again. With his good arm, he snatched up the spine he'd broken off and drove it into the palm. It screamed and shook. Then it whipped back and threw him.

He landed in the water but managed to hold tight to his broken spine. He kicked for the surface. When he broke through, the beast came down at him from above. Injured, desperate. He caught a glimpse of its soft underbelly.

Bakr snapped up his sword-like spine as the beast fell on him. It pierced through the creature's skin like a hot knife through halva. The creature screeched, but the sound was different. Not fury or intimidation, just profound pain. It crackled and faded at the edges.

He yanked out the spine with both hands, hot orange blood that smelled like rancid fruit bubbling over him.

Bakr shoved the spike down the front of his jacket, a mild nipping acid on his skin. With all his strength, he swam for the platform and yanked himself up. When he found his feet, the beast was still flailing. A cascading whir of blue lightning filled its mouth, choking it. Bakr backed up to the far edge of the platform until his back touched iron. He threw the broken spine in the air and caught it, wielding it like a spear. Then he took a running start and flung it at the creature's exposed neck.

The spine hit true, and the beast screamed, a torrent of thick orange blood pouring forth, saturating the water below. It moaned and fell, the head coming down mere inches from him.

Bakr stood fixed, watching as it writhed and fell silent. He pressed his hand over the bleeding wound in his bicep and staggered closer. The lightning in the mouth and the thick yellow eyes had gone out too. He used his foot to dislodge his sword from the creature's mouth. He was panting, shivering.

Bakr shook out his bad arm. Not broken. He grinned and lifted the blade in both hands then hacked the head off. Orange stringy blood painted his chest and arms. When the deed was done, the dislodged body was pulled down by the weight. It disappeared under the water, leaving him alone with the head on the platform.

He wiped his blade on the creature's long snout, then threaded it back into his frog. He took off his jacket and looked at the wound in his upper arm. Blood oozed out slowly, his shirt sleeve dyed red. Still, it didn't look nearly as bad as it felt. He could still use it.

He stepped closer to the head, then leaned down and peered into its sticky yellow eye. "Does that mean I'm innocent? Do I get to sit in a cistern and judge strangers from now on?" He sniffed and glanced around the chamber. "I'm gonna redecorate."

He wiped his face with his jacket, then put it back on. Then after a few slow breaths, he went to the iron door and kicked it. "Hey, boys! You can come back now."

It was sometime before the door was opened, and tentatively at that. When the two yellow-bearded guards saw the monster's head lying cut from its body, they gasped and moved back.

"What have you done?" said the one.

Bakr coughed out an incredulous laugh. "What's it look like?"

"You killed Cetus," said the other.

The one shook his head. "You can't do that."

Bakr walked to the head and hefted the huge foul-smelling thing onto his shoulders by its slimy whiskers. Its nose dragged on the ground as he carted it up twisting rows of stairs. The guards followed him, but they didn't say anything more, not to him or each other.

He climbed what felt like forty flights of stairs, though it was probably only five or six, and finally came through a door into a marble hall filled with soft white and green torchlight, burning without smoke in decorative sconces. He glanced back and forth, trying to decide which way to go when he heard the clank of glasses, soft music, and the murmur of many voices from down the hall. The banquet. He'd almost forgotten.

He wiped his nose on his shoulder and loped in that direction. The head must have weighed a hundred pounds but carrying it up all those stairs on his back, it had felt much heavier.

Bakr kicked open the door and tramped inside. Every eye turned. Some fifty of Ahmar's courtiers in their perfect sparkly clothes, all seated at a long sparkly table. Qadira was at the head, dressed in a brand new gaudy and ridiculous outfit, with a brand new gaudy and ridiculous headdress. Sezan sat on her right, looking dignified and gorgeous. An Ahmaran man he did not recognize was sitting at her side and moved his arm in front of her protectively, glaring at Bakr as if he were a wild animal. The music ground to a stop, and the queen's mouth opened in a wide 'o' as he strode towards the table, his body dripping with black water, globs of orange blood, and his own red human flavor mixed with it all.

"You got rats," he announced with a fiery glare at Qadira. Grunting with effort, he slung the massive, decapitated, bloody head of the monster up onto the table in front of her, crushing all the food and scattering the plates. "I took care of it."

Courtiers scurried back from their destroyed plates. He flopped into an empty chair on Qadira's left, leaned far back, and kicked his slimy, disgusting boots up onto the glimmering table. He snatched up a goblet and took a long, satisfying drink of something dark and sweet, then belched loudly and smiled. "Now. About that vineyard."

CHAPTER SIXTEEN

Sezan

Bakr had finally done it.

After years of seeking his own death through ridiculous stunts and sheer brashness, fighting monsters instead of attending dinner, it was his putrid boots on the table that would finally do him in.

Qadira screamed, stumbling back so quickly, glitter still dotted the air where she had just stood. The courtiers filed to the edges of the room or left altogether, hands clasped to their mouths and their faces paling.

"Bakr!" Sezan gasped, looking between his dripping, torn clothes and the slimy, tentacled head that *thunked* onto the wood. One of its dead yellow eyes oozed from its sockets. A matching wound gushed from a tear on Bakr's upper arm, a sickly pus color from an already raging infection.

Ajmal immediately pulled her back and placed an arm in front of her, the other clutching his nose. Then his face changed from horror to mild fascination.

"Is that Cetus?"

"It *is* Cetus," Bakr said, turning his bright white smile on Ajmal. "Or so I've been told."

"You weren't supposed to kill him, you son of a pigdog!" Qadira shrieked.

Bakr's smile hardened into an animalistic snarl. "If you didn't want me to kill him, you shouldn't have introduced us. Because I have to tell you, he had a rough personality."

Hearing the monster's name sent realization tumbling through Sezan's mind. "You sent Bakr to be Tried by Truth?" Her mouth hung open, unsure whether to burst out laughing or grind her teeth in anger, his weeping wound in the corner of her vision. "A representative and citizen of Shihala without due process?" She pulled her eyes away from the horrid, suction-cup-covered beast and flicked her fiery gaze to Qadira. "That is a breach of international peace accords. Even if he did deserve it."

A pale flash of pink anxiety touched Qadira's eyes. She opened her mouth, but Bakr cut her off as he snapped his gaze onto Sezan, "Can't you back me up just one time?"

"What do you think I'm doing?" Sezan said sharply. "Thanks to you, you aren't my first priority here in Ahmar. Making sure Qadira follows the rules so we all don't go to war is. Be thankful for what you get."

"She wouldn't know how to follow a rule if you tied her to it," he grumbled.

"I have a right to know if there is a spy in my palace," Qadira snapped, finding some of her composure.

"And how do you expect to make peace with Shihala if you assume we are all spies?" Sezan leaned over the table toward Qadira, the disgusting smell of something akin to decaying fish mixed with drakonte urine wafting up between them from the head. "And if you thought we had sent a spy, it is horribly offensive you'd think we'd send someone as terrible as Bakr to do the job."

"He'd make a perfect spy," she seethed, "with his dead eyes."

Bakr growled. "You know what—"

Ajmal cleared his throat with something between a chuckle and groan. "I think things just got out of hand a little. Qadira has been trying to kill Cetus off for years now. Haven't you, cousin?"

Her eyes muddied with brown malice, but she nodded.

"So, thank you." He formally bowed to Bakr. "For taking care of our rat problem. We shall honor Sezan *and* you with our feast." He flicked his hand and two servants appeared. With barely concealed grimaces, they hefted the monster away, slipping on its blood.

"That's more like it." Bakr held out his empty goblet and snapped his fingers at one of the servants.

Sezan's lips were so tightly pressed together that she couldn't feel them anymore. Ajmal put his hand on her shoulder and guided her farther down the long table, then pulled out a chair. She smiled at him, grateful someone in the room wasn't a temperamental baby. He had handled the situation beautifully, even if she would go to her suite and write a novel to Jahmil about Qadira's blatant indiscretions. Ajmal sat on her right, and she made sure to turn entirely towards him and lean in so she wouldn't have to see even the blurry image of Bakr in her periphery. His gaping wound nagged at her. It didn't matter what she sacrificed; she'd always be stuck trying to save his life while he risked it with cavalier disregard.

She focused on the steady, reliable man sitting in front of her. "Thank you, Ajmal," she said, touching his arm.

He smiled gently, his light blue eyes cooling her temper. "Anything to make your life easier." He slipped his gaze past her for a moment, then refocused. "Though I believe you'll be the one answering questions for me on our date to the library."

She stopped after that, drowned out as Qadira and Bakr exchanged clipped, angry words at the end of the table behind her, punctuated by a copious amount of cursing on his part and a lot of name-calling on hers.

After a few moments of trying to ignore their petty ruckus, Sezan sighed. "They're not going to stop as long as they remain in the same room together." She leaned back and relished the simplicity of sitting in a chair while having a normal conversation before giving a resigned shake of her head and standing back up.

"Bakr," she snipped, not needing to yell. He knew better than to make her say his name twice. "Come." She pointed to the door and stormed past him.

He finished his wine, bared his teeth at Qadira one last time, and smashed the crystal goblet on the tile. Then he dutifully turned and followed her.

The moment they were out of the room, she whipped around, grabbed the collar of his shirt, and dragged him all the way to her room. There, she shut the door discretely and rammed a finger into his chest.

"Explain!"

"What's to explain? Qadira tried to have me fed to that thing. I'm alright, by the way. Thanks for asking." He shook out his arm, the jagged wound still oozing blood. Then he shrugged off his torn, mucus-covered jacket, which hit the floor with a *glop*.

She forced her fingers loose, a weakness wheedling through her at the sight. A desire bloomed to tend to him, to protect him from a danger he probably deserved and which he had already faced. Like a little girl wanting to bring home a flea-infested namur.

"Yes, the entire palace heard that part. My question is, why?" She went to Lila's sewing basket to look for fabric scraps. "There's a hot bath ready that Lila had prepared for me after dinner. I suggest you make use of it."

Bakr moaned as he pulled off his shirt, dropping it on the floor beside his jacket. The tattoo of the Rukh bird that wrapped around his chest shivered as he breathed, his muscles as taut and sinewy as ever. Though it was the blood dripping down his arm that held her attention. "Because she's an evil madwoman," he called over his shoulder, walking into the bathroom. "I thought that was well established."

"Exactly." She pulled out a few long pieces of muslin and snapped them taut twice. "Everyone in all of Qaf knows she's a madwoman. So why on earth do you insist on testing her temper? Has your death wish finally reached its pinnacle?"

"Apparently not." The sound of a buckle hit the tile along with a squishy glop as he dropped his pants. She could see his outline moving in the bathroom, naked skin the color of dark caramel. Then came the slosh of water as he got into her tub. "I'll have to try harder next time."

"You're an ungrateful son of a snake."

She stifled a growl, then marched after him into the washroom. He was sitting in the tub, dirtying the rose-scented bathwater. White bubbles concealed everything but his shoulders and arms. He rubbed some water over the wound, but it was still weeping blood and pus.

He sucked a pained breath through his teeth, then closed his eyes and leaned back on the porcelain headrest.

"You need to flush that cut before I wrap it up," Sezan said with a shake of her head.

He kept his gaze on the floor and answered in a slow, careful voice. "Would you mind? I feel a little shaky."

Sezan folded her arms and glared at him. Then relented with a huff. She disappeared into her washroom and came back with a bowl of hot water mixed with Lila's herbs. Her lip threatened to curl at the putrid smell of his gash, but she forced it smooth. There was no point in complaining. He was going to do whatever he wanted either way. And as much as she scolded herself for it, she would always be there to clean him up afterward. She slipped the bowl onto the stand by the bath and dipped one of the muslin pieces into the fragrant tincture. The thin cloth soaked up the healing waters until the cream-colored threads turned the soft green of sage and sorrel, of taluli blossoms and the pungent puti root.

Then she knelt down next to the tub. "Don't yell at me when this hurts."

He lifted his pale green eyes to hers and showed a soft, close-lipped smile. "Thanks."

She set to work cleansing the wound from the outside in. Occasionally, the water would hiss and pop with the smell of rot wherever it touched saliva or blood or whatever else the creature had spewed over him. But her efforts proved fruitful. Already, the redness began to ease.

"You were right," he said, looking down. "About me and Qadira. I was trying to wear her out so she wouldn't crash Jahmil's wedding. It was really, really stupid."

She pursed her lips and continued to dab, not wanting to hear about him doing anything with any woman, much less the vindictive and petty Queen of Ahmar.. "Why not just find a normal, stable girl to sleep with for once? Or keep it in your pants? But no one wants to hear what I have to say on that issue."

He sighed. "Normal, stable girls don't go for me."

"I'm not fooled by you," she said, dipping the cloth in and swirling the red of his blood into the water, green turning brown. "You're charming enough you could have anyone, even if for one night. You just like trouble."

He rubbed his forehead with his free hand. "Look, I think it's pretty clear my being here is going to hurt your chances of brokering a deal with the so-called queen. I don't want to mess this up for you."

"I have a strong suspicion you could be anywhere in the kingdom and still mess it up for me, seeing as you can't change the past."

Bakr's face pinched, and he sucked his cheek between his teeth.

She wiped off the rest of the wound and wrapped a clean, dry piece over his bicep, tight enough to stop the bleeding but not cut off the flow. "And either way, it doesn't matter. I need you here." Which was true. She needed to keep him in Ahmar until she could work up the courage to ask about Fajar, his precious Rukh, and prepare everything for a journey to Ard. It would take time and delicacy. Neither of which Bakr could appreciate.

"No, you don't." Bakr pulled his arm back and pushed himself up from the water. She stood and turned her back, then snatched a towel from the cabinet and held it out to him without looking back. He took it, his finger lightly brushing hers. "I brought along a horde of loyal soldiers to protect you. Besides, it seems prince whatever has already fallen under your spell. And I've got one or two tiny things I need to attend to."

Sezan turned and eyed his face carefully. His cavalier sense of pity was normal, but something else hid in his constant eyes. Whatever it was, she couldn't allow it to stop her plan.

"You make it sound like I bewitched the prince when really it is I who finds him quite charming."

"So do I."

She let out a tiny, exasperated giggle. "Shall I step out of the way so you can have a chance?"

"If I wanted him, he'd be mine." He wiggled his eyebrows, then stepped out of the tub and grabbed another expensive cotton foutas to dry his hair. "He reminds me of Jahmil a bit. Just without the temper and all that delightful self-loathing." He chuckled, but it sounded sad. "I think you can trust him."

"I'm certain I can," she said, pressing her lips together. She felt strange, discussing another man with Bakr without him flying into a fit. It should have felt good. Like they had reached something—a mutual understanding they never had before. Instead, it felt like a hollowed-out pit. One of many confirmations that she meant very little to him. "But I still need you here. It is non-negotiable."

"Why? And don't say it's just to torture me."

She chuckled. "I would never dream of bringing you discomfort." She poked his wound. "But no, that's not why."

He winced and snarled at her playfully. "Is it me, or are you refusing to tell me?"

Sezan looked away from him, the smile falling from her lips. She was crazy for even considering trying to convince Bakr to take her to his Fajar and fly her to the floating city in Ard. She was also determined to do just that. But Bakr would be gone by morning if she didn't do something that would hold his interest.

She took a deep breath and met his eyes. "If I tell you, do you promise to do what I ask? Even if it sounds crazy?"

He moaned, deep and gravelly in his throat. "Yes?"

"I need to hear a *yes*," she said, dropping the word down at the end.

He turned from her and walked back into the bedroom. A small parcel of clothing had been left at the door, folded crisp by Lila's practiced hand. She always understood the nuance of anything involving Bakr. It was the only reason she had allowed him in her rooms at all, much less let him get naked. Lila would be discreet. Lila would keep it quiet. And Sezan would repay her for it all someday.

Bakr opened the parcel and pulled on the pants, which fit his waist perfectly. He walked to her bed and took a seat, tossing the shirt between his hands. Then, he rubbed the towel over his hair, sighed deeply, and slouched. All so painstakingly slowly. Was he honestly mulling over whether he was willing to help her or just trying to torture her? She tried and failed not to watch the muscles in his back roll under his skin, now shiny, clean, and smelling of roses.

"If you really need something from me, Zan, you got it," he said at last. "You know that."

Sezan twitched her lips side to side, then flicked her gaze to his. She stepped closer. Then a little more so their knees touched. With a hand on his shoulder, she leaned down so their lips almost touched and slid her hand behind his neck, her fingers twining themselves into the hair at his nape.

She smiled as his breath picked up. "Remember when we snuck into the royal suites and hid from the guards in the king's personal baths?"

He grinned and bit his bottom lip.

"And remember how after all the bubbles had long melted into rose-scented waters and all that was left was you and me and our glistening reflections on the crystal ceiling, I told you it was the most wondrous place I'd ever been?"

He nodded slowly. "I promised to take you to the hot springs at Pamukkale someday."

She nodded, looking up through heavy lashes and running her tongue over her top lip. "I want to go."

He chuckled. "To Pamukkale?"

She nodded, praying their shared heat and tender memories would be enough to stay his questions.

"I'm confused. Why do I need to stay in Ahmar to take you to Pamukkale?" He flickered his gaze towards her bathroom door. "There's a hot bath right there."

She kept her eyes honey, focusing on the scar on his cheek to keep the colors from flashing and giving her away. "I was hoping for a few days to... prepare myself." She tugged his hair softly and sighed resignedly. "But you're right. And don't expect me to admit that again. Why have you wait around for a fling in the hot springs? You may leave Ahmar. I've just been dreaming of seeing Ard's sun and feeling its warmth..." She flashed her eyes to his. "Or someone else's on my bare skin. But I suppose I could have Ajmal take me. He seems rather keen to be by my side."

He grabbed her and threw her onto the bed, then jumped on top of her. Her yelp of surprise melted into giggles, despite herself. He kissed her hard, his hands moving along her waist.

"It's heat you want, is it?" he said and pulled at the strings holding together the front of her dress. She grabbed his hand to slow his advance, and he kissed her neck. The brush of his scruffy chin sent tingles across her chest, while his growls set her senses ablaze.

"Bakr," she tried to admonish him, but the words were caught up in breathy laughter. He laid kisses all along her bare clavicles, then down along her stomach in the gap that showed her belly button between her top and pants. He looped a finger under the hem and tugged.

Her breath caught. He had ventured too far. A hint of her rosy fire tingled across her skin, reflecting softly in Bakr's eager eyes and reminding her why she had started this flirtation to begin with. What was she doing?

"Bakr, wait," she said.

He looked up at her and wiggled his eyebrows, his brilliant smile as genuine and hopeful as any she had ever seen. "Bath?"

She laughed, each brush of his hand on her skin a wave of pleasure. "No, not here. I want to be with you on Ard."

He gripped her thighs, kissing and nibbling through the fabric. "Take us, then. You don't even have to get dressed. Humans can't see you on Ard. They'll just think I'm insane, and I don't care."

He quickly crawled up her body to kiss her lips, slow and passionate, drinking her in as he had the other night on the balcony. The kiss that made her forget everything. Like the worth of her soul, untainted, in Allah's eyes the first time she gave into him and every time after. And like how her goal was to get him to stay longer in Ahmar, not fall prey to his wiles and ruin it all.

Pressing his forehead against hers, he said, "If I think about the place, could you find it?"

"Of course," she said, breathing in his spicy scent and trying to keep her head. "But I can't go to Ard like this. Half-undressed and completely distracted." She brushed a thumb over his bottom lip, trying to suppress her fire's glow on her skin. It only ever emboldened him. "It's dangerous for djinn."

"I would never let anything happen to you. Besides, I was just kidding. There won't be anyone there. It's completely isolated." He kissed her thumb and sucked on it gently. "It's so beautiful there, Zan. The water is the same color as your skin." He ran his hands through her hair and kissed her neck. "And to watch your hair sparkle in the sunshine..."

Sezan bit her lip and turned her eyes so the colors would not betray her like the rest of her body. She truly longed to go with him to the hot springs, to run away as she had always wanted when she was young and foolish. But her magic would still vanish if she didn't find Sulayman's Seal, and she needed a few days to prepare for the trek to the Rukh and Ard. Besides, she reminded herself forcefully, there was no way Bakr would stay once they came back. He always left when the adventure was over and things got serious or real.

"Stop thinking so much," he said. "Let's just go. I promise we'll come back. And I'll stay."

His last word caught her off-guard, as if he had read her mind, and she knew her eyes were flashing hints of foolish, hopeful blue. "For how long?"

"Until you're sick of me."

"Bakr..." She stifled a soft groan. Why was the eager look on his face always so convincing? "You don't mean that..."

"Stop it," he whined. "You're murdering me."

"I rather thought I was doing the opposite."

"Please, don't make me talk anymore. I always ruin it when you make me talk. Let's just go. Now. Don't think. Just let me keep my promise."

She bit her cheek, every one of his desperate, pleading words stretching her chest farther and farther apart so the ache was cavernous. She grabbed his cheeks and pulled him up to face her, nose to nose. Then she closed her eyes, and they vanished into Ard.

CHAPTER SEVENTEEN

Bakr

Their clothes lay scattered in crumpled piles. The hot springs spread down one side of the hill like interlocking bowls. Salt deposits clung to the sides like stalactites, giving them the appearance of frost, but the air was hot and humid. When they arrived, he'd stripped off his pants, grabbed Sezan by the waist, and yanked her into a pool. She laughed like he hadn't heard in years, free and easy as the sun itself. Her wet hair immediately curled, like it always did, free of the torture and tonics she used to keep it straight. As he kissed her, it clung to him, streaks of pure light, glimmering in the sunshine like it never could in the twilight world of Qaf.

The turquoise water welcomed her as if she were returning home, sparkling against her impossible skin. Everything about her was soft. Her palms of satin running over his chest and back. The sweep of her curves, untainted. Her lips anxious, yielding. And her eyes, the fiery glow that filled him with a need for sunlight when he was in Qaf, were tempered by the light of earth, a sweet honey and amber that he wanted to dive into and swim in forever.

The first time was frantic, their hands grasping for each other like they were both scrambling to keep from falling off cliffs. His vision was blurry, and he could barely breathe. There was nothing but her skin, her hair, her mouth. His own rushing blood, fire and ice in his veins. A tightening in his stomach. His heart-pounding. Sky-flowers and thunder. It ended quickly.

The second time was achingly slow, kissing her and watching the freckles in her eyes until he couldn't bear it anymore. He pressed his face into her hair and breathed her in.

The water washed away her floral perfume leaving nothing but the scent of her, sweet and fruity. Everything he had wanted to do and say. He allowed himself to imagine everything he had wanted to be for her since he lost her, and even before then. Emboldened by the sun, which he had missed these last years, almost as much as he had her, he let the roiling pain in his guts leak to the surface like sweat through his pores. The gaping ache he'd been nursing for so long—her body fit into it like the missing shard of broken glass when she was so close, so trusting. Rising to his every caress and silently begging for more. He drank her in with his fingertips and when it was over, he held her tight to his chest and trembled.

When they had first arrived, the glorious sun had been high in the sky. Now it was sinking into the west, casting ribbons of color over the horizon and painting the pools in shades of red and yellow. He watched it as he leaned on the edge of the pool and stroked her hair, her legs tangled with his, her skin pressed so close. The light hurt his eyes just enough to let him know he was alive.

But in all the glory of light and softness and beauty, a feeling of dread was creeping into Bakr's bones. She would expect him to say something soon, and he didn't want to. He wanted to pretend that the only things that existed were him and her, water, and a sunset. Words were an affliction.

But the blissful silence could never last. Eventually, Sezan sighed and tilted her face up to him, chin on his chest. "See what you've been missing?"

He laughed and squeezed her shoulders. "How could I ever forget?"

"Yet you stayed away so long."

"Didn't we already talk about this?" he said, a sting in his chest like a tiny sharp knife being pushed in slowly. Why couldn't they have one moment without dragging up the past?

She frowned, her eyes creased with hurt. "Sorry," she said, then put her head back down, staring into the water instead of him.

A dozen words spoken, and he'd already ruined the moment. What in hellfire was the matter with him? He chewed freely on his cheek, comforted that she couldn't see.

Say something, he chided himself. Tell her you're sorry. Tell her how much you've missed her. Tell her why you left. Tell her...

"It's beautiful here, isn't it?" he said.

"I don't think I've ever felt so warm or bright in my life."

He rubbed her shoulder and squeezed her closer. "Me neither."

She pushed a hand against his chest and pulled away, her hair streaming in rivulets down her skin. "What time is it? Back in Ahmar?"

"I don't know." He squinted at the sky. "We've probably been here about forty-five degrees."

She touched a finger to her lip, looking to the sky and deep in thought. "Then I have ten or so yet before we must get back."

His gut clenched, and his eyes tightened. He leaned his head back on the lip of the pool, the stretch in his throat lending a casual tone to his voice. "Big plans?"

She eyed him from the side, then flicked her gaze away as a blush colored her cheek. "I'm going to visit the library."

"What is my little bookworm studying these days?"

"What else besides seals and contracts?"

He groaned and stretched his shoulders. The wound in his arm ached like he'd been punched hard, but the flesh had already sealed over. "That sounds like a date worth missing."

She glared at him even as the purple on her cheeks deepened. "At least he takes me on dates."

"What do you call this?" Bakr skimmed the water with an even palm to splash the horizon. Of all the cheap, dirty things to say, why was she bringing up the princeling? As if she was going to go meet him in the library in ten degrees. It would take her half a night and six jars of oil just to fix what he had just done to her hair.

"As I remember it, I took *you* here. Not the other way around."

"You want to throw in my face that I'm apparationally inept?" he scoffed. "Racist."

She slapped the water so it splashed in his face. "I have never for a day in our knowing each other treated you differently because of your mother or your father. You could take me anywhere in Qaf, and you still don't." Then a glimmer caught in her eye as she settled back into the water. "There is a place I've been wanting to go, though, if you'd like to make it up to me."

Bakr actively suppressed a sneer as he wiped his face with his hand and blinked stinging saltwater from his eyes. "Where's that?"

She looked to the sky then down to him. "Have you ever heard of Eayima?"

He narrowed his eyes suspiciously and bit back the first sentence that came to mind. Why would Sezan be bringing up Eayima, the very place Rahik's infernal mission was sending him to? Had she been spying on him? She had told the disgusting hagfish that he was harassing her, asked Rahik to *cut him down*. She wouldn't be in bed with that creature, would she?

He scoffed at himself and shook his head. It was ridiculous, but the thought stuck into him like a burr. "What is it?"

"A floating city," she said evasively. "Here on Ard. I only thought you may have heard of it because of the time you nearly burned all your flesh being a dolt."

He tipped his chin back and grinned. "You're going to have to be more specific."

She smiled, cool and easy as the breeze once again. "Tell me again about your special friend."

"Fajar?" He smiled at the bittersweet memory, even as Sezan's sudden interest put him on edge. "She's more like a child than a friend."

"Are you actually able to ride her? Or were you just blowing hot air the entire year you were twenty?"

"Sometimes I was asleep." He closed his eyes and leaned his head back on the rim of the pool. "I rode her all the time. I wish you could meet her. She was my first love."

Sezan traced imaginary shapes in the water so the ripples expanded and lapped against his chest. "Why can't I meet her? Would she not like me?" She raised her wide, amber eyes to his. "Or is this a jealousy thing? Because I think it'd be a grand time, we three, riding off to an adventure on a floating island. No one and nothing to answer to."

"I told you. I had to let her go. As far as I know, she's somewhere in the mountains of Zabriya, hiding from all djinn if she remembers anything I taught her."

"So, you give up on and abandon everyone you love?" Her face soured. "Or am I too presumptuous to assume I'm on the list of those you truly care for?"

Bakr's stomach clenched. Why was she so interested? She never wanted to hear about his bird. Not really. Whenever he talked about Fajar, Sezan got jealous like he was discussing an ex-lover, which was ridiculous. He remembered so many times stealing into her room in the harem, and she would lie on his chest, tracing his tattoo, and half-jokingly pout that he had Fajar imprinted on his skin, but not her. And that it must've meant he loved the bird more. Bakr always fanned those flames because he loved the way Sezan twitched and pursed her lips when she was feeling possessive.

He pressed his palm over his forehead to smooth out the furrows. This was nothing like that.

"I didn't abandon her," he said, hurt by the implication. "She wasn't safe with me. There are too many people who want her, who would do horrible things to her if they found her. Try to make her a slave, or worse. It broke my heart to let her go."

"That you lump me in with monsters like that is all I need to know." She tilted her head, a scowl on her face as she analyzed every movement and twitch he made. "And thank you for so clearly elucidating my future. Because no one's safe with you, right? Everyone's better off without you around? Wonderful." She covered her breasts and swept out of the water, sunlight reflecting off her sparkling hair and wet skin. She marched over to her clothes, donning first her hijab to cover her hair, then working to pull on her pants as the superfluous fabric stuck to all the wet patches.

"Last time I checked, you weren't a giant immortal bird." He turned in the pool and folded his arms on the rock ledge, watching as she struggled into her dress. "I did the right thing."

She paused with her fiddling and looked at him, her eyes softening for the briefest moment before burning once again. "Congratulations on a first."

His instinct was to argue, but he was feeling so raw. Hurt that she would bring up the princeling after what they had just shared. Hurt that she would imply that he had somehow done an injustice to Fajar by setting her free. Hurt that she only ever saw the worst in him. Just hurt and aching and wanting nothing more than for her to hold him. He wanted to fold into her, bury his face in her bosom, and cry and confess everything he had been through in the last two years since Rahik and his poison drove him from her side. But not unlike his mother—the only other woman Bakr had ever loved—Sezan had no patience for his pain. She refused to even acknowledge it.

"Letting go of Fajar was probably the only time in my life I ever did anything that wasn't selfish."

"Good thing you spent it on a bird." She finally managed to pull her dress up and over her shoulders, though her hands shook as she tried to do up her laces. They were ripped, anyway.

"Fajar is not just a bird. She's like... she's..." He sighed and looked away.

Maybe he should ask Sezan to come with him, to introduce her to Fajar so she could finally understand and let go of her jealousy. He opened his mouth to say so, but Rahik's burbling, ugly voice was in the back of his brain. Sezan didn't know what her monstrous uncle had done, what he had put her through and subsequently forced out of Bakr. What sort of lies might Rahik have told her? He knew how much Bakr cared for her; that was the reason he was in this mess. If Rahik was going to use anyone to try to get at Fajar, it would have to be Sezan. But Bakr couldn't risk Fajar any more than he could risk endangering the mission that would finally give Sezan her life back.

He'd been sucking on his cheek for a few seconds before he realized he was doing it and let go. Little prickles tightened the back of his neck. "Never mind about Fajar. She's gone. What were you saying about this place you wanted me to take you? What was it called? Yuma?"

"Eayima," she said with a sigh. "And what do you mean never mind about Fajar? You love that bird more than the flesh on your back."

"Yeah. I like a lot of things better than the flesh on my back." He rubbed his tongue over his teeth. "And since when do you want to talk about her? You never want to hear about my bird."

"I never want to hear about her because usually, you won't stop talking about her. Now the one time I ask, and you have closed lips? I know you feel the need to be difficult about everything, but I was certain Fajar was the one constant in your life. Allah certainly knows I'm not."

"I haven't seen her in years. You call that constant?" He scoffed, but there was a painful boil in his guts, throbbing and twitching like it was about to burst and coat his insides in sickly smelling slime. "You just want to be mad at me so you don't have to feel guilty about your little princeling."

Sezan snapped her chin up. She was fully dressed again, which only emphasized the difference between them. "And why should I feel guilty about him or anything else? You chose your namur, now ride it. The only mistake I made was wanting to visit a lovely place with a less than lovely person."

Another jab. He should have been used to them by now. Numb to her incessant, cruel prodding that tore at his ego as much as it did his soul. As sweet as her words could be one moment, she could be just as cruel the next. Why could she never just be nice to him? Not intense and passionate or cold and biting. Just nice.

"I hope you enjoy your noble, civilized library date not two degrees after hooking up with the likes of me. Almost makes me feel sorry for the sack of silver."

The gold in her eyes dimmed so much, they looked nearly human. She bit the corner of her lip as her face crumpled and she turned away. "I just wanted to go Eayima with you. I thought... after all this time you'd finally want to run away with me. To have an adventure. To finally share the part of you that you always keep hidden. But I keep asking and you keep saying no." Her shoulders slumped, the angle foreign to her frame. "Why I am so stupid?"

"You're the one that just jumped out of the spring and said you had to get back to Ahmar. I will never be able to follow the script you've worked out in your head for me. You never actually listen to anything I say, you just judge whether or not it was what you were expecting. If you want slow and steady, boring and predictable, go have that." His voice tried to choke, to save him from his own brain. He powered through. "You'd rather just be angry with me because you're jealous of a bird."

"No Bakr." She raised her eyes slowly to his and squeezed water from her hair from under her hijab. "Because I'm tired of watching you run away without me."

He held her gaze, and it took everything in him not to tell her. He couldn't tell her.

"I'm right here," he said at last, looking down at his naked body in the warm saltwater. "I haven't moved."

She watched him for a moment before crouching down at the edge of the pool and reaching out her hand. "Then come with me to Eayima. You, me, and Fajar."

"I told you, Fajar is gone." Bakr rolled to his knees and pushed himself up. He took her hand and pulled her nearer, his eyes scanning hers for every stray flicker of color. "Why can't we just stay here? After all this time, why can't we just be in one place for a while?"

"Stay in one place?" she scoffed softly. "You? There's a higher chance of a uptka fish taking flight and wedding a drakonte. Yet I offer you an adventure in Ard, your home, and you refuse. Why?"

He knew she would never actually run away with him. Leave her palace and servants and all her beautiful expensive things behind to live the way he lived. She would never give anything up for him. It was just a fantasy to her. *He* was just a fantasy to her, and one that the flesh-and-blood Bakr could never, ever live up to.

He let go of her and sank back into the pool. This time she was the one leaving, and still, she managed to make it all his fault. Maybe it was better that way. In fact, it definitely was. How long might it be before he saw her again? Would he ever see her again?

"You look beautiful," he sighed sadly.

"If only you enjoyed me for my company." Sezan grabbed her slippers and shoved them on her feet. She fussed some more with her ties then let them go in a flurry of frustration. She pulled a string loose and throwing it to the ground. Then another and another until three lay at her feet.

"I like the way your hair curls when it's wet. And the natural color of your lips. I wish you could just be yourself more often. All that crap you put on, it's… I don't know. It's a shame."

She placed a hand over her heart. "Now I know what it's like to not live up to someone else's expectations. Thank you for the meaningful life lesson that I somehow missed every single day of my childhood under my mother's glare. And what I look like isn't who I am, Bakr. Not that you would know that." She flipped her hair over her shoulders, then bent over and grabbed his clothes carefully out from under his sword so that the metal did not touch her.

"I know who you are," he said, a little bite at the edge of his voice that he didn't intend. But there it was because she was leaving. And all the things he might say to stop her simply wouldn't form on his tongue. He tried to push through. "You're smart, and dedicated, and a lot more sensitive than you like to let on. I also know you feel suffocated."

"By you? Always."

"Not me."

Sezan glanced between the clothes in her hands and him. "I'll send your servant to come get you. Just don't—don't…." She bit her lip with a pained look, then vanished with his clothes.

Bakr straightened his back and scanned the earth where she had been. On the ground lay a barely formed triangle formed from the strings of her top. The simple shape was the gate for all djinn to return to Qaf from Ard and took nothing more than their fire and a bit of stamina. Even when she ran she planned ahead. And even if he had planned, he could never do what they did, the magicless lump of flesh that he was.

He closed his eyes and pressed a hand over them. It was exactly what he had expected she would do, so why was he at all disappointed that she had done it? Little tingles of regret rippled through him, forced back only by his suspicion. What he had said shouldn't have elicited such a reaction, not unless he was right in thinking she had ulterior motives for inquiring about Fajar. Perhaps Rahik was just manipulating her, and she didn't understand the implications of what she was saying, but the outcome was the same.

He turned in the pool and looked at the sunset again, the stars glimmering on the horizon. Qaf rising again to eclipse the beauty of the sun that he longed for with all his heart.

He could have said anything and she would have stormed off. He could have leaped on a pedestal and declared his undying love for all the empire to hear, and she would have stormed off. She liked to say she wanted to be with him. That she would change her life and make love to him as seven moons sailed the heavens. Leave the world behind. Leave behind her magical, luxurious existence to be with him. But it wasn't true. She didn't trust him, would never trust him. And that wasn't her fault. All her sweet words and kind nothings were just echoes of an old fantasy, of a time before she knew better.

She thought he only cared about the way she looked, that he didn't know anything about her. That stung more than anything. Not because she thought he was shallow; he was. But she should have known better. He'd tried to tell her so many times.

He hadn't broken his promise. He'd said he would stay until she got sick of him. In her romantic fantasy, maybe she hoped that meant he would stay forever. He was far more realistic. That it had taken a full six hours was practically a record.

She hadn't needed to take his clothes, though. That was petty.

Whatever. He wasn't going to wait around for her to send a full-blooded djinn to fetch him like a dog. Like a child. Like an inferior. He had told her he had a few things to take care of, and he had already wasted enough time. She loved him, she hated him, she would give her life for him, she wished he were dead. She was willingly or unwittingly working for Rahik. It didn't matter. He still had to save her life, even though she didn't realize it was in danger. Even though it would mean nothing to her. Even though she wouldn't believe him if he told her the truth. Or would she believe and still find a way to make him feel like a fool?

And now she was rushing off for a date with a prince. The sort of man she had always wanted. The sort of man she deserved. A man who dressed in embroidered silk, maintained an immaculate shave, and wore cream in his hair. A man who could meet her in a library and actually have anything to say about what he found there. Bakr had meant it when he said he thought Ajmal was charming. Anybody who can deal with Qadira on a regular basis and not become a cackling toddler afraid of his own shadow had a level of integrity, nobility, and serenity that Bakr could only dream of.

Sezan deserved someone like Ajmal. A handsome, serene, and learned prince. Deep down in her heart of hearts, that was what she had always wanted. Bakr had only ever been a distraction. A bad idea. He'd come to terms with it.

So, why was his face pinching harder and harder the more he thought about it? Why did he have a stomachache?

He hopped out of the pool as the final light of the sun purpled and faded into nothing. No, he would not be going back to Ahmar. Perhaps ever. He may be a half-breed with virtually no powers save a little extra strength, a little extra agility, and a little extra ability to heal from a nasty hit, but that didn't mean he was helpless. People had been making that assumption about him his entire life, human and djinn alike. And Sezan was just as wrong as the rest of them.

He scoffed thinking about it. She didn't know him at all.

He let the anger bubble until it burst on the surface and then it was gone. It didn't really matter because he didn't care what happened to him. He just needed to get to Zabriya as quickly as possible, to find Fajar and be done with it. He didn't have time to charter a boat or any of that nonsense, never mind he happened to be on the wrong world. There was one person who could take him exactly where he needed to be.

The thought of calling her and asking for her help twisted painfully through his skull, leaking like acid down his throat into his stomach. But what difference did it make now? Had it ever made? He was living in a fantasy too, pretending, if only briefly, that he could be somebody else. Somebody who was normal and happy, who could love a woman and have her love him back. But that wasn't in the cards. He was a demon's slave with no way out. The least he could do was try to wrangle the occasional perk out of it.

He picked up his sword and pressed the tip into the ground. Leaning his weight on the pommel, he took a few steadying breaths.

"Shaytana," he whispered.

Instantly, a mist of gray twirled to life before him like a dirt devil. He watched her figure quickly coalesce as if from starlight. Her shoulders were slumped to one side, her skin like the very kiss of a shadow. She stood on the water, long elegant legs accentuated by a dress of furs that covered nothing.

When she opened her shining, yellow eyes and saw him standing there dressed only in air, her sharp sultry lips curved into a smile. "Why hello, lover. What a pleasant surprise."

CHAPTER EIGHTEEN

SEZAN

"DON'T LEAVE," WAS WHAT Sezan had wanted to say as she left Bakr in the springs, what her heart pleaded with her to utter while her lips refused.

She returned to her rooms, threw herself on her bed, and let herself cry pathetic little tears until there was nothing left, and the corners of her eyes stung in the light overhead. Then she wiped the dribble of snot from her nose and the stain of salt from her cheeks and called in Lila. She didn't let her say a single word before commanding her to send one of Bakr's men to fetch him from the springs at Pamukkale, outside İzmir. She had taken his clothes, hoping that would keep him there instead of wandering off to never be seen again, but she knew there was a better chance of seeing a Jasraib mer-djinn in the deserts of Ghaluma.

Lila's eyes widened at the mention of the Ardish city, but she did what she was told, thank Allah. Then Sezan went into her washroom and scrubbed furiously at her skin, trying to erase the scent of Agarwood and sweat from her body. Sin and sulfur. Her faith in the goodness of Shihala was fading. Or maybe it was her faith that she deserved anything at all from Shihala after everything she had done. She had so badly wanted to stay with Bakr that leaving him there felt like a ghoul had ripped out her heart and chewed on it before squishing it back in her chest in mangled pieces. That would have been better than reality.

She must have sounded so petty to him. So spiteful and childish. But being cruel was all she could do to get away. And she had to get away even if he was not willing to be the one to take her. His access to the Rukh bird and his knowledge of Ard had been her only hope of salvation. And he hadn't even trusted her enough to share it with her. She asked him to take her to the floating city, and all he could do was croon about his first love. A bird. Who he valued more than her and who was the only being he'd ever have on his stupid list. Maybe Jahmil. And that made her all the more upset.

She had offered for the second time in a week to run away with him on an adventure, and he had said no twice. Even the offer of a floating, magical city and being with his Rukh had not been enough. And while she needed to get to Eayima to save herself, the more she talked about leaving, the more she realized she *did* want to go live a new life with him and leave everything behind. But he did not want that with her. And he had made it abundantly clear he would not share the tenderest piece of his heart with her, either.

Now, she had nothing. Why had she let him convince her to go there in the first place? Why was she so weak when he was near? So desperate for his touch? Did she have to be in mortal danger for him to actually show up?

Because even when he had promised to stay with her, she had known that was a lie, too. It always was a lie, even though she desperately, foolishly, idiotically hoped otherwise. So what was a little push to send him on his way? He'd simply think the worst of her, tell himself he was doing everyone a favor by leaving and that she didn't want him around in the first place, and then disappear. Especially with how disdainfully he had talked about his inability to apparate. If he hated that about himself, his quasi-lack of magic, then he would hate it even more when she had none. Just like everyone else. If he didn't even want her at her full potential, why would he want something less?

A knock sounded on the door.

Bakr? Her heart skipped a beat, both angry and desperately hopeful. Had he returned and come to yell at her already? To storm in and grab his clothes and her along with them? And why did she care? But oh, how she did.

Sezan hurriedly scooped any sign of unkempt hair into her hijab. She looked a mess, but as a diplomat, she was consigned to take a meeting whenever called. And if it was Bakr, he'd prefer it that way. Allah, why did she hope it was Bakr even after what they had just gone through?

She took a rushed breath and opened the door. The fidgety messenger before her had neither shiny smile nor jade-green eyes, but the second she saw the letter in his hands, she knew exactly what it was. The narrow script told her as readily as the thick blue seal. Her *elder brother* and amir checking in on her, no doubt.

Swallowing a groan, she took the parchment with a bow and shut the door. Using a pearl letter opener, she cut the thick, blue seal of Shihala and tossed the smooth knife onto her desk.

Honorable Ambassador Sezan bint Malik Bajul,

Tahanina. News has reached Shihala of your party's successful admittance to the court of Ahmar without incident. This, however, is little measure of success, merely an opportunity that must not be wasted. It has come to my attention that the queen has mustered troops on the border of Shihala, ten thousand strong at least. And while their blades do not yet point fixedly, it would take but a word from the queen to change their orientation.

This cannot be allowed to happen. War must be avoided at all costs. Consider this missive an official endorsement of your power to concede whatever you believe is necessary to Ahmar in the interest of peace, including monies, lands, and marriage contracts. On the recommendation of both General Bakr and Ayelet Amira, I am placing tremendous trust in your abilities.

Do not give me reason to regret this leap of faith. And please understand that if you fail to broker a successful treaty, your career as a diplomat for Shihala will end as quickly as it began.

I expect detailed daily updates on your progress.

With respect and amity, etc.

And at the bottom instead of a signature, Jahmil Amir's official seal.

She tossed the epistle on her dresser and rubbed a hand over her bare face. Like she had anything to say to him on either front. *Stop a war, Sezan. Quell the beast of my own making. Just do the job, Sezan, or you will end as quickly as you began.*

She slid her hands off her face and looked in the mirror. Her hair was still frizzy and curly underneath her hijab, and her lips were a pale pink instead of their usual bright red. A mess. Bakr only liked her looking that way because it meant he had gotten his way through persistent wheedling. What did he know of her anyway? Cruelly joking about her worth after *hooking up* with him when he knew very well he was the only one for whom she had ever sacrificed her virtue. That their intimacy was both sacred to her and a source of pain as long as they remained unwed. And she had been foolish enough to hope he knocked on her door.

The wound in her heart gaped farther and farther until she could hardly breathe. She pressed a hand to stifle the agony, to provide herself with some relief. It helped a little. Enough that she could set to work fixing herself up for Ajmal Amir—the person she *should* have thought was at the door, come to take her on their date. She smoothed her hair with oil and heat and applied her powders and charcoals and rouge until she looked as if she had never wandered lost into Bakr's arms at all.

"Pretty," a voice crooned.

Sezan froze, her bones so cold she doubted she could summon her fire even if she wished.

"No hello?" the husky voice pouted.

She turned like a wheat mill, not wanting to see the shimmering gray skin she knew awaited her. "Lilith," she said through clenched teeth.

"Hi, boo."

"Do you need something?"

"Not particularly," the lilith said, pawing at Sezan's hijab. She sat on her dresser, one knee draped lazily over the other and a menacing smile of sharp teeth on full display. "I just wanted to congratulate you on your steamy romp in the hot springs. You're absolutely glowing."

Sezan didn't have the emotional wherewithal to cringe at her words. "What is it to you what I do with the last two weeks of my life?"

The pointy smile widened. "I'm just reveling in the irony."

"What irony?" Sezan snapped.

"That for all your time studying deals in those pretentious Eastern Elm libraries, you're still so wretched at making them. And that for all of Bakr's efforts to die so he doesn't hurt anyone, he perpetually lives, wreaking havoc wherever he goes."

"Leave Bakr out of this," Sezan snipped. She took a step toward the lilith, though the creature could fry her in a snap.

"I like how feisty you are," the lilith scrunched her nose and chomped her teeth playfully. "And *I* didn't involve myself in his matters today. He called me."

Sezan's boldness slipped like water through her fingers. "What are you talking about?"

"Sorry, sugar. I don't kiss and tell."

"Could have fooled me."

The lilith cocked her head in a movement so birdlike her hair seemed to ruffle like feathers. "I heard you say you're looking for the city of Eayima."

Sezan's eyes widened. Had the lilith come to kill her for trying to break their contract? Or exact the payment early? She brushed the top of her desk and slid the letter opener into the palm of her hand.

The lilith giggled. "If you want to stab me, aim right here," she tapped her temple. "It gives me such a high."

Sezan squeezed the cold handle. "If you want to stab me, you won't get my magic."

"I have more magic in my pinky than you do in your entire body," the lilith stroked her little finger under Sezan's jaw. Then she snapped it back. "I simply wished to tell you there is more than one way to get to Eayima. I know how much you want to break the contract."

"Why would you want to help me?" Sezan asked, narrowing her eyes.

"Who says I'm helping *you*?" The lilith's eyes glowed with a hint of umber. "And if you want to get to the floating city, talk to your new boy toy, the stately and oh-so-royal amir. Love the shade of your lipstick, by the way." She picked the cherry red tube from the dresser and winked.

A knock sounded on the door once more, causing Sezan to jump and look. When she turned back around, the lilith had gone, her lipstick in hand, just a hint of smoke and burnt cinnamon lingering in her place. Sezan's eye twitched. She checked herself in the mirror before going to the door, far more frazzled than hopeful. Then walked back to her reflection and squinted. She grabbed a washcloth and rubbed her lips painfully clean. She looked strange without the color, like she wore someone else's face, someone who was weaker and softer, but she refused to wear anything that monster liked.

This time she was not so foolish as to hope for Bakr, but her heart pinched all the same. She threw open the doors and nearly hit Ajmal.

"*Marhabaan*, Sezan," Ajmal said, stepping back just in time. "Bad day?" He offered her a gentle smile.

Such manners from her *oh-so-royal amir*. What havoc would the lilith wreak in his life if she involved him, too?

She plunged into a bow. "I'm sorry. I thought you were—" What? A demon woman? A man she'd left naked in the hot springs? Another servant from the disdainful Jahmil? There was no good answer. "My apologies."

"Don't apologize to me, I'm afraid I'll be the one begging your forgiveness, shortly."

Sezan raised a brow, but before he could answer, a shrill voice echoed down the hallway.

"Where have you been?" Qadira demanded, acid in her tone as she approached in a gaudy silver dress that had more sequins than there were stars in the skies of Orkeshi.

"Me?" Sezan asked with a few blinks. Her mind had fractured into strings, one with Jahmil, one with the snakelike lilith, one with putting on a show, and another rope-full with Bakr on Ard.

"Yes you, you stupid woman. I've been sending servants around to find you and looking like a fool all the while. Do you intend for me to look like a fool?" She squinted cynically; her pointy lips pursed into a squishy spear.

Sezan bowed twice more. "Of course not, Your Astonishingness. I had to attend to some official business. My deepest apologies for the inconvenience."

"It was my fault, Qadira," Ajmal said apologetically. "I required her help on several important matters. You can take it out on me later in a game of Mangala." He turned to Sezan. "Never once have I beaten my merciless cousin. She is too clever."

Qadira's frown lessened a hair's width, but her eyes glanced around the room in scurrying bursts. Dart. Frown. Dart. Scowl. Dart... "You little spy!" She stormed over to the dresser and held up Jahmil's letter. "How dare you bring anything of *his* into my palace?"

Sezan furrowed her brow, too hopeless to put up much of a front. "I beg your pardon, Astonishingness, but how am I to broker peace between two nations if I am only allowed to speak with one? Jahmil Amir, faults and all, is still my amir."

"Exactly why I can't trust you."

"Then tell me how to prove myself," she said, one snip away from losing her temper. What did it matter anyway? The lilith was probably lying about another way to Eayima, laughing at the chance to send her on a wild goose chase before her time ran out. Her fate was sealed. The least she could do was keep Qadira from obliterating Shihala for two more weeks. Maybe that would provide some restitution for her soul after betraying her birthright and giving what was left of it to an uncaring Bakr.

Qadira opened her mouth, snapped it shut, then repeated. Three more times she moved her lips like a turtle drinking rain before snapping her head straight. She scowled and glared at Jahmil's letter, reading every last word, probably hoping it contained a reason to behead Sezan then and there. Then her hand stiffened, and she looked up. "Change your allegiance."

"I'm sorry?" Sezan said.

"Qadira," Ajmal interjected. "You cannot ask her to commit treason."

"Oh, shut up, Ajmal," Qadira bit. "I do not speak of treason. I wouldn't want to break any more international laws and have this ugly woman tattle on me."

Sezan pulled her chin in, turning her gaze to the floor on her right. She had heard about the queen's temper, but her vitriolic love of common insults caught Sezan off-guard every time. It was effective, using the insults of peasants against royal courtiers instead of flowery prose that got lost in the haze of perfumes and politics. Only people who knew very little suffering could happily misinterpret passive-aggressive phrases like "this is why everyone talks about you when you leave the room," as a good thing.

Qadira leaned in so close, that Sezan could count her eyelashes. Then she flashed a confident, eye-cutting smile. "How do you feel about ceremony, Ambassador?"

Sezan's chest tightened. She clasped her hands loosely in front of her to prevent them from wringing the loose, crimson tunic she wore over her harem pants. "*Malikati*?"

Qadira turned to Ajmal. "You are old."

He chuckled, but a pink-tinted wariness flashed in his usually clear eyes. If whatever Qadira was up to made him nervous, she didn't stand a chance. And for some reason that made Sezan strangely calm. Like fate was telling her that even if she had fixed her magic mess, she was doomed to fail anyway. It was just her lot in life. She had cast off any man who would vouch for her in a world made for men, and now she would drown in her hubris.

"Out with it, Qadira," Ajmal admonished. "Your teasing is creating undue stress for our dear ambassador."

Qadira looked as if she'd break into a cackle at any moment. "Why is Shihala having to beg Ahmar to honor old ties?"

Sezan raised a brow. "I believe you made it clear you don't want me to mention his name within your palace walls."

"Good girl." Qadira smiled cruelly. "And that is because that man, your pathetic prince, broke his marriage vow. He shattered the uniting bond of Shihala and Ahmar. And there is only one way to fix a rift like that."

Ajmal's good-natured smile vanished. His back went board-straight and stiff for the first time since she'd met him. His eyes, too, were a kaleidoscope of color, moving too quickly for any one to stand out. Sezan looked desperately between the two, clawing through her brain for the realization that had clearly struck him while leaving her in the dark.

Qadira snapped her finger and two servants materialized from the shadows. "Measure her," she said, pointing a blood-red fingernail at Sezan. "Order the finest silks, procure the best jewels. Call in all the favors owed me by the courtiers of both Ahmar and Shihala."

Sezan shook her head as the truth of Qadira's words finally hit her.

"And order a new kaftan and robes for Ajmal. We must host an extravagant banquet tonight to announce the betrothal of Ahmar's honored Ajmal Amir and Shihala's Ambassador Sheikha Sezan bint Malik Bajul."

A whirlwind of commotion followed Qadira's proclamation. Servants zipping in and out in a flurry of color and gossip. They were to marry in a week. They would have children immediately. Three, by the way, two boys and a girl. They would live in the west palace. They would eat baklava on their wedding night. But the only thing that truly registered through Sezan's shock was Qadira's smile, giddy with cruelty.

In her numb state, it all meant nothing. The drone of gnats over the corpse of an animal long dead. Either this would be her fate, saving her from her ruin just long enough for Qadira to realize her lack of magic and behead her in triumph, or she would be saved by the one man she could count on only when things were most dire. And matters were dire, indeed.

Sezan blinked in the surrounding commotion, living only in the briefest moments when her eyelids sealed. In the end, she had done the best she could. And in the end, she had only made things worse. Now she could only hope. Hope one last time for a miracle that never came.

A soft paper slipped into her hand, rousing her from her stunned stupor long enough for her to glance down and read the awful words.

I'm sorry, eazeziun. Bakr is gone.

CHAPTER NINETEEN

BAKR

When djinn apparated through the veil from Qaf to Ard, the time spent in between was negligible. A second at most of glimmering white light, insubstantial and forgettable. But as he and Shaytana moved through the veil between Ard and Qaf, Bakr held his breath. This was the first time he had ever called on her for a ride, but he knew how she operated. If she was busy or uninterested, they would pass right through to their destination. But if she wanted to talk to him, or do anything else, they would linger in the unnamed place between worlds.

It was an ability unique to the lilith, one which djinn did not share. Out of curiosity, he'd once casually brought the idea up to Jahmil, just to see if he could do it. He couldn't, not even with Ayelet's help. With a bit of experimenting and the aid of a small triangle he was able to maintain an open portal between Ard and Qaf, but he couldn't extend the time spent in the in-between by a fraction of a second. But Shaytana...

At her side, he had spent weeks, months, perhaps even years, lingering in the formless nothing. There was no time there, no consequences. She could keep him there for a century and he wouldn't age, and when she pushed him out the other side not a second would have passed.

The white light rushed over him. He closed his eyes and held his breath, but that was purely psychological. There was a feeling to the place that let him know instantly whether they were in or out.

No quick passage today.

He opened his eyes on the whiteness, the figure of Shaytana at its center, standing just a foot away from him. Beautiful as ever, a lithe and petite body, gray skin that shimmered like clouds filled with starlight. And sharp, yet delicate features. Her lips were the most distracting thing about her — pink and full, sweeping to every perfect feminine point.

She pressed those lips together and ran her fingers over his cheek. "You look upset, baby."

He cleared his throat and lifted the corners of his lips. "I'm fine."

She pouted "Do you want to talk about it?"

"There's nothing to talk about."

"Well, you certainly didn't get to Ard on your own." She pushed her hand over her mouth to stifle a laugh. She was always poking at him and never failed to find the most tender spots.

She ran her finger down the entire length of the scar on his neck and chest, sending shivers through him. He would never forget the day they first met, after the Battle of Karzusan. The high walls that protected the city had always been impenetrable, but one of Vespar's magic users set off a powerful explosive of compressed djinn fire. Huge blocks of stone were sent a hundred cubits high and three thousand Shihalan soldiers had lost their lives in a single flash. Limbs sprayed the sky with geysers of blood like something from a nightmare.

With Vespar's fire spiders casting powerful barriers over the palace to stop apparation, the only way to get the royal family out was on the back of a drakonte. King Bajul issued the order to hold the breach in order to buy time for Takisha Alqayid to get the queen and prince out. Jahmil protested having to flee, but Bakr knew that if he died the war would end right then and there. Shihala itself would end. And he owed Jahmil so much.

Bakr had already been fighting for a day and a night, his body drenched in blood and muck, his armor biting into him, chafing all over. Muscles like bags of hot sand, barely responding to entreaties. But he held his ground, slashing his iron sword in circles and leaving dozens of Vespar bodies at the wayside. There came a moment of hope when he saw Takisha's drakonte, Thueban, rising from the rubble of the broken palace. But there were only two passengers on her back.

Bakr's heart froze and he stumbled closer. He squinted against the light of the First Moon, trying to make certain the missing rider was not Jahmil.

Distracted, Bakr didn't see the berserker coming straight at him wielding a thin, razor-sharp Vesparian rapier. It went in at his neck and cut down his chest, the sharp sword tearing through his already frayed armor. Blood exploded and Bakr went down with the force of the blow. He found the wherewithal to thrust up his own sword into his assailant, impaling him between his legs. He screamed wildly as the iron scorched and sizzled in his entrails. The bastard fell and the light went from his eyes, even as all the energy went from Bakr. He was certain he was going to die.

Sezan was the last thing on his mind. He prayed Allah would be merciful. That the divine would allow him to see her just one last time—allow him the chance to tell her the truth—before he was plunged into the Eternal Fires of Jahannam, where he knew he belonged.

His eyes closed as he failed to take one choking breath after another. Then there was nothing, a beautiful infinite blackness without time. Just nothing and no sense of himself. Then slowly, light crept back in. Sounds. Smells. Sensations. Like a formless mist, a memory and a dream drifting over a dark ocean. Shaytana was at the center of it all.

Shaytana had come for him, scraped his limp body from the battlefield, and stolen away with it to her home on the coast of the Sea of Bahamut. She used her magic to draw him out from the hands of death and sealed up his wounds. She bathed his body in the milk of the legendary Talimad tree and wrapped him in a bed of storm clouds. And while he lay comatose, the lilith had slipped in beside him and kissed his lips. That was all it took—a single kiss to build an unbreakable gateway into his psyche, which she could make use of over and over and into eternity. From that moment there had never been any chance of escape.

The next several months passed in a blur. He didn't understand it now any better than he had then. Shaytana led him through a series of lucid dreams. Mixtures of memories and fantasies, every part of himself, from the purest hopes and joys to the darkest nightmares. She rode with him on the back of the Rukh bird, made love to him under Arabian starlight, kissed his brain, and wove her fingers into his heart. She watched with glee as he leaped from the back of a drakonte, barreling towards the earth at terminal velocity, only to save him with a cushion of cloud before he touched the ground. She danced with him in fire and pressed his back to the bottom of the ocean.

But she was also cruel, delving into his past and bringing it to the present just to see how broken he could become. She would mock him with images of Sezan, showing her twisting and dying on the floor. Reaching for him and begging with her sunny eyes. Or he would see her dressed in red silks on the day of her *nikah*, happy with another man and gazing at him like he was everything in her world. Bakr would see the two of them laughing together, mocking him for ever believing he could be good enough for her.

Other times Shaytana would show him as a child, weeping from hunger and covered in filth as his mother gazed at the nothing of the desert and whispered the word *musikh*, over and over.

"Monster," she would say. "Leave me be. Allah forgive me, and save me from my sin."

Shaytana's favorite roleplay was the night his mother had finally abandoned him. Ten years old, she had taken him to a Sufi mystic who knew how to call a djinn to invoke the three lines and open a door to Qaf. His mother had been saving for years to pay the exorbitant fee. She gave the mystic everything she had. The man accepted and drew a triangle on the floor in the blood of a chicken. His mother had said nothing to him and left the tent before the man pushed him into the center, and he fell through the nameless place into Qaf. He found himself alone in the shadows of the strange forests of Shihala. Screaming and crying and begging the wind for his mother to take him back. Promising to be better.

And Shaytana would laugh, and laugh, and laugh.

Bakr closed his eyes, trying to force back the memories that always simmered beneath the surface whenever Shaytana came near. He hated her. Was terrified of her. Wished on her nothing but pain. Yet, he could not deny how his body ached for hers, no matter how he chastised it. It was strangely comfortable being around her. He had nothing to hide from her because she already knew everything about him. And she treated him with the flippancy and disdain he always expected from everyone else.

Like longing for the love of a mother who despised him, his body ached for the embrace of Shaytana and her evil.

"I don't really see the point in talking," he said, returning his mind to the present and knowing no time had passed at all.

She sighed and tilted her head to one side. "That dizzy girl sure is silly the way she fusses over a common slut like you."

Bakr smirked. "That makes two of you."

"We're feeling bold today, aren't we?" She snatched his testicles in her hand and squeezed them hard enough that he growled in pain and bent at the waist. "But you're not wrong." She let go and took a step back, laying one of her long fingernails on her bottom lip. "Of course, unlike her, I can afford to indulge in frivolous things. Silly, handsome, little things that can't be left alone for ten minutes without breaking something."

"You've been talking about her a lot lately." Iron wires tightened around his chest as he narrowed his eyes. "What is your interest in her?"

"What's yours? I dare say, I've never understood it. I mean, what has she ever done for you that's of any value? All she does is yell at you and make you feel bad about being the vile, self-destructive, little slut that you are." She pouted and flipped her shaggy hair over one shoulder. "Some of us like you just the way you are, Bakr. Don't ever change."

He couldn't help but laugh even as her words burrowed into his heart like flesh-eating ratzin worms. She was laying it on thick today.

"No problem," he said.

"So, if I understand your plan, you want me to drop you off, wet and completely naked, with nothing but your sword, in the mountains of Zabriya, where it is currently snowing, by the way, so you can go look for your pet bird?" Her shoulders trembled as laughter trickled over her like rain. "I think that is the most frivolous and suicidal thing I have ever heard. Just like how calling me after making such passionate love to the woman you've been pining over for the last two years is probably the sluttiest." She pressed her hand to her chest, curling over it as she tried to rein in her girlish giggles. "In rare form today, Bakr!"

"If you feel like giving me clothes, I wouldn't say no."

She pouted and lifted her slight shoulders. "Now, does that sound like the sort of thing I'd do?"

He shrugged. "That's why I didn't ask."

She pressed a finger to her lips. "I'll give you clothes, but I want something in return."

He raised arms to the sides, his weather-beaten sword hanging limp in his grasp. "Would you care for a pound of flesh?"

"Maybe later." She flicked her gaze down his body, then winked. "Right now, I want you to hold on to something for me."

He put out his hand, palm up.

"Just like that?" Laughter quivered through her again. "That is what I love about you: no hesitation."

He lifted his shoulders and smiled. "You don't get a reputation as a vile, self-destructive slut by thinking things through, now do you?"

"How very true." She patted his cheek lightly. With her other hand, she set something cold and metal in his open palm. An ugly copper ring with a lump of scorched metal in the spot where a stone ought to be. "Put it on."

"It's ugly."

"It's... unfinished. It suits you."

He shrugged. "What does it do?"

"Nothing that concerns you."

"I find that difficult to believe."

"But you're going to wear it anyway, aren't you?"

He sighed and looked up at her eyes. "Will it hurt my Rukh bird, Shaytana?"

Her lips twitched in irritation when he said her name, like they always did. She had never meant for him to learn it. One night as they tumbled together in the powdery sands of the sparkling shores of Bahamut she had simply allowed herself to be too open. The syllables had come into his mind, and though she tried to remove them, they remained. Like a tattoo. When he said her name, she had to come to him, no matter where she was or what she was doing. And when he said her name, she had to tell him the truth. It was the only card he had against her, and so far, he'd kept it tight against his chest, knowing that if he played it too often, she would kill him to get it back.

"No," she said, her cool smile returning. "It will not hurt your precious bird."

"And what about Sezan, Shaytana?"

She grumbled. "No, it will not hurt your precious cow either. It won't hurt anybody you care about."

He licked his lips and slid the ring onto the middle finger of his left hand. "Clothes? Maybe some supplies? Wine would be appreciated."

"Sure thing, buttercup." She wiggled her nose and a leather bag appeared at his feet. Folded pants, a shirt, and a jacket were piled on top, thick furry boots beside the bundle.

He could've asked her to take him to the top of the mountain, but he didn't want Shaytana anywhere near Fajar.

He grabbed the pants and slid them on, but before he could tie up the strings of the fly, she stepped closer to him and put her hands on his shoulders. "Kiss me, lover," she said, her voice husky and wet.

He closed his eyes and turned away, a painful sigh depressing his chest that he could not stifle.

"I know you don't want to. You want to keep pretending you had a pure moment with your little harem girl. But I can't allow it." She wrapped her arms around his neck and pressed herself against him. The touch sent shivers through him, the intense smell of stargazer lilies. "You're letting yourself dream again, losing sight of who you are. You weren't born for love letters and flowers. Especially not love letters." She giggled in his face. "You're not a good person, Bakr. You don't get to fall in love. Or at least, nobody cares if you do."

He nodded, her words settling over him like turkey vultures on carrion. She was right, so he grabbed her by the back of her lithe neck and kissed her. He felt like a filthier sack of blood than he ever had before. The meager contents of his stomach curdled in disgust. Not for Shaytana. She was just being what she always was, what all liliths were. He was disgusted by himself, by the truth she had told. He kissed her, soft and careful, her tongue playing against his as she pulled herself close to his chest. Her silken skin, icy and hot and so familiar. Her hands slipped down the back of his pants and gripped his butt, yanking him hard against her. She was right about everything, so he may as well kiss her. He may as well do everything she wanted. Shaytana was the closest thing to a companion he would ever get, the companion that he deserved.

Hours later when she'd taken everything she wanted from him, she let him slip through the veil back into Qaf. Alone. At last.

His bare feet landed in a pile of powdery snow. Snowflakes as large as his palm fell against his skin, awakening him to reality. He pulled on the clothes she had given him. The landscape was obscured in a gray mist, but he could see the crests of the Zabriyan mountains in the distance, taller than any that existed on Earth, at least any he had seen. Gray stone with white caps on jagged rocks; not a color in sight.

Bakr slung the backpack over his shoulder and trekked slowly into the drift.

CHAPTER TWENTY

Sezan

Sezan had not let go of the note Lila sent her. Not when too-chatty servants ushered her, numb, around the palace. Not when an equally miserable Ajmal cast her concerned glances. Not even when she changed out of her clothes and stepped into the bath. The water was fire against her skin and soaked the paper into shredded flakes that sunk to the bottom. The gentle pressure of the clear liquid was a cruel reminder of earlier in the day when she had been happy. But that's what bad contracts did. They took two parties and completely destroyed one while giving the other everything. The lilith was right. She was wretched at her job.

And out of her sour deal with the lilith, Bakr had gotten everything. Life, freedom, a trip to Ard for a romp with an old fling. *Gug.* Sezan sank farther into the bubbles. She might as well have just given him her powers. Then at least her humiliation and stupidity would be complete and he would, in fact, have taken everything from her. She had been so foolish thinking he would come for her at all anymore. The back and forth that spotted their relationship history died when he left for the war, the hot springs merely a last visit to the grave. Their parting was permanent this time and the thought slowly cracked through her like water through the fissures in ice. Why was she always so stupid when it came to Bakr?

Sezan looked at her empty, uninviting bed in her cold, sterile room and couldn't do it. She wrapped a light robe around her shoulders and slipped out into the palace hallways. Shadows lingered and stretched off of statues, and the fifth and sixth moons that shone through the crystal ceiling breathed light over the tile just enough for her to see. She started slow, one foot in front of the other like a turtle on the sand, but soon enough she was running. Sprinting and slipping on the buffed stone toward the worst idea she could imagine.

Because why not? That stupid lilith was right. Bakr wasn't only foolish, he tempted death with everything he did. So, if all her years preparing to make informed split-second decisions resulted only in her being magicless and betrothed to a man she barely knew, why think or prepare at all? Especially when she didn't have a future, anyway. She rounded another corner and headed towards the room at the end of the hallway. Stately but unassuming. Ornate without being garish. She stopped in front of the light olive-wood door and touched a finger to the softwood. She was panting, her breath coming and going in quick, silent gasps. A mist of sweat dampened her neck and smelled of sweetgrass. She raised her knuckles when the door creaked open on its own.

Her heart spasmed. She stepped backward and nearly tripped over her robe.

"Sezan?" Ajmal asked, his brows pinched and raised.

"I—I—"

A crinkle appeared above his nose, and his light blue eyes stared into hers. He wore a sage green robe that wrapped so thickly and snuggly around him, he could have been wearing an entire bear.

"I'm so sorry," she said and turned to flee.

He grabbed her hand. "Sezan, wait. I was coming to find you, too. Please, come in and talk to me."

She started running through the list of reasons not to, then stopped cold as Lila's words flashed before her mind like flickers of flame. *Bakr is gone. Bakr is gone.* So why not in Jahannam?

She conceded, hurrying so quickly into his room that she ended up pulling him through with her.

"Is everything okay?" he asked.

But before he could say anything else, she threw her arms around his neck and kissed him. He was startled at first, hands out to the side, then gently touched her waist and pulled her off. He bent low enough to look at her face straight-on, like he thought her a lost, little child. His eyes were kind and yielding.

"You've had a bad day."

"I have not," she pouted. "My day has been fine."

"Sezan...." He raised a brow skeptically.

"Hush," she said and kissed him again. Bakr was right. Words ruined everything.

He held her chin in his hand and brushed her cheekbone with his finger. Then he pulled away once more. "Is this about what Qadira said earlier?"

"You mean about what she declared to the entire kingdom without my consent?" Sezan darted her gaze away from his. She had not meant it as an insult to him, but it had sounded like one.

"Yes," he said.

"Does it matter?" She flashed her eyes back to his, using her fire to pour all the honey and sun she could into them the way royal concubines did to snare their prey, the way her mother had taught her. She could see the halo of her eyes in his. Like Ard's sun in a beautiful blue sky. And again, she tried to feel something.

"Yes," he said again with a sigh. "I decided long ago that I would never marry by force. For contracts or titles. Even to a woman as cultured and elegant as you are. Besides, Qadira can't force you without Shihala's consent."

"I have power to grant Shihala's consent," Sezan replied.

"It doesn't change the fact that neither of us had a chance to decide this for ourselves."

"So, let's decide now."

Ajmal straightened and quirked a brow. "And how do you propose we do that when everything is already looming over us?"

Sezan bit her bottom lip, missing the tang of her cherry-flavored lipstick. The first time she had decided to trust Bakr had been through a game, and since he was the only person she had ever been with, that seemed as good an idea as she could muster.

"One question. One truth. One act."

He rubbed a finger across his tea tree-oiled beard. "Why not? It's no crazier than agreeing to marry someone without discussing it like adults first."

She gave one sharp nod. Nothing either of them said would matter to her, not as long as she got him to help her bury her pain and sealed the fate of their potential marriage. "My question for you is what is most important to you in a wife?" She expected him to lean back, to cross his arms, and get a glitter to his eyes that aimed at putting her in her place. Almost every man she met got that look eventually when they talked to a woman. Except for Bakr, probably because he didn't listen most of the time, anyway. But instead of contemptuous disregard, Ajmal's eyes rounded with softness.

"I rather prescribe to the notion that I should only expect of my wife what I expect of myself. Honesty. Love. General affability." He smiled. "An interested mind and a desire to

do more than laze away the days with impractical matters. Though vacations are allowed."
He winked.

Sezan smiled, though there was nothing to hold it up. An admirable answer. The best she could have hoped for. "What's your question for me?"

He paced his opulent room, hands clasped loosely behind his back. The plush mats and pillows that made up his sleeping arrangements were all in soft hues, like the sheen of an opal. Stacked next to the pulled-back curtains were several piles of books and half-written scrolls that smelled so strongly of vanilla and sweetgrass she could breathe in the comforting scent from where she stood by the door.

At last, he finished his circuit of the room and returned to stand before her. His lips were set in a straight line, neutral, but there was the ghost of envious green in his eyes. "What is your relationship with General Bakr?"

She waved her hand airily, her insides too hollow to feel anything about anyone anymore. Especially *him*. If all she had to do to get Ajmal to marry her and stop a war was convince him how little she cared for the flighty, prideful half-human, it would not be so hard. Nothing mattered anyway.

"He is an impulsive, reckless man but a fantastic leader. He is also a close friend of Jahmil Amir, which is how I came to meet him when I was still blooming into a woman. I've been cleaning up his messes ever since and will be glad to be rid of him when the matters of Shihala and Ahmar are sealed with peace. That is if he hasn't already run from his duties and fled the palace."

He tilted closer, leaning on his toes and scrutinizing her words. Her face. Her airy wave. "He does not plan to stay?"

"As far as I understand, he has already left. And I would not let him stay even if he did plan to."

Ajmal's lips dipped into a tiny frown, brows tightening together, before relaxing back into a smile. "On to truth. Ladies first." He bowed.

Sezan wanted to smile. It was the right time for that sort of thing. But her body no longer cared for what her mind had to say. Instead, she angled herself away from him, scrunching her brows and pursing her lips so she would look deep in thought. "I also vowed as the child of a courtesan to never let myself be married as an object in a contract or to a man who would have many wives and concubines. While I'm willing to capitulate to the first to save two kingdoms from a dreadful war, I refuse to negotiate the second. While I can ignore any past dalliances you had, or any you will have before the day of our union, if we marry and you ever take the bed of another woman, I will kill myself. Or you." She breathed out a heavy sigh and turned fierce eyes on Ajmal, waiting for his blustery excuses.

"Ah," he said, his tone very serious. Two steps brought him to her, and he tapped her chin so she looked up at him. "I see. You are one of those strong, independent, smart women who know what they're worth and won't settle for any man who refuses to see their value." He *tsked* deep in his throat. "Whatever shall I do with such a treasure? Besides cherish only her forever, think only of her when the Fourth Moon sets and the first one rises, and see only her and her beautiful smile and glittering hair every day of my life."

She looked up at him, eyes betraying her surprise with a gentle flash of golden honey. His warm smile was genuine, a dimple in his cheek hiding beneath dark whiskers. He smelled clean and crisp, like freshly washed linen that had cooled in the breeze. She waited. Nothing.

"Now my truth." He pulled a strand of hair loose from behind her ears, following along the faint twist of curl she had not fully subjugated. A hint of unexpected orange dappled his eyes and some of the warmth from his smile faded. Shame? He looked at his feet. "I will trust this to you because I can see in your eyes that you are kind and wise."

Sezan nodded, her chest empty of the usual interest that would stir at the mention of a secret.

He breathed out a heavy sigh. "I am unable to have children."

"Really?" she asked, her voice wobbling between mild shock and vague interest.

She pushed her lips side to side. If she had not but a week after their marriage before she was ruined, this would surely give her pause. Having no heir would greatly reduce her status and leave her and her husband's positions open for scavenging among the greedy, lower courtiers. It was probably the reason he had yet to marry despite his age. And the very reason he had been allowed to live during Qadira's bloody ascension to the throne. Luckily or not, her circumstances now freed her from such worries. She wasn't supposed to be thinking anyway.

Sezan gathered what physical responses were still within her reach and placed a hand on his shoulders, copying the gentle smile he usually wore. Now all she had to do was muster up some vaguely poetic words. "The lives of two nations saved is more than the one I could ever grow inside me."

He looked up at her through thick lashes, his eyes creased at the corners and as soulful and round as a baby drakonte's. "Sweeter words I'd never hoped to hear in all my days in Qaf." He kissed her forehead and stepped back, his hand sliding into a pocket in his robe. He stood at his full height, shoulders much straighter than before, as if he had been carrying a load the whole time she'd known him and had finally placed it down for a rest.

And finally, emotions stirred within her. The first, an ugly, dark swarm of guilt because she hid the truth of her future from him when he had so trustingly laid his bare. The second, a tiny wistful nudge to tell him about her deal, but she could do nothing but ignore it. She must let him find out a week after they were married so he could spurn her, cast her out in heated rage, a tit-for-tat over what Jahmil had done to Qadira. It would be poetic. And ensure justice. She would be cast off from Shihala and Ahmar forever. The kingdom of Elm, strict with rules and tradition, would hardly take her, and she'd be forced to travel the lone mountains of Zabriya or the anarchy of Western Elm, or maybe she would be cast from Qaf altogether.

"Not one woman in all of Qaf is like you, Sezan," Ajmal grinned, eagerness lending energy to his normally calm frame.

She held her smile, blacking out large swaths of memories filled with Bakr looking the same way, genuine and vulnerable. It had always made her heart ache and her chest swoon when he would share pieces of himself with her. It had been part of the reason she had loved him so, that candid frankness that caught people's breaths in their throats. But that feeling did not come with Ajmal. Maybe she was too broken to feel it again. Maybe she knew those soft eyes would fade to revulsion when her magic was gone, and he chased her from the city after such a grievous lie of omission. Maybe only a week left of being herself meant it didn't matter.

"Now for the act," she said resolutely.

If Ajmal's tender eyes and sweet words, quick mind, and absolute safety weren't enough to sway her heart, maybe she had been wrong all along. Maybe men, in their coarse way, had been right all along. Maybe physicality was what truly mattered. She had only ever loved Bakr. She had only ever slept with Bakr. To move on from him, she had to do this, if nothing more than to bond Ajmal to her for a short time.

She hadn't known what to expect her first time, except what she'd heard from the maids and other young courtesans. Men could be greedy, clumsy, or harsh. Soft, kind, or patient.

Sezan felt she already had a sense of what Ajmal would be like. No fire. No feverish embraces and volcanic eruptions of eager desperation. No kisses that drank her in until neither of them could breathe, then crashed away like waves on a beach. Ajmal would be like a river—strong, steady, and predictable.

She took his hand and tugged him toward the mats.

He hesitated. "Sezan…"

"You wish to do something else for our one act?" She raised an eyebrow, tempted to put up the classic concubine pouty lip. Instead, she let her lips lay natural, slightly parted as her eyes searched his.

"What I wish and what I should wish are very different things. I would love nothing more than to sit with you reading books. I remembered your question about the Seal the other day and scrounged up an old book my nursemaid had that talks about the Rukh bird and a copper ring—"

Sezan pressed a finger to his soft lips. She did not want to hear any more about her damnation. She kissed him again, soft and inviting and devoid of the almost-painful burn Bakr left whenever he embraced her.

Ajmal resisted a moment more before tightening his fingers around hers and leading her to his mats. He gently slid the robe from her shoulder and laid her down so her hijab fell back and her hair spilled across the pillows in glistening black, cooled lava beneath the glinting sun.

His lips moved over her cheeks, her jaw, her neck, and down. And he was as strong, steady, and predictable as she had imagined he would be. He did everything right, lingering where her body curved and brushing by her ears and nape so her skin tingled just so in response. And when he brought her close and clung only to her, as he promised he would when they were married, she felt nothing but hollow, hopeless shame.

CHAPTER TWENTY-ONE

Bakr

It took him a day and a half to reach the summit. It should have taken longer, but he never stopped to sleep. Shaytana had been generous, providing him with ropes and climbing gear as well as food and water. He had to concentrate hard as he moved up from the base, clinging to the side of the icy mountain, constantly searching for his next hold and forcing himself not to look down. It didn't leave him much time to think and exhausted his body, for which he was thankful. The cold chewed on his skin, frost clinging to his ears, the tips of his nose. His hair had been wet when he arrived and had frozen into a bowl.

When Bakr pulled himself over the summit his energy went out in an instant. He couldn't stand to gaze in wonder over the side at the feat he had accomplished. There on the edge of the mountain—a precipice yawning below like the mouth of a great eimlaq, teeth of ice and breath of frost—Bakr closed his eyes and told himself not to fall asleep.

His deepest reserves of adrenaline were spent, and even the cavernous pit in his heart could not convince him. For all the energy he'd just put into it, there was a part of him that just wanted to roll off the edge and rip his body to shreds on the rocks on the way down.

But if he killed himself, Sezan would die. First he had to finish this, and then it could all be over.

Bakr rolled the other way over hard packs of ice that had probably been on top of the mountain for ten thousand years. He was well beyond the powdery snow, beyond even the clouds. The air was thin and crisp.

He opened blurry eyes to the gloriously clear sky of Qaf. The moons pulsed in his vision. Four? Maybe five. Spiral arms of stars streaked the sky, so much light it was impossible to tell where one ended and another began. He smiled at the beauty, feeling a pull on his tired bones as if heaven itself were lifting him up. As high as he had ever been, yet still so low.

"I wish you were here," he whispered, a memory of Sezan's warmth as she lay on his chest ripping at his heartstrings. The words were carried off by the scraping wind and ripped into meaningless confetti.

He let his lids fall closed and pushed her away, remembering the secrets in her eyes as she ran from him. Right now, Sezan would be lying in a warm bed, wrapped in safety and stability. She never would have wanted to lay with him on this desolate mountaintop: freezing, isolated, exhausted. Gazing at wild stars with nothing but him and the embrace of the universe to keep her company. With so many stars, and each one a universe in itself. The life of one person, or two, didn't count at all.

And there was comfort in that, in the meaninglessness. Yet here he was for the life of one person who only ever wanted him around when she gave into her weakness. He was a character flaw, nothing more. And that made perfect sense.

Bakr dragged himself to his feet and took in his full-circle view. He breathed slowly and wrapped his arms around himself, his fingers stroking his tattoo through his coat. He had drawn it himself on a piece of lambskin, using one of Fajar's feathers as a quill and the ash from her immortal embers as ink. She had laid behind him, with all her hulking mass, her head stretched up by his side to watch him do it. He'd always liked drawing, though he rarely got time to, save stupid scribbles in the dust as he sat by a campfire. And he'd never thought he had any talent for it. But that day, the lines had flowed from his hand as if by magic.

When he was done, Fajar had pushed her head against him—her great, heavy head that was as large as an elephant. And she'd blown a breath of white fire onto the picture. In an instant it had come to life, the wings moving gently as if riding a high current, the talons twitching. And her eyes sparkling with sunlight. The bird from the picture had taken flight and come to roost on his back, then moved around the side as if yearning for his heart. It was his way back to her.

He took off his jacket and his shirt, dropping them in the snow. The blast of wind sent him shivering, skin paling and turning blue. But the tattoo was glowing with hints of orange and red, warming him from the outside in. She was close.

He closed his eyes and took slow, steadying breaths. When he had sent her away, she had promised that she would always be there should he need her. All he had to do was climb to the summit and call her name. He'd never thought he would take her up on it, but his heart pounded at the prospect of seeing her again. She had been missing from him for so long.

"Fajar," he breathed, and the word felt like a prayer on his lips. Then he lifted his cracked, frayed voice and shouted it into the sky with every remaining drop of his strength. "Fajar!"

Every muscle clenched, and he waited. Waited.

What if something had happened to her? What if instead of protecting her by sending her into these isolated mountains, he had instead signed her death warrant? Was it possible that she had needed him to stay more than she needed him to leave? Had he been wrong in thinking he was being selfless by letting her go?

But no. The tattoo was glowing. She was not only alive but close enough to hear him. And still, she didn't come.

He fell to his knees and pressed his fists into the ice. Had she forgotten him?

She wouldn't do that, would she? She was the only child he would ever have, and he was her only parent. Her mother, her father. Her protector. But he had left her—*abandoned her*, as Sezan had said. Maybe she despised him. Maybe she'd given up on him long ago and moved on with her life, though he wasn't exactly sure what that meant for her. Maybe she'd found a nice man bird who was cultured and loyal and useful and true. Fajar didn't need him any more than anyone else did. He was a burden. More likely she'd heard his call and closed her ears against it, waiting for him to go away.

"Fajar," he said again. Tears descended, and he felt as if his throat would crack open. He fell further to the ground, curling in on himself. The cliff looked more and more tempting.

Moments later, light touched his eyelids, soft and distant. He lifted his head. Far on the horizon, he saw the dawn rising in the dip between two triangular peaks.

Bakr staggered to his feet. Not dawn, nothing so simple. The light burst over the edge of the horizon and rushed towards him. He exhaled sharply as a dumbfounded, open-mouthed smile stretched his lips. For a long time, she was so far away, like an orb of red-orange fire. Then he saw the tips of her wings, the shine of her golden beak and talons. The sparkle of long tail feathers like a peacock, eyes of pure red heat. Her musical cry filled the air, so loud and biting it nearly knocked him back.

He stood frozen as she swooped past him and made a circle around the peak, her beautiful plumage sizzling with flames and sparkling like the embers of a campfire on a moonless night. She swooped and dived, did backflips and rolls. Showing off for him like she always used to. He started to laugh, and a beautiful honesty overtook him, body and soul. It warmed his frozen skin as his tattoo glowed brighter, imitating her.

Swooping closer, Fajar dropped something so it landed in a spattering heap beside him—covered in golden fur and screaming. He narrowed his eyes at the lump and slowly recognized the twisted broken body of a mountain ram. A present.

"For me?" he laughed as the poor, half-eaten creature writhed in agony. "Oh, baby girl, you shouldn't have."

Fajar cawed brightly and swooped back towards the peak. Rushing to the edge, Bakr leaped off and landed on the nape of her neck. Then he sank down into her downy warmth and hugged her with his entire body. "I've missed you."

She made a tiny, whining coo in her throat and he knew what she meant. He always knew what she meant.

She rocketed up into the air, higher than any other beast. Higher than Bubbles. High enough to touch the stars. High enough to steal the air from his lungs, but Bakr knew from experience to hold his breath until she swooped back down, angling her body to go as fast as possible. He clung to her with all his strength and laughed, just enjoying the impossible ride, leaving his brain behind to live only in his heart and body for every glorious moment. He had his baby back.

After quite some time of looping and corkscrewing, making him as dizzy as a drunk, she settled into a low glide through the mountains, towards wherever she felt like taking him. He didn't care at this moment. He pressed his face into her feathers, snuggling closer and closer.

But even as they flew, the stretched smile on his face faded, lower and lower until it was nothing.

"I wish you were here," he whispered again, and this time the stars ripped it away even faster than the wind had, leaving a chill like a drop of ice water running down the dip of his spine.

Fajar landed on a ledge. They were now far deeper in the mountains, deeper than djinn ever ventured. Somewhere beyond the crest of those mountains was the Kingdom of Fyre, the only country in all of Qaf that was ruled and populated by humans. He didn't know much about it, other than it was the birth place of all drakonte. The Court of Shihala had a long-standing contract with them that gave them exclusive rights to purchase the animals. But those negotiations always took place in Karzusan. Djinn were not allowed within the borders of Fyre.

Fajar flattened her neck against the ground so Bakr could slip off, landing on unsteady feet. He stumbled, but she caught him with the side of her beak. He fell against her and stroked the feathers between her eyes with both hands. She purred like she always did and flopped down on her stomach, making the rock quiver.

Pulling back, she blew a fire around him, melting all the frost from him so his hair dried in a fluffy poof. He scooted closer and rested his back against the feathers on her chest, and she slung a massive wing over him like a tent. There was joy and relief in her heat, but also a sadness he'd never once felt in her before. He understood the feeling the moment he touched it. The feeling that was such an inextricable part of his life, it almost felt like it belonged to him.

Fajar had been lonely here on her own, waiting for him to come back. She greeted the day with hope and ended it with resigned desperation. She had never wanted him to leave, he could feel it in her soft fire that sparkled over his skin. He had hoped she would come to terms with it, find happiness in the freedom. He had expected her to be thankful to be rid of him, but that hadn't happened. She was as lonely today as she had been the moment he left. And her heart hurt thinking he hadn't missed her too.

The thoughts that had shrouded him earlier about how she was angry at him or had simply forgotten him now dug into his guts like a knife. How could he ever think that about her? He deserved to be forgotten, to be reviled, but she would never feel that. She was good and she loved him, the only creatures in all of Allah's worlds that did. And it dug at him that even now he had ulterior motives for coming to see her.

He silently begged her for forgiveness, which she gave as easily as a breath. They were together again. The past didn't matter. And she was the only being that he could ever have that with. Never with another person because people learned and became jaded. But Fajar was so innocent, so naïve.

Cocooned in her softness—in innocence that not even he could taint—Bakr drifted off to sleep. Again, Sezan was the last thing on his mind. And the embrace of dreams transformed her into a sparkling turquoise star on the horizon that he could walk towards for a thousand years, yet never draw any nearer. And perhaps that was for the best, too.

CHAPTER TWENTY-TWO

Sezan

A̶JMAL HAD LEFT EARLY to tend to several state matters. In a truly honorable fashion, he had requested a generous breakfast without taking a bite and gave his servants the morning off so no one would discover her there. She had been considerably less kind to her servants, leaving them to pace the palace halls in hopes of finding her before Qadira did. Lila would be furious. All the more reason to stay in bed, read some books, and eat Ajmal's breakfast of bananas and almonds, of hummus and savory chicken over naan.

Sezan had slept well, considering the cold lack of dreams and the unfamiliar body next to her. It was the sleep of someone who had accepted their fate and was no longer burdened by hope. She crunched into a cinnamon-dusted almond and opened the top book on the bed next to her. Ajmal had pointed it out before apologetically bowing out of the room. It was the same tome he had mentioned the night before, the one about Rukh birds and rings.

She flipped through the first few pages, leaving sienna-colored fingerprints on the edges. She paused, looking between her smudgy fingers and the stains on the paper, then shrugged. If there was a silver lining to impending doom, it was that nothing mattered anymore. Not really.

At last, she reached the page Ajmal had bookmarked with a thin mahogany plate imprinted with fig leaves and topped with a green tassel. The chapter head had an image of a Rukh bird in full flames diving through the air, the shadow of a man on its back.

She blinked, running a finger over the picture, and lingering on the rider. She had not been Bakr's first love, which meant she never once had his heart.

Sezan smooshed the remaining cinnamon from her fingers into the image before licking the tips with a smack. No, she had lost that title to a bird. A bird she knew in her belly he could find if he wanted to. Even after all this time, she was still losing to the beaked creature. He had even tattooed it on his side, for Allah's sake.

She wiped her fingertips on the blanket like a plebeian and flipped the page. Again and again, she sifted through the delicate book, skimming the words as she looked for something interesting to occupy her time. Her fingers lighted on a beige page with inky black borders and inscribed with ancient languages she didn't know. In the center sat a picture of a copper ring. Hadn't Ajmal mentioned that last night? She leaned back into the pillows with a puff and opened the book so wide the spine creaked for easy reading.

Perhaps the most alarming legend of the magnificent Rukh and the floating city of Eayima concerns one Keid Izar, the alchemy sahir of Baghdad who sought the Seal fervently throughout his life. Determined to ride the un-rideable Rukh bird and reach the floating city, Izar fashioned two rings, one of copper and one of onyx, as conduits of magical energy, and a magic spell to make the copper ring master of the onyx. He then began to lure djinn to him and drain their fire so he could gain the strength to ride the Rukh and claim his kingdoms.

Thus, Izar grew in power and attracted the attention of a lilith. He gave her the onyx ring, but struck by her beauty, could not bring himself to drain her power, thinking he fell in love. However, he soon realized his love had only been a cruel dream brought on by a single kiss. Enraged at the lilith's trickery, Izar used the ring to catch and mount the Rukh, calling on the lilith's ancient well of magic to stave off fiery death. He rode the magnificent bird toward Eayima.

But Izar had underestimated the evil magic and cruel cleverness of earth's oldest demon. The lilith had cast an illusion, making the onyx ring appear to be copper and the copper onyx. She had then gifted him the power to fly to the floating city, only to suck it back out upon his arrival through the very curse he had used to bleed magic from the djinn. His heart collapsed and his body fell back to earth where his apprentices, fearing his fate had been Allah's judgment, left his body for the caragans to find so they would not invoke the Evil Eye.

The only mercy in this terrible outcome was that the lilith withdrew her magic from Izar too soon, causing him to fall to his death before he procured the infamous Seal of Sulayman that resided in Eayima, sparing both worlds an untold fate.

Sezan stared at the black and white drawings of Izar prostrate upon a mountain as vultures, wolves, and even an effrit fed on the fallen sorcerer's body, his terrified apprentice watching in horror from behind some trees. The ring remained on his lifeless finger. His death was as terrible as hers would be, for she too would lose her magic to a lilith for the folly of love, and the Rukh bird could not save her either. She sighed heavily and closed her eyes.

"My flower?" The door creaked open, and Ajmal clipped into the room, an alyasmin in his hand and a smile on his face. "I'm pleased to see you awake. Did you sleep well?"

She nodded and managed a half-smile as he bent down to kiss her forehead.

"Ah, I see you took a look at the pages I found. Fascinating, aren't they? Though I find this story particularly unbelievable."

"Oh?" Sezan asked, tossing a slice of caramelized banana into her mouth. The sweet, warm flavor helped ease the tension in her shoulders that had crept in when he neared. "I thought you were open to the possibility of impossibilities."

"Don't mistake my skepticism, dear Sezan. I adamantly believe in the impossible. Even so, no man could ever love a lilith, no matter how much magic they endured. The creatures are vile."

She smiled without having to force it for the first time since... The corners of her lips fell again. "I couldn't agree more. But I find the idea of the rings interesting. Are they just any old rings as long as you have the spell? That seems like a powerful weapon for any human to wield."

Ajmal chuckled. "It would, indeed. But no, the copper ring has been lost since the time of Izar and rumors abound concerning the location of the onyx ring. Though the lost spell to bind the two would be hard enough to find on its own."

Sezan plucked another piece of banana and slid the browned sugar onto her tongue, mulling over Ajmal's words. Another dead end, no doubt, but her curiosity was piqued. If the lilith or one of her kind was last in possession of the copper ring, was that how she planned to drain Sezan of her powers?

"And where do *you* suppose the onyx ring is?" Sezan asked.

His eyes sparkled ice blue with a benign playfulness. "That information will come at the cost of one kiss." He leaned down, and she flinched away. He pulled back, eyes hurt, and straightened.

Al'abalah, she cursed herself. Then smiled apologetically. "Come again, *habibi.* I was still chewing my food. I did not mean to push you away."

He eyed her warily before bending slowly to try once more. She grabbed his face and pulled him down to her, twining her fingers in his hair and breathing in his crisp soapiness. At last, she released him. He grinned, shifting so he lay next to her, and slid his arm under her head. She fought with all she had to keep the muscles in her shoulders from knotting like the ball of yarn the first time she wove her mother a shawl.

"You were saying?" she asked, her voice half a pitch higher and dripping with innocence.

"This shall be another secret between us," he said and tapped a finger on her nose.

She scooted closer to him and lay a hand on his chest, intertwining her legs with his. "On my honor."

He ran his hand through her hair, his fingers brushing gently against her uncovered scalp, and kissed her nose. When he pulled back, he brought his hand around and held the back up to her. Then he reached over and pressed a small clasp on the bone ring he wore. It popped open to reveal an onyx ring of the deepest black that seemed to shine with hints of garnet.

She let out a tiny gasp before cynicism crept in. "You are fooling me, Ajmal Amir." She raised onto her elbow so she could scold him properly. "Playing with my curiosity for the chance of more kisses."

"I do not," he said, chuckling.

"And how would you have the magical ring from a forgotten fairy tale?"

"Because my ancestor was the apprentice who found Izar dead on the mountain."

She scrunched her face and pulled the open book from off the mats next to her. "This guy?" she asked, pointing at the image of a sniveling man in tattered clothes staring dejectedly at his former master. "The ugly human?"

"The very one. Only, he was no human. He lived in disguise, using his fire to change his skin, and was on strict orders from his father, King of Ahmar, to claim the Seal of Sulayman as soon as Izar descended from Eayima."

"He looks nothing like you."

"My thanks." Ajmal's chuckle deepened. "A good many beautiful women have helped to ease the burden of such an ugly face in the gene pool. And if you still don't believe me, look here, at the inscription." He held out his ring.

She leaned close to see an engraving of an 'x' with four strange symbols made of circles and lines, one each per triangle on every side. It matched the image in the book, for whatever that was worth.

Her scowl softened into curiosity. Say he did have the onyx ring and the lilith had the copper one... could she prevent her fate by destroying Ajmal's ring? For his was the ring that stole power, not took it, and the lilith *had* told her to seek Ajmal out. Maybe his ring had been part of the plan all along. A trick or a ruse to see if she would take it. And if the lilith did have the copper ring, could Sezan alter the spell and change the flow of magic?

The creases on the bridge of her nose deepened. "If that's truly the ring that can drain power from a djinn, why would you wear it?" She reached a finger to touch it, then pulled back. "Aren't you worried the lilith still has the other and could drain your power at any moment?"

He twisted the ring so the shineless black flashed another hint of red. "I suppose the impossible could be possible." And for a moment, the dark of the onyx caught in his pooling eyes. "But the spell is lost to all but one. Besides, none of my ancestors before me have ever been drained."

"You say there is one who knows of the spell. Who is it? Do they live?"

"They live, flower." Ajmal ran a thumb over the creases in her brow, smoothing them out. "But no one who knows such secrets can be trusted."

"I did not ask if they could be trusted," she snipped. Biting her lip so hard she could taste blood on her tongue, she took a breath and made her voice sweeter than the caramelized bananas. "I'm infernally curious, my love, please forgive my eagerness."

"Love?" he asked, pulling his head back and gazing at her with a skeptical sheen in his perfectly kind eyes.

She ran her hand across his chest and hid the colors in her own gaze beneath her blackened eyelashes, only incredibly guilty and disgusted she had used yet another of her mother's shallow techniques to bamboozle a man. It made her feel cheap and dirty, but she also knew it would work. "You don't mind if I call you that, do you?"

The sharp look in his eyes melted into a pleasant glow. "Of course not."

She waited an entire degree, listening to his breathing, before asking her question again. "Who knows the spell to make the rings work?"

He let out a quick breath of air and inhaled roughly. "Faris Khayin D'Jaush." He said at last. "Traitor of Shihala and prisoner of Ashkult."

Sezan's fingers tightened around his shirt. Murderer of thousands. Betrayer of his oath. Errant knight of the Nine Kingdoms. And a disgusting, evil lump of a djinn if the stories were to be believed. But those were not the only stories she had heard of him recently. For Ayelet had mentioned the very same monster over their game of Mangala when describing her path to becoming the Chosen One. Jahmil had made a deal to kill the immortal djinn in exchange for three questions. Two of which were left unused.

"Come, *my love*," Ajmal repeated her platitudes. "We must go meet Qadira for dinner and officially concede to the terms of our marriage." He paused, and a shyness crept over his face. "That is if you still want to proceed after my one question, one truth, and one... act." His cheeks warmed with a rosy blush.

It took everything she had not to barrel full force into hoping once more. But the seed of it was there. She could make marriage to Ajmal work if she retained her powers, even if she did not love him. Her stomach folded upon itself in needle-like waves as Bakr's pleading eyes flashed before her mind. Her hold on Ajmal's shirt tightened, and she twisted her tongue upon itself to force the words.

"I wish to proceed."

He pulled her closer and hugged her tight, and she folded willingly. She would proceed to save Shihala, and she would proceed because Ajmal actually wanted her for a lifetime, not a nighttime. She would not be the fool Izar was. The fool she had already been. She would not continue to wallow in the hopelessness she had felt just that morning, not when her bucket of useless sand could yet be turned into shining glass.

She sat up, leaving his embrace. Her long hair tickled bare skin as it cascaded across her shoulders. "I must go to my rooms now. Lila will be in an absolute tizzy."

He pushed aside her hair so the sparkles caught the light and danced on the walls and kissed the back of her neck. "I shall miss you every degree you're away."

She turned her head so he would not see the pain that tightened her lips or the purple she was sure clouded her eyes. "Me too, my love. Me too."

CHAPTER TWENTY-THREE

Bakr

Fajar knew why he had come to see her. That he was there because he needed something from her, not because of how much he had missed her. It hurt her, but she forgave him with a sad sort of sweetness because she understood the reason he hadn't come earlier wasn't that he hadn't missed her. It was that he was frightened that being near her would hurt her.

As Bakr had climbed the mountain, everything that had been said between him and Sezan and him and Shaytana swirling through his brain, he'd made a decision. He'd decided that once the business with Rahik was at an end, he was going to kill himself. But being near Fajar again, he quickly changed his mind. Instead, when all was done in Eayima, they would go away together to the proverbial island on Ard. Just him and Bubbles and Fajar. And that made her coo, knock him to the ground with her beak, and sweep him around affectionately until he had abrasions on his back.

He didn't have to ask for help to get to Eayima. She knew what he was thinking and feeling. Not in that creepy, invasive way that Shaytana did. It was like she could understand what he meant to say before his tongue had an opportunity to ruin it. And she never hid anything from him, except the occasional stockpile of dead horses that she kept as snacks and did not want to share.

Fajar's feathers could be used to apparate anywhere on Qaf, or anywhere on Ard if that was where she happened to be, but she could not move between worlds like a djinn or a lilith. And that meant they had to go the long way around. The Muthalath al'Ard, or Great Triangle of Ard, was found at the center of the Muthalath Sea that separated the

Upper Continent from the Lower. Situated at the very heart of Qaf, the Triangle was invisible to a magically unaided eye, written in the currents of the oceans and draughts of the wind. Each of its equal sides stretched for fifty parasangs. There was a similar triangle on Ard—one that would bring an unsuspecting human to Qaf should they unwittingly sail through it. The triangle stretched from the edge of heaven to the bottom of the sea, so the ocean of Muthalath was teeming with Ardish creatures—dolphins, manatees, and parrotfish. It was rumored that the Jasraib—a race of djinn with fishlike tails who lived virtually all their lives underwater—moved so freely through the Triangle that their civilization sprawled through the oceans of Qaf and Ard alike.

The journey was long and potentially dangerous given the wild hippogriffs that called the Muthalath Sea home, so Fajar went out to hunt to make sure she was starting off with a full belly. As he waited for her in the cave, he sipped the bottle of wine Shaytana had given him. He always expected her gifts to taste of her bitter magic, but they were nothing.

Bakr warmed himself by a small white-hot fire Fajar had left burning. He did not know what might be waiting for him in Eayima, so he needed to be prepared for anything. He had his sword, which was really all he needed, but had left everything else in Ahmar. His money, changes of clothes. Bubbles. A single feather from Fajar could slip him through the veil to Ahmar to retrieve his things. And maybe while he was there, Sezan would be willing to talk to him again...

He still didn't fully understand why she had gotten so angry at him, but he knew she would be very upset that he hadn't waited around for someone to pick him up. That he hadn't gone back to Ahmar the way he had promised, even if she was sick of him. Jahmil was going to be irritated about that too, but that seemed a lot less important at the moment.

He had realized something while flying on Fajar. Sezan had been waiting for him to say he was sorry. Sorry for staying away from her for so long. Sorry for not writing. Sorry for leaving while she was so sick. Sorry for not saying goodbye before going to fight the Vespars. She also had been waiting for him to say that he had missed her, which he still hadn't been able to bring himself to say. Not out loud. Not to her face. And he couldn't help thinking that when she had asked if she was presumptuous for assuming she was on the list of people he cared about, he was probably supposed to have reassured her that she was.

Maybe if he managed to say those things, in the right order, in the right tone of voice, without letting her distract him or make him angry, maybe he would be able to convince her to come with him to Eayima. She had asked him to take her anyway, to meet his darling. If he could bring it up in such a way as to say, *I-know-you've-been-spying-on-me-but-I-don't-care*, maybe things could be alright between them again.

Or maybe, he should just take Bubbles and go straight to Ard. Maybe he was right the first time and leaving her alone was the kindest thing to do. Give her little prince a chance to woo her, or for her to woo him, or however that situation was working out. Maybe it didn't matter what he said anymore. After all, Sezan was not a giant magical bird with whom he could communicate telepathically. Different rules applied.

He found a flat stone inside Fajar's cave and etched a cross on one side, then poised it on his thumbnail. Smooth side, he would make a quick trip back to Ahmar; 'X' and he would just go straight to Ard.

He flipped it and let it fall to the ground.

X.

No trip back to Ahmar.

"Two out of three," he said to himself and flipped it again.

X.

He pressed his face into his hand. Maybe this was fate trying to tell him something. That saving her was more important than seeing her.

He never should have signed that stupid contract with Rahik, but he had been so scared in that moment, he hadn't seen any alternative. He still didn't. Rahik's spies had figured out that he cared about Sezan—that he had been on the verge of asking her to be his wife. The bloated hagfish's instinct had been to exploit that fact.

Bakr had never wanted to be a prince, no more than Sezan really wanted to be a princess. And so, they decided they were going to run away together. The night they were meant to leave, Bakr sneaked up to Sezan's balcony. He could still remember the feeling of the smile he'd warn that night: so large it was painful, stretching the skin of his face. His life had been about to begin. A life with a woman who loved him—truly loved him in spite of the fact that she knew him well. They were going to be together and be a family. He had never felt more ready for anything.

The ring was in his pocket.

He came into her room in the harem, the part of Karzusan palace reserved for the women and children of the royal family. But when he stepped into Sezan's room, he found her lying on the floor with blood on her lips, barely breathing. Bakr's heart stopped and he rushed to her side, lifting her into his lap. Her pulse was slowing under his fingers.

Blue lips. That was when Rahik stepped out of the shadows and explained that she'd been poisoned.

Bakr snatched him by the throat and thrust him against a wall, ready to break his neck if he didn't give up the antidote. But Rahik just grinned and thrust that infernal contract in his face. Sezan's breath had taken on a death rattle. With no time to think, Bakr signed.

The Seal flashed bright green, making the contract permanent. At that very moment, the battle horn of Karzusan sounded. The city was under attack. As Rahik slithered away into the shadows, Bakr called Lila into the room and ordered to take an unconscious Sezan to the summer palace in Ranabar. They got out seconds before the Vesparian spiders cast fire barriers over the city to trap everybody inside.

Bakr didn't know everything that was in the contract. He knew he wasn't allowed to kill Rahik or himself, not without condemning Sezan to the same fate. And if he failed to live up to the terms, the magical antidote that even now flowed through Sezan's blood would expire and she would drop dead. The only way to make the effects permanent was to fulfill the contract.

It was his fault. He had endangered her because he had let himself get close to her, close enough that anybody with half a brain could see how he felt, even if she could never seem to figure it out. He had to finish out the contract and make sure she would be safe forever, with or without him.

Probably without him.

"Three out of five." He flipped the stone again.

X.

He threw the thing off the cliff. He would go to Ahmar. One hour, that was all. Just one hour to make sure she was okay. One hour to gather all his things, to find Bubbles, and to try to explain, Allah's mercy be with him, why he had left. But he couldn't tell her the truth. She would be terrified if she found out that her life was in his hands, so little did she trust them.

He closed his eyes and called out to Fajar with his mind, knowing she could hear. She was hunting down an entire pack of wild pigs, scooping them up in her talons and dropping them, dashing all their brains against rocks, before she would sit down to her feast. But she heard him and when he promised he would come right back, she believed him with no hint of suspicion. It was so refreshing.

He plucked a few of her small downy feathers from the walls of the cave. One to get there, one to get back, and a dozen more just in case. Back when he and Fajar were together, he used her feathers to teleport all the time. It was almost exactly the same as when a djinn moved him through the veil—a flash of fire, a negligible slip through the nameless place, and then appearing at the destination in a puff of white smoke. Though, with Fajar's feathers, he didn't have to make a stop-over in Ard to get where he was going. And he could go anywhere he wanted, not just to places he had already been, so long as he knew the lay of the land.

He lifted one feather in his palm and thought about where he wanted to be, then he blew it off. It drifted towards the ground and when it hit, he was pulled through to the nameless place. He expected to slip right through it, as he always had in the past. Instead, he lingered. His blood curdled and his eyes darted around the whiteness, expecting to see Shaytana holding him there. But there was nothing. He was alone.

Shaytana had left him alone in her Namelessness many times, sometimes locked in a cell, sometimes lounging in silk sheets like a king. But something about this felt different.

He took a step, turning in all directions. Nothing. He opened his mouth and let out a high trill for anyone that may be near. Looking for an echo, a reverberation. Anything.

Nothing.

"Interesting," he said. He stood there for a while, just taking in the nameless nothingness, the utter un-magic of the place. The timelessness and lifelessness that stretched for eternity in every direction. A single-toned vastness that assaulted his senses with its passionate insistence to be nothing.

It was boring.

He thought of Ahmar again. He hadn't been assigned chambers in the palace, and he didn't know the layout. There was the front courtyard where he and Sezan's retinue had originally entered The City of Pearls.

He tried to move, but something pushed back. The way was open. He could sense the gaping hole his thoughts had made in the Namelessness. But there was a barrier holding him back.

A fire barrier, he realized. Protection cast over the palace to keep riff-raff djinn from apparating in any time they chose. He would've thought the power of Fajar's feathers could force their way through such a thing. But when his heart reached out, trying to touch the bit of her that lived in every single plume, all he felt of her presence was his own tattoo.

The feather had fizzled out in the Namelessness. Fajar's power wasn't holding him in place. Neither was Shaytana's. He was just *here*.

Prickles of panic brushed his neck but Bakr took a deep breath, refusing to lose his cool just yet. Taking it as read that his thoughts were somehow influencing the surrounding space, Bakr conjured up thoughts of Bubbles. Shihalan drakonte would not have been kept in the royal stables with the delicate Ahmaran pegasi. They might not even be on the island, but on the other side across the Buhayra.

Suddenly, Bakr fell. Like snapping to wake from a short drop through sleep, he opened his eyes and he was in the stables next to his baby drakonte.

Bubbles' pretty snake eyes popped and she lunged at him to wrap him up in one of her cold, nearly suffocating hugs that left him tingly, slightly terrified, and giggling.

"I missed you too, bubbly baby." He petted her head and kissed her between the eyes. After another ultra-tight squeeze, she set him down in the middle of her coils, boxing him in. Her snake eyes narrowed as if to ask him where he had been. He patted her nose. "I was always coming back for you. Calm down."

She pouted and squeezed him tight enough that he coughed. "I'm sorry! I'm sorry! Okay?"

She set him down, but she flicked her chin off to one side and pouted even harder.

"I just need you to stay here and be quiet for a little while longer," he continued. "I have one little thing I need to take care of."

She nodded and drifted into the corner to finish off the goat she'd been given for dinner.

He stepped out of the royal stables, his gaze darting around the massive palace complex. Huge open-air squares were connected by veins of pearl-studded porticos. Bakr did not know where the apartments were that Sezan had been assigned to. So, he decided to head towards the main palace, hoping to find someone who could point him in the right direction.

The front door was open but guarded. Given the time, near lunch, he decided to check the dining hall. He went around the side of the palace and went in through a window. As he turned a corner, trying to be as sneaky as possible but too distracted to do it well, he bumped into a man so hard that he nearly knocked him down. On instinct, Bakr reached out and snatched his wrist.

"*Alqarf*," he cursed, and quickly smacked wrinkles out of the man's jacket. "I'm sorry. Are you okay?"

"That's quite alright..."

Bakr glanced at his face. Pastel purple skin. A perfect quaff of oiled hair like every other princeling he had ever known. Trim beard that he obviously spent hours shaping just so. And pale blue eyes that had barely flashed with color on the night Bakr and Qadira had nearly sent two countries to war.

"Ajmal Amir," said Bakr, forcing a congenial smile. "Good to see you."

"And you, general. I had been informed you had already left Ahmar."

He laughed and rolled his shoulders. "I leave, I come back. It's what djinn do."

"Indeed." Ajmal smiled tightly and widened his eyes. "While it is a delight running into you without announcement, is there a reason you are lingering in the hallway?"

"I'm not lingering. I—"

"Is that you, Ajmal?" called a cold, high-pitched voice.

Ajmal widened his eyes still further.

"Say no more," said Bakr, and he ducked behind a thick column. The click of heels brought a bouquet of jasmine, oleander, acacia, honey, and so much else wafting into the room. He peeked around the edge as Qadira swaggered into view in what looked like riding gear — ultra-tight leather pants, boots, and her usual bandeau in an iridescent shade of yellow. Her long hair was wrapped in brown and green ribbons and her sparkles were golden. A more earthy feel today, but consistently ridiculous.

"*Marhabaan*, cousin," said Ajmal. "I've come to finalize the terms of the marriage."

She turned her nails in and examined them carefully. "Where is the fat, ugly one?"

"Ambassador Sezan bint Bajul is simply composing herself before joining us."

"You're being tedious again," said Qadira. "Although, my servants tell me she's been sleeping in your room."

Bakr's lips parted, a sharp pain stabbing into his chest. He almost stumbled.

Qadira pinched Ajmal's side playfully, and he squirmed. "Well done. I dare say, I thought you were going to cause me a lot more trouble. It is a relief to have your elderly, depressing butt married off without having to pay an exorbitant bride price. Plus, it helps to smooth things over with that Sack-of-Silver Amir of Shi-stinking-hala. Double win. You should be congratulating me."

"Congratulations, cousin," he said, but there was an unmistakable smile hidden behind his careful expression. A smile that Bakr recognized as easily as he did the color blue. "Sezan and I are a good match."

Bakr dropped a feather and disappeared back to the top of the mountain. He should have listened to fate. She had tried to warn him.

CHAPTER TWENTY-FOUR

SEZAN

WHEN SEZAN WENT TO meet Ajmal for her formal sitting with Qadira, she could have sworn she smelled the kick of Agarwood lingering in the hallway. It made her furious. Every time she thought of him did, but only at herself for leaving him in Ard. For having the best day of her life and walking away from it because of a bad deal she made while he was at war. Not that she regretted saving Bakr, she would do so again even now, but because she had thought of nothing better to give the lilith than everything she had ever worked for. She couldn't focus on that now, though. There were only a few days left before her wedding, and she needed to make a trip first.

She had sent Jahmil a letter asking for one of Faris Khayin's answers as the only way to prevent war with Ahmar. It was half a calculated choice and half an impulsive one; the gray space she lived in these days. But she couldn't help it, even if it meant asking her irritating elder brother for a favor. Of course, being dismissed from her ambassadorship if he found out she was lying would be humiliating, but with her magic intact, her marriage to Ajmal Amir would be enough to sustain her place in society and the goodwill between the nations, even if he couldn't have an heir. She could focus her efforts on creating a new space for herself in the treacherous courts of Ahmar and leave behind Shihala altogether. And then maybe, she'd finally secure herself in a stable marriage to a stable man, free from the whims of Bakr and his unpredictable passion and pet demon. Surely, that was worth broaching the subject, even if it was with Jahmil.

Either way, her suspicious amir had granted her request and said he would meet her at Ashkult as soon as possible. She could finalize her marriage contract, playing ambassador and future cousin-in-law for a few degrees, and then tend to what really mattered. She simply had to go to Ashkult, secure a private meeting with the traitor, and ask her question with Jahmil's blessing.

Sezan took a breath and shook loose her shoulders before tugging her dark blue hijab over her hair and straightening the sapphire that hung on her forehead. Her stomach did flips like she was diving off a cliff though she stood solidly on the ground. *Queasy* was the term her mother had used when chastising her, and it was something her mother had beaten out of her when she was young. Why was her body starting to feel so off now? Had her nerves frayed so far?

"Ready?" Ajmal asked, appearing by her side. Today, his creamy kaftan was embroidered in gold stitching in the shape of feathers.

She nodded, afraid to look into his eyes lest the flicker of pink betray her doubts.

Ajmal took her limp hand, kissed it, and slipped it into the crook of his elbow. "I'm glad you made it on time."

"Why wouldn't I have?" The tickle of worry in her stomach made her sick.

He patted her hand and chuckled. "My apologies, my love. I did not mean to offend. I saw General Bakr in the hallway not five degrees ago and thought he may have been bringing you some official business from Shihala."

She pinched the fabric of his sleeve before realizing her mistake and quickly smoothed it out. The scent in the hallway... She closed her eyes just in time to hide the flash of yellow.

"Bakr brought me nothing." Just like always. "In fact, he didn't come to see me at all." Just like always. "He doesn't matter." She kept her eyes on the door straight ahead, refusing to look up at her prince. Her soon-to-be officially betrothed.

"Sezan..." Ajmal said with a sigh. "When we played your game the other night, I didn't want it to be just one truth you ever told me. I want all your truths." He turned her to face him. "Why does General Bakr anger you so? He is supposed to be here to protect you, and the only time I've seen you together, *you* were protecting *him* from Qadira. It is strange." He stopped talking and looked away from her. "It seems as if you avoid each other, and yet are entirely comfortable in each other's presence. I've heard of General Bakr's inability to be tamed, his wild impulses and problems with authority, and in one whispered snap of his name he followed you out of the banquet hall with a smile on his face."

With every one of his words, she could feel the heat dripping out of her cheeks and into her upset stomach. She had been so worried about Ajmal discovering her glaring lie of omission that she hadn't considered getting caught for her smaller untruths. She needed to decide what to tell people about her and Bakr's relationship since he couldn't seem to stop popping up in her life and destroying everything. Preventative damage control. Wetting the forest before the fire.

"I'm sorry, my love," she turned a pained face to him, relieved that for once the emotion she showed him came naturally. "He and Jahmil Amir are very close, as are he and Ayelet Amira. I have been given special charge of tending to his affairs while here at the palace."

"Like a babysitter?" Ajmal asked, his tone incredulous.

"Unfortunately, exactly like a babysitter. He only obeys me because Jahmil has decreed it so, and he acts so casually around me because he finds joy in my discomfort. I'm but one big joke to him."

"Hmm." Ajmal patted her hand once again, this time absent-mindedly. "Maybe Qadira had been right to send him to Cetus." She smiled, then his hand tightened over hers. "But I cannot allow my future wife to be treated so disrespectfully by the very throne she serves with such passion. It is intolerable. I will write to Jahmil Amir today and insist he apologize for diminishing a Sheikha of your caliber to a mere babysitter."

Sezan's eyes widened. "No, Ajmal. No. I appreciate the thought, but I am to meet my amir as soon as we are done and plan to explain everything to him then. To tell him I'm betrothed for the sake of Shihala, and that I cannot be a loyal and good wife while having to think of another man." Which was most certainly true, though Jahmil Amir had no control over that.

Ajmal frowned, the downturn of his lips unnatural against the beard he had shaped for smiling. "I suppose it would do no good to inflame your unpredictable prince at such a tenuous time." The weight on her chest lifted. "I'll talk to Bakr instead, prince to halfling."

"Wait," she said, her throat closing in tight.

He released her hand and turned, scanning the hallways up and down. "Where is he?"

"Who knows," she said hastily. "And it doesn't matter. We have a marriage contract to finalize."

"Ah, about that," he said, turning to her with eyebrows tilted toward each other. "I'm pretty sure Qadira intentionally forgot our appointment and plans to make us wait half the day. She was in full riding gear on her way out of the palace just before you arrived."

Sezan hid the glare burning behind her eyes. Maybe if she locked Qadira and Bakr in a room together, they would just kill each other off. Then again, no one could lock Bakr in anything and expect him to stay. He was water; hard as ice when you needed him to yield and vaporous as steam when you wanted him to appear. And all the while running and pouring and bubbling away down a path that had no end.

In the end, the risk of Ajmal finding out too much about the situation from Jahmil was far lower than he would with Bakr, one being as tight-lipped as the other was a loud-mouth.

Sezan stifled a sigh so big it hurt her nasal cavities just to keep it in. "Perhaps you could escort me to the lake of silver outside Ashkult. Rumors say the place is so devoid of magic, djinn feel the draining effects for days."

Ajmal stopped searching the hall and turned to her. "Of course," he clasped her hand. "I would be happy to."

Within five degrees, they were on the back of one of Ahmar's stunning winged horses. The muscles of the mare moved smoothly underneath feathered fur, white with dappled gray, that grew bigger and bigger until feathers longer than her arm branched out to the tips of ten-foot wings. The ride was smooth and full of playful dips as the pegasus rubbed her nose at passing birds and skimmed the ground for tasty flowers. They passed a waterfall, and Sezan smiled against the mist-coated breeze, thinking of nothing but the wind against her face and the moons' light upon her skin. It took half the passage of the Third Moon to arrive. Fortunately, she and Ajmal had spoken very little as she leaned against his back with her arms around his waist.

He would be a good husband, she told herself at least seven times. Respectable. Caring. Intelligent. Punctual. Protective. Responsible. Articulate. Safe. In fact, everything she hated about Bakr, he had covered in spades. But she had to pinch the back of her hand for that thought, determined as she was not to compare Ajmal to him anymore. No one deserved that. To be put up against a man who was utterly impossible.

How could she compare the two anyway? Impeccable penmanship and throwing oneself off a cliff were hardly relative. Bakr was a superb soldier and commander, she supposed, but Ajmal preferred no one go to war in the first place. And then there was the matter of articulation. While Ajmal said everything in a melodic, perfect way and never caused her emotional turmoil, Bakr... Bakr just said whatever blunt or rough or sarcastic thing came to mind first. Or locked his eyes on her like she was the only person in the entire universe, pleading and desperate as if he would die without her and even his bones would ache for her in the grave.

She pinched her hand again, much harder this time. She was impossible.

The wings of their mare stopped their methodical flapping and coasted toward the earth. Below lay a deep, motionless lake of quicksilver that sent shivers through her skin. One touch of the liquid would sear her skin and maim her forever, magic or no. Next to the lake stood Jahmil Amir and a giant drakonte that hissed and bared its spear-like teeth at their approach. The mare whinnied in protest, but with a gentle nudge from Ajmal, landed dutifully upon the earth several dozen yards from the flying snake.

"You're late," Jahmil said, glancing at the First Moon, his lips a flat line of disdain.

"*Amiri*," Sezan said with a shallow bow.

She was more than happy to let Ajmal make his own introduction. The two men spent the next two degrees crafting precise sentences, sizing each other up, and making perfunctory assessments of their kingdoms' current affairs.

"Come," Jahmil said at last, beckoning her like she was finally worth his time. "Let us get this over with."

She ran a hand down Ajmal's arm. "I'll be right back."

He bowed as Jahmil raised an eyebrow.

"He comes, too," Jahmil said, taking a wide step into the little boat. The red-skinned Ghaluman at the front of the boat sneered as the vessel teetered back and forth, threatening the amir with impending doom.

"Your Highness," Sezan began to protest, but Jahmil shot her an ice-cold warning.

He was not in a good mood. Perhaps it was the giant Ahmaran army milling about on his border. Regardless, Sezan had not intended for Ajmal to come inside the prison, and Jahmil's nosy insistence that he did irked her. She hesitated, but Ajmal took her elbow and helped her step into the boat. He followed, wrapping his arm around her protectively. Jahmil's other eyebrow raised, and his eyes glittered with calculation.

He was looking for fault in her. For a lie or a mistake. And she was hiding plenty. He could not suspect her ulterior motives, but he had a way of needling her that made her look petty. Especially when he brought up Bakr. And he always brought up Bakr. If he found out she lied to him in front of Ajmal, her circumstances would get exponentially worse. Altogether, the situation tasted like bitter sumac.

Maybe she could distract the two by announcing the news of their engagement. But the words sat dry on the tip of her tongue. Qadira commanding them to marry was one thing. Sezan agreeing to the match in front of her air was an entirely different matter. She would not be able to change her mind without becoming a traitor to Shihala, even if Jahmil himself had done the same thing, not a year past.

They arrived at the shore long before she worked up the courage to say anything. The barren, white walls of the prison shot straight into a sky of the same color, giving the illusion that they never ended. There were more Ghaluman guards inside, the prison residing in their desolate lands, all staring at her with narrowed eyes. Maybe it was her skin, a bright bastion of calming color in a prison full of rage. Or maybe it was because the natural sparkles in a loosened strand of her hair reflected its own internal light against the darkness of this place. The last of her family's Jasraib ancestry shining through, her great-great-grandmother having belonged to the stunning silver and gold-skinned people of the northern isles. Or maybe, it was that she still had her hair at all. Every prisoner that snarled at her had been shaved entirely bald.

After a long, silent walk, they arrived at an iron door with three tiny slats for a prisoner to peak out. Heavy metal studs bolted the frame to the wall every two fingers' width, and an 'x' made of brass reinforced the door's strength through the middle. Excessive, really. Unless they were trying to hold back an eimlaq, and then it would not have been nearly enough. She stood on her tiptoes to see through the slats, but there was only abyss. She tightened her hijab and shivered against the cold lack of magic.

"Khayin D'Jaush," Jahmil called. "The time has come to give your second answer."

The creature hissed from inside the cell before eyes darker than the black behind him appeared beneath wrinkly blue-gray folds. "You've come to waste your second question?"

Jahmil narrowed his eyes before turning to Sezan. He touched her arm and led her away from the door a few steps. "What is the exact question that you need to ask?"

Sezan froze, hating that her eyes shined like Ard's sun in the shadows of this terrible place. She had not considered that the question might need to be asked through him. She simply thought she needed his permission to ask it. But men often forced their presence on others when it was unnecessary. She should have thought of that. Maybe she was as foolish as Izar. "Your Highness, I was hoping to speak with the traitor myself."

Jahmil narrowed his eyes at her. "He is too dangerous."

"And what can he do locked up in this place when I am on the other side of the door?"

"More than you would expect. He carries magic with him and there is no metal on Ard or Qaf that could remove it."

"Do you not trust that I can keep myself safe or do you not trust that I can do the job you assigned me?"

"Frankly, no. I do not trust you. I think you are trying to play your own game." Jahmil sighed and looked away, his fists clenching as if trying to hold back his temper. "The only reason I deigned to grant this request is because my wife would not leave me alone about it."

Sezan pressed her teeth hard together. Jahmil only ever deigned to do anything. "You are too magnanimous, *amiri*." She offered a pert curtsy. "Though I should think you would trust me a little more since I've managed to broker lasting peace between Ahmar and Shihala."

"Lasting peace?" he scoffed. "Are you out of your mind? An Ahmaran army is parked on my northern border, and whatever guarantees Qadira may have given you are as flimsy as gossamer until written in blood."

"And who's fault is that?" She took an extra-long breath. "You gave me power on behalf of Shihala to make concessions to the queen. I have done so. An arranged marriage between her cousin, Ajmal Amir, who so respectfully stands behind you."

They both glanced back at Ajmal, who was slowly strolling the line of cell doors out of earshot. When Jahmil turned back to her, he looked as if he had just eaten a bitter cucumber. "You're going to marry him?"

"As ambassador, I promised my life for that of Shihala. Qadira suggested this union as a way to mend the one you broke. And I accepted the offer. We sign the contracts as soon as I return from this place."

"What about Bakr?"

"What about him?" she asked, looking away. His words reached through her chest and ground her heart into bits of dust. "Didn't you just try to marry me off to the King of Elm? Where was your concern for Bakr then?"

"Those were very different times." He sighed and shook his head, his hands on his hips. "If you're determined to marry this... whatever. Felicitations, I guess. But Qadira is as slippery as a wet snake. If this was her idea, it is probably a bad one."

"For all your disdain for the Queen of Ahmar, Your Highness, her kingdom is in far better shape than yours."

"Than *ours*, sheikha," he snapped. "And I can't imagine the Vespars had anything to do with that."

"You're quick to place all your troubles on the shoulders of others, brother."

Jahmil scoffed and shook his head. "Yes. That's always been my problem."

She glared at him. "Do not judge me so harshly when I do for Shihala what you would not." She clenched her fist and a soft halo of pink flame burst around it. But not her rose pink. A dirtier, lighter, and more orange glow. She quickly shook it out, a dread too terrible to think about oozing into her stomach.

"You speak above your station, ambassador." His eyes flashed white, bright enough it was like a strike of lightning in the middle of the hall. Ajmal's head turned to look at them and Jahmil snorted out a sigh. "Do as you wish, Sezan. But even nobles are entitled to some happiness."

She snorted out a cold laugh, the tapestry of her life unraveling far faster than he ever thought. "You are only free to do as you wish because you have ambassadors like me to smooth over your impulsive decisions. There is no happiness for me, *amiri*. And even less when you mention the name Bakr in my presence."

"You love him, you hate him, you love him, you hate him. The cycle goes on, exactly as I knew it would. You two are incapable of being happy. Perhaps it is for the best if you marry this..." He smirked and shook his head. "And nobody is given freedom. You have to take it and be uncompromising in keeping it. Everyone will make a slave of you if you let them."

She chuckled, but it was hollow. "You tell me to grab freedom in the same breath you order me around. You're disillusioned as our father. And it's too late. I am already a slave. To you, to Shihala, to—" She dug a nail into her palm and took a shaky breath.

"What I am is tired of all your circuitous nonsense. You will not speak to Faris Khayin. The two remaining questions belong to me, and I will not waste one if you refuse to even tell me what it is."

Sezan pressed her fingers into her palm even harder. She should not engage so recklessly with her amir. He could make the last week she had to do anything about her circumstances even more difficult. She forced up a smile, the anger from their argument giving her the strength. "Fine. I'll capitulate. I want to know from the traitor a spell."

He lifted his eyebrows.

"I need to know the incantation Keid Izar used to drain magic from the djinn through a copper and onyx ring."

"And how does this relate to your peacemaking work in Ahmar?"

"Because if I do not find out, Qadira will learn of a great injustice in a week's time, and I'll make sure she takes it out on you."

"Are you threatening me?"

"Are you willing to take the risk with ten thousand Ahmaran soldiers at your border?"

"*Our* border." He narrowed his eyes at her still further until they were nothing but tiny slits of white. "Where is Bakr? What does he think of all this?"

"Bakr?" She spat the name. "Where do you think he is? Anywhere but where duty requires. He promised me he would stay and then disappeared without so much as a word. To think you make decisions based on his counsel is baffling."

"He may be reckless, but he is loyal, which is more than I can say about you."

"Bakr is not loyal."

"He is to me," he said, smiling with one corner of his mouth. "And if he chose to leave Ahmar at this time, I trust he had important business to attend to which could not wait. You see, I trust him. Do you have any idea what that's like, sheikha? To trust someone?"

"And why should I? All you know of me is what you saw looking down your nose at dinners, unaware of anything I was going through until it served your purposes as a pawn in your kingdom. And what of Bakr? He abandoned me without a word, yet you still defend him. What male in my life has been worthy of trust? The answer, brother, is none."

He slid his gaze over his shoulder at Ajmal and then back to Sezan. "Interesting."

She only half concealed her growl, her hands itching to slap his face. "Can we ask the traitor my question and get on with this? Or do I have to listen to your ridiculous statements about marriage and trust and the nobility of being a stupid man in Shihala? I don't believe either of us enjoys the other's company much, and my dear betrothed is waiting for me patiently behind you."

"On the contrary, I rather enjoy our little tête-à-têtes. But, duty calls." He walked back up to Khayin's door, then lifted his hand, permitting her to speak her question.

She hesitated, then caught sight of Ajmal's encouraging smile. "Traitor, what is the spell the magician Izar used to pull magic between rings?"

CHAPTER TWENTY-FIVE

Bakr

Fajar took a loop over the Muthalath Ocean. The sea was still and silent, the sky clear so every star shone like a back lit diamond. No clouds for monsters to hide behind. When they passed through the Great Triangle, the change was gradual and soft. The moons and shimmering nebulas of Qaf faded from the light of Ard's brilliant sun, like flying into the dawn. Soon the cold winds faded to nothing as brilliant heat that only Ard could provide warmed his bones.

Bakr was grateful that they did not have to pass through the nameless place. The last two times he'd used Fajar's feathers to teleport, Bakr had found himself stuck there, lingering until he gave himself a push to the other side. He hadn't felt frightened at all, which he realized now was a little ridiculous. Alone in that place without Shaytana, the Namelessness had felt strangely natural, if a little dull. Perhaps the reason he was getting stuck was that he had simply spent so much time there, or maybe there was something more to it. He didn't understand what it meant if it meant anything at all, and there were too many other things dashing through his brain to worry about it too much.

Brilliant crystal-blue waters and a gleaming sun hit his eyes, stinging and beautiful all at once. Tropical lands carpeted in vibrant green lay to the west, so Fajar immediately turned east and climbed higher into the sky so that nobody could see her. He had warned her—continued to warn her—what humans would do if they saw her. There were some that would watch her with awe, even fall down to worship her. Others would stop at nothing until she was dead. She needed to stay high up, out of range of even the most ingenious weapons, which humans never seemed to have any shortage of.

She knew where she was going, the location of the island as much an instinct as the ability to fly or hunt, so Bakr just watched the movement of the sun's rays on the impossibly blue waves.

Sezan marrying Ajmal was for the best, exactly what he would have expected. Perfect. Wonderful. He felt really good about it all. It was about time and had been a very long time coming. It just proved how wrong Sezan always was about everything, and how right he had been. He had always known how things would end, had always said so. She'd finally wised up and listened to him. Why should he blame her for that?

No. Everything was exactly as it should be. He would finish his mission, go to Qaf and deliver the stupid seal to Rahik, even though he still did not know what it was or what it did, and then he was going straight back to Ard. Forever. Qaf could burn for all he cared. He would build an isolated house in the middle of nowhere, perhaps on a deserted island. He would grow coconuts, and Fajar and Bubbles could fish for whales in the surrounding waters. It would be quiet and peaceful, and when he felt like having company, he could just pluck one of Fajar's feathers and go party in Istanbul, or Damascus, or Baghdad whenever he wanted. For as long as he wanted. And he could leave just as quickly, back to his isolated house where humans and djinn were not allowed. And he could sunbathe naked on his own personal beach, drink as much as he wanted with no one to lecture him, grow out his beard, and not give a wet pile of crap what anybody thought, or said, or did ever again.

He just wished Sezan could have told him the truth instead of trying to hide behind anger. She had pressed him to go with her to the hot springs so that she could say goodbye. One last romp with the vile, self-destructive mongrel before she moved on to more serious matters. But why couldn't she just have the guts to say it out loud? It was simple enough to articulate, wasn't it? Especially for someone so in love with words as she. *I don't love you anymore, so I'm going to marry this uptight prince who is much smarter and more mature than you, and together we'll have lots of vaguely purple babies and live a good long life.*

Would that have been so hard? He wouldn't have gotten angry. He wouldn't even have asked any follow-up questions. He certainly wouldn't have asked if the prince's kiss made her feel the same way his did. He wouldn't have asked if it felt the same when he drew her close or said her name. The last thing he would have done was fly off the handle, scream at her, break all her furniture, and swear on Allah, and Iblis, and the universe itself that he would die a thousand deaths before he allowed the ceremony to go on. That he would kill the prince, no matter how charming he was, before he let him touch her again.

He wouldn't have said any of that.

The floating island came into view on the horizon, at first just a dot and then growing in size and clarity. It was vaguely heart-shaped, a floating crater with high sides that protected the center from wind and everything else. Completely gray with whispers of scraggly trees and bushes, and grasses that curled their way to the stars instead of standing straight up. Most of it was hidden behind the high, natural cliff-faces. But water flowed through it in a quiet river, three small falls pouring off one edge and fading into clouds long before hitting the ocean below.

A ledge jutted out at one side, like a dock. Fajar could just perch on it, the rock crumbling a little under the grip of her massive talons. As he examined the shape of the rock, he realized it had been made especially for this purpose—for a bird just like her to land on it and let off her rider.

She extended her wing and Bakr slid down it onto a rocky ledge. It was so cold this high up and the air so thin, even more so than on the peak. The sun was still up, the sky a vibrant shade of blue, as puffy clouds sailed below like fog on the ocean.

He took a few deep breaths, then rolled his shoulders and squared himself towards the center of the island. Fajar whined and nudged him with her beak. He could tell she wanted to come along, but she hardly could have fit between the jagged cliffs that rose like curtains all along the sides of the island, save in one space where a path meandered through.

Bakr patted her beak. "I won't be long. Just stay here and keep a lookout."

Fajar cocked her head and narrowed her eyes, silently asking what exactly she was supposed to be looking out for.

He laughed and shook his head. "Fine, fine. Just stay here."

Bakr hurried down the path of large square stones until he came upon a staircase that led up towards a large building. It looked almost like a Christian church, as well as he remembered having seen one in the Kingdom of Jerusalem many years ago on a sojourn with Jahmil. All gray stone and high columns, double doors of that same stone and engraved with black swirls of Arabic script. A giant circular window of blue and white glass reposed over the door: a massive Nazar charm, protection against the Evil Eye.

Bakr didn't pray much but found himself murmuring the *Bismallah* as he mounted the long stairs.

He wondered if he was truly alone up here. If he said her name, would Shaytana be able to come to him here?

Bakr sucked his lower lip between his teeth. Fajar was special. He knew that. And this place was special, a place that only she could bring him to. Did that mean he would be safe from Shaytana up here?

"Shay—" he said, then stopped himself. What if he was wrong? The last thing he wanted was for her to pop into existence at his side. Bakr shook his head hard to force back his curiosity on the matter and kept walking.

When he reached the door, he tried the handle, expecting it to be locked, but it swung open with barely a groan. A breath of barren air rushed against his skin, cold and bereft of life. He staggered with the chill.

Bakr swallowed hard and stepped inside. The space was empty—a square chamber with no features save a single small platform in the middle, circular and uninteresting. Similar to the squat columns he'd seen in Istanbul and Edirne to display ancient Roman busts. He approached cautiously, the soft soles of his boots silent in the dust.

Lying at the center on a small pillow of dusty velvet was a rusted iron circle, like a large coin. On the front was a symbol of a six-pointed star with little scrawls of Arabic all around and throughout. It was about a quarter of his palm in size, small and ordinary, nothing worthy of all this nonsense. In fact, it was rather damaged, rusty, and unattractive.

It couldn't be this easy, could it?

Bakr looked over both his shoulders, checking to make sure he was alone. Then he gave a shrug and reached for the Seal.

"Are you sure you want to do that?" a voice said from behind. The most familiar voice.

Bakr turned and found himself staring into his own eyes. The man standing before him was a perfect duplicate of himself, though dressed differently in his Shihalan uniform of gray-green leather. The jacket which Cetus had destroyed. He had a clean shave and no circles under his pale green eyes that shined so prettily in the soft blue light. And on his hip was an exact copy of Bakr's crusader blade.

"Hey, handsome." Bakr gave a befuddled, little smile. "What are you doing here?"

The duplicate smiled back. "Didn't anyone ever teach you not to take things that aren't yours?"

"Nobody ever taught me anything."

"Not for lack of trying," said the copy, strolling casually around to the other side of the pedestal and looking Bakr in the eye. "*Khātam Sulaymān*, the most powerful hunk of iron in all of Allah's worlds."

Bakr yawned. "Is it now?"

"Bestowed by Allah himself to King Sulayman, the Wise. When this seal is used on a written command, it has the power to bind spirits, both good and evil. Humans, djinn, effrit, eimlaq. All the king had to do was put his will to paper and stamp it with the seal, and King Sulayman was able to enslave ten thousand djinn to build his great temple, to call angels to him so he could move from place to place without walking, even into the realm of Qaf. And he could command the angels and demons to teach him the secrets of eternity."

A shiver raced down Bakr's spine. Everything the copy was saying was so heavy and ominous it sounded like a pile of *alqarf*, yet here he was in a magic temple with a legendary bird. What had become of his life?

Bakr scoffed and shook his head. "You're joking."

One corner of the copy's mouth lifted into a charming smirk. "No, buddy. This is very serious. The Seal of Sulayman is the most dangerous and powerful artifact of magic in all of Allah's many worlds."

Bakr bit his bottom lip and looked at the rough iron circle again. "If it's so dangerous, you'd think they'd hide it better."

The copy laughed and shook his head. "The only way to reach it is by riding the Rukh from Qaf through to Ard, and up to a floating fortress. And only one man in ten generations is able to do such a thing because only one Rukh bird is born every thousand years, and she only ever chooses one rider. She is the only creature alive that knows how to find this island."

Bakr pushed his lips to one side and cocked his chin at the seal. "Well, that's me. So, that means it's mine to do with as I please." He reached for the seal, but the copy snatched his wrist in his strong, strangely comforting, grip.

"It belongs to no one. You must leave it where it lies."

Bakr flicked his gaze back to his own eyes. "I need it."

"If the seal is taken from this place, there will be dire consequences. Wars will be fought. Famine and pestilence will sweep the land. Entire races may be enslaved and forced to create weapons of such unfathomable destruction that you will long for death many years before it reaches you."

Bakr scoffed. "You're exaggerating."

"Only the wisest of kings was ever granted Allah's permission to wield such power," the copy replied. "In the hands of all others, it would be the undoing of both worlds."

Bakr looked back at the seal. He wished it would glow or something so he could believe what he was saying to himself about its powers. He didn't want anybody enslaved or forced to fight wars of unfathomable destruction any more than he wanted such power for himself. Still, his heart thrummed in his chest as his hands grew slimy with cold sweat.

"Is there another way to save her?" he said slowly, quietly. A normal person may not have heard him.

The copy shook his head warily. "I'm sorry. The life of one person is worth very little in the grand scheme of eternity."

"You can't expect me—"

"There is no such thing as innocence," he heard his own voice say. "Only the difference between sins of the past, present, and future."

"Then why should I worry about plague and death?" Again, he reached for the seal.

The copy snatched his wrist a second time. He was so fast, so coordinated. So handsome. "How can you judge anything except based on what it is right now?"

"That doesn't even make any sense," Bakr scoffed. "On one hand you judge a person based on who they are at any given moment, and on the other you say nobody can be innocent because someday they will do something bad, and so you judge them on that..." He swallowed hard, dry and heavy. "You're just making excuses to hate everybody."

The copy shrugged and put on a wide smile that looked more menacing than it did pleasant. "All people are untrustworthy, isn't that right?"

"Yes." Bakr's jaw twitched, the word hot on his tongue like a poker fresh from the fire. "I mean, most of them are."

"But they are all selfish."

He nodded, even as his bottom lip curled into a sneer. "If this seal thing can command the spirit of a djinn, I could use it to force Rahik to break the contract. Then I wouldn't have to give it to him. Nobody even needs to know I had it, and I could bring it right back."

The copy's face slumped in condescending incredulity. "You would trust yourself with that much power? Do you truly believe that with the ability to call angels and demons to do your bidding—to remake the world in your own image—you would just bring the seal back after undoing one contract?"

"Demons?" Bakr nibbled the inside of his cheek. "Does it work on demons?"

The doppelgänger shrugged. "Some of them."

Bakr's eyes darted from side to side, then he coughed out a laugh. "Why in the name of all that is holy would I want to remake the world in my image?"

"The Seal has the power to find anyone, living or dead. To bring them before you."

"What do I care? Who would I—?"

"Your father."

The copy's words echoed in the cavernous chamber and a chill of disgust ran over Bakr's skin. He tried to laugh it off, but the breath caught in his throat. His face was hot, and his neck was sweating.

"Are you trying to convince me to take it or not to take it?"

The copy smiled and glanced off to one side. "I'm trying to show you the tremendous temptation you are exposing yourself to. You have never been able to resist temptation, even the most benign. Such a powerful artifact in your hands will spell disaster for both worlds. You know that."

Bakr bit his tongue, turning his gaze back to the iron seal. "But there is no other way to save Sezan's life."

"What is one life? And the life of one who has already decided she will have nothing to do with you? Is she worth risking the fate of every living creature?"

Bakr stared at the seal, all the words they had both said racing through his head like a stampede. They were all good arguments, but none of them made the slightest bit of difference.

Yes. Sezan's life was worth risking the fate of every creature. Of every mountain and every ocean. Of the stars themselves. He would plunge all of Allah's worlds into Eternal Fire if it meant saving her.

One contract, that was all. He would fix Rahik and then bring the Seal right back.

Although, there were so many other things that he would change if he could. He could solve all the problems Jahmil was having with Qadira, secure the trade routes, and broker true and lasting peace all over Qaf. He could not only punish his father, but find his mother and tell her... Tell her everything he had ever wanted to say. And maybe he could even...

Bakr shook his head hard. One contract. One act and that was all. He would not allow himself to be tempted. After all, there was a life of abject solitude on a deserted island he had to get to.

"I'm sorry," he said, then he snatched up the ring.

The image of himself bared his teeth, a cruel snarl bubbling up from within. "I didn't want to have to do this to you, buddy," he said and drew the iron sword from his hip, confidently resting it on his thigh in a fool's guard.

The seal was tied on a heavy chain, so Bakr put it around his neck. It didn't feel like anything other than cold and a bit sharp from all the rust. "There's no point to this," he said, drawing his sword from the holster. He set the tip on the ground, resting the blade across his leg, imitating his copy perfectly. "I promise, I will bring it right back."

"You will take it nowhere," the doppelgänger growled. He was still wearing Bakr's face, but the voice had transformed into something deeper and more menacing, a dozen dark cries wrapped into one shrieking harmony.

Without warning, the duplicate brought up his sword and lunged.

CHAPTER TWENTY-SIX

Sezan

Several hours had passed since their return from Ashkult, and Sezan had not left her room. She missed a meeting with her tailors, dinner with Ajmal, and hadn't opened the door when Qadira came pounding. That, however, was not for lack of trying. She simply could do nothing but clap a hand to her mouth the second she neared the door and run back to the ceramic bowl in her washroom to throw up the little bile she had left to give. Eventually, she had stopped trying to leave—a slave to the will of yet another entity—and lay her cheek on the mercifully cool tile.

The door to her main chambers opened, and footsteps rushed into the room. "Sezan?" Lila called.

"In here," Sezan said, slapping her hand once more over her mouth as her stomach objected to the disturbance.

Lila's tan sandals appeared over the cool white marble in Sezan's limited view of the floor. She bent down and pressed a hand to Sezan's cheeks. "What happened? Are you sick? You're not running a fever, but you're ghostly pale. Did you catch a bug? Will you be well enough for your wedding? Your wedding! Ajmal's been looking for you, he needs to know."

"Lila," Sezan said, reaching for her friend's hand and pressing it once more to her cheek. "Stay with me."

Lila collapsed next to her, her soft yellow skirts embroidered with salmon-colored flowers and forest green leaves folded around them both. "What is the matter, *eazeziun*? You have not been yourself these last few days."

"I just spent myself too much at Ashkult," she said as much to reassure herself as Lila. "The magicless walls there suppress your very fire and make it hard to breathe. And then I lost my temper with Jahmil and—"

"You did what?" Lila gasped. "Are we done for, now? Will we have to move back to Elm?"

"No, Lila, no. I am still the ambassador."

Lila bent down to see her eyes, eyebrows dipping in the middle and wrinkles forming in between. "How could you be so foolish? You've spent your whole life collecting your emotions before they spill from your mouth so you could create fortune, not disaster."

"I know," Sezan said, no energy to snap as she had wished. "I've just been so angry lately. Angry at Qadira—at being forced into a relationship that might have formed on its own without the pressure—at that snot, Jahmil Amir..."

"And with Bakr?"

"Why does everyone keep asking me about Bakr?" She pushed herself up and immediately regretted it. Little fuzzy dots of color formed on the edges of her vision, and her view of the room swung side to side like a pendulum.

"Because it hasn't been the last few days you've been acting off, my dear. It has been the last few weeks. Ever since he returned from war with a scar so big everyone knows he should have died."

Sezan laid her head back down and closed her eyes as warm tears filled the corners and slid over the bridge of her nose to collect on the floor. "He hurts me so, Lila. I ache." Her shoulders shook with weakness and misery, and the formerly comforting cool of the floor became a wretched chill. "I asked him to let me be with him. Twice I asked him. And twice he ran away. So why can't I stop wishing he were here?"

Lila brushed a hand over her back. She pulled back Sezan's hijab and collected her hair from off her neck, draping it over the side. "You are *taw'um alruwh*. Soulmates. You hunger for each other. It is small comfort to know he hurts for you just as much as you do for him."

"How can we be soulmates when we do nothing but fight?"

"The same way two people could fit together perfectly and be extremely happy in each others' presence but still hunger for someone else."

She meant Ajmal. A fresh wave of guilt twisted Sezan's stomach, and she spit up more bile, her stomach seizing in knots as it rebelled against the gnawing nothings left inside her. "How can my fire hunger for a man who barely has his own?"

Lila chided her softly with the gentle sound of rustling leaves. "You and Bakr are more than simple *taw'um nar, eazeziun*. Fire mates flame and die out. You two have been at it since the beginning. It is your souls who decide, not the magic within you. And if he had djinn eyes, they would burn more than the red of lust for you. They'd burn blue with hope to see you again. Green with envy when any other man neared you. Copper whenever he swung you into his arms for a kiss. And black when you are hurt, because the only times I've ever seen his eyes full of fear have been for you."

Sezan took comfort in Lila's gentle words and soothing touch, knowing her eyes, too, would be shining blue, hoping they were true. She sniffed, then said, "I am ruined, Lila. You must find a new lady to serve before everyone finds out."

Lila's hand paused on her lower back, then continued in soft circles. "Nonsense. My family has served your mother's for three generations. And we do not do so for station."

"You cannot serve an ignominious peasant, Lila."

"I may serve whomever I wish." She stopped her stroking and laid a hand once more on Sezan's cheek. "This hopelessness isn't like you. Tell me what's wrong, and we shall fix it together."

"I made a deal with a lilith," Sezan said, relieved the words came so easily. She was expelling her emotional bile now, desperate to be rid of it.

"Sezan!" Lila slapped her forehead with two fingers. She deserved far worse. "What did you promise?"

"My fire and its magic on my twenty-fifth birthday. All but the flicker that will keep me alive."

Lila inhaled sharply. "That was very foolish of you."

Sezan sighed and closed her eyes tightly to fight back a wave of nausea. "Are you going to ask what I traded it for?"

Lila went silent. Sezan opened her eyes and turned to see her face. Her coppery eyes were soft, creased around the edges, and glimmering with purple. Sorrow. Pity.

"You know," Sezan said, casting her eyes away.

"Who else would you give so much for?"

"You." Sezan sighed and reached her hand out for the only friend she had in the world.

"Oh pish," Lila said, but she squeezed Sezan's fingers in return. "We can navigate life without magic as long as your spark of life remains. We will avoid certain events, certain people. And beg for mercy if we are found out. And if that doesn't work, we can leave Shihala and the City of Pearls and head to Al Madinat. There, anyone can live and make something of themselves, magic fire or no. But Ajmal is tender for you. If you produce him an heir quickly…"

"He is infertile," Sezan said simply.

Lila squeezed tighter.

"And I am pregnant."

Lila crushed her fingers so hard, Sezan yelped in pain. "Your sickness. It's the merging of two fires… so early, even for most djinn. That means it grows strong inside you."

"Its fire already warms me."

Lila let go of her hands and placed them on her hips. "You must tell him."

"I know," Sezan said, pressing her fingers into the cool marble for relief. "I will tell Ajmal my shame as soon as I can stand."

"Not him," Lila said quickly. "Bakr."

Sezan shot up, and the room spun around her. She shut her eyes to find stability, then focused on Lila. "I cannot."

"You must."

"He will be furious."

"He may be at first, but I think he'd be a fantastic father. You've seen him with his drakonte and the children of the court. And you said Al'amirat Ayelet adored how great he was with Sheikha Serap. And we've all heard how much he dotes on his bird. He is gentle and attentive."

"He will never leave me." Sezan's eyes widened painfully at the realization. "He will finally stay forever, and I shall bask every day in his gut-wrenching smile and light jade eyes knowing he stayed only for the child and not for me."

Lila allowed her a moment of silence. "You must tell him."

Sezan cringed. "And how shall I find him? He could be anywhere between the worlds."

Lila raised one brow and looked away. "Just as Shihala's bloodline and that of each of the heirs of the Nine Kingdoms, Ahmar's royal bloodline carries a special gift of Elm. Theirs? The power to teleport to a person instead of a place."

Was Ajmal's gift what the lilith had been talking about? Sezan's shaking increased, grinding her joints together. "You can't honestly expect me to ask that of Ajmal?" She could taste the terror on her tongue, metallic and burning like she had swallowed a coin.

The door knocked, startling both women to sit up. "Sezan?" came Ajmal's concerned voice.

"You must," Lila said with a resolute pat on her head. Sezan watched in horror as she stood to answer the door.

"But what if the lilith taking my fire takes the baby's?" Sezan whispered frantically as yet another realization dawned on her.

Lila said nothing, the admonishment in her eyes quite enough to silence Sezan. She swung the door wide. "Amir." Lila bowed respectfully, then hurried from the room.

Ajmal rushed to her side, his hands touching her head and neck and back and face as he searched for a cause of Sezan's affliction. "My love, I've been so worried."

"Ajmal," she pulled back, undeserving of his ardency. "It is time to tell you all my truths."

Ajmal stood stock still as Sezan explained her evils with the lilith, her past with Bakr that caused Ajmal's eyes to flicker green, and ended with the child growing inside her. She had even let slip Bakr's Rukh bird and the true reason she had gone to Ashkult. And when she was done, she lay her forehead on her hands at his feet.

"If you hate me, I understand," she said, her voice pleading. "If you want to send me from the court or shame me, I will submit. I like you Ajmal, and I want your happiness. But I came here already broken, already doomed, and even though I'm worse than the dust of Ard, I still must ask you a favor."

His shoulders stiffened. She glanced up, and his blue eyes pulled away from the wall behind her and slid to look at her.

"I need you to take me to... Bakr." She could barely say his name through her clenched throat. "I don't know where he is. I beg of you the use of your gift of Elm given to you by the royal line of Ahmar. I need to tell him and... and afterward, you can leave me on Ard if you wish as my punishment. I promise I will stay, and then in a week's time, I will not be able to return to Qaf ever again."

Ajmal did not fly into a rage. His eyes did not flood the room with icy light. He didn't even get a halo of fire around his fist. He was as calm and steady as always.

"You're sure you're pregnant?" he asked, at last.

She called fire into her palm, and the orangey glow erupted between them. "My fire burns pink. A new life, a new magic weeps into mine and changes its hue."

He frowned, the deepest one she had seen upon him yet. Then it vanished. "We will marry and raise the child."

"What?" She nearly collapsed from exhaustion and sickness at his ludicrous words.

"You and I will marry for the sake of our countries and raise the child as our own."

"But you are unable to have children."

"Something only you, Qadira, and the royal physician know."

"There's a good chance its skin color..." she tripped over her tongue.

"If the baby does not come out with any shade of your brilliant turquoise, sorcerers can change the hue of its skin, but I doubt it will be an issue. Crystal eyes and gem-toned skin are dominant traits when mixed with lesser blood. And the father is half-djinn already. The child shall be only a quarter short."

She flinched at his qualification, so crassly said. "But you said you wouldn't allow yourself to be forced to marry a woman over a contract." She backed away, head shaking despite the headache it brought to her temples. "I can't imagine there's any other reason you'd want to marry me now."

"I would not be bound by contract alone. Despite your transgressions, Sezan, you said you would forgive me any dalliances before our wedding night, and I said I would expect only from my wife as I would of myself. It would only be proper for me to extend that courtesy to you and forgive any stray beddings before our wedding day. Besides, I..." He paused, voice softening. "I've always wanted to be a father. As long as Bakr isn't around, we shall proceed and make a good life of it."

"Bakr will not leave his child," she whispered, not sure why she was fighting so hard against Ajmal's gracious offer. He would still marry her knowing she would have no magic and someone else's child. He was offering her salvation. So why didn't she shut up, throw her arms around him, and accept?

"Is he so selfish that he would deny the child a loving mother and father and a home in the court of Ahmar where all his needs will be met?"

She opened her mouth and left it that way. She was almost certain he would be. He still carried the gaping hole his horrible father and cruel mother had gouged out of him as a child. He would never leave his own, not for all the armies in Qaf. Even if it was what was best for it.

But was it?

"I will take you to him." Ajmal held out his hand, the bone-covered onyx ring shining in the light between them. "So you may end things once and for all and focus on what truly matters. Our family. But this will be the last time you shall think of that man. My heart simply cannot take it," he said with sorrowful eyes. Then they sharpened. "Understood?"

"You want to go now?" she asked, streaks of cold shooting down her shoulders.

"Immediately, yes. Go get changed. We have just enough time to inform Bakr he is not welcome back in Ahmar and get back here to sign the contract before tomorrow's nuptials." He walked to her armoire and pulled out a pink tunic with sparkling harem pants. "Don't forget your ambassador's seal. We shall not be stopping back in your room before the official signing, and you'll need Shihala's authority to finalize the marriage contract."

She bit her lip and nodded, walking to her bathroom to change in a daze and sliding out the box with her unused seal. Ajmal's hand lingered mid-air, waiting for her to grab hold. She did.

"You don't have to do this," she said, more for her own sake than his. She was not ready to face Bakr again. She probably never would be.

"And miss out on a chance to visit Eayima?"

Her eyes darted to his. "What are you talking about?"

"Bakr controls the Rukh, does he not?"

"Yes..." she said slowly, eyes tight. "Though he claims he does not know where it is."

"I can fix that easily enough, can I not? Pop in and have him take us to your salvation."

"I do not think he would oblige," she said bitterly. "He's very protective of his bird."

"Fair point, but what did the lilith offer as an alternative solution to your problems? Me." He lifted his arms out to the side, palms up. "You don't need Bakr to share the location of his bird. You simply need him to be with it and you to be with me. I will take you to him and the Rukh."

"And if he is not with it?" Sezan asked, shaking her head. "He left it alone to keep it safe. And even if we find it, what if the creature won't let us ride it? Legend says it only allows the one it truly loves."

"To be honest... we may not need to ride it." A smile twitched on Ajmal's lips. "We may not need the Rukh at all."

She narrowed her eyes. "Whatever do you mean?"

"My belief," Ajmal said, leaning in, "is that the lilith wants you to find the Seal and be foolish enough to leave the barren island with the powerful talisman so she can snatch it from your fingers and use it as she likes. If she tortures Bakr as you mentioned—"

Sezan flinched.

"—Then she would know where he is and be trying to manipulate him as well. I think he's gone to get the Seal for her and that by using me, we will arrive not just with Bakr, but on Eayima itself." His eyes glittered with the last word, a childish eagerness on his face. "What do you think? Will you go on this grand adventure with me, my love?"

She twitched at the last two words, not because he said them with spite or mockery, but because they sounded the same as they always had, as if nothing at all had changed between them or how he felt.

She squeezed his hand tighter. It seemed to her that apparating to a person instead of a place would be fraught with peril. If Bakr rode his Rukh bird, Fajar, at the time they apparated, would they burn to death as they materialized on its back? Or what if he was not in Eayima—something she doubted, indeed—but in the middle of his favorite pastime? She was fairly certain, merging fire sickness or not, that she would not have the wherewithal to keep from stabbing whoever he slept with. Still, the royal Ahmaran line continued through no help of their own. Apperating to a person not a place couldn't be that dangerous. Either way, Lila was right. She had to tell him... something. To get closure, or not. To force him to be her family, or not. She didn't know. But trying to talk to him was the first step.

So, she did as Ajmal asked and thought of Bakr. Of his tenderness with Bubbles. His laughter. The genuine mirth he carried in his eyes and the smile that melted her every time she saw it. Of the night they spent swimming under the stars. Of their day in Ard. And once again of how he would stay for the sake of the baby and resent her for it the rest of his life.

The fires of Qaf took them, and in a whirl of churning colors that twisted her stomach and made her wretch, they alighted inside an ancient palace fabricated in the style of Rome. Vast columns lined the walls, and at the front of the cavernous room, two men fought fiercely with giant iron swords.

"Bakr?" she said, wishing to rush to him, but Ajmal tightened his grasp on her wrist. He took a step back, pulling her with him until she saw what had made his lavender face go white. There were not one, but two of the man she had come to see. "Bakr..."

CHAPTER TWENTY-SEVEN

Bakr

The doppelgänger did not just look like him—those perfect cheekbones, irresistible eyes, and the physique of a demigod—he moved like him, too. He anticipated every strike and parried every blow. The advantage was, he couldn't get a strike in on him either. It was a stalemate and no matter how he tried, Bakr couldn't break it. Their fight ranged all around the temple. Thrust, parry, riposte. Repeat. The best duel he'd ever had.

But as time went on, Bakr came to a horrible realization. He was not evenly matched with his bizarre, impromptu copy. Because as his muscles began to weary, the duel continuing well past ten degrees, the copy was as fresh as when it first began.

If he couldn't find a way to out think himself, he was going to lose, run through with his own blade. By his own smiling, idiotic face. Not that he couldn't appreciate the irony.

He had what he had come for, he reminded himself. He didn't have to win this fight. All he really needed was to get away, get back to Fajar. There was no copy of her, at least not as far as he knew. If he could get to her, she could get him out, and the magic of this place would not be able to follow. He hoped.

But every time he rushed for the door, he would block himself. He was impossible.

Bakr's brain poured over increasingly insane ideas, trying to come up with something he would never do in a fight to throw the thing off. But the copy was doing the same.

A burst of pale blue light filled one corner. Bakr glanced towards it but couldn't focus before the opportunistic son of a snake tried to use it to cut his belly open. Bakr caught the blow and kicked him back, but the copy saw it coming and barely stumbled. They came back in and their blades met, circling. He laughed. He laughed.

Oh, it was irritating.

Bakr caught him in a hard parry and managed to push him off, giving himself a chance for riposte, but he used his free second to glance at where the flash of blue had been. When he saw Sezan standing there staring at him—and him—her mouth slightly open, and her stinking fiancé with his stinking hands on her, Bakr momentarily forgot that he was in a duel. The copy didn't and got in his first good strike, dragging the iron sword down Bakr's thigh, splitting open his pants and his flesh.

Bakr hissed in pain and stumbled. The copy tried to capitalize, but Bakr swung his blade up, knocking him off balance. He kicked him back with what was now his bad leg.

"Sezan!" cried the copy. "What are you doing here?"

"Shut up!" Bakr swung at his legs. "You son of a snake!"

"Don't talk about my mother that way!"

Bakr spat out a cruel laugh. "She's not *your* mother!"

"Sezan!" The copy rolled to one side. "You should not have come here!"

"I said shut up!" Bakr lunged at him, smacking him in the gut with the top of his head and knocking him to his back.

He stabbed at him, trying to impale him like a piece of garbage. Quick as a six-tailed *tset aldhayle* and twice as nimble, the copy leaped to his feet and darted away.

"Hold still and let me kill you!" cried Bakr, chasing after him.

"Bakr," Sezan snipped from across the room in that tone that meant he was going to get it. "Stop it."

"You must go, Sezan," said the copy, pausing to look at her. "It is too dangerous for you here."

"Did I say you could talk to her?" snarled Bakr, coming in with a rush of wild swings. At last, he got in his first hit, the blade cutting open the copy's forearm so blood spit out.

The copy turned and rushed away a few paces, then once again called out to Sezan. "Help me! Cast your fire at him!"

Sezan looked between her hands and the two of them, her brows deeply creased and her lips slanted with uncertainty. Then an ice-blue blast burst in the air between him and the copy, pushing them farther apart.

Bakr drew back, his gaze turning to the intervening princeling. He snarled, his grip tightening on the pommel of his sword.

"Good," said the copy, rolling his shoulders. "Now, finish him."

A bright blue ball began to form above their heads, splinters of lightning flashing from the edges as it grew bigger and bigger.

"Ajmal," Sezan cried, tugging at the princeling's outstretched arms. "Stop!"

"This is ridiculous," Bakr grunted, then leveled his sword like a pike and hurled it across the room at the copy. The idiot doppelgänger was gawping at the stupid blue ball and didn't see it coming. It cut into his chest, spearing him to the wall. Blood formed on his lips as his eyes swept the room. Then he fell limp.

"Bakr!" Sezan cried and ran halfway to the copy's lifeless body. A shock of blue blocked her path, and she turned, running for him instead. Again, another flash of blue corralled her back. Distress streaked her face, her hair falling free from her hijab in loose curls around her face.

"What in Jahannam do you think you're doing?" Bakr snarled at Ajmal.

"Protecting my future wife from your dangerous nonsense."

"You're frightening her, you idiot." He walked across the room and yanked his sword from the copy's chest. When the other Bakr hit the ground, it shattered into pieces like a broken statue. The ball of blue flashed once more, then fizzled out.

Relief flashed honey in Sezan's eyes, and she fell to her knees and began to retch.

Seeing her like that sent a shock of fear through Bakr's blood that quickly congealed into rage. "If you're trying to protect her, what are you doing *here*?"

Ajmal walked over to her, placing a protective hand on her shoulder. "I am here to support her. Something you have consistently failed at. Now, where's the Seal of Sulayman?"

"Up my ass." Bakr hurried closer to Sezan and knelt at her side. She was pale as an Orkeshi, her hands trembling. He'd never seen her look so un-put-together. His hand itched to reach for her. Instead, he gripped his sword tighter. "Are you okay?"

She nodded feebly, wiping her lips with the back of her hand.

"She'll be fine as soon as you get your stink away from her," Ajmal said. "As you can see, she's in a delicate state, and arriving on this scene of sorcery has done nothing to help that."

"I'm gonna need you to shut up."

"Threaten me again, half-breed," Ajmal flashed blue from his fists.

Bakr swept up and in one quick move, grabbed Ajmal by his collar and put his iron sword to his throat. "You think I'm scared of djinn fire, *habibi*?" He touched the blade to Ajmal's skin so it hissed, just enough that it would leave a scar. Black fear and the yellow of disdain pooled in the prince's eyes but he did not look away. "You got something to say?"

"Bakr," Sezan said before retching once more, clear spit tinted with bile that came up in a pathetic little dribble. "Please."

He looked down at her, then back at Ajmal. He pushed the prince away hard so he stumbled and fell on his backside, then quickened to Sezan's side. "What is happening? What is wrong with you?" He touched her shoulder, his gaze searching her face for any clues. "What do you need?"

Her eyes softened as she looked upon him, then slid heavily to the floor. "Who was that? Or *what* was that thing you were fighting?"

He chuckled a little, pushing her hair back behind her shoulders. He wrapped her hijab around it gently to keep it out of her face. "I have no idea."

"Sezan," Ajmal said as he got to his feet. "Tell the mongrel what you came to say and let's go. Our wedding is less than a day away and you clearly need your rest."

She winced.

Bakr took a cloth from his pocket and wiped a bit of spittle from her chin. "I've changed my mind. I don't find him charming at all."

"He's just worried, Bakr," she said half-heartedly, still not meeting his eyes. "I have not been so kind to him."

"That's not what I've heard."

Her eyes darted to his, wide and round and caught off-guard. "What does that mean?"

He forced himself to shrug, but he was holding his sword so tight his skin felt like it would blister. "I mean, you're marrying him."

Her brows sank, and she hid her eyes beneath her lashes. "He has stayed with me," she whispered, "even when I did not deserve it."

"Sezan," Ajmal clipped. He strode to where she sat and thrust a hand out for her to grab. "Stand up. You're stronger than this, and you have nothing to fear. Shall I tell Bakr for you?"

"Don't make me bite you." Bakr clenched his teeth and looked up at Ajmal. "Don't you have enough faith in your fiancée to let her have a conversation? Or are you one of those men who thinks women should be seen and not heard?"

Ajmal raised his hand but curled it closed before swinging it back. "I'm certain in the few days I've known Sezan we have exchanged more words than in all the years you've known her combined."

Bakr wanted to bite back, but that assertion was so absurd it didn't deserve acknowledgment. He turned his gaze to Sezan. "Real fishwife you've got here."

Instead of letting fly her usual sassy remark, she simply nodded and laid her cheek on the stone floor.

His heart cracked looking at her. He leaned down close and set his hand on the back of her hair. "What is wrong with you? Are you sick? What are you doing here?"

"Obviously she's sick," Ajmal snapped. "The better question is, what are *you* doing here? And where is the Seal?"

"Up my ass, I told you." He leaned down close to Sezan so his cheek was on the floor beside hers. "What are you doing here?" he whispered.

"I came to see you," she said and smiled weakly. "And because Lila told me I had to."

He took the skin from his belt and uncorked it, then offered it to her. "It's just water," he said, knowing what she might ask.

Another shadow of a smile. She sat up and took the flask, drinking a few swallows. "Thank you," she said, her eyes amber and clear.

He laid his hand on her back to steady her, worried she might swoon again. "Why would Lila send you to see me? Do I owe her money?" he joked, desperate to see her expression look anything other than pained.

She slid a hand over her mouth and closed her eyes. "Her opinion of you has recently changed."

Ajmal pushed Bakr's hand off her back with his foot.

Bakr's instinct was to swing his sword up and impale the prince, stick him to the wall exactly as he had done his doppelgänger. And why not? The mincing little courtier obviously had a death wish.

But he was Sezan's fiancé. The man she chose. The man she deserved.

Bakr bit his cheek as hard as he ever had. "Zan, I am going to kill your fiancé if he touches me again. And I'm sorry if that sends Shihala and Ahmar to war. I really don't care."

"You don't care about anything," Ajmal muttered, but he turned his head coldly and stared at the opposite wall. "It is time to finish things up, Sezan. I have been patient and fair with you, and the time to sign our marriage contract is fast approaching."

"I'm sorry, Ajmal," she said quietly. "You have, that's true. I just need a little more space to talk to Bakr. You know what I have to say is not easy. And then I'll come with you, and we can go get married."

Her words wrapped around Bakr's heart like frozen iron wires. He bit his cheek so hard that he tasted blood and forced himself to stare at the floor.

Ajmal's shoulders tensed, then released. "As you wish." He walked out of the temple doors. Bakr had an instinct to bark at him like a wild dog, but he bit that back, too.

The man she chose. The man she deserved. The man she was going to marry.

"Are you okay, Bakr?" Sezan asked, touching a finger to his cheek now that they were alone. It burned his skin like hot oil.

He looked up at her and tried so hard to smile, but it just wouldn't come. So many things were tumbling through his brain, things he had needed to say weeks ago. Years ago. It was all too late, now.

"Bakr?" she tilted her head down so all he could see were her sunny eyes. Then she shuddered and looked away as her hand slipped once more to cover her mouth.

"I'm sorry," he said quickly, though he tried to hold it in. It fell out of his mouth like the muscles in his lips had reached a point of exhaustion, yanking his breath out with it. He let go of his sword, pushing it far enough away so Sezan might not accidentally touch it.

Her trembling stopped after she took another sip of water. "For what?" she asked, her eyes trailing the scar on his brow, the one on his cheek, and down his neck. He really was a broken doll, stitched together with magic and misery.

"Just for..." Bakr swallowed hard. "You know... Everything. Just all of it."

Her eyes flicked up to his, round and whole. "Now I'm certain you are sicker than I."

Laughing, he ran his fingernails back and forth over his forehead, searching for a little bite of new pain. "I'm sure I am."

"Thank you." She touched his other hand with fingers chilly from the floor, spinning the copper ring that Shaytana had given him before pulling back from the light sting of the metal on her skin.

He looked up and met her eyes. He felt like his chest was folding in on itself, his ribs collapsing, piercing his heart and his lungs. His mouth was dry. He wrapped her chilled fingers in his sweaty hand. His lips twitched for something to say.

Her face went pale once more, and she lay her head against his chest, breathing deeply. "I'm sorry, too, you know. Especially for the hot springs. I didn't want to leave. I didn't want to be mad."

He wrapped her in his arms, frightened to squeeze her tight but desperate to have her closer. He pet her hair with one hand. "You know you're on the list," he said.

She wrapped her fingers into his shirt. "I don't know how I could be. I don't understand why you run when I ask to be with you. Why you always run without saying goodbye. Why you ran the night I almost died just hours after you promised to be with me."

He swallowed the hot, hard lump of burning coal in his throat. "Because I break everything. I'm not a good person. And I don't want you to think I'm weak. That I need full-bloods to do things for me."

"Why is magic so important to you?" Sezan asked, pulling away and looking at him. "I never bring it up. It is always you."

"I don't care about magic. I've just had to live in stupid Qaf. Why do you think I want to go back to Ard so badly?" He heaved a sigh. "I just want to *be* and stop worrying about all the... everybody calling me a damn mongrel."

"You're not planning to stay in Qaf?" she asked, her voice low and her brows knit in dainty ripples.

He shrugged, his gaze falling to the floor. "Does it matter? I can't imagine prince prissy pants is going to let you see me once you get married." He looked up and narrowed his eyes at her. "Why are you marrying him?"

Some of the softness shining in her eyes vanished. "I already answered that. Because he's always there for me no matter what I say. Because it will save Shihala, and because it's what I deserve." She tried to stand and wobbled before straightening. "I deserve everything I'm about to get. Did you find the Seal?"

Every word she spoke was like a thorn growing into his heart. The prince was what she wanted. He wasn't good enough for her. He had never been and never could be. He already knew that, but she'd never said it outright before. Or maybe she had said it and he'd just never heard it.

And even now she hadn't come to see him. She'd come for the seal. Did that mean his instinct about her at the hot springs had been right? Was she really in bed with Rahik?

But, no. That didn't make any sense. She wanted the Seal for herself for some reason—some noble, diplomatic, *the-angels-only-knew-what* reason.

"That's why you came here." He rose to her side, steadying her with a hand on her forearm. "For the Seal."

"Well, no... I came to see you, to tell you something, not knowing where you'd be. I need to tell you that..." She stopped and shook her head. "But you don't plan to stay in Qaf, so it doesn't matter now. And in that case, I guess I came to say goodbye."

"I won't say goodbye to you." He understood the full truth of the words even as he said them. If he'd had fire, his eyes would have been twisting like a kaleidoscope. "I know he's better for you. He's the prince you've been hoping for since long before I even met you. So, I won't... I mean, I shouldn't..."

He pulled away from her suddenly and punched himself in the forehead.

"Ah." Sezan's face crumpled. Deep purple clouded her bright eyes. "Please, please don't do this to me again, Bakr." She pressed her hand to her eyes. "Please... please."

He corrected his jaw, trying to keep himself silent. His blood boiled and viscous steam pushed the words from his throat. "Don't marry him."

"And do what, instead? Watch you come and go in my life until I'm banished and you abandon me altogether?"

"What do you think of me?" He snarled, but then the rest of her words came to nest in his stomach, and he slowly narrowed his gaze. "Banished? Who threatened to banish you? Was it Jahmil? I'll break his legs."

She smiled, though it did not reach her heartbreaking eyes. "Only I am at fault for my future. The time has passed for it to be any of your concern."

"You've been talking so strangely lately. But you refuse to tell me why. Maybe I could help. Or is it so shameful asking for my help?"

"I should ask you the same thing. I know there's a deal between you and my uncle, and that a darkness lives in your eyes since you returned from the war, but you won't tell me any more than I've told you."

His shoulders slumped. "I don't remember being asked either of those questions."

"That's because when I ask you questions, you jump off balconies and cliffs and the backs of drakonte."

He laughed and shook his head. That was fair enough, even if it stung. Then he looked down at her, so fragile, trembling, and everything in him sunk. She wouldn't even tell him what was wrong, so little did she trust him. Still, he could not help himself from taking her hand. He had to ask. He would never forgive himself if he didn't.

"Jump with me," he said.

She pulled her hand from his, sending a ten-thousand pound weight crashing into what little hope he'd had left. "You've thrice refused to be with me already. Who says you won't change your mind ten minutes from now? I couldn't bear you leaving me again, not when I need someone to stand by me more than ever." She looked away and dropped her hand to her stomach. "My life is a mess. A disaster. I'm going to lose everything, Bakr." She stared at him, the pink of her fire shining in the back as it so rarely did. Then she turned her head away and folded her arms across her chest. "So go, before it hurts too much."

He chewed on his bottom lip. She wanted some truth, that was what she had said. If he was going to convince her—and he could never forgive himself if he didn't try—he had to give her something. Something real and honest and raw. He couldn't tell her about the deal with Rahik. It would only frighten her. But perhaps there was one thing he could confess, one truth he'd never told anyone, that could finally convince her, and himself, that he was capable of opening up.

It was his last hope.

"You never asked me how I survived Karzusan." He cast his gaze to the dull, gray cobbles underfoot and ran a finger absently over the scar on his throat. "Everybody in Shihala has asked me, but you never did."

"You've never been one to gloat about war."

"This is not about war," he said, turning his gaze to her once more. "It's about darkness."

She glanced at him through the sides of her lashes. "The darkness in your eyes is because of how you survived Karzusan?"

"Not all of it. But whatever it is that you can see that wasn't there before. I don't know what exactly, because you are the only person who can see anything in these *dead eyes* of mine. But it is because of Karzusan, or everything that happened afterward. Everything that is still happening."

Sezan clenched her fist around her tunic so hard her knuckles whitened. "Well, I'm so—" She bit back whatever sarcasm-laced retort she had been about to say. "*Still* happening? What does that mean?"

"I've never told anybody. Not really. It's... hard to explain..." He sucked in a long breath, his tongue threatening to seize up.

Don't think, he told himself. Just take the plunge.

"I have a demon," he said. "Or she has me. I'm not sure." He looked up and forced himself to look into her eyes. "Her name is Shaytana."

Bakr flinched as he said her name, knowing how angry she would be if she found out he'd spoken it to another living soul. But something told him she couldn't follow him here. After all, his doppelgänger had said the power of the Seal of Sulayman had the power to control all of Allah's other creatures. Which meant if they'd had the ability to pop onto the island whenever they wanted, the whole business with the Rukh bird would have been moot.

He waited, holding his breath. Nothing happened.

Sezan's eyes widened as quickly as they narrowed. "You owe her nothing, do you hear me?"

"She saved my life. She scraped me off the battlefield and healed me, then she took me to her nightmares. And her dreams. And she did…" He pressed his face into his hands. He'd never even told Jahmil any of the details of what Shaytana had done to him, just that a lilith had rescued his life. Even that had been hard to force from his throat. He dug his fingernails into his palm. He had to say it.

"I can't even tell you everything she has done to me. What she still… What I did, not knowing." He sighed and wiped the water from his eyes with his thumb knuckles, trying to hide it from her behind his palm.

"Do you wish you had died that day? Back in Karzusan?" Sezan asked so softly he barely heard.

"I did for a long time. I was sure I was going to. I was ready for it. It even felt good, in a way. Like my nasty life was finally at its end before I had a chance to really mess it up, and I could even die with some glory, some purpose. Something somebody might even be proud of. Maybe I've been trying to die since then. My brain isn't the same as it used to be. She's always there, right on the edge of everything. She takes everything from me, and gives sometimes, but always for a price…"

Sezan bared her teeth and turned toward him. A wave of white washed her face and she spat out whatever had come up her throat. "Stop." Her fists clenched, shaking. "Stop talking about her. Don't even—I can't even believe her. And you. And myself." Pink fire with flecks of orange bloomed around her fists.

"I'm trying to tell you the truth about something. Like you asked." He looked at the ground and shook his head, determined not to fall back on silence. "She terrifies me. And you know, I'm not scared of much. But she… she's powerful. And she knows everything. She knows everything. She can read my mind."

"Stop! For Allah's sake, stop. I can't hear about what I did to you anymore. I can't." She turned her swimming eyes away from him, took a shaky stand, and rushed toward the doors of the temple.

"Sezan! Wait!" He took a few long strides after her. "Why are you running away again?"

But she was gone. He turned his back on her and fell to his knees on the cold floor. Shaytana was going to cut him to ribbons for everything he'd said, and Sezan just ran off on him anyway. Why did he always let himself get taken in? She was hours from marrying another man, and that's when he decides to bear his pitiful soul, thinking that would make any difference?

How stupid could he possibly be?

And how had she somehow managed to twist everything he had said into being her own fault? It had nothing to do with her. She was just feeling guilty. Guilty because he still couldn't let it go. Let *her* go. But he still couldn't find the grip to fully hold on.

Don't marry him, he had said. And she had taken that to mean he wanted her to be a spinster, just available for whenever he felt like going to see her until he got bored and she somehow, inexplicably, got banished from Shihala.

Ayelet had been so very wrong when she said nobody in the court of Shihala thought less of him than he did. Sezan thought less. A lot less. And nothing he said made any difference.

Do you wish you had died at Karzusan, she had asked.

He did now.

CHAPTER TWENTY-EIGHT

Sezan

Sezan ran through the doors as Bakr called out behind her. Lila had been wrong. So wrong about all this. How could she tell him anything when he was all questions and heart-wrenching stories about how she had destroyed him?

Shaytana, she thought, the name venom in her mind, in her blood, and on her tongue. Sezan stumbled her way to the edge of the cloud and followed the edges, aimless and hurting. She found a jut of rock and climbed upon it, staring at the feathery white sky too high for bird or beast.

"Shaytana!" she yelled into the abyss just to get the name of the monster out of her lungs. The wind whipped and whirled around her, and the whisper of a thunderstorm darkened and cracked the sky far in the distance. She pressed a hand to her stomach as another wave of nausea hit her like a splash of cold water.

Why did Bakr have to look at her with those eyes? Those eyes that broke down all that she was and looked at the ugliness that was left and said kind things. She had come to tell him one thing. To tell him he would be the amazing, loving father of her child and that she wanted him to save her from her marriage. Hoping and hating how he would jump at the chance and how she would finally get to keep him. But it would be a lie. A mirage of love she would cocoon herself in until one day the child would grow up, and he would peel back her armor so she could watch as he left again.

Jump with me, he said. But he had never wanted to jump with her before. And even if she could ignore that, it wasn't just him she would be jumping with. It was him and *his* demon. He spoke of her the same way he had Fajar. Stumbling over words as he tried to describe just how he felt about the lilith when he so easily found them with her. Uptight. Stupid. Vain. A shame. Even if he agreed to stay for the baby, it wouldn't be just him and her raising it, it would be him and her and *Shaytana*, the demon who put the darkness in his eyes because Sezan asked her to save him and made him wish he would die.

So she wouldn't say anything. She would go back to Ahmar, marry a disenchanted Ajmal, and owe him for the rest of her life for not kicking her out. It was different from the life of a concubine in name only. But at least her baby would be away from that immortal monster. She rubbed her face in her hands until her nose warmed against the cold, thin air. She turned her back against the raging sky and picked her way through blocks of old ruins and strange plants with vines that curled like fingers and shone like stars. Ajmal would be about somewhere, and so she kept a wary eye on each jut between crag and cliff, not wanting to see him and not wanting to be seen. If she stuck to the edge of the tufty gray and pink cloud, she'd make it back to the entrance of the temple, eventually. Though she couldn't help but lean over every once in a while and scoop up a ball of fluff that melted in her hands like sugar in water.

Around a ridged column, a gargantuan blot of bright red and orange appeared on a rock. Sezan inhaled sharply. A Rukh. Bakr's Rukh. The love of his life. His first love.

She stared at the bird, curious and sorry for herself at the same time. At least he had said sorry. It was a small salve for her gaping heart, a bandage far too small, but kind, nonetheless. Why was he always just kind enough to make her heart sting even more?

She moved with purpose, trying not to startle the magnificent bird as she approached. The Rukh turned its head and watched her approach. But it did not ruffle its feathers, squawk, or snap at her. It simply stared until she was a stone's throw away. Its shiny feathers were brighter than poppies and its beak curved like the arm of a lyre. Two intelligent, dark eyes sized her up, fire flickering inside as it does within the charred wood of a sleeping campfire.

"Fajar?" she asked, not sure what to expect.

The Rukh tilted its head and sent a ruffle down its neck and into its body. She took another step and reached her hand out to pet the feathers on its massive wing that looked sharp as glass and soft as the smoke of Shihala. As soon as she touched the sun-fire down, she felt warm. Her shoulders bunched up as she waited for the warmth to turn into a bone-consuming heat, but it stayed steady, a gentle hum of embers washing through her veins and lacing itself with her own inner fire. The Rukh bobbed its head and crooned, then squawked a sweet little noise.

Sezan grinned and bit her bottom lip. "So, you're Bakr's sweetheart?"

Another ruffle and twist of its neck made it so the Rukh stared directly at her.

"He loves you, you know. More than anything in the entire world. Even more than Jahmil." She patted the feathers, then ran her hand the length of the wing, walking down and back up to start all over again.

Fajar nudged Sezan's arm on one of her trips back to the top. Its fire still bubbled within her, warm and safe, easing the nausea within her stomach, like soap suds frothing up the sides of a pot and cleaning away the dirt. She placed a hand on her belly and sighed.

"Thank you, little Rukh. Apparently, I am to suffer greatly during this pregnancy as my mother did with me." She sighed. "I had hoped to be one of those glowing mothers." She petted the feathers once more, then twisted her lips to the side. "May I sit with you?" she asked, even though it sounded crazy talking to a bird.

Fajar cocked her head to the side and lifted her wing. Then she nudged Sezan under the downy tent, her golden beak lingering on Sezan's stomach and crooning. Sezan ran a hand over the bird's head and traced the lines of its beak. Fine. Maybe Bakr had a right to be enamored with a creature so innocent and sweet. And everything she'd done recently, she wouldn't choose herself over the bird, either. What did she have to offer Bakr, anyway? Besides a baby anchor she couldn't bear to tell him about. She offered nothing in bed he couldn't find elsewhere. She *did* get mad at him far too often, though she'd never tell him that. They liked different things. His best friend was the worst. And neither of them told the other anything that really mattered. And worst of all, she still couldn't make herself trust him. The yawning hole he dug in her when he left two years ago was just too big to fill, especially since he continued to do so. And now he had a demon hanging on his shoulder which meant they'd never truly be alone together.

Taw'um alruwh, Lila had said. Would a soulmate be so selfish to save their love from death just to have him tortured mercilessly by an evil monster? And all because she couldn't bear the thought of him not being around? Allah, if she had known just how evil and obsessive the liliths were, she would have made a deal to send it to the other side of Ard, not into the arms of Bakr. She chuckled coldly at herself and nestled into the Rukh's silky feathers. No, if she had known the true cost, surely she could have found another way.

"What do you think, Fajar?" she asked, rubbing her nose into the bird's sides and breathing in the scent of campfire. "Is Bakr crazy for continuing to come around me? Am

I one of those destructive adrenaline rushes he seeks like when he barrels into forest fires or jumps off of cliffs?"

Fajar trilled a little melody, and Sezan's heart swelled with heat. Not the kind that trickled through her veins like a salve, but a powerful rush of feelings that throbbed with pain and joy at the same time. Then came the pulses of memories, not her own. First of him tending to a yolk-covered hatchling, frightened in the forest. Then of him teaching her to fly, to hunt, to sing little songs under the light of the moon. Of his drawing a picture of the Rukh and imprinting it on his skin as a gift of love from Fajar. Safety. Family. Father. Love. Then the images shifted to those of Sezan smiling, laughing, of her wrapped in white sheets with no makeup on. Others, too, of her tears, eyes full of hurt or joy or anger or ecstasy, and always flashing brighter than real life in hues of gold and dandelion, of amber and honey. His memories of her he had shared with his first love, his family. And the desire to be a part of their little nest wrapped so fiercely around her, she wished for it with all her heart. It was the most hopeless thing she had ever done.

She wove her fingers into the smooth feathers and buried her face in the magical warmth, feeling for the first time that Bakr had cared for her, at least at some point, even if he was wretched at showing it. And saying it. And wanting it. And even if it didn't matter. The price of keeping him alive was darkness and the hated monster that came with it. He'd hate her, too, when he found out.

Fajar nudged her again, looking between her and her stomach in short, curious, bird-like glances.

"Yes," she said with a sigh. "There's a little Bakr in there. Heaven, help me."

She rested a hand over her stomach. It would be a disaster if the little one had his sage eyes, but she wished for it, nonetheless. For a piece of him she could take with her wherever she went.

Sezan stretched, about to bury herself further into Fajar's wings when the bird's head snapped to the side. Something dark flung itself from off the cloud, and in one graceful motion, Fajar released her and jumped into the air and over the edge of the island, crimson vanishing into white. And just as suddenly, the cold of the air crept into her bones. Sezan scrambled to the side to see Fajar catch her falling rider. Bakr was gone. Again. And again, it was her fault.

She wished she had been brave enough to jump.

"Sezan!"

She flinched and turned. "Ajmal?"

"Are you okay?" he jogged over and took her hand in his. "I went to explore the grounds, and when I returned, you had gone. I was worried I had lost my chance at finding the famed Seal and my bride."

"I'm fine," she said and touched his cheek.

"Did you tell him?" Ajmal asked, unable to keep his true concern hidden for long.

"No. You were right. We shall keep it to ourselves."

The flicker of colors in his topaz eyes cleared. "It is for the best, my love. I shall love the little one as my own, the child I never thought I'd have. We'll be our own little family."

Sezan cast her gaze toward the fomenting clouds,. Her heart wished for a different family, but she knew it was impossible.

"Was the floating city everything you wished it to be?" she asked, turning a sickly smile to her betrothed.

He grinned wider than she had ever seen. "Absolutely. Though the Seal of Sulayman was nowhere to be found. I even checked the temple once more. Maybe *that* part of the story was just a myth. Unless Bakr found it. I still don't trust him." Ajmal narrowed his eyes and scratched at his chin. "The Seal of Sulayman in the hands of a half-breed would be disastrous."

"Don't call him that," Sezan said.

"What?"

"Half-breed. Mongrel. My sister-in-law is human and a friend and it offends me when you say those words. Especially considering this child will be one, too."

Ajmal's eye's flickered with yellows and purples and greens before clearing and widening. "You are right, my love. I let my passions overtake my sense of reason. I do not trust that... man around you. I'm sorry for the way I behaved. Forgive me?" He plucked up her hand and gave it a kiss, eyebrow raised in question.

"Of course," she nodded graciously, but the spell of innocence between them had been broken. Still, she had lied to Bakr in the temple. She deserved far worse than what she was getting.

"So, no seal?" Ajmal asked once more.

"No seal. But... the ring on his right hand was copper," she said, realizing that instant what she had been looking at now that Bakr was gone. "With an engraving just like your onyx one, in fact. Oh, why hadn't I realized it before?"

Ajmal's arms went stiff at his sides. "Are you saying that your old fling has Izar's magic-stealing ring?"

"It's possible," she said, brows furrowing as she tried to remember what exactly she saw and wondering why the devil she had not asked him about it. "If we can't find the Seal of Sulayman, the rings could be the next best thing."

"Well, that would have been good to know when he was still here. You didn't tell him the spell you got from Faris Khayin, did you?" he asked, nervously twisting his ring as if afraid Bakr would steal his fire right then.

"Of course not," she said with a shake of her head. If Bakr knew he could drain *prissy pants'* powers, they'd be gone already. Then another idea crept into her mind. "Why don't you let me wear your onyx ring."

Ajmal furrowed his brow and twisted the ring round and round on his finger.

"Hear me out," she said, following the words Bakr always used to persuade people into his ludicrous ideas. "I'm about to lose my powers anyway, right? And I can see that ring is very important to you. I'll wear it as my engagement and wedding ring and keep it close to my heart, thinking of you and knowing that I am keeping you safe." She held out her hand, fingers spread apart. "What do you say? May I wear your ring for you?"

A small smile turned the corners of his lips. "As you wish, my love," he said and slipped the ring off his finger and onto hers. "But we must get back now, or we'll miss the ceremony altogether."

"We wouldn't want that," she said, looking past him and into the clouds once more. Bakr had looked so free when he threw himself off the falls and into the lake, and she wondered how it would feel to take a leap of faith like that.

CHAPTER TWENTY-NINE

BAKR

BAKR ARRIVED AT KARZUSAN on the back of Fajar. Bubbles flew at their side, the twenty-foot-long snake looking like a dragonfly compared to Fajar's enormity. There was only one place big enough for her to perch in the whole city—the high tower of the palace. Nobles and peasants alike came out to watch the spectacle. Nobody could deny the grandeur of his entrance this time.

Fajar's talons wrapped around the spire of quartz, crunching some decorative emerald beams under her girth. And just to prove she was his, she let out a beautiful cry that boomed through the city. He patted the back of her neck. What a show-off.

"You okay up here for a little while, baby girl?" he asked. She cooed out a yes, and he got the distinct impression that she was going to enjoy a bit of people watching. She had been stuck up on her own in the mountains for years, and she really was a social butterfly.

He told her how sorry he was again, and again she forgave him.

"There's a field of antelope goats to the west. Go nuts." He patted her neck one last time, then slid down her outstretched wing until he slipped off the tip. There were still another forty feet to the ground, so Bakr tightened himself up and did a few spirals before he hit, coming down running so he wouldn't break his legs. The gathered crowd exploded with applause and called his name. He smiled and bowed, but it all felt so hollow. Even more so than usual.

"Bakr!" a loud, deep voice parted the crowd, revealing the regal figure of Jahmil Amir in all his finery with his perfectly quaffed hair and expertly trimmed beard. How was it that such things could look so charming on one man and so execrable on another?

"Praise Allah that you are well," Jahmil said, smiling. Golden happiness rimmed his bright diamond eyes. "Where have you been?"

Bakr walked closer and threw his arms around the stiff amir, pulling him into a bear hug. Jahmil's rough exterior melted immediately like it always did. For somebody so tough, uncompromising, and downright nasty at times, he had a soft, gooey center. Like candy covered in baked clay. You just had to know how to break through and get at it. And only Ayelet, Serap, and Bakr had hammers.

Allah forbid, Jahmil ever had a daughter. Such a creature would surely be able to render him into a puddle with a single flash of her eyes.

"Are you well?" Jahmil asked, pulling away to hold him at arms' length. His brilliant eyes hid nothing, flashing with every color in his heart. Anger, disappointment, concern, love, apprehension, happiness, excitement, fear. All of it. He was so honest. Little wonder he had such a hard time in politics.

"I'm fine," said Bakr, smiling.

"Is that who I think it is?" He pointed up at Fajar.

"That's my baby girl!" Bakr called up to her, spreading an arm out to one side and then clasping it to his heart. "My true love." She cooed down at him and ruffled the feathers around her neck.

Bubbles shrieked and lunged at the bird's neck.

"No, wait!" Bakr cried. "I didn't mean it like that. You're my true love, too."

Fajar bapped Bubbles away easily with a quick shake of her head. Bubbles did a loop-de-loop in anger, then spat a giant loogie. It shimmered like a massive opal as it fell, then splashed into the crowd. Sputum shot two stories high as djinn scattered from the impact.

"Don't take it like that, bubbly baby." Bakr glanced at Jahmil and shrugged helplessly. "She's ticked off I didn't take her to Zabriya."

"Okay," said Jahmil, smiling in that delightfully baffled way of his.

Bakr clapped a hand onto Jahmil's shoulder. "Hamam?"

"That's more like it."

Bakr slung his arm over his shoulder, and they walked together to the bathhouse. Several officials rushed up to Jahmil with a dozen questions, but he brushed them all away, telling them it could wait until he'd had his bath. Most of them wanted more information about the giant flaming bird that had just become an unofficial mascot for the city, but Jahmil didn't have much to say on the matter. Bakr paused just long enough to let somebody know what was going to happen to the antelope goats in the western field, and that if anybody so much as put a feather out of order of Fajar's head, he was going to skin them alive.

It *was* a very effective threat.

They spent the day together, steaming in the hot room, getting oiled, scraped, scrubbed, and massaged. Bakr finally got his wounds properly cared for, sealed up with extremely expensive healing potions. He called a notary into the massage room and dictated a contract, the whole thing right in front of Jahmil because he didn't care anymore.

"Every contract between Marqiz Rahik al-Shihala and Bakr al-Ard is null and void," he said. "Sezan is released from the hold of the poison with no ill effects as if it never happened... Oh, and Rahik will be afflicted by several horrific skin diseases."

Bakr had considered just killing him, but there were worse things. He wanted to watch him suffer for years to come.

"Also, he's impotent," Bakr continued, "in every sense of the word. He cannot have sex, he cannot fight, he cannot hold a conversation. And he smells like old mushrooms and a soldiers' privy."

"What in all of Allah's mercy are you doing?" asked Jahmil.

"You got all that?"

The pale-faced notary nodded. He dusted the paper with something to set the ink, then passed it over to Bakr. The notary lit a small fire in his finger and held up a tube of wax, then dropped it onto the paper. Taking a fat candle from its holder on the wall, Bakr pulled the Seal out of his shirt and pressed it into the wax.

The heat from the wax nipped at his fingertips. When he pulled his hand back, the Seal left behind glowed and shimmered. The light spread out from there to touch the ink, bleeding into the words until they shined like liquid gold.

"What is that thing?" asked Jahmil.

"Is that it?" Bakr wondered aloud. "Did it work?"

"What did you just do?"

Bakr picked up the glowing note, rolled it up, and set it up on a shelf with his other belongings. Then he hung the Seal around his neck again, seal-side in so it just looked like a hunk of rusted iron. He steadfastly refused to answer any of Jahmil's questions with anything other than, "It doesn't matter anymore."

Ever since he'd picked up the Seal everything he might do with it had been running through his brain. What he could do to Qadira, to Ajmal... to Shaytana. Would the Seal work on her? The doppelgänger had said the Seal had the power to bind djinn, humans, effrit, and eimlaqs. But what about lilith?

He was frightened to hope and nervous to try, knowing what Shaytana might do to him if he attempted to use magic on her. And what would he do? What would he say? Bind her into her Namelessness? Forbid her from ever coming near him again? What command could he write that he could also explain away in case it didn't work?

Could the Seal kill an immortal lilith?

Now wasn't the time. First, he needed to find a way back to himself after everything he had been through. He was wound up tighter than a man being stretched on a rack and his head was not straight. Sezan was safe, and that meant he had time now. All the time in both worlds.

He and Jahmil went back to the steam room where Bakr drank, and drank, and drank until even Jahmil, who knew him well, asked him why he was drinking so much. In response, Bakr decided to tell him all about his adventures in the land of Qadira.

Jahmil was horrified, listening with eyes and mouth in wide, stretched circles. Bakr couldn't stop laughing.

"How could you?" Jahmil said again and again, and he shivered until his body was about to break apart. "With her? Have you completely lost your mind?"

"I've already paid for it."

"I'm the one who will pay for it, you idiot."

"You've already caused as much damage with her as any idiot could," laughed Bakr.

"Ick," Jahmil growled, then shivered again. "Gross. How could you? Did you at least use protection?"

"Like a fire barrier?" he asked, incredulous. That was what sexual protection meant among djinn, one or the other focusing their fire to burn between them and incinerate any impregnating material as it tried to pass. But being only half a djinn with no fire of his own, having fire burn at the tip of his... you know... had a tendency to put him off the mood.

"I'm sure Qadira did something," Bakr said. "She'd never let herself get pregnant with a mongrel, half-breed, Shihalan baby. She'd rather die."

"Did you take a bath before you stood beside me at my wedding?" said Jahmil seriously.

"No." Bakr rolled onto his back on the ledge of the quartz slab, laughing so hard that his towel fell undone.

"You are a disgusting animal, you know that?" Jahmil snatched up another towel and threw it at him. "Cover yourself up. I don't want to look at that thing. Especially knowing where it's been."

Bakr howled with laughter, rolling over onto his knees and slapping the bench.

"You're drunk," said Jahmil reproachfully.

Bakr wiped tears from his eyes, trying to gain control of himself. "What gave it away?"

He was on his sixth bottle of wine by the time he and Jahmil left the hamaam to join Ayelet for dinner, or at least that was where they were headed before Jahmil announced he thought Bakr was too drunk for polite company.

"Polite." Bakr sighed like a horse, his lips flubbing. "Ayelet's more fun than you any day, even if she could get drunk off spring water. God forbid a woman gets drunk, huh?"

"Keep your voice down," Jahmil hissed.

"God forbid a woman cuts loose and has a good time. And *God forbid* she actually enjoys having sex. No, she's got to worry about her stupid reputation all the time. She's got to press her hair with hot irons to make it flat and then yell at me about it!"

"We're not talking about Ayelet anymore, are we?"

"You're a racist, just like everybody else." He shrugged dismissively. "Leave me alone."

Jahmil snapped his fingers, calling a servant to his side. "Muhammad, will you please see the General to a room?"

"Yes, Your Highness." The stiff-backed chamberlain bowed. His turban was strapped so tightly to his head, it didn't even shift.

"What's up, Muhammad?" Bakr slung his arm around him and let his head loll onto the djinn's shoulder. "You're not a racist, are you? Nah, you're my bubby."

"Yes, General."

Bakr staggered down the hall and Muhammad deposited him in an opulent bedroom, then drew the heavy velvet curtains to hide the bright light of the setting First Moon. As Muhammad shuffled towards the exit, Bakr called out to him. "I need dinner."

He turned sharply. "Yes, General. What would you like?"

"Puh. Everything. All of the things. And I need wine."

"Wine is forbidden in the Palace of Karzusan."

"Are you talking back to me, you djinn bastard? I'll cut your—" Bakr stumbled to his feet, tried to pull out his sword, failed, twirled on one heel, and fell back into bed.

"Nah. You're alright." He rolled onto his back and gazed up at the massive, bulb-shaped chandelier. Red, blue, and silver glass twisted above him like fireworks. "You can get me some poppy wax instead. And the tears of golden adders. And some good old-fashioned Ardish hash, if it is on the menu."

"I would advise against it, sir."

"Don't make me change my mind about you, again."

Muhammad stifled a very obvious sigh. "Yes, General."

"And some dancers."

"His Highness, Jahmil Amir, has abolished both the harem and the House of Nymphs."

"What?" He tried to sit up and glare at the man with incredulity, but he didn't stand a chance. "Jahmil killed the House of Nymphs? What a prick. Just cause he's in love and blissfully happy he has to ruin everything for the rest of us miserable bastards. We'll see about that."

Bakr flopped onto his stomach and pointed his finger at the chamberlain's pudgy, navy-colored face. "Take a memo, Muhammad."

"Yes, sir." He lifted his hands. A pad of paper and quill puffed into existence out of nothing. He looked at Bakr with a raised brow. "Whenever you're ready."

"The House of Nymphs is hereby reestablished and there are five of them on their way up here right now."

"I beg your pardon, Sir?"

"Just write it."

He scribbled out the paper, then dried the ink with a quick dust of fire.

"I need a wax."

"Is this a letter, sir?"

"You are getting on my last nerve, Muhammad!"

"Apologies, sir." He produced the wax and dripped a small puddle. Even before Bakr had lifted the Seal from the wax, he heard the chatter of girls coming down the hall, accompanied by the merry strings and pipes of a Qasir Band.

Muhammad excused himself as the dancers funneled into the room. Bakr lay on his back. The world was soft and blurry, twirling in time with the music. The dancers barely even looked like women, just colors drifting in and out of a breeze. He told them to put on more scarves and dangly jewels so he could watch the movement. He fell asleep like that—on his back with his head dangling off the edge of the bed where his feet ought to be, listening to music, watching pretty colors.

Time and again Sezan crept back into his mind. The way she had turned from him and ran. Rejected him. He wished he could just figure out how to hate her.

Bakr awoke to cool fingers stroking his chest. His eyes twitched, body compressed by some invisible force. Frozen in space. Fear gripped him. He tried desperately to bring up his arm and slam it down again, to startle himself awake, but he could not get it to move. All the while, those hands were moving over his body. His neck, his chest. Kisses lingering on his abs.

He caught a flash of turquoise skin and sparkling black hair and the soft moans of a delicate, careful voice.

It was a dream. Just a stupid dream. And it hurt so much because he knew that's all it was. He would wake soon, and she would be gone. Again. Forever.

But he could not stop himself when her fruity sweetness filled up his senses, lifting him closer to the light. He tried to reach for her, and at last, his hands moved.

Suddenly, his body was alive, fear replaced by demanding anguish. He sat up, grabbed her, and kissed her, tasting that cherry lipstick that he was always so anxious to get off. Heat overwhelmed him, desperate and aching as he always was. As she became when he drew her near. Yielding to him and overpowering him with her urgent craving. She entwined her fingers with his and climbed on top of him. His head rolled back. She lifted one of his hands to her mouth and sucked on his finger, deep into the back of her throat. He yanked down the strap on her little fur dress so he could kiss more of her skin.

A fur dress.

Bakr shot bolt upright, and his eyes snapped open. Shaytana straddled him, her dress hanging down from her shoulders. Her pink lips pushed together in a superior smile. "Hello, lover."

He shoved her off and recoiled to the edge of the bed. "What do you want?"

"I thought you might be lonely," she purred, pursuing him. She ran her long, pointed nails down his back. "Considering today is Sezan's wedding day."

"I'm never lonely for you."

"Why are you trying to hurt me?" She wrapped her body around his back, pressing her bare skin against him. He tried to pull away but couldn't. Like a fly caught in a web, he knew no matter how he struggled, the hold would only get tighter.

He didn't stand a chance. Though his pulse quickened and cold sweat formed on his brow, he didn't want to give her the satisfaction of tasting her favorite appetizer.

Fear

Shaytana leaned over his shoulder and nibbled on his earlobe so hard that it stung. "What a silly thing she is, making such a sacrifice for you and then just letting you get away. If I were her, I would never let you out of my sight. I would kill for you. Lie and steal. Anything to keep you with me."

"You do all those things, anyway."

She giggled and slipped her tongue inside of his ear. "She thinks she's given up so much."

He turned to look over his shoulder at her. "What did she give up?"

"Oh, never mind about that."

"Tell me the truth, Shaytana," he snapped.

She pouted and opened her eyes wide so they sparkled in the dim light, her shoulders falling in like a child that had just been caught with her hand in a cookie jar. "She sent me to save your life. She promised to give me all her magic if I protected you from dying in the war."

Bakr's breath caught in his throat. He searched Shaytana's twinkling eyes, but they gave nothing away. "What?"

"Only a few more days to go until she'll be all mine." Shaytana perked up as quickly as she had fallen into a pout. "She thinks I'm just going to drain her magic from her, but I think I'll leave it in. That way, I can move her around like a puppet and make her do whatever I want. And she'll just have to watch in silence, trapped inside her own body."

"You're lying," he growled. "Sezan never would have…"

She giggled, her gray skin shivering like midnight waters. "I can't lie when you say my name, stud. You know that."

Breath puffed out of him in angry gusts. He clenched his teeth so hard they creaked. "I won't let you."

"There's nothing you can do to stop me."

"Oh, really?" He lifted a hand to his neck to grasp the Seal, but the necklace was gone.

"Looking for this?" She lifted her finger, the chain dangling off the end.

He tried to snatch it away, but she pulled out of his grasp and blinked it out of existence. Beyond his scope of it, anyway.

"Oh, Bakr." She giggled and shook her head. "You make it too easy."

"Please, don't do this." Bakr raked his nails down his own cheeks. "Just leave her alone. Take me."

"I already have you, muffin." She winked. "And her. But if you ever miss Sezan, I can always crawl inside her body for an evening. It will be like roleplaying. "

"You vile bitch!" He jumped to his feet, snatched his sword off the ground, and plunged it into her chest.

There was no blood, no gasp. She didn't even flinch.

Shaytana looked down at the blade, then back up at him. She pursed her lips and cocked her head to one side. "I'm going to have to punish you for that."

Then she smiled, and a gray mist wrapped over them both. He tried to pull back, but it was hopeless. They slipped into the nameless place where the bite of her razor-like nails tore into his skin.

CHAPTER THIRTY

Sezan

When Ajmal flashed them back into Ahmar, he had them land right next to the officiator. Sezan looked at him reproachfully, to which he patted her hand comfortingly. It did little to assuage her surprise. She still felt woozy on her feet, the water Bakr had given her the only thing she hadn't fully forcefully expelled the entire day. Her head hurt, and her brain swam with speckles of exhaustion. But Fajar's shared memories were crystal clear, everything else blurring like heat to the sides. Beautiful, warm images of family, of Bakr.

"We're ready," Ajmal announced to the room, though only the officiator and a few government dogs were there. This was just a formality that would bind their souls in the eyes of Ahmar and Shihala, of Allah and Qaf. Utterly mundane and completely life-altering.

"Ajmal," she said in a dulcet tone, trying not to raise the officiator's eyebrows any further. "May I speak with you a moment?"

He took one step back and swept his hand across his body. "What is it, my love?"

"I just think with everything that has happened, we should talk."

"Of course," he said, a slight tightening around his eyes that quickly smoothed. "I'm sure you're devastated after dealing with that absurd... bastard?"

"Ajmal!" she scolded in a whisper.

"You said not to call him mongrel. I did not. And he is one. I'm sorry, what would you have me call him?"

She clamped her teeth over a growl. "It's not about Bakr—"

"I should think not. Especially after you broke his heart by not letting him go sooner. You must be devastated, knowing the lilith you made a deal with obliterated everything good he ever had. But at least you've done what's right now. You've let him go. Now you may both work toward healing."

She ran the fabric of her tunic through pinched fingers, each one of his words an iron knife in her lungs, her throat, her heart. "I didn't—"

"I even feel sorry for him, the way he's so desperate to please people, to please you when it's destroying him." He dropped his voice to a whisper. "He didn't stand a chance. Though I'm not sure which one of you has done more damage. I'm certain if you hadn't come to your senses with me, he would continue to do what he always has: stay just long enough to trick you into thinking you love him only to leave again. And again. And *again*. If you let it continue, he would come and go and come and go until you were mad enough to make another terrible deal. Maybe with an effrit next time. Didn't he leave you on your deathbed hours before the Vespars descended on Shihala?"

Her eyes flashed to his, and her tired bones shook.

"The rumors surrounding Shihala's highest-ranking sheikha are tragic. The woman who was overcome with an evil sickness and spurned by her love the second she started dying spread as far as Ahmar and much farther. Though the other rumor goes that he left first and you nearly died of a broken heart."

She shook her head, throat aching with emptiness. The burn of his words ate through Fajar's memories like flame to paper. The Rukh had only shared Bakr's good memories because he hadn't shared any dark ones with her. Fajar didn't know the ink Sezan and the lilith had cast over his heart. Nor did she know of the black hole Bakr had scooped out of Sezan's own heart when he abandoned her so completely.

"It is time to end the destructive cycle between you two. Now that I know this childish General Bakr is the same man from the stories, I can't see you get hurt any longer." Ajmal ran a hand across her shoulder and behind her neck, sliding her into the crook of his arm. "And he *will* hurt you. He's left you, Sezan. Over and over and over... and he'll never stop. He can't anymore than you can risk him doing so with a child on the way. Give yourself and your child the home and life you deserve. Let me be for you what you need."

With her still pressed against him, he guided her forward to the oak-wood podium and set a pen in her fingers.

"Save him," he whispered, his breath hot against her cheek. "Save your baby and yourself."

She blinked at the golden words, the blanched parchment, and Ajmal's seal already gleaming on the paper. He touched her elbow, guiding her hand to her pocket where her seal resided, untouched, in its official box. She slipped a hand inside, touching the cool glass of Ayelet's gift before finding the smoothed wood of her seal. She had been so proud of it. So proud to make her own life. Now, her first official act as an ambassador, as a free woman, would be to make it her last. But Ajmal was right. He had to be. This was what was best. For her, for her baby, and for Bakr.

Ajmal took her other limp hand and plunged the obsidian tip of a yellow-feathered pen into her skin. She didn't even wince, the pain suffocated under renewed devastation. A wound that had never healed, the edges jagged and infected. He held her fingertip to Shihala's official seal, teaming with Jahmil's magic and waiting for hers. Her blood and fire slipped quickly inside the seal so it flashed Jahmil's white and her pink, untainted by the baby's. It was not the little one's burden to bear. She looked at the seal blankly, then let her hand fall onto the paper, the glowing mark, blurred and smeared, flared bright before fading into permanent ink. It was done.

***

The rest of the day and the night passed quickly. The next morning, Sezan sat stiffly on an emerald-green settee in the official waiting room outside the ceremonial hall waiting for the blast of trumpets to announce her and Ajmal's nuptials.

The red, heavy silks of her wedding dress, brocaded in golden thread, hung around her like curtains. She had a yellow diamond draped across her forehead to match her eyes and thick coal in her lashes to create allure. Golden boots adorned her feet in the softest leather, and her bodice was breath-squeezing tight and embroidered heavily with beads. She had a vague memory of being pricked several times by shaky hands as servants sewed her into it. The only thing loose on her body was a small satchel with her seal and Ayelet's gift, slung loosely on a chain of pearl beads around her waist. Lila had been in and out in a constant tizzy, trying to tend to Sezan's needs when she wouldn't speak a word. Her mother would have approved if she had been allowed to come to her only daughter's wedding. But she was not free to make her own choices. If only Sezan could use that excuse for how terribly her life had turned out.

Ajmal, dressed smartly in his red-embroidered ceremonial kaftan, stood by her side. A smile turned his lips, though it dipped whenever he looked at her. "You look miserable, my love. At this rate, I'm surprised you haven't written to the King of Eastern Elm to see if he could help release you from your deal with the lilith. I hear he has also taken a fancy to you, though your current circumstances may make things tricky." He knelt in front of her and patted her hands. "I count myself blessed that you have chosen me."

"Yes. But a free favor has not once been given nor received by anyone in the Eastern Elm since the Nine Gifts of Fire," she said flatly, affixing her blurry gaze to the powder blue ewer on the chest across the room. "It is why Jahmil Amir likes them as allies so much. Everything is equal, fair, or otherwise written in the blood of Qaf. I would get nothing from the king even if I begged."

"You said the contract with the lilith wasn't sealed by his powers. Surely flexing his power against another immortal being would prove useful to him."

Sezan could only manage tiny little breaths in her bodice, and even that hurt against the pinching seams. "It wasn't, but the king of deals isn't about to go around breaking a contract just because his name isn't on the document. It would be a slight on his millennia-old reputation."

Ajmal sighed and paced the room.

Through the corners of her lashes. Sezan caught a genuine look of dismay in his downcast eyes and frustrated brows. She blinked, wanting to feel guilt or anything when looking at him, but came up as empty as ever.

She turned her gaze back to the ewer.

"I think only of you," he continued. "I wish I could find some way to break the deal with that vicious lilith and free you from your agony. I can't stand that you're paying the price for someone so ungrateful."

"Bakr pays his own price," she said, the stir of feeling returning to her chest. "I paid my magic to keep Bakr alive, and she continues to torment him. He believes he owes her something, and she won't leave him alone. She's received twice the payment for the same deal."

"Surely the King of Elm would help you then," Ajmal exhaled the words. "Let Bakr's suffering pay the price and free you, instead."

"You're unbelievable," she said, an ambiguous mist of disgust beginning to form inside her.

"Is it so unbelievable that I would want our child to retain its magical abilities? That I should want my official wife to still be a djinn."

"I'd still be a djinn," she said bitterly, looking at him fully for the first time.

"In blood only," he growled, breaking his silky tone at last. "I want freedom from the lilith so her evil doesn't hang over our marriage."

Sezan said nothing, so long it felt since she had given up that hope.

"Maybe you can convince Bakr to trade you rings."

"What?" she asked, willing herself to the present more fully. She forced the stiff fabric of her robes to bend so she could stand. Her shoulders felt as if a silky plank of wood tied them together.

"If you switched rings," Ajmal continued, his pacing faster, "You could use Izar's spell and gain magic instead of losing it. That was the plan, right? I'm certain with how he looks at you, he'd gladly give you the ring. Then, after the lilith takes your magic, you can... you know, borrow his."

Sezan rubbed a hand along her pinched ribs, face flush with the horror of what he was suggesting. "I wanted to reverse the spell and suck the magic from the lilith. But that was before I learned that Bakr, not her, wore the ring. *You* want me to become just like the lilith and steal some innocent person's magic!"

"Not *some* person's. There's only one person wearing the other ring."

"You mean Bakr," she accused, her voice sharp as glass.

He shrugged. "It's only half the proper amount of magic, but that's better than none. His djinn half shouldn't have to mix with his human half anymore. They aren't meant to be together."

"Absolutely not." She tried to cross her arms but could feel the seams of her dress pulling against the strain. "You wish to make me like Izar so I will reach for magic that is not my own and fall to my death. Only, your reward isn't the Seal, but a baby who is an acceptable level of djinn. You are deplorable."

"Why would I want you dead?" He opened his palms to her, exasperation clear in his open mouth. "I don't know what you've decided about me, what *he* might have persuaded you into believing, but I love you, Sezan. And Izar fell because he got too close to a lilith. It sounds like Bakr's the one destined for her cruelty in this story. The least you can do is put his magic to use before the succubus drains you both. He'd want that, right? For the baby? He doesn't even like it here in Qaf. Let him go be a human like he wants."

Sezan stopped herself from biting her lip. Getting her hair and makeup right had taken all morning, and she couldn't risk reapplying and getting rouge on her gown. Or having to hear the maids blather on anymore. And aside from his manifesting manipulation and ulterior motives, whatever they may be, Ajmal had made some interesting, practical points. If she asked Bakr for his magic, he would give it. He never cared for that part of himself. Had never really cared for djinn in general. And why would he? But there was no way she would ask Bakr for anything. Let her be abandoned after marriage and exiled for all eternity. The baby would have a safe home, magic or not. She couldn't stand to see

Bakr's face twisted with agony anymore. To know for all she tried, she had made his life worse than death. She deserved to suffer ten times over for making a deal that ruined them both.

And yet, if she agreed to Ajmal's plan… would he take her to see Bakr one last time? This time she did bite her lip and gasped in frustration. That would be one of the most selfish things she had ever done, second only to keeping him alive in the first place. What would he do if she showed up before him in her wedding gown about to be married to another man? He would put on his wide eyes that pierced straight to her core and tell her not to, and that would hurt worse than his iron sword in her chest.

"I'm sorry to put you through this on our wedding day," Sezan said at last. "But I cannot take Bakr's powers, or anyone else's. The lilith has won. I shall curse her bitter name forever."

Ajmal's head snapped up. "What did you say?"

"I said the lilith has won."

"After that. You said you'd curse her name," he said, moving forward in long, quick steps. "Did she give you her name?" he asked, the shake of incredulity in his voice.

"No." Sezan eyed him warily. "She must have told Bakr, or he learned it when she imprisoned him in her mind or whatever happened." Remembering the look on his face when he bared his shredded soul made her sick. She reached for a small ceramic cup on a table next to the settee and drank tiny sips.

"Ha!" Ajmal snapped up. "Say it!"

"Her name?"

"Yes," he nodded, his eyes sparkling with a deep blue.

Sezan narrowed her eyes. "Why don't you do it?"

"Because I don't know it. And because you already made a deal with her. You don't want both the baby's parents cursed by a lilith do you?"

Both the baby's parents *were* cursed by one, but she kept that to herself. "What will calling her name do?"

"Make her come to you," he said with a wide smile.

"And why would I want that monster here on my wedding day and so near my unborn child?"

"To see if the rumors are true," Ajmal said. "That she has to tell the truth. That she must obey."

"They can't be." Sezan shook her head dismissively. "Or else Bakr would not be tortured so."

His face fell a little, then brightened back up. "Not if Bakr doesn't know. He's kind of an idiot."

She opened her mouth to protest then shut it. "There's a good chance he learned her name by accident..." She sighed. "But maybe we should try this after we get married. Who knows what she'll do, and we have a room full of people waiting to be indulged with ceremony."

"And who are they here for but us? They can wait."

"You love ceremony, though," Sezan said, her eyes narrowing even more in suspicion. "And hate being late."

"Call me curious. Dreadfully so. Besides, won't we both feel better sealing our union without this magic nonsense hanging over our heads?"

Sezan spun the bone and onyx ring around her finger. She had taken off the casing, not afraid to show the stone known for dampening magic, the cursed black meant to drain a djinn's powers. Now that she thought about it, why *was* Ajmal so invested in all this? In magical rings that gave and drained power, in seals that could control djinn? In favors from Eastern Elm and commanding a lilith? An unease far worse than morning sickness made a nest in her belly as more questions piled up. Why had Ajmal agreed to take her to the floating city when he hated Bakr and wished not to tell him about the baby at all? Why had he agreed to leave them alone in the temple?

"I think we should marry first," she said, trying to suss out his intentions.

"Sezan," he sighed, grabbing her hands and patting them. "If you can command the lilith, you can keep your magic and..." His face twisted as if he ate a mouthful of raw caraway seeds. "You can save Bakr from the torment you inflicted upon him."

He was manipulating her, she could see that now, and she realized she'd been so caught up in her misery that he'd been guiding her with a gentle, intentional hand for a while. But his words still pressed like a thousand needles into her flesh. She would not call the lilith for herself. But for Bakr...

"No!" she snapped, more at herself than Ajmal. "Playing games with magic is what got me into this mess."

"And how will you ever get out of the mess you made if you lose yours altogether?" His eyes hardened, jagged lines fracturing the edges of his crystal blue eyes like ice chipping away from a glacier.

"What are you talking about?" she snipped. "Since when has my life been in peril?"

"Do you think the lilith won't take everything she can? Are you so selfish to let that monster take the baby's powers, too? What if it kills our child? What if taking the fire from you extinguishes both your lives?"

Sezan's lips parted. She had not considered that. With another creak of her near-bursting seams, she looked down at her belly. She had so wanted to be one of those glowing mothers...

"Sezan?" Ajmal asked, fingers thrumming against his ceremonial jacket.

She lifted her gaze from her belly to the center of the room, slow as snow melting in spring.

"Shaytana," she called to the crisp silence between held breaths. "Come."

CHAPTER THIRTY-ONE

BAKR

BAKR LAY ON HIS back in the nameless place, gazing up at nothing. He was bleeding, but not too badly. Shaytana knew he had a high tolerance for physical pain, so she didn't bother with it too much. Besides, she liked him. In her twisted way, she always had. He saw that plainly now. She didn't want to destroy him completely, just keep him broken. A little doll with popped seams that she could hide under her bed and take out to play with whenever she was bored. Until he was so broken, he wasn't fun anymore, then like a cat with an injured mouse, she would abandon him to die.

"Thanks, lover," Shaytana said, standing up and shimmying back into her ragged little dress. "That was amazing. I'll have to figure out how to get you angry more often."

Naked and exhausted, he curled into a ball and covered his head with his hands. He'd never raised a hand to her before because she had always told him what would happen. Exactly what had happened.

"Shaytana," he whispered. "Please, don't do this. You don't need Sezan's fire. Just leave her alone."

"You can say my name as much as you want, Bakr, it isn't going to make any difference." She sat on a cloud of nothing and crossed her legs. A vial of liquid silver appeared in the air beside her, and she took a little brush from the top and used it to paint her nails. She'd chipped them doing what she did to him.

Bakr ran his fingers roughly over his scalp, then sat up and forced himself to look at her. The back of his throat caught, and his stomach roiled in pain. Her smell was everywhere around him. Inside of him. Like poison racing through his veins. It seemed every time she touched him was worse than the time before. More painful. And always permanent.

"I'll keep you with me forever, Shaytana. I'll just say your name over and over so you can never leave."

"Great plan, lover. Except I don't have to actually be next to Sezan on the day of reckoning to take her fire. A deal with a lilith fulfills itself. For the contract to be valid, we aren't allowed to lie. And people certainly can't catch us up on those kinds of technicalities." She laughed and shook her head. "I bet she wishes she'd talked to a lawyer before summoning me. She was in Elm when we made the deal, too, so there's really no excuse. Lawyers are Elm's only export."

"Besides," Shaytana continued with a flip of her hair, "why should you care? She's already signed the troth's plight with my dear Ajmal. In just a few hours the deal will be done. He gets everything, and she gets... well, me." She smiled at him like a wolf with a rabbit. He could practically see the blood on her teeth.

Bakr's head fell into his hands, hopelessness rushing over him like a frozen ocean. The barbs of her words scraped down his skin until one caught and he looked up. "Did you say *your dear Ajmal?*"

"He's just a client." She shrugged. "You have nothing to worry about."

"Ajmal is your client?"

"He has his virtues, Bakr. If you give him a chance. He's such a good liar, his eyes don't even flash." She poked him playfully in the gut with her toe. "Bit of a cold fish, but then again, no djinn could hold a Roman candle to the fire in your blood, lover. That silly harem girl is going to be chilly the rest of her days. Good thing there won't be too many."

Bakr dragged himself to his feet and pulled on his pants. His fingers still felt numb. Until a moment ago he'd had half a mind simply to lie in the nothingness until time consumed him. His bones still felt ragged, his voice parched.

"Tell me about Ajmal? What are you doing for him?"

She waved him off without looking up. "Just lending a helping hand to djinn in need. I really am such a philanthropist."

"What does Ajmal want, Shaytana?"

A short petulant breath rushed from her nostrils. "To get rid of Qadira, of course. What would you want if you were him?"

"What does he want with Sezan?"

"Well, he's not after her for her personality, that's for sure." Shaytana giggled, the little silver bottle disappearing in a puff of thin air. She took a step forward and opened her mouth to speak, but then her head snapped quickly to one side as if she'd heard something. "Who in the world—?"

She puffed out of existence.

Bakr clenched his fists and growled in frustration, every muscle in his body cinching tight. He couldn't stand these stupid games anymore.

For years he had avoided using Shaytana's name too often, frightened of what she might do to him if he annoyed her. But what did he have to be frightened of any more? She was going to continue doing more of the same for eternity no matter what he did.

"Shaytana," he snapped.

She popped back into existence in front of him, but everything about her demeanor had changed. A snarl clung to her lips and her eyes were sharp and hot with rage. "What did you do?"

Bakr forced himself to stand up straight. "I'm not done talking to you."

"What did you say to me?" Her eyes flashed, and she stomped closer. She snatched him by the throat and yanked him off his feet. Bakr grabbed for her hands, his legs kicking in the air though he knew it was pointless. Her razor-like fingernails dug into his neck, drawing stinging blood. Then her whole body twitched, and she growled in frustration before disappearing again.

Bakr fell limp and landed softly in the nothingness. He wiped a hand over the back of his neck and growled, "This isn't over."

He pushed himself onto his hands and knees then back up to his unsteady feet. "Shaytana!"

She popped back in and cocked her head at him. "I warned you..."

"I said, I'm not done talking to you."

Shaytana looked like she was about to pounce on him and rip his skin off like a hungry lioness. He braced for it. But then, she took a long slow breath, shook out her shoulders, and donned a sickeningly sweet smile. "Bakr, have you been telling people about me?"

He glanced quickly to one side, searching his brain for either a lie or a truth that made sense of her question. But no. Screw her question. He was the one who had questions.

"I asked what deal you made with Ajmal, Shaytana."

She laughed and checked her nails. "I find it incredible that it never occurred to you that Sezan is the daughter of King Bajul's official chief courtesan. Her *only* child."

He searched his brain, looking for the epiphany that was apparently supposed to be coming. "So?"

"And Jahmil is the *only* legitimate heir."

Bakr's lips twitched. "So?"

"Oh, Bakr. So handsome. So stupid." She patted his head. "Should something ever happen to Jahmil—Allah forbid anything happening to those eyes—then the power of Shihala wouldn't pass to his human, peasant wife who is so clueless about the affairs of state she hasn't bothered to produce an heir yet."

"Rahik would be king."

"Nuh-uh." She shook her head. "New blood supersedes old in Shihalan law. The son or grandson of the old king always comes before brothers or uncles. Besides, Jahmil forbade Rahik's ascension."

"I don't understand."

"Of course, you don't!" She spat out a laugh that snapped off at the end like brittle iron. "I'm warning you, Bakr, I have been setting this up for years, and I am not going to sit back and watch you destroy it, no matter how cute your butt is. So keep out of it."

Her threat rolled over his skin like sharpened blades, but still, he refused to look away from her eyes. "And what do you get out of all of this?"

"There it is again." Her head snapped up, like she'd just heard a bell, then she pressed a fingernail into his chest. "If you call me back here one more time, I will cut your head off on principal."

Shaytana puffed out of existence. Bakr chewed on his lip. He was tempted to yank her right back, but the little hole her fingernail had left in his chest warned him against it. His brain was being pulled in so many directions, he felt like he was on the rack, his bones slowly being stretched by a sadistic madwoman. He might have preferred that to the psychological torment currently ripping through his psyche. Shaytana had said so much, and at the same time, so little. Ajmal was her client. Sezan was her client. Was there anybody in the Nine Kingdoms that did not owe that evil vulture a favor?

He didn't, he realized. He never had.

Sezan had given everything she had that she thought was of value to save him. He hadn't even sent her a stupid letter. And when he finally came back, he had immediately sent her into Ahmar like a lamb to the slaughter.

Now Shaytana had the Seal. He may as well have gift-wrapped it for her. Was that why Ajmal had come to the floating island, to look after his side of the deal, whatever it was?

He'd asked about the Seal. All he'd wanted was the Seal. And Sezan, too. Was Shaytana the reason she was looking for it? To find a way out of the binds she had tied herself into when she made a deal with a demon?

Bakr needed to get to Jahmil, to come clean about everything. To warn him about Qadira's plans. But he still didn't understand them. Something about Sezan and a legitimate male heir. Was Ajmal supposed to get her pregnant? A child with the purple skin of Ahmar to sit on the Shihalan throne after the current queen and prince regent were disposed of?

Bakr thought back to every time he'd met Ajmal. His words. His behavior. The colors of his eyes. Bakr hadn't paid him much attention; he'd been trying so hard to convince himself that he wasn't jealous of him. Now, he let images of the Ahmaran prince float freely through his mind.

Ajmal had been rough with Sezan in the temple, possessive and insistent. He kept playing at his role of being the perfect fiancé, but he'd messed up. It had been painfully obvious there was something in that room he cared about a lot more than he did her. Frightening her with his stupid fire, constantly cutting her off. And as she knelt on the cold stone, barely able to speak and fighting so hard to keep her stomach, he had marched up to her and demanded that she stand and get on with things. Bakr had thought he was just jealous. Maybe there was more to it than that.

Bakr had also been impressed, albeit begrudgingly, by Ajmal's fortitude. There were not many djinn who would go toe to toe with him, especially not after feeling the burn of his sword. Bakr knew his reputation across Qaf was one of an unhinged killer with supernatural strength and speed, who had a complete disregard for his own life, not to mention as many as a thousand notches in his iron blade from fallen enemies. Ajmal should not have been able to look him in the eye. But he had, over and over. Was it love that had given him such courage, or something more tangible?

There was one thing he was sure about. Ajmal hated Qadira. Hated her with all his soul. Was humiliated by her, resented her, wished he could replace her with a more competent, cool-headed ruler...

Prince prissy pants was playing his own game.

Bakr itched to go to Ahmar, to march in there and start cutting people apart. To run Qadira and Ajmal through in one stroke, throw Sezan over his shoulder, and run off with her. Again, he was being horribly unrealistic. Bakr was one tough son of a snake, but he couldn't take on the entire court of Ahmar. And if Shaytana was working with them, things were even stickier. Besides, he hadn't brought his bag of Fajar's feathers. If he went to Ahmar without it, he wouldn't be able to get out again.

He didn't have to make a rash decision. He was still in the nameless place, in the white void, the timeless boring whatever. When he returned to Qaf, it would be as if not a second had passed.

Bakr stood and paced through the Nothing. Then he ran, hoping a bit of exercise would help him think more clearly, expel some of his useless anger and frustration, his guilt and shame. Just get him out of his brain enough to be able to think of a plan. He'd never been good at it. Even in the war, he wasn't that kind of general. He had never studied books of tactics or played a single war game. He relied on instinct, on the random things that popped into his head at any given moment. And it had always served him well. Perhaps he was just lucky. Or perhaps, there was something about his brain that just worked better when it was under pressure.

He could only hope.

He would go to Shihala first and warn Jahmil about everything, and then go to Ahmar to warn Sezan. He would have to sneak in quietly to scope everything out and then decide what to do.

But even as he laid his plan out in his mind, his heart caught on another burr. Would Sezan even listen to him?

It made no difference. He had to try.

As Bakr readied himself to slip out of the void back into Qaf, aiming for the royal chambers, he noticed something far in the distance where there should have been nothing. A tiny dot of black, almost too small for the eye to see. He blinked, thinking it was probably a flaw in his vision. He had never seen anything in the nameless place other than himself and Shaytana.

The dot remained. Step by step, Bakr moved towards it, slowly at first and then faster and faster until he was running full-tilt. For a long time, it seemed to be retreating, and he felt like a dog chasing a bone dangled from a stick lashed to its own back. But slowly, very slowly, it grew. What had been a pinprick soon was the size of a thumbnail, then a fist, then a dinner plate. And the more he ran, the faster it grew. He stopped once to try to catch his breath, and the black circle immediately began to shrink.

He chased it, throwing all his energy into his legs until they ached from the strain and his face and chest were drenched in sweat. The thing was the size of a tunnel now, big enough to fly Bubbles through. And then, all at once, it stopped, and he ran into it. The sterile white nothingness was gone in an instant, replaced by a cascade of black. He was falling through it, deeper and deeper, unable to stop, picking up speed. Deeper shades of black rushed him from below as the white nothing shrank into the distance until it was but a pinprick. He thought of Shihala, of the place he wanted to be, trying desperately to slip back through the veil. Nothing happened. He continued to plummet through nothing, towards nothing.

What had he done?

CHAPTER THIRTY-TWO

Sezan

The first time Sezan called Shaytana's name, nothing came but a faint wisp of cinnamon smoke. She glanced anxiously at Ajmal who shrugged and prodded her to try once more. The second time, she had to will herself not to flinch as the lilith popped into the room, lithe hands already upon Sezan's chest and her sneering face a mere finger's-width away.

"He told you, that naughty boy, didn't he?"

Sezan snuffed out the air in her nose, the strong pot-pourri of the lilith overwhelming her sensitive stomach. "Why won't you leave Bakr alone?"

Shaytana chomped her teeth playfully, then pulled back, the slip of her dress doing nothing for her. "Because he's tasty."

"Shaytana," Sezan said, her tongue curling with the bitterness of the creature's name. "Step back."

The lilith's eyes widened. She stepped back. Sezan glanced to an eager-faced Ajmal who nodded encouragingly. "Raise your arm."

Shaytana did.

"And your other."

Again Shaytana obeyed. They stood, staring at one another until the lilith's face broke into a gleeful laugh and her arms fell, clutching her stomach as she doubled over.

"Oh, Sezan, you're such a tease."

The air was suddenly hot and stifling. "What?"

"*Raise your arm, Shaytana,*" the lilith mocked, giggling hysterically. "You thought you had it within your power to control a lilith and that's what you commanded me to do? I really don't get what he sees in you." Her laughter cut off as abruptly as it had begun. "Now if you'll excuse me," she said and popped out of the room.

Sezan stared blankly at the carpet, as surprised that the lilith was gone as she was that she had shown up in the first place.

"Call her back," Ajmal said.

"Why?" Sezan asked sharply. "I can't control her."

"But you can make her tell you the truth," he said. "I know *that* one is true. Isn't there anything you wish you could ask her?"

Again, his eagerness slipped down her spine like oil. And again, he had made a fair point.

"Shaytana," she said more sharply this time. "Come."

The lilith blinked back into the room, irritation replacing the playfulness in her eyes. "What?" she snapped.

"I just wanted to see if you'd come," Sezan said with a shrug. "Like a common mutt."

Shaytana snarled.

"But now that you're here, tell me why you want to drain my magic when you have more than enough for anything you could ever need."

"Kicks and giggles." The lilith bared a sharp-toothed grin, arms folded.

"Is it to kill me?"

"I have a million other ways that would be far more fun. You djinn sure are attractive, but you're dumb as rocks. Magic and life force are two different things. Just because they're both tied to your fire doesn't mean they're inextricable from each other."

"You must tell me why you want to take my magic, Shaytana."

The lilith's eyes narrowed into glistening slits. "I have no intention of draining your pathetic fire."

"Then why make the deal?"

"How's marital bliss, sugar?"

Sezan glanced at Ajmal, who was pressed against the far wall, a mixture of fascination and something else cascading across his face. Something dark.

"Ajmal's a good boy," Shaytana continued. "Aren't you?" She turned and curled her finger, beckoning him to come.

He slid off the wall and walked over, not even the decency of a sheepish slump curving his shoulders. Sezan scanned his eyes, but except for a tiny haze of yellow, they were clear.

"You are lucky to have him," Shaytana said resolutely. "At least for the eightish months until your baby is born. I don't know what he plans to do with you after that."

"Our marriage is not your concern," Sezan said, forcing her shoulders to stay relaxed while the tips of her fingers trembled.

"That's not very grateful, now is it, Ajmal?" Shaytana pouted.

He shook his head, not saying a word. And for a moment, Sezan could see that darkness in his eyes that lived in Bakr's, only a thousand times smaller. The mark of Shaytana's tortures.

"You don't ask for thanks when you do favors. You take blood or souls or magic in return. What was your price, Ajmal?" Sezan turned to him. "And what was your payment?"

He looked to the ceiling.

"Ajmal," Sezan snapped.

Shaytana grinned, her sharp little teeth glistening. "This sounds like a marital affair. I'll leave you two to it." She popped out of the room once more.

When the glimmer of smoke had faded from the room, Ajmal's eyes fell to hers. "I'm sorry, Sezan, that it was you who got wrapped up in all this. I asked her for a kingdom. My own to rule. I hate Qadira. She ruins the lives of everyone and knows nothing about how to take care of Ahmar, which she gained control of unprepared. She will run it to the ground and every Ahmaran with it."

"Your payment?" Sezan asked, her eyes flashing an angry gold across his light skin.

He looked away. "Marry you."

"That's it?"

He shrugged.

That didn't make any sense. "Why would you marrying me be helpful to her?" she asked.

"Because of your rank in the Shihalan line of succession."

She snorted. "To rank at all as a woman I'd have to—" Her hand flew to her stomach. "Shaytana!" she yelled.

The lilith popped into the room, arms draped lazily over Sezan's shoulders from behind. "Alright, kitten, next time you summon me, you're paying in blood." She ran a long fingernail across her skin, and Sezan nearly choked at what she saw. Sliding over

Sezan's shoulder with a rusty gleam was the *Khātam Sulaymān* on a heavy chain, the pattern exactly as it had been drawn in her books.

Sezan froze, building her fire within to find the courage to speak with those pointy teeth so close to her neck. She wanted to know how Shaytana got the Seal, why she bothered with trivial matters like theirs when she could command anyone in Qaf to do as she wished. But another matter anchored her heart in the storm of uncertainty, and she knew she may get only one or two more questions before she would have to start paying in blood.

"You didn't know I was pregnant when you had Ajmal seek me out."

"True," Shaytana purred.

"So how exactly did you plan to get me pregnant with an infertile husband?"

"Look at him," Shaytana said, pointing at Ajmal as she slumped further over Sezan's shoulders. "He's a bumpkin."

Ajmal stiffened, looking smaller and smaller as his good posture crumbled under her words.

"Naturally, I assumed you'd get bored soon enough and stray. Especially when a certain green-eyed flame sauntered by." She fluttered her eyelashes.

"So your plans do involve my baby," Sezan said, as satisfied as she was sick with finding out the answer. Her stomach swirled, and she felt the heat drain from her face.

Shaytana traced Sezan's clavicle, digging in at the edge so hard a drop of red dripped out, purpling over her turquoise. "Playing games, are we, sweetheart?"

Sezan jerked her head away from the lilith but held back the cry of pain that wanted to seep out through her teeth. "You want my baby to live. And you want it to be Bakr's. And you don't want to drain my magic, which means you want to use it... in me somehow."

Shaytana pushed her nail harder and harder until Sezan gasped. Then slipped from her back and sashayed around the front so the Seal swung back and forth, a wicked look in her eye. "Did you call me to make wild accusations or were you actually going to ask me something?"

Sezan inhaled slowly until her lungs felt like they would burst, then let it out in one sigh. "What are you planning to do with my magic, Shaytana? With my baby?"

The lilith's eyes glittered with black and pink for the briefest moment before she smiled far too wide. "Play house," she booped Sezan's nose. "Now if you don't mind, my lover boy is waiting. With how we went at each other just before popping off to see you, I'm sure he's eagerly awaiting my return."

The skin around Sezan's eyes tightened so much it hurt. Her revulsion prodded an already sick stomach, and she retched, her stomach heaving without releasing a thing.

"Oh," Shaytana tsked through her lips and patted Sezan's cheek. "Poor thing. I'll tell him you said hi, though, sweetie." She bit her lip, her body shimmering behind heatwaves, like she had decided to teleport and then changed her mind. "I always knew his fire was insatiable, but when he dreams I'm you..." She shivered, her shoulder slipping free from her fur dress, starlit and smooth. Then she winked and vanished.

Sezan rounded on Ajmal, ready to take her anger out on someone. "How could you?"

"You lied to me, too," he said, his cool demeanor slowly returning. "Marriage will always be a political animal. My offer is still the best you'll get. And besides, you've already signed the contract, we might as well make the best of it." He reached for her hand. She smacked it away.

"Why did you have me summon her?"

"It is as I said, I wanted to see if the rumors were true. Whether a lilith could be controlled if you knew her name. Only her tongue, it turns out, and even then, she plays games."

"And the second time?"

His eyes slid to the floor. "To see the demon squirm a bit. To hear her utter a truth for the first time in her life. I don't know."

No one could love a lilith, he had said to her in the halls of the palace. He hated her, too. He was just like Bakr, and it sent sparks across her skin. "If you wanted to go against Shaytana, why have you been so *muhbat* helpful to her?"

"I wasn't always helping her. I went to Eayima to see if I could find the Seal and stop her from meddling in my life—in yours, too. Once I realized you'd marry me without her forcing... well, I didn't need her anymore." Then he pointed at the ring on her finger. "The rest of the time was because she threatened to drain my powers if I failed."

"Shaytana gave this to you?" she asked, holding it up to the light. Not even a glint of light reflected off its surface. "You said it was passed down for generations... with a straight face and clear eyes."

"I'm a good liar," he said with an infuriating degree of nonchalance.

"Why didn't you just take off the ring, then?"

He shrugged. "It's cursed. It can only be removed from one's finger if another person asks to wear it and places it on theirs. Something Shaytana did to punish the people stupid enough to put it on."

Sezan winced at the stupid remark and took consolation in the fact that if he wore it, he must have been stupid, too. She rubbed the pads of her fingers together. "Izar…" she said, light dawning. "Shaytana must be the lilith from the story. She still feels betrayed by Izar, just as he felt betrayed by her. They never could trust the other, could they?" Then a more immediate realization hit her. She grabbed the ring and yanked. It didn't budge. "Ajmal!" she accused, wide-eyed.

"I'm sorry, Sezan. You asked and… what fool would I have been not to remove that burden?"

"You said you loved me without even a twitch."

He pointed to his crystal-clear eyes and sighed. "I do like you well enough, though. We're sort of perfect for each other in a messy way. I'm still glad to marry you and raise our child, with or without magic, so the ring doesn't make a difference now that it's on your finger."

"Marry you?" She took two steps back. "I'm not marrying you."

"So, you'd rather die than be with someone who isn't perfect? Or is it because you have some fetish for dead-eyed half-humans?"

"Die? Why would I die if I don't marry you?" She clenched her fist, a dim halo of her and the baby's fire glowing around her whitening knuckles.

"Because those are your only options," Ajmal said with a shrug. "You really should have read the contract before you signed it."

She shot him a glare that should have caught him on fire.

"You agreed to follow through with the marriage by sundown today or die. You also agreed that the second the sun goes down, your child belongs to the courts of Ahmar no matter whether we divorce or not."

"What?" She fell back onto the couch, his words too awful to process. "What do you mean?"

"Your baby is an Ahmaran no matter what you do. You can leave. Bakr can try to claim it. Both of you could die, or not die, and it won't matter one flick. The baby is mine. So wouldn't you rather be with your child?"

Her jaw fell open, and her eyes blurred. "I don't believe it. I would have caught that. I would have…" She pressed her palms to her eyes.

Ajmal walked over to the desk on the far side and picked up the contract, the seal still glittering on the parchment. "You're welcome to read it for yourself. You really shouldn't sign important documents without reading the contract. That's ambassador basics. I'm surprised at you."

"You son of a—" Sezan punched the settee. What had she done? Allah, what had she done? The one time she didn't read a contract had been the most important one of her life. Bakr would never forgive her. Never. Ever. She would never forgive herself either. It would have been better if she had been swallowed up into Jahannam than suffer this fate.

"Our contract was sealed by the King of Elm," Ajmal continued, tapping the contract. "And remember, if you die by breaking the contract, so does your baby." Ajmal walked behind her and placed his hands on her shaking shoulders. "It would be easier on everyone if you put up a smile and followed me out of this room as my wife."

"Shaytana will not leave you alone after this," she said through the bars of her teeth. "Didn't you hear her? She plans to *play house*. She will ruin you, me, and take the baby just like you took it from me. And then you will be ruler of nothing."

"I already am the ruler of nothing, Sezan," he said with a candid resignation. "So you're all I've got and I'm all you've got. Now smile, pretty, I want you happy on our wedding day."

"I'll smile, right after I do this." She pulled her arm back and punched him in the nose so hard blood burst out from the bottom.

His head jerked back, and he staggered. "How dare you?" he spluttered, cupping his nose in his palm. The sticky blood leaked through the cracks. He grabbed her wrist with the other hand. "You're trying my patience. Don't tempt me, or I'll cast you out as soon as that child is born and raise it to spit on your name."

She clenched her teeth, yanking on her held wrist. It was stupid of her to have hit him—he even took on Bakr in one of his legendary rages—but it had felt so good. Had he ever expressed being afraid of anything?

She turned to Ajmal, grinned, and touched a hand to the pouch at her waist. He raised a suspicious brow. Then she reached inside and pulled out Ayelet's gift of bottled magic.

"A present from my human princess," she said and took pleasure in watching his eyes widen. "I'm sure you can guess what it is. So believe me when I say I will rip this through your lungs and out your eyes just as Al'amirat Ayelet did in the stories about the redemption of Qaf."

He threw her arm to the side with a sneer. Blood trickled down his lips. "What do you want?" he asked. A rainbow of color finally leaked from eyes that watched the vial of magic as if it were a blade aimed at his heart.

"For you to fulfill your obligation in our marriage contract and do everything within your power to help me break my deal with the lilith. I have until sunset before the contract expires, and then I die, and your future with me. Don't test me."

"How am I supposed to help?" he asked, licking his lips nervously.

"By taking me to Bakr."

"Sezan," he growled.

She put a hand to the cork of the bottle of magic and tipped it under his nose. "Now."

CHAPTER THIRTY-THREE

BAKR

BAKR LANDED. OR AT least, he stopped falling. He opened his eyes, or at least it felt like he did. It was impossible to know in such blackness. He had nothing. His sword Shaytana had left in his room when she took him into the nameless place, and now... This was even worse. No light, nothing to say that he was even still alive.

Panic tried to swell in his chest, but for how strange the place was there was a familiarity that helped quell the fear. He closed his eyes and breathed—focused in on his thoughts—and tried to push back through to Qaf or Ard, or even back to Shaytana's immutable expansive void.

Nothing happened. He was trapped.

Time passed as if it were nothing, as if *he* were nothing. Wasn't that what he had always hoped for? To find a place where he could pretend, even for a moment, that he no longer existed. Like death. Not the death promised by Allah, or Shihala, or magic, or the poetry of punishment and paradise. But true death. Nothing.

But he was still *here*. Still alive and conscious, even if he couldn't move. He could not rise to his feet. Did he even have feet?

There was no pain, no sensation. A nose without smells, ears without sound.

"Hello?" he called. It echoed back to him from a thousand miles away. Distant. Fading. Nothing.

He screamed with all his strength, and in this place, there was no end to it. No echo. No breath. He could have screamed forever. Still, it came back to him. Hollow.

A flash of gray in the darkness. Bakr's mind tightened. That was all he had here. He watched, unblinking and only feeling. A sense of dread. When he saw such dusky gray skin in the past, it had only ever belonged to one person. His savior. His nightmare. The one that defined him.

"Shaytana?" he called, almost hoping that she would pop back into existence at his side.

Nothing. And that meant one of two things. Either she was already there, or...

The gray drew closer, carried on its own mist until he was looking at a stranger. Gray skin. Small horns peaking through a mane of black hair. Eyes of shining, pure jade. Familiar, though he had never seen them before.

The man came close enough to smell him. Spicy and woody. He was tall, muscles defining his frame. A white smile with spiky canines. As cold as winter in the Zabriyan peaks, yet perfect. Timeless, ageless beauty just like her.

"Hello, Bakr," the man said, his impossible smile broadening until his face could barely hold it, like a snake about to ingest his prey. The man had dark thick eyebrows, sharp cheekbones, and a spade-shaped jaw. His voice was a viscous mixture of amusement and disdain. "I was starting to think you were never going to make it."

Bakr found the wherewithal to look down at himself and was startled to discover his body was as he had left it. Barefoot. Bare-chested. Slumped to the ground with bent knees. He could see himself as clearly as he could the man. The dirt under his nails. The smear of hashish wax on his forearm. He narrowed his eyes up at the man and tried to rise to his feet, but he had no energy.

"I've been trying to call you here for quite a while," the man laughed, bracing his hands on slender hips. "Finally managed to peel your eyes away from Shaytana, hmm?"

Bakr watched him in silence before finding a voice trapped deep in the back of his throat. "Where am I?"

"We call it *makan majhul*," he said, his voice as flat and disinterested as if sharing the time. "We all have one." Laughter quivered over his gray skin like glitter. "At least, all full-bloods do. I don't know about half-breeds. It's never come up."

Bakr shook his head, straining to understand what being a half-breed had to do with anything now. "Who are you?"

"Is that a question?" The stranger offered his hand, lifting his dark eyebrows and giving a charming, entirely animalistic, smile.

Bakr looked at the man's hand. Broad and strong, thick nails of pure black. He didn't take it, instead forcing himself to stand on his own.

The man put a hand to his own heart and leaned back. "You hurt me, son. You really do."

"I don't give an *alqarf* about you." He groaned and glanced down at his chest, expecting to see the many wounds Shaytana had left on him. Everything had been healed. "What in Jahannam is going on?"

"I guess it is a lot to take in, you being half-human and all. I know your brains are a bit bogged down with all that mortality stuff. What a shame." The man crossed his arms over his chest, chuckles shivering all over his body. "But just look at you, boy. You've done your old man proud. Better than I could have hoped for."

"My old man...?" Bakr couldn't finish the question. It trailed off, stolen by a silent and immobile breeze, and lost in the infinite darkness. He looked down and shook his head. "This is another of Shaytana's tricks."

"No. I got you out of her *majhul*, and not a moment too soon. Watching you with her these past years, seeing what she's done to you. I almost reached in and plucked you out so many times. But she was right about one thing. You had to be ready to come to me on your own."

Bakr allowed a haughty laugh to bubble up his throat. He was certain this was just another of Shaytana's tricks, no matter what the imaginary man said or how real and fundamentally different he seemed. This was just another trial she had invented for him to endure, and not even an especially clever one.

She was punishing him for calling her back so many times, that's all this was.

"It was good for you," the gray-skinned man continued. "Almost like she eased you into all of this for me. I suppose I should thank her, but she is such a gloating *alkalba*. I'd have to listen to it for centuries."

"Listen to what?" Bakr tossed the question casually over his shoulder and began to walk a slow circle in the darkness. He was prepared to talk to this new hallucination and say whatever it needed to hear to get back to reality quicker.

"That she found you first. I had a close eye on you back when you were still with your mother, but when she sent you off to Qaf..." The gray-skinned man cast his gaze askance, irritation twisting his perfect features. "I had not expected that. She was always so weak before that, so easy to bend. I never would have thought she had the stomach to send you away. But when opportunity knocks, you answer, I suppose. Ten years and she'd just been waiting for a good excuse."

Bakr scoffed coldly. Mention of his mother was always painful, no matter how he tried to steel himself against it. But it was an old and beloved game for Shaytana. Nothing made him twitch and ache quite like talking about his mother did.

"You know how women are," the gray man sighed. "Stupid, malleable animals. All you have to do is hold one down for a few seconds and show her who is in charge, and you have her for life, provided your boys are strong swimmers."

All the implications of the horrible words settled on Bakr's shoulders like hot ash. He shivered to shake them off, but his skin was already scorched.

"I've had enough, Shaytana," Bakr hissed, making a slow circle around the man. "If you want to torment me, at least have the decency to show yourself and stop insulting my intelligence with this nonsense."

"I'm not Shaytana, kid," the gray man said, his empty eyes meeting Bakr's and staying fixed. "I'm a lilu."

"A what?"

Genuine irritation flashed in the black and jade-colored eyes. Not like a djinn—with their bright, audacious colors. This was more muted, almost human. And so quick that it would have been easy to miss.

"We're rare," the gray man said. "As far as I know, there are only five of us left in existence. Six, if we count you, so I don't see why not. I suppose the easiest way to explain is to say I am a male lilith. All the same powers, but with twice the upper-body strength."

"You're a lilith?" Bakr scoffed.

"Lilu," he said again. "*Incupi. Pori. Karabasan.* We have many names."

"And I'm supposed to believe that you are my father?"

"I *am* your father." He shook his head and his body quivered again as a fit of laughter overtook him. "It still sounds strange to me, too. Lilitu can't breed together, so we have to rely on djinn and humans, and that virtually never works either. I hope you appreciate how rare you are. I have been trying—sometimes ten to twelve times a day—for literally thousands of years to make a child. And you are the only one." He put a hand out to one side and gave a regal bow. "Congratulations."

Bakr laughed. He had to laugh to keep from screaming, lunging at the man, and gouging his eyes out with his thumbs. But after the way Shaytana had punished him the last time he attacked her, he wasn't yet ready for a repeat performance.

"So, you're trying to tell me I'm half lilith?" Bakr scoffed.

"Lilu," the gray man corrected again, his voice tight. "And yes, you are. Honestly, I'm surprised you never questioned the whole *djinn* theory. If you're half-djinn, where's your fire? Where is your fire, Bakr?"

Bakr shook his head. He didn't have an answer to that question. He never had. In twenty-four years of a nomadic and social life, he'd met a few other half-djinn. All of them had rainbow skin, muddied only a little with human brown. And all of them had fire, popping from their palms and flashing in his eyes. He figured all half-djinn got different things from the transaction. Some got fire; some got screwed.

He pinched his nose between his thumb and forefinger. Why was he even thinking about that right now?

"Shaytana, why are you showing me these stupid fictions?" Bakr spat. "Come as you are and let that be the end of this."

"She can't hear you," said the man, his voice cold and slow and sharp as ice growing on the roof of Ashkult prison. "Nobody can. You're in my space. There is no way in or out unless I grant it."

Bakr turned back to him, all the muscles tightening in his face and neck. He scanned the lilitu again, both with his eyes and with his heart. Usually he could tell—*feel*—the characters Shaytana played in his dreams were actually her. But when he looked at the gray man—really looked at him—he didn't feel any of that.

"This is impossible," Bakr breathed.

"I tried for years to make you a little brother or sister," said the lilu. "I thought there must have been something special about your mother to have made you. Nothing ever came of it.."

"You what?" Bakr whispered. A large part of him still believed this was another of Shaytana's tricks, but the words still bit into him as deep as any that ever came before.

"At least I got you out of the bargain, hmm? And just look at you!" The gray man stepped closer and punched him in the shoulder. "A strapping young man if I ever saw one. A real chip off the old block. I bet you've been breaking hearts all over two worlds. Isn't that right?"

Bakr's mouth hung open, jaw twitching. "You're lying."

"You don't have to answer. It's better if you don't, actually. Keep a bit of mystery for yourself, isn't that right boy?" The horrid gray demon clapped his arm around Bakr's back.

"Don't..." He flinched, his shoulders tightening. "Don't touch me."

"Don't be that way, kiddo." He flashed his hideous snake smile again. Too wide. Too many teeth. Uncanny. "I know it's been a bit of a rough journey so far..."

"No. You can't be my father. You can't."

"I'm afraid it's true. I'd say ask your mother, but I guess she wouldn't recognize me either, hmm?" He spat out a braying laugh. The sound of it ignited a white-hot flame in Bakr's brain that quickly eclipsed his vision and all sense of reason. He lunged at the horrible gray man, nails bared to rip out chunks of the flesh on his neck.

"Woah!" the demon threw up a hand and Bakr was knocked back as if by a sharp gust of wind. "Sit down, boy."

He skittered across the blackness, then ripped back up to his feet. "You raped my mother!"

"Psh." The gray man waved a hand dismissively. "Women."

"Shaytana showed me what you did. I've experienced what you did." Bakr shuddered at the memory, the nightmare of being inside of his mother's body while the invisible monster tore at her flesh and her soul.

He pressed his face into his hands, running his fingers into his hair so the ragged nails raked the scalp. If what this monster said was true, his mother had endured much more than one nightmare. A recurring horror night after night. For years.

And that meant every day when she awakened and saw him—the offspring of a monster—she had a fresh memory of horror in her mind.

No wonder she hated him.

"Don't worry about her, kid. She abandoned you. Sent you to Qaf to be murdered by who-knows-what? She didn't care." The demon put his hand on his shoulder again. "Baba's here now."

Bakr was flooded by a flash of fire, extending from those twisted black claws. "I said don't touch me!"

Bakr snatched the wrist and twisted. He flipped the demon over his shoulders, slamming him down onto the flat of his back. Then he brought his foot down to smash that horrible grinning face, but it landed on nothing. He whipped around to see the monster standing behind him, cackling. And the noise traced his skin in rivulets of burning metal.

"Okay, kiddo. I can see you need some time to come to grips with things. We'll talk later."

Bakr screamed maniacally and lunged for him, but he disappeared in a puff of gray smoke and the world around him began to churn. His stomach lurched and his vision blurred. When he looked up again, the blackness was gone. He was alone in his room at Karzusan, the same room where he'd watched the dancing girls before being tricked and robbed by Shaytana. It still smelled of opium and hashish, as if not a moment had passed.

Screaming, Bakr picked up a stone tea table and threw it at the wall. It crashed, bottles and hookah shattering. What that monster said was a lie. It had to be a lie, another of Shaytana's tricks. He wanted to say her name. To call her back to him and demand an answer, but his tongue was like a rock in his mouth.

He fell to his knees and cradled his head in his hands.

CHAPTER THIRTY-FOUR

SEZAN

SEZAN LET GO OF Ajmal's arm the second they landed. They stood in the halls of Shihala's palace, her royal blood allowing them through the fire barriers. The royal blue tiling was as familiar as the hijab on her head. She blinked through the fading smoke and scanned the surrounding space.

"Where is he?" she snipped.

Ajmal shrugged. "Teleporting to a person is not an exact magic."

"Why not? It's the one stupid perk for being an Ahmaran royal."

"He's somewhere in the proximity," Ajmal growled back. "And if he's not, that's your fault, not mine."

She glared at him when a sharp, familiar voice called out from behind. "*Bihaqi aljahima*? Ambassador Sezan?"

Jahmil came marching down the hallway towards her, his eyes flashing with irritated streaks of white lightning.

"This is not a good time, Highness," she quipped, not even bothering to bow. What was the point considering what she was about to go through?

"What are you doing here?" His gaze darted from her to Ajmal and back again.

"You don't want to know," Sezan said. "Have you seen Bakr?"

He opened his mouth wide and scoffed. "Excuse me. This is my palace. I have a right to know. And if you're here, who is in Ahmar keeping track of everything?"

"What is there to keep track of? All of Ahmar is at a wedding." She pushed past Jahmil, searching the hallway before turning to the door to her left. She would have to kick it. "Open this." She turned to Jahmil.

"You mean *your* wedding?" he demanded, ignoring her order.

"Yes, my wedding. But look, I've brought the groom with me, unlike when you left yours. Problem solved. Now stop talking and open the door." She paused, then added, "Please."

"I ought to have you brought up on treason," he said, shaking his head in disbelief.

"Oh, get off it, Jahmil," she dropped his title. "I'm trying to prevent you from losing your throne, not to be the cause of it."

He clenched a fist, white fire exploding from his knuckles. He muttered curses to himself as he pointed at the door to the room. The lock clicked open. "I'll have you both flogged in the public square," he said, mostly to himself. "By Allah's might, I will."

She slapped him on the shoulder as she rushed past. "Thanks, brother."

It took a moment for her eyes to adjust to the dimly lit room, and the smell of hashish, sweat, and opium made her gag. Allah, it stank. He was definitely in there somewhere.

"Bakr?" she called, wiping her mouth clean.

A shadow moved by the window. A soft breeze blew the curtain, starlight illuminating one half of his face. He leaned against the sill, one leg propped up with an elbow draped across the knee. Deep lines cut between his brows, around his cracked lips. The whites of his eyes were so red that the color shined in the darkness.

"Sezan?" he said, his voice cold and raspy.

She rushed to him and placed her cool hands on his warm cheeks, not caring if Ajmal or Jahmil or anybody else watched. "What's happened to you? The darkness in your eyes has consumed all of you."

"Don't marry him," he said, no energy in his voice. "He's a liar. He just wants to use you."

Sezan huffed. "Same ole Bakr, harping on the same points over and over again, thinking I never listen. Wash your face, I need you standing."

He stood slowly and wiped his hands over his face. "He's in league with Shay... with the lilith. They all are. You have to get out."

"Yes, yes," she said, pulling him the rest of the way to his feet. "You have the ring?"

"She took the Seal." He lifted his right hand into the light. "She took it. I'm so stupid."

Sezan froze. "That's how she got the Seal." She shook her head. "You are a fool, Bakr. But I'm not here for the Seal. Not right now." She grabbed his hand and sighed with relief when she saw the copper lump on his middle finger.

"This?" He grabbed the ring and yanked at it, but it was stuck. He licked his finger and pulled it off. "You want it?"

"Uch. Not after you licked it. Put it back on," she sighed and flinched away from the metal. "This would be a lot easier if you were sober, you son of a snake."

"I'm sober," said Bakr, a tired smile flinching on his lips. "It's been hours since I had anything. Days, maybe."

She growled at him. "Why are you a useless lump the one time I need you to be your passionate, idiotic self?" She turned to Jahmil who stood stiff and uncomfortable by the door. "Please tell me there's something you can do. I need him... I need his fire." Faris Khayin had said the spell would only work if the bearer of the copper ring yearned for something in the other. This Bakr could barely stand, much less yearn.

"Don't look at me," Jahmil quipped, though his eyebrows knit together in concern.

"I don't have any fire," Bakr said. "I never did."

"Great," Sezan snipped. "The amir's graciousness ends with opening doors, and you don't have any fire."

"My graciousness did end with your antics," Jahmil said coolly with a shake of his head. "I don't need to be privy to the mess you two have made. I'll be outside." He took one more glance at them before mumbling and stepping into the hallway.

Sezan turned back to Bakr. "It's not about djinn fire. I just need whatever it is that makes you *you*. So find it."

"Why?" He took a step past her and groaned as he bent to pick up his sword. "What do you want me to do?"

She almost slapped the blade from his hand, remembering last second it would sear her flesh. "Put that down. All I want from you is a kiss. But not a... a lumpy kiss. I need *you*."

He choked on a tired laugh. "What in the name of all that is horrid is a lumpy kiss?"

"You know what I mean." She smiled and chuckled with him. "Please?"

The sword fell from his grasp, tinkling in the broken glass that covered the carpet. He put his arm around her waist and pulled her body flush against his, his eyes scanning up and down her face. "Does this mean you've changed your mind?"

She turned away from his scrutiny. What was she to say to that? Yes? And give him false hope that there was life after a broken contract sealed by Elm? No? And have him refuse to kiss her?

"I have decided to make my own way."

"Good enough for me," he said and kissed her so hard it almost hurt.

She wrapped her arms around his neck, every part of her flickering and begging to be closer. Closer. Her tight throat, her desperate fingers, the shaking in her chest. And her fire and the baby's rising to a blazing roar that filled her vision with light as warm as Ard. This could have been her family.

And then his kiss did hurt. She pulled him closer and ran through the spell Faris Khayin had told her over and over in her head. The onyx ring on her finger burned cold, like a bolt of lightning straight to her bone. She gasped at the pain but held him to her. It was the only way. The only way to keep the baby safe from Shaytana.

A waft of cinnamon coated the room.

Sezan's stomach clenched. Their time was almost up. She clung tighter to Bakr as the warmth drained from her bones and channeled what was left through her stomach, to ease the loss of magic from the life that lay there, hoping it would be enough. Hoping that Shaytana would not want a magicless baby or its empty mother.

"You gave her the ring, you stupid bumpkin!" Shaytana shrieked. A crash cut the air, followed by a pained cry from Ajmal.

Bakr pulled her to him tightly—tighter and more delicately than anybody else ever could—his open palms pressing into her back. He moaned into her mouth, a dry, painful little sound, but he didn't pull away.

"Get your hands off of him," said Shaytana, focusing her ire on Sezan like a blast of burning air. Nails dug deep into Sezan's neck. Shaytana grabbed Sezan's hair through her hijab and ripped her from Bakr.

She had never felt so weak. So cold. But she turned to Shaytana and grinned. "Too late."

"I will rip your heart out," Shaytana said and lifted her hand.

"What in Jahannam's name is going on!" screamed Jahmil, pounding on the door that was now locked tight with magic he couldn't even undo.

Sezan lunged forward, ripping the seams in her dress and grabbing hold of the lump of iron dangling from Shaytana's neck. She waited for it to sear her pale blue-green skin. Stinging, blisters, but not the fire of death she had expected. She tried to pull it off, but Shaytana sunk her teeth into Sezan's shoulder. Pain tore through her flesh, fire on fire in pulsing agony. Sezan couldn't hold on. She pushed the monster's face away and stumbled back. Shaytana lifted her hand, her silver nails lengthening into daggers. She slashed down.

Sezan braced, hands wrapped tightly around her stomach, but Bakr stepped in front of her and caught Shaytana's wrist. "Shaytana, stop this. I'll do anything you want. Just leave her out of it."

Sezan darted her eyes to Ajmal's twitching body near the door as another wave of nausea hit her. Was he dead? She pressed her lips to her shoulder to keep back the vomit so she wouldn't have to let go of her baby. If he died, what would that mean for her contract? She'd be free. But if he died in Bakr's rooms, no one else would be. Ahmar would demand Bakr's death and when Jahmil inevitably refused to hand him over, war would break out for certain. Who would believe a demon had killed the prince?

She closed her eyes, waiting for her nausea to pass. Then she looked between Bakr and Shaytana. To how their skin touched each other. To how Shaytana already leaned into him. To their familiarity. A sick closeness she couldn't help but feel was her fault. She snapped.

"Stop giving her what she wants, Bakr. Stop treating her like you owe her anything."

"I know I don't." He turned his gaze to her slowly. "She told me."

"Then why do you kowtow to her like that? You never once lay down and take it from me so easily. So why her? Why now, after everything I've done? Why am I never enough for you?"

"He lays down and takes it cause I give it so good." Shaytana's nails retracted back into her usual three-inch points. Bakr released her wrist, and she took a step back and straightened her little dress. "I may not be able to take your fire anymore, kitten. But that doesn't mean you aren't going to suffer for this." Her twinkling pink and black eyes twitched to Bakr. "And I'll need a word with you, muffin."

Gray mist wrapped around her, and she quickened out of existence.

"Why are you like that?" Sezan spat where the lilith had stood and rounded on Bakr.

"I don't want her to hurt you."

"So you'll fight ten thousand Vespars for Jahmil, but not one demon for me?"

"Vespars die when you stab them." He shrugged and slumped down on the bed. "I've already tried that with her. That's my move. I don't know what else to do."

"And here I thought your move was seducing hapless women into bed. Just get the Seal back, Bakr! How many times have you laid with her since she's had it on and you've left it there? That's probably how she got it in the first place, isn't it?"

"Leave me alone. You don't know anything about it."

Sezan sighed, regretting the coldness in her words. Without her fire, everything seemed sharper, like her pink flames had softened the world and warmed it for her. Now she saw as Bakr did.

"I know she's a monster. And I know I can't understand what she's done to you. But I don't believe for one second that you're too weak to fight it. You go around fighting everyone else's battles but not your own. And if you doubt it, then take my strength with you and... and stand up for yourself for once."

He shook his head slowly, pressed a hand over his eyes, and rubbed them harshly. "I just can't stand it anymore. I don't want to be like her."

"Who said you were anything like her?" Sezan asked, trying to follow his windy way of talking through things when her body ached and her stomach slushed and her skin crept with cold.

"I'm exactly like her. Like all of them. I always have been. You've said so yourself many times. I seduce hapless women. I lie to them. I hurt them. I use them. That's what I do." He covered his face with his hands, folding over himself. "I don't want to do it anymore. I don't want her to..."

She scooted over to where he lay and stroked his hair. Fear about him failing hit her for the first time. She had not expected this. She had placed her hope in the shining Bakr who could overcome anything. Who would protect her at all costs. It was why she had thought of no one else to hold her magic, their baby's. It had to be him. Even if the lilith had torn him down, had broken his spirit and parts of his mind. A wave of protectiveness washed through her. A need to get him out of Shihala and away from the lilith and the wounded amir who she couldn't bring herself to look at.

"And since when have you cared what pretentious, judgemental, vain courtiers think? A vapid lot, they are. Myself included." She smiled, then let it fall when he didn't look up. "You are not like the lilith, Bakr. She creates pain. You hide from it. Embrace it even, if you think it's right. But you don't deserve it. You never have." She stopped short of bearing the rest of her heart. Of confessing everything, including her love, because she would just hurt him, too. She saw that now.

Her love was destroying him.

He wiped his face quickly and turned his eyes to meet hers. "I'll do whatever you want me to do. You want me to go back to her? Sleep with her? Try to steal the Seal? Is that the idea?"

"Allah, no."

"I'll do it." He yanked himself up from the bed, rolled his shoulders, and swung his arms around. Then he smacked himself in the face a couple of times. "Let me just find my shirt." He sighed. "Screw it. I don't need it."

Sezan watched him openly, knowing for the first time her fire wouldn't give away the sadness eating away at her heart. "I spoke out of rage earlier, Bakr. It was not fair for me to place this burden on you. I had only meant to give you life, not to bring you pain, and yet that's all I've done. Just take Fajar and go live on the floating city. The demon cannot get to you there."

"And leave you to clean up this mess?" He shot her a smile over his shoulder, but it was the saddest expression she had ever seen. "Are you out of your mind?"

"My hero," she said, a wince in her smile. "There is no more mess to clean up. No more burdens to bear. I know what you really want is to be free from her nightmares, so do that. Soak up Fajar's love. She's a sweet little thing. And in time, I—" She stopped short of telling him about the child. It would do nothing but send him to death at Shaytana's hands. "Be free, Bakr. And stop worrying about me, or Jahmil, or the demon, or anyone else."

"You should know by now that is literally impossible." He walked over to her and knelt down in the glass to look at her eyes. "You're really stupid, did you know that?"

She scoffed. "You don't care about what I've done here or why, and I'm the stupid one?"

"Yes, you are. You made a deal with her. And then you lied to me about it over and over and over…"

"And you told me you wanted to be with me forever and on the same night left me for two years without a word. Besides, that's not true," she said stiffly. "I told you exactly what I did at the celebration after Jahmil's wedding when you finally decided to talk to me."

"I believe I would remember that conversation."

"I am not responsible for what you believe."

He narrowed his eyes at her. "What did you say?"

"You were teasing me about missing you. And I said that I spent the nights drinking away my sorrows and making deals with demons just to see your face again."

His face softened, and he set his hand on her knee. "Oh, so you aren't just stupid. You're hopeless. And impossible."

She smiled and bit her lip. "You knew what you were getting into." Then she slid out from under his hand and turned towards Ajmal's battered body. She clenched her teeth but kept her voice level "I'm serious, though, Bakr. I have to take Ajmal to the royal healer after what the lilith has done and then finish my contract. And you should leave, escape while you still can. I know what you've always wanted is to be free."

His face fell and then tightened into knots. "Are you kidding me? Finish your contract?"

"Yes," she shook her head with a huff. "That's what I said. I told you I'm forging my own way, and I am."

"You're still going to marry him?" he hissed through clenched teeth. "After barging back into my life and demanding that I kiss you with fire? Why don't you just pick up that sword and run me through while you're at it, you vicious woman?"

His words ate at her like rust through iron so all she wanted to do was crumple in on herself and weep. But that would solve nothing. She found the strength to keep standing. "So you would rather I die? Because that's what will happen at sunset in Ahmar if I don't sign that contract."

"What are you talking about!" He stood and smacked a chair across the room. "For once, could you just speak plainly?"

His growing rage set her in a place of calm, especially since she could see a flicker of fire, her own and the baby's, beginning to shine in his eyes. Did he not feel her very heat burning inside him? Or did he simply not care?

"Fine. I'll speak plainly. I already signed an engagement contract sealed by the King of Eastern Elm that states I will marry Ajmal today by the fall of the First Moon. If I don't, I'll die. Is that plain enough for you?"

"Why would you do something so unbelievably stupid?"

She held her chin up, though it trembled, hurting her teeth. "Does it matter after everything we've both been through? After everything we've done to each other? I'm trying to let you do what you've always wanted, guilt-free and with no strings attached, and you're mad at me?"

"What a load of hot crap," he spat. "Do you have anything else you want to tell me? Any other secrets that you think might concern me, Sezan?" He spoke her name like a curse, staring daggers at her, his fists clenched. "Or do you think I'm a halfbreed idiot just like everybody else?"

She pointed to his fists and the soft glow that formed around them for the first time in his life. It was strange seeing her fire lick someone else's skin. And already she missed the little orange ember that had been her baby's magic. "A gift."

He shook his head hard. "A sacrifice."

"That I already made over a year ago. At least now I am with you."

"Not just you."

Her eyes widened and she looked away. "What do you mean?" she asked for lack of any excuse.

"You really do think I'm stupid," he scoffed and shook his head. "You just pushed two colors of fire into me. I've lived among djinn most of my life. You think I don't know what that means?"

"I thought you'd be too prideful to acknowledge what I'd done in the first place. Which was true."

"I was getting around to it," he snarled.

"Ah well, let me just lay back and wait for you, then." She flashed her eyes back to him, a sharp pain pricking her heart when no amber glow came with it. "It's not like I'm on a time clock or anything. And I thought you'd be... I thought the news would..." She couldn't finish the words as the fissures in her heart filled with fire and ice.

"Is it mine?"

"Yours?" She wrapped her fingers in her tunic and squeezed tight. His words were a cool salve that somehow left her raw. He did not realize what he kept safe within his body. That the baby was his. But what good would telling him he's a father do when his baby would belong to another as soon as the contract was fulfilled at sunset? The baby belonged to them by blood but to Ajmal by dictate. She could never live down the shame of it, and Bakr would never stop fighting and never win until they were both destroyed. She sighed and formed the half-truth on her dry tongue. "The child belongs to the court of Ahmar."

All the color drained from his face. "You put another man's child's fire inside of me?"

"I had to, Bakr."

His lip twitched, eyes wide and tinged with purple light as they darted up to meet hers. "How could you do that to me?"

"Because your demon is after my baby, because the baby is innocent and doesn't deserve my fate... and because—" She looked away, her voice dropping to a whisper. "Because you're you. No one else would do. Not ever."

Seeing her own angry fire glowing back at her was punishment enough, but the sorrow in his sage green eyes showed through, crushing her into dust. Already she wished to take back her half-truth. To make amends. To beg his forgiveness, but it wouldn't change the situation. She still had to marry Ajmal. And then the baby would belong to him. And

Bakr would never know. And if he did, he would hate her forever knowing what she'd done.

"I did it the same way I've done everything I have for you. So call me stupid and vicious." Her chest tightened, and her voice rasped. "And take comfort in the fact that I will suffer every day for what I've done."

"If not today." Bakr turned his back on her. He picked up his sword and stumbled across the room to where Ajmal lay unconscious, blood trickling down his face from where Shaytana had smashed his head against the wardrobe. Bakr set the tip of his blade on his stomach and the flesh immediately began to sizzle. He laid his other hand on the pommel. "So much for Elm," he said, and his shoulders tensed.

"No!" Sezan leaped forward and grabbed the sword. Blisters coiled to life on her fingers. He shoved her back hard with his elbow. She stumbled, barely catching herself from falling. He had never struck her before. Not ever. Her whole body trembled.

"Don't kill anybody, please," she said, desperately searching the room for something to stop Bakr and regretting that Jahmil had left. He was the only other person Bakr would listen to.

"I can't stand for this." He turned to look at her, the tip of his blade burning a hole in Ajmal's belly so the room filled with the smell of scorched flesh and singed hair. "I'm not a good person, Sezan. What did you think I would do when you told me about all this?"

"Not this," she said, covering her mouth with her hand. "Bakr, stop. Please. I'll fix it. Is it the fire? I'll find a way to get it out of you. Is it... I need you to not do this. Please, trust me. The baby... the baby needs a father. And you will be exiled."

"You are not marrying him. It's just not happening."

"What part of a contract of peace are you not understanding? If I break the contract, I die. If you kill him, Shihalans will die. Is that what you want?"

"I don't care!" he yelled, pressing the scorching blade deeper into Ajmal's tender flesh. Her body shook in terror, horror, revulsion. "This bastard set you up with a contract where you die—you die!—if you don't marry him. So I kill him; end of contract."

"And how will I ever be able to look at you again?"

"I've been a killer the entire time you've known me. What do you think I was doing in Orkeshi? Negotiating contracts?" He chuckled through his bared, leonine teeth, then turned his furious gaze on Ajmal. "If I let him live, you're still gone. If I kill the lying little bastard, at least I can say I tried to stop it."

"Bakr," she said softly. "You are not like Shay... like that demon. And you are not responsible for my mistakes. If you kill him... they will kill you. Even Jahmil won't be able to protect you. And... I need you alive."

He laughed coldly. "Let them try to kill me. I can't die!" He turned back to her, his pale eyes glowing brighter than ever and sparkling with orange fire. "You don't need me. Nobody does. I might as well embrace it. I *am* like the lilith, more so than you will ever understand. Maybe I'll make a deal with her. I'll make a thousand. And I'll fix the stupid war. Or maybe I'll make it worse. Either way, my bills are paid."

"What are you talking about?" Sezan shook her head to make sense of his words. "What do you mean you can't die? The whole reason I made the deal with that awful demon in the first place was because you're a dumb mortal who thinks he's invincible but isn't."

"Not so dumb, baby. Intuitive." He flashed a bright smile, made all the brighter by the broiling sunshine in his eyes. "I laid on that field with blood coming out of my neck for three days before she came and got me. Do you know how dead I should have been after three days? After three degrees." He growled and shook his head. "No. No, you are no longer entitled to my secrets."

"It is your secrets that made this mess worse. The only reason I entered this marriage was to fix the problems I made in my deal with the lilith. But if you can't die, that contract is void. The lilith didn't save anything. So now I'm marrying Ajmal solely for the fact that *you* didn't trust *me* and gave the Seal of Sulayman to the lilith, yet you stand over *him* with a sword?"

"You're the one who ran off from the hot springs. You're the one that pushed me away. You're the one that slept with the lying pig. You're the one that signed that contract. And you're the one who called the lilith. I never asked you to. And you kept it from me all this time, pushing me away at every opportunity because you knew I wouldn't have wanted you to. I would give anything to go back and stop you from doing it."

"Even now?" She dropped her yelling to a whisper. "Even after all I've done?"

He laughed in her face. "Especially now. Especially after all you've done. You didn't have to do any of it because I can't die. You didn't have to do any of it, period." He lifted his free hand to his eyes to look at the multicolored fire dancing on his fingertips. "And now I have this taint on me. Another one. This filth's disgusting spawn glowing in my blood."

"That disgusting spawn is the love of my life. It is my Rukh. My one and only. And an innocent child in all of this. You could have ended things with the lilith when you had the

Seal, that is not my fault. If you wanted so badly to get out, maybe you should have done something about it for once instead of cowering to her and blaming everyone else."

"Keep it then. And I'll keep its fire just so it will never have it." He lifted his sword and slid it into the holster at his hip, then spat on Ajmal's face. "I loved you, Sezan," he breathed, looking up to meet her eyes once again. "I've loved you for years." He tightened his lips and shook his head. "No more."

A vat of quicksilver straight down her throat would have burned less than the words that fell from his mouth. There would be no forgiveness for signing his baby over to Qadira's court—the worst sin of negligence she ever made—or for her hiding the secret of his fatherhood. She didn't even deserve redemption. He had finally been able to tell her he loved her and now it was no more.

"I deserve all that I shall get," she said and laid face down on the bed. "Thank you, Bakr. For keeping the fire safe. I knew... I knew you would."

He walked over to her and put out his hand. "Give me the ring."

The hold the onyx had on her finger loosened, and the oversized ring slipped down to her middle knuckle. She slid her limp arm so it dangled over the edge of the bed. He snatched up her hand and yanked it off, then ripped the copper ring from his own finger and threw it on the bed beside her.

Sezan slipped farther into darkness, wrapping the blankets tighter.

He stormed over to the nightstand and yanked the drawer open with so much force it pulled clean out. A pile of small, fiery feathers inside fluffed with the wind. He lifted one to his mouth and blew it off. When it touched the ground, he disappeared in a burst of yellow fire.

Even with her magic flowing through his veins, he still would not use it. He still thought her love for him made him weak.

Only the thought of her little one gave her the strength to slide out of the bed and crawl her way to Ajmal. She slapped his face and for lack of any water threw whatever alcohol Bakr had left lying around over his skin. When he still did not wake, she called for help. Servants and healers and tsking courtiers flowed in and out of the room as Sezan's world darkened into abyss.

The beating from Shaytana, the burn of iron on his skin, it had all been too much.

Ajmal was dead.

CHAPTER THIRTY-FIVE

Bakr

Bakr appeared in the nameless place. He was nervous to open his eyes, thinking he might have found himself back in his father's infinite blackness, but endless white cocooned him. It was strangely comforting. Familiar. Everything he had come to know and trust because it was the one thing that had never gone away. Still, he didn't want to be there, alone in the worthless nothingness with his thoughts, and least of all his feelings. His heart was thrumming in his chest, thrashing against the bones, trying to break free to something better. His skin was flush, muscles tense, itching desperately for action. Trembling with so much built-up energy, a bolt of lightning not yet expelled. His mouth was so dry his tongue scraped his hard palate like sandpaper, though his teeth were clenched so tight the muscle could hardly move.

His thoughts kept running over the same points again and again, and with each pass, his shaking intensified.

How could she do that to him? How could she?

A flash of gray and brown swept his eyes up to where Shaytana sat a few feet away. She had a pile of papers laid out in front of her and a quill in her hand, scribbling furiously and then pressing the Seal into the bottom of each so they ignited with that golden sparkle. Her head snapped up to look at him, and she rolled her eyes and pressed her lips over to one side. "Oh, it's you."

Looking at her, a wave of relief crashed over him. He was grateful to have something, anything to focus on that wasn't a memory of Sezan. To push out the frenetic thoughts that threatened to consume him. The energy drove him to her side. She was all he had left, the only creature in the world that still wanted him.

Shaytana was the only woman that he deserved. He saw that now. She was a hideous monster belched out from the pits of hell. And so was he.

Bakr snatched her into his arms, squeezing her body with more force than he ever would have dared touch a human or djinn woman. Then he dipped her low and kissed her passionately.

She giggled and ran her fingernails through his hair. "I thought you were mad at me."

He turned his gaze up to her face, lingering. Her pink lips curved in a coquettish smile, her black and pink eyes sparkling like stars. He moved in closer like he was about to kiss her, then snapped down and nibbled her neck.

She moaned and wrapped her arms and legs around him. He grabbed her thighs and lifted her up, thrusting his hips forward to balance her. "I wanted to thank you," he said.

"Thank me?" She dipped her shoulders sideways. "For what?"

"For killing prince prissy pants." Bakr lifted his brow. Saying the words brought the flood of anger back full force. He dug his fingers into Shaytana's thighs and lifted her up so he could nip at her dress. She squealed and squirmed.

The moment he had touched his sword to the prince's belly, and he hadn't writhed in agony, Bakr had known Ajmal was either already dead or so far gone that he was beyond saving. Perhaps it was cruel, to torture Sezan by pretending her weasel of a prince stood a chance of standing up and walking away. But he didn't care. He wanted her to think that he had murdered him, especially after the way she had pleaded for his miserable life.

Bakr forcibly stopped himself from going down that road, reminding himself that he didn't give a damn what she thought or felt about anything. Never again. She had betrayed him, humiliated him, rejected him. Again.

"Wait, wait." Shaytana pushed on his shoulders until he lowered her back down to eye level, but she kept her legs wrapped around his waist. "Is Ajmal really dead?"

"Very."

Shaytana put a finger between her lips and widened her eyes. "Oops." She held the guilty expression as long as she could, but when he cocked an eyebrow at her, she burst out laughing. "Don't make me laugh." She slapped his chest. "It isn't funny."

Bakr smiled coolly. "It's a little funny."

"Okay, fine. Maybe a little. But it is still very irritating. I worked hard setting all this up, and him dying before signing the final contract means Qadira has no claim on the baby."

He shrugged. "Why are you interested in that little abomination, anyway?"

"I'm sure it will all work out one way or another." She lifted the Seal of Sulayman to eye level and smiled at it. A chill raced down Bakr's spine, wondering what horrible plans were tumbling through that capricious brain of hers. He still didn't fully understand the extent of what the Seal was capable of. Did she?

"That's what that traitor gets," Shaytana said. "I mean, I didn't explicitly tell Ajmal not to take off the ring, but it was strongly implied."

"You know royals—always searching for a way to wriggle out of a contract." Bakr took a deep breath. His hands were burning where he held her, and his stomach was churning in disgust. But she was his woman. He'd made up his mind. He was in so much pain, all he really wanted was for someone to hold him. And the monster who haunted him, raped him, tortured him, and constantly reminded him that he was nothing, was the closest thing to a friend he had left.

Even though he didn't care anymore—could never care about Sezan ever again—a little fly was buzzing the back of his brain, and it forced him to ask, "What was your plan for the princeling anyway?"

"I suppose it makes no difference now." She drew up her shoulders and pouted, her eyes turning askance. "It was supposed to be a present."

"A present?"

"For you, honey." Her long, cold fingers caressed his cheek. "Once I was done with him, I was going to drain his power into you. Give you that djinn fire you've always wanted, even though you don't need it. I thought ice blue would go with your eyes, and I wanted you to gain his special teleporting powers so it would be easier for you to move around, at least until you learn how to use your lilith powers properly."

Bakr furrowed his brow and gazed into her eyes, looking for a giveaway that never came. "Is that true, Shaytana?"

"Cross my heart, lover."

His belly warmed as her words slithered over him. It was a nice thought, although he would rather have died than have that bastard's fire bursting in his channels.

Bakr ran his fingers through her shaggy hair. "That's so kind of you."

"I'm very kind. People often forget that about me." She showed him a big smile filled with bright white, slightly pointy teeth. Bakr tongued his own canines, realizing they had always been quite pronounced, his smile unstoppably white. That was the monster shining through.

"It's a shame he died before I could take his power," Shaytana said. "Though, it seems you got some djinn fire anyway."

His heart smarted at the mention of it—at the reminder of what that vicious, heartless woman had forced into his throat. She was no different from Shaytana, worse even. When had she ever asked what he wanted? What mattered to him.

She didn't care. She never had.

Bile churned in Bakr's guts. A weak voice whispered that it wasn't true. That she had loved him once. He buried it alive deep in the shadows of his psyche where even he was afraid to look.

She had put another man's baby's fire inside of him. It was unforgivable, not that she had asked for forgiveness.

Kiss me with fire... He clenched his teeth.

The magic was there now, and there was nothing he could do to change that. A tattoo on his soul and a frequent reminder of just how stupid he was.

He might as well embrace that, too.

He lifted his hand between their faces and summoned the rose and orange flames that danced on his fingertips like a sunset.

"Another plan foiled." Shaytana sighed and shook out her hair. "When I realized what she'd done, I was so angry. I didn't want you to have that uptight cow's fire inside of you. But now I'm looking at it, it's actually kind of nice. It'll be like she's in the room watching us."

Bakr's heart tried to seize with spasms of pain and fury, but he forced them down with a loud laugh. And just to make sure he took his mind off of it, he kissed Shaytana. Her magical body was like a drug. Hot and sweet and soothing and the source of all his problems and shame all at once. He may as well have been a Dragon junkie, his tongue rotting from his mouth and his brain drying up in his skull as he prostrated himself before gangsters and begged for one more fix.

Moaning, Shaytana pulled herself in deeper, opening her mouth so he could drink in her tongue. She tightened her legs around his hips and grabbed his cheeks, running her palms over his stubble.

"It really was an accident," she breathed, her hands running freely over his chest. "I guess I just don't know my own strength."

"I understand that's often a problem for us," he said into her mouth.

"Us?" She pulled back a bit and looked into his eyes. What did she see there? Certainly, they wouldn't be dead anymore; he had no experience in trying to control djinn fire. Sezan's fire, the fire of her lover's child. It was a liability, nothing more. That's all she had ever been. A liability and a distraction, a soft spot that he had left exposed for far too long. Maybe now it would finally scar over.

His muscles tried to seize up with black, smoky fury—a veneer for the misery pooling in his gut. Anguish pounded in his brain like the worst hangover he had ever experienced. He ignored all of it and ran his hands over Shaytana's perfect thighs and laid kisses all over her neck, hoping the intoxicating sensations that her magical body always brought would be enough to soothe him.

And it did help. A little. He knew he'd wake up tomorrow feeling even worse, but that didn't matter yet. All that mattered was now.

"He got to you, didn't he?" she said.

"I don't know what you're talking about," he laughed, not looking up from nibbling her collarbone with his lips.

"That sneaky backstabber has been trying to steal you out from under me as long as I've known you." She pulled herself away from his embrace, her feet landing delicately on nothing. She straightened her skirt. "Listen to me, lover. There is absolutely nothing your father can teach you I can't teach you better."

He cocked his head to one side. "Teach me?"

"About your powers. I've been getting you ready for years now. That was always his game, the lazy bastard. Let me do all the work so he can just come in and swoop you out from under me." She shook her head hard, then laughed and spun the Seal around her finger. "It's never going to happen now. It is written. I wrote it. He can't have you."

A painful realization overcame him at that moment. When he still had the Seal, he could have used it to defeat Shaytana. But he had been overcome with an unspoken dread in case it didn't work. And so he hesitated, too afraid to jump in with both feet. That wasn't like him. Then again, he was never himself when he was around her.

"Is my father the reason you're so interested in me?" he asked.

"It's really hard for me to find men, okay?" She folded her arms across her chest and turned her back on him. "It's always the same. I meet somebody I like and after just a week or two he's completely insane or his limbs are falling off."

"I can see how that would be a problem." He laughed, walked up behind her, and wrapped his arms around her waist, pressing himself into her back. She sighed huskily and let her body lean into his. She smelled like the sweet release of death.

"Basically, the only men I can really be with are lilu," she said, letting the back of her head fall onto his shoulder. "And there's only five of them. I have been with all of them so many times, for centuries and centuries. I am so bored with all their stupid faces." She rolled her head to one side, so she was gazing at him. "I hate them all so much, Bakr. The idea of sleeping with one makes me physically ill. They're all cold and gray and dead inside."

"Like you?"

"Yeah, but I wear it better." She looped one of her arms over the back of his head, guiding his lips back to her neck. "I have been alive for three and a half thousand years."

"You look amazing."

"In all that time, the number of babies born to my kind, I can count on my fingers. You are number nine in three and a half thousand years."

"Wow." He set his chin on her shoulder, eyes gazing into the void.

"You're also the first male in five thousand years."

"Really?"

"We have a tendency towards femaleness. I mean, there's like twenty liliths and five lilu."

Bakr scrunched up his nose. "Where did the first lilith come from?"

"Go ask Adam," she scoffed.

"What does that mean?"

"Let's just say we weren't cut out to be human."

"There's twenty-five of us?"

"There's only one of me, honey. And there's only one of you. I found you by pure luck when I responded to Sezan's summoning spell. And ever since, I've kept you my little secret. My dirty, beautiful little secret. And this..." She lifted her necklace to show him the glowing Seal of Sulayman. "This ensures none of those malicious harpies can take you from me, including your so-called father."

"Good," he said, and he meant it. The last thing he needed was another lilith gnawing away at his bones. One was more than enough to suck all the joy he'd ever had from his life, leaving him a broken useless husk. Loveless, and hopeless, and unable to just die.

Spiraling back towards the deep well of his own hatred, Bakr pulled himself up by kissing Shaytana's neck. He wanted to cut her head off and rip out her entrails with his bare hand. This seemed like the next best thing until he someday found the opportunity.

"There is nothing cold or dead about you," she moaned, shivering against him. "You are so hot, inside and out. All I have to do is look at you and I feel an inferno brewing inside of me."

"I want to stay with you, Shaytana," he said into her ear, hot and breathy. "I want you to teach me everything there is to know about myself."

"Oh, lover. I thought you'd never ask." She flipped around and pressed her mouth against his, as hungry and desperate a kiss as she had ever given him. He tangled his fingers in her hair, then gripped her by her horns like handles and pulled her back so he could look at her.

His eye glanced at the Seal dangling from her neck. Sezan had scoffed at him, insulted him, and mocked him for losing it. Nothing he ever did was ever good enough for her. She'd wanted him to go and sleep with the demon to get it back.

Fine. He'd get it back. And once he did, he wouldn't use it to fix Ahmar or to hurt Qadira. He wouldn't use it to help Sezan or her baby. Rahik's contract was done and lilith or not, it was time he was done, too.

"Will you marry me, Shaytana?" he said.

"Marry you?" she scoffed. "Now I know you really have lost your mind."

"Hear me out," he said and forced a smile, which he knew from years of practice was charming. "You've made all of these other contracts with that Seal. You know, the one that I went and stole from a damn flying island."

"You mean the one I snatched off you in a hundredth of a degree, you drunken idiot."

"You're the one who said you wanted to be with me. Isn't that the reason you've been doing all of this?"

"You're trying to lock me down, is that what I'm hearing?" She giggled and tried to look away, but he held her in place by her horns, forcing her to look into his eyes. She could have pulled away if she wanted to, but she seemed happy to play the submissive role for a change.

"Is that so absurd?" he smirked, then downcast his eyes coyly. "I don't want to get taken by my father."

"I told you, stud. That is not going to happen." She ran a finger over her chin, nose squinching in thought. "But I'm intrigued. You'd be willing to sign a contract binding yourself to me forever?"

"There's nobody else for me," he said, and the truth of words hit him like a thousand hot needles digging into his liver. "I see that now. I only want you. I just need to know that you want me, too. That you aren't going to abandon me."

"Oh, Bakr. I think that is the saddest, most pathetic thing I have ever heard." Her eyes shifted from side to side, twinkling with an inscrutable pink glitter. "Are you doing this to try to get me to leave your sad little Shihala alone?"

He frowned hard. He hadn't thought of that. "Would that be so bad? Jahmil is my friend. I practically have him in my pocket. Isn't that better than having to deal with Qadira?"

"Why are you so against poor Qadira?" She covered her mouth to hide a loud, snorting laugh. Then she squeezed her stomach and doubled over.

"To hell with Ahmar, that's why," he declared in a loud voice, mirroring her and matching her energy. "To hell with Qadira, and all her relatives, and all her people. And while I'm making a list, to hell with Sezan and her baby, too." The last sentence came out in a sharp snarl that he had not intended. He swallowed hard and tried to regroup.

"You are turning me on so much right now."

"Is that a yes?"

She stared at him in silence long enough he started to wonder if he had overplayed his hand. Then suddenly she cried, "Why not? Three and a half thousand years and I've never been married before. It could be fun." She lifted her finger and wiggled it. "You better get me a good ring."

He smiled and showed her the onyx ring on his finger. "Good enough?"

Her eyes snapped wide, and she stomped closer. "You're not supposed to wear that, you idiot! Give it to me."

The ring seemed to slip down his finger all on its own. Bakr furrowed his brow at it, then shrugged and passed it over. He wasn't completely certain what it did, only that he had felt its power when Sezan used it to force her baby's fire into him. And the ring he'd been wearing—the one he left with Sezan—had pulled the magic like a magnet.

Shaytana absently slipped the ring onto her finger. "Where's the copper one I gave you?"

"In my room at the palace," he said with a shrug. Bakr sucked his cheek between his teeth, hoping she would leave it at that.

"You are so stupid it's a wonder you're still alive." She gripped the bridge of her nose and shook her head. "We need to go back for it."

"Can't it wait?"

"No. It's important."

He couldn't let her rush off to get the ring. As much as it clawed at his heart, worry over Sezan was still pulsing through him. He didn't want Shaytana anywhere near her. He also didn't want to be alone.

His destiny was a sinking ship. Bakr was ready to go down with it and drag Shaytana with him like a dead kraken speared on a bowsprit.

"Please, Shaytana," he whispered hoarsely, body quivering as he reached for her. "I need you right now. If I'm not inside of you soon, I am going to lose my mind."

She bit her lip, eyes darting from side to side. Then she rushed at him and leaped into his arms, knocking him down to the flat of his back to devour him. It was everything he deserved from love. A drug and a punishment. And just as he had hoped, it left him feeling dead inside.

CHAPTER THIRTY-SIX

SEZAN

SEZAN'S ANGER WAS NOTHING without her fire, and her stomach ached like a piece of it had been ripped out of her throat. Which was more or less true. Her body hungered for her fire, for her baby's, and her heart hungered for Bakr.

She did not blame him for the way he acted. She had done so many awful things, some intentional, some not. But she had never thought he'd murder a man as he lay unconscious on the floor. And that's how she knew she was a terrible person, too. Because she wasn't sad at all that Ajmal was dead. She hadn't pleaded for his life because of who he was or for the principle of the thing. She had begged Bakr to stop because she knew he would be hunted for the rest of his life. A traitor. An enemy of Shihala and Ahmar. Of his own best friend. A cell in Ashkult awaited him right next to Faris Khayin. She had not wanted that for him. For the father of her child. And what she wanted had not mattered.

Now she lay locked up in Bakr's room. *House arrest,* she was told by a furious, spluttering, flaming Jahmil. Until he could *clean up their mess.* She was certain by the way Jahmil's hand, white with lightning, trembled near her that he would have burned her alive if it weren't for a life of princely training, and for once she appreciated his cool demeanor and self-restraint. His insistence on asking all those infernal, prying questions before he made a judgment.

He had offered to send her to her rooms, then had insisted on it when she declined, but she refused to budge, staying face-down on Bakr's bed, breathing in his spice. She would stay like this forever, sleeping in his fading warmth. And so, Jahmil left her, but soldiers came in and removed the body and maids bustled through, cleaning up the mess and the smell. She found the strength to snatch the copper ring from busy hands and slip it on her finger. The metal stung just a little on her magicless skin. They tried to remove the sheets, but Sezan snarled, and they left her be.

As the last of the servants and maids left and silence consumed the room, she fell into a merciful sleep. And as she slept, she dreamt.

Moon and swirling galaxies moved on their paths through the Shihalan sky, only faster, as if the world were racing beneath her. She was swimming, hair streaming out behind her, lilies kissing her skin as they floated by. Bakr too, bare-chested and grinning at her with those insatiable eyes. Green as jade. Pure joy. Divinity. Love. Then the sky fell around her, stars splashing into water and the moon melting away in a smear. The green eyes brightened, sharpened like square-cut emeralds lit with fire.

And then she was on the floor of her old bedroom, twitching, spasming, choking for life as white foam seeped from her mouth. Her skin was more white than blue, leeched by whatever demonic sickness had taken her. Her back arched, she cried in pain, and Bakr laid a hand on her head, face strained with worry, tears streaming from his eyes as he called and begged for help. Then he smiled, a cruel, twisted thing, and vanished. Only green eyes remained. Her body on the floor crumbled into dust that blew away like chaff in the wind. Then the rest of the scene went with it, crashing around her like tumbling blocks that broke into glitter and faded away like embers escaped from the fire, leaving her in utter, painful darkness.

She lay there, unmoving in the cold nothingness for what felt like forever, convinced that draining her magic had finally killed her. She tried to feel her baby within her, to know it was somehow still with her, but she felt nothing.

What else besides death could explain the sheer lack of anything around her? Her body felt weightless, her eyes, whether opened or closed, saw only abyss, and nothing stirred about her, not a whisper or sigh or hint of a breeze. She would have believed she no longer even breathed except every inhale brought her excruciating torment as she relived the nightmarish scenes over and over. Felt the genuine love and joy of swimming with Bakr and the agonizing rejection of waking from scraping death to find him cruelly gone. Again and again and over and over, and the only thing that changed was Bakr's smile at the end growing wider and wider and wider.

She gasped and sat up, unable to take anymore. And there before her in the eating black, were green, sparkling eyes.

"Hello, Sezan," a pleasant, tenor voice said.

The green eyes moved closer until a handsome face appeared beneath, lit by an unseen source. Perhaps his own fire, though he was not djinn. He was painfully beautiful, whoever he was; one of those people you could stare at without caring whether they saw or not because they knew what they were and wanted everyone to enjoy. Bakr looked like that sometimes, when the fire caught his lovely brown skin and reflected in his human eyes, though she wanted to drink him in always.

"Who are you?" she asked, expecting her voice to echo into the abyss. Instead, the dark air suppressed the sound to a whisper.

"A fan of yours," he said, smiling in a way that made her body pinch with heat. His words were as smooth as glass that slipped down her spine.

"Where am I?"

"Wherever I want you to be."

Sezan frowned, the memories she had been reliving still spilling across her mind, making her dizzy.

"Why?" was all she managed to say.

"Because, right now, you and your child are more valuable to me than anything in both worlds."

"Shaytana?" she asked, rubbing a hand over her eyes. She knew that wasn't right, but the feeling here was the same as Shaytana's breath and the wavy lines that helped her travel between realms.

The green eyes glinted. "You won't need to concern yourself with her anymore. I don't plan on having that ancient minx around this time."

Sezan pushed herself up into a stand, not knowing where to find a hold but finding one everywhere she tried. "Is this where the traitors of Shihala go when they die?" The thought should have alarmed her, but instead, it swam warm in her mind like bees in honey. She cradled her stomach just the same.

The man laughed, hazelnuts pouring out over a cedar table. "I wouldn't be here if it were. That sounds like a real drag."

She pushed her nails into her palms, crushed her eyes shut, and shot them back open, then held her breath for as long as she could, but nothing changed.

They stood in silence for what felt like hours, then days, then years. Or maybe just minutes.

"What do you want?" she asked at last.

"To ensure the safety of my grandchild."

"What?"

He sighed. "You djinn are quite tedious, did you know that? Sexy..." He paused for a playful, terrifying growl. "But stupid."

"You're not *my* father," she said, assuredly fulfilling the man's intellectual expectations. "I mean... Bakr doesn't have a father."

"Of course, Bakr has a father. Though we've only just met."

Sezan's eyes widened. Or they didn't. Or maybe they narrowed. The numb nothingness made it impossible to tell. "He didn't tell me that."

"And why would he?" The man laughed. "The affairs of lilu are none of your business."

"Is that what you are?"

"I am."

Sezan stared at the beautiful face, the only light in all the world as far as she could tell, and the pieces began to shift into place. "So, Bakr is..."

The man—no, the lilu raised his brow.

"Half-lilu?" she said at last. "Not half-djinn."

"Your lips look exquisitely delicious when you say the word lilu." He glanced down at her, his bottom lip tucked between his teeth. "It's going to be hard resisting you." He moved closer, and a hand joined his face in the dark, touching her cheeks, her chin, and circling down to her clavicles.

She slapped his advance away, grateful that her own hand existed at all as it took shape near the lilu's body. "What are you talking about?"

He chuckled. "I want the little bean to grow strong and healthy before I try anything."

His words managed to wake her stomach in the darkness. It pitched and squeezed.

The lilu blinked out then reappeared, one arm wrapped around her waist, pulling her flush against his smoke-scented body, and the other tangling painfully in her hair. "I can see why he picked you, Sezan." Her name sounded filthy in his mouth. "Why he fell to his human half in his devotion to you." He scooped her hair up and breathed in the scent of it with a deep inhale. Then he blinked away once more, appearing farther in the distance.

"Oh, you temptress," he scolded, but his laughter rang out all around her. "Just a few more months until the little lilu is born. I'm sure Shaytana will keep Bakr busy long enough that he'll never know. Not that he seems particularly keen on you these days, good boy. Or knows the baby is his at all, good girl," he winked. "Then when the baby's born—"

"You'll kill me," Sezan said, his flickering face jumbled in the mess of memories still blurry in her purview.

"Of course not, my stunning star. I plan to keep you for myself. It is a rare woman indeed who can grow and birth a lilu. I should like to have a go myself. A decade or so of trying before I turn you ragged back to Bakr and see if he has any luck. You're welcome."

She shuddered so hard the bones in her knees creaked. "But my baby doesn't have any power or fire. Not anymore."

He waved his hand dismissively. "Trifles. Blood is blood. Fire is pathetic djinn fire. The lilu genes are enough. Calling the power back into the little heartbreaker will be easy. Especially since you have the magic ring. You know..." The lilu's green eyes sparkled maliciously. "You could suck back your and the baby's power at any time. And take the rest of Bakr's. The baby would be nearly full lilu at that point."

Sezan tightened her hold on her stomach. She felt sick and nothing at the same time. She would never take anything from Bakr. And she wouldn't risk taking her baby's fire back as long as Shaytana lived. "Why are you doing this to me?"

"I just told you why," the lilu said, bored.

"I mean, why the memories, the... nightmares." They still hung on the edge of her periphery, giggling at her without sound. She remembered Bakr's eyes. His words. The things he said Shaytana did to him. The things he did... without knowing.

"Thousands of years is a long time to live, beautiful. And lilu can't dream. So, sometimes I like to borrow them, live in them, and—" He smirked. "Well, you'll find out what else later. Though the death-by-poison scene is quite compelling. Usually, mortal fears are quite trite. Falling off cliffs, the dark—" He wiggled his fingers and eyebrows. "—Spiders. Nonsense like that. But your body seizing in horrible agony as Bakr walks away..." His smirk widened, shadows that had not existed before playing on the dips in his perfect face. "He makes me proud."

Sezan wished again for her fire so she could see more than the looming nightmare that hovered before her. But she was nothing. Trapped, as Bakr must have been with Shaytana, unable to teleport, to escape. And she knew then in that inextricable moment, there was darkness in her eyes, now, too.

"Why do you think it was poison?" she asked, trying to grab onto something tangible. "That didn't come from my memories."

"Ah, my voluptuous woman, anyone could see it, with your face all contorted and unbecoming, and the white foam dripping out. Quite a nice memory of that you have. But I'll indulge why I really knew because it's quite the riot."

A bitter cold slipped up from the nothingness, over her sandals and into her toes. It began to work its way up with every word he said.

"Your family is a mess, did you know? You'd make great lilith and lilu with how backstabbing and vindictive you are. When Rahik called me to make a deal, I had a good laugh."

"Rahik..." she said his name like she had Mangala pieces in her mouth. A faded memory of a sweaty, bulbous, and bald man floated past her mind's eye. How long had she been in the darkness? She refocused on his words, trying not to slip in and out of the black like a mirage. "Why would Rahik want me dead?"

"Because I wanted you dead. And because he wanted to harm my boy. It all worked out splendidly."

Finally, a sharpness, and a cold glint of herself surfaced in the Nothing. "Why would you want to hurt your own son?" she asked, instinctively laying her hand back over her stomach.

"Because he's half-human and needed a little molding to squeeze that part out of him."

She thought about that, about what he said, and as she did, she began to gain a sense of this place. Time didn't matter. And neither did she. So, she took her non-time time. Watched the gorgeously handsome demon face. And occasionally slipped into terrible memories or the sweet reveries Fajar had shown her in Eayima.

"You wanted to kill me because he loved me," she finally concluded.

"Correct," he smiled. Then he was at her side again, brushing her cheek and running his hands down her back and tugging at her buttons and laces.

"He left me..." she said as her mind swam through muck. "He left me on the floor to make the deal with Rahik. To save my life."

"It's part of the nobility in him I'm trying to stamp out. Though you shoving his own baby's fire inside him and having him think it belongs to another man has done far more than anything I or Shaytana could." He chuckled again, and this time it rumbled on unseen walls around her. "Such a clever girl."

She winced because he was right and tried to hold on to the truth laid bare before her. All this time. All this time she had felt betrayed, had felt as if she could not trust him for leaving her to die, and all this time he had been the one who saved her.

Emptiness again. Time and no time to process reality, to let anger slip out of her veins as easily as blood through a gaping wound, taking the toxins with it so she could heal.

"Bakr must have beaten you because I didn't die."

He growled a laugh against her neck, and the touch of his skin on hers brought the chill from her toes up into her spine. His smoky smell tempted her eyelids to close and her body to lean in.

"Nobody beats me, you silly, curvaceous creature." His hands pressed hard where her hips slid into her waist. He groaned against her nape, weaving his fingers once more into her hair and across her scalp. "He was sent to get the *Khātam Sulaymān* and bring it to Rahik to give to me so I could break Jahmil Amir's stupid little contract that barred the bald idiot from taking the throne. At least that's what I told him. As soon as it was done, I, of course, planned to torture him for all eternity and subjugate both worlds to my whim even as Iblis himself would."

Silence.

Complete black.

Hands sweeping her skin and then not and then tugging on her hair and brushing her lips.

She shot her eyes open, unaware that they had slipped shut. Again, time eluded her, and she reminded herself it didn't matter. But Bakr did. To her.

"Then why does Shaytana have the ring?"

He gripped her arm hard enough to bruise, his fingers dimpling in her flesh. "That was an unfortunate mistake. Luckily, while she holds the power to control both worlds, Shaytana dreams small. The little brat must think she's so clever having nipped the ring from me, though she does nothing but plan petty wars and play house. However, time is patient. As long as the Seal isn't on Eayima I will have my hands on it soon enough." He bit her ear so she winced and growled once more before popping far away into the dark, his head a star against an infernal night sky. "Now, that's enough for you. There's no rush. We have all of your short mortal life to get to know each other better. To build up your character and break your spirit. It's going to be so much fun."

"Wait," she called as he vanished, and she wondered why. Why had she wanted the monster to come back?

The inky nothing shattered around her in a mix of soft smoke and glass. She sat up in Bakr's bed, the last rustle of a maid's skirt leaving the room and screamed.

CHAPTER THIRTY-SEVEN

BAKR

BAKR LAY ON HIS side in the white nothing.

Naked. Cold, even though there was no temperature. Alone.

Was Shaytana even there anymore? He didn't care. She had made love to him as he had wanted, as close to love as a demon like her was capable. As a demon like him. He had hoped her embrace would take him further away from himself. Away from the dark room filled with smoke and broken glass where everything inside of him that had ever pretended at being good had finally breathed its last.

At least he'd bought a little time. Not literally, as time didn't really flow in the Namelessness. But he had distracted Shaytana long enough for her to forget about the copper ring he had left behind in his bedroom. When Sezan pushed the baby's fire into him, Bakr had felt the magic from the ring catching on to Sezan's power and drawing it into himself. He didn't know much, and he may have already given Shaytana the Seal of Sulayman—*the most powerful hunk of metal in Allah's many worlds*—but he didn't want to give her anything more.

He had hoped sleeping with Shaytana would distract him in equal measure. Instead, she had taken him back to that moment as she took everything she wanted from him. She twisted her fingers into his brain and sent him spiraling, forcing him to relive the argument with Sezan, the worst they had ever had. Making him re-watch the terror in her eyes as he raged at her, as he stood over Ajmal with his sword. The palpable pain in her eyes when he told her for the first time that he had loved her, and that he didn't love her anymore. Shaytana made him look at the monster that he had allowed himself to become in his anger, and all the while she whispered that he had been right and justified. That he should have done more. That he should have plunged his sword into Ajmal without hesitation before turning his fury on Sezan. She made him watch and listen to her raucous laughter as an image of himself cornered Sezan and cut her apart.

Bakr clenched his eyes closed and turned his face into his hands. Why had he coaxed Shaytana into sleeping with him when he knew exactly what she would do? She could never resist a fresh wound. Watching him suffer was what she liked, what made her body quiver with spasms of delight, and she was so good at getting the right response out of him. Why did he let her? Why did he encourage her? Every time she ran her hands over his skin, or kissed him, or pressed him inside of her, he felt like he was dying. Coming into this place had been a kind of suicide.

It was what he deserved. Not the softness of a kind lover, but the hatred and disdain of a captor. He couldn't change what he was. A monster, just like her. Perhaps somewhere deep down, he had always known about the darkness inside of him, the eternal hatred that would never let him rest. Never allow him to be fully comfortable around anyone. He had always known that he was destined to hurt anybody who came too close, and so he had run from virtually everyone who tried.

He never had to worry about hurting Shaytana. She was unhurtable. He longed to see her in pain. To watch her writhe and beg for his mercy. To see the pink lights in her eyes go out and never have to suffer her touch, her words, or her nightmares ever again.

But that was a fantasy, and a fleeting one at that. He belonged to her. It was what he deserved.

He laid his hand in front of his face and summoned pink fire to his fingertips. How many times since he was abandoned in Qaf had he longed to see this very light on his own skin? To fit in with the djinn and the world he was unwillingly thrust upon. Now, he wished it gone with everything. The rosy hue that had once so enraptured him, glowing over Sezan's skin when she let her guard down and let herself fully be with him. He remembered times encircled in its warmth, the closest he had ever come to a feeling of belonging. Like he was wanted—truly wanted—and that he wanted to be wanted.

He remembered a night before the war, before Rahik and his poison and the unhinged cruelty of the Vespars had barged into his life and torn everything to shreds. He had been lying in bed with Sezan, his head in her lap as she ran her fingers through his hair, streaming her fire through him. After months together, he had finally found it in him to tell her about his life on earth, about his mother and what little he knew of his father.

About what the invisible monster had done. He had never spoken about it to anyone, and he hadn't wanted to tell her, but it had fallen out of him like a stone through wet paper. Wrapped in her warmth, the defenses he'd built up had fallen apart and all of it had come out at once. And it had felt right and good as if he finally had someone to help him carry the weight he had borne alone for so long.

"Who your parents are is not who you are," Sezan had whispered, her soft fire glowing all around him. "You are nothing like them. Either of them."

Curled up with his head resting so trustingly in Sezan's lap as she stroked him and hugged him and rocked him, he had almost started to believe it. To believe that maybe, with her, things could be different. That he could be somebody worth loving.

A little tinge of orange flickered at the tips of the rose-colored flames, and Bakr's heart seized with pain. The white-hot anger that had filled his senses earlier was gone, replaced only with sadness. That day at the hot springs had been his last chance. He could have stopped her from leaving, he knew that. If he had gotten up from the water and walked over to her as she struggled into her dress. If he had wrapped his arms around her and told her in no uncertain terms that not only was she on his list, she was at the very top. If he had let his tongue form the words that were in his heart when she asked if he knew what he had been missing.

He knew. And he had died every day without her.

He had driven her into Ajmal's arms with his pride and evasiveness. If only he could go back to that night in the tent and scream *yes* when she asked him if he would be with her.

He focused on the baby's fire, the soft orange mist of flames. Slowly, Sezan's blushing rose died away until only the orange remained. The light of Sezan's child that could have been his, but wasn't. A dead father, a broken mother, and demons fighting over its soul. It was all so familiar. The innocent creature could not be but a week old, safe in its mother's womb and unaware of all the chains already being placed upon its neck. It had yet even to breathe and already the world worked to suffocate it. Why did Sezan sign that stupid contract? It was one thing to sleep with the prince, as furious as the thought made him, but to agree to marry him? And to agree to such hideous terms, promising to die should she change her mind? How could she have been so cruel, endangering not just her own life but the life of her innocent child?

The last thought stuck in his throat like vomit. She hadn't given him her fire as a gift, a sacrifice, or even as a punishment. It was a plea for help. She was frightened for her child because Shaytana was coming for it—desperate to protect the baby from the monsters closing in around them.

But then why give it to him?

Was it possible that despite all the compelling arguments to do the opposite Sezan still trusted him? Maybe not to stay and maybe not to love her, but to protect her. She could have simply asked him to give her the copper ring and he would have. She knew that. And then she could have moved the fire into anyone. But still, she put it in him.

She wanted whatever it was that made him who he was to protect her child.

Whether the child was planned or an accident, it was not the child's fault. At least Sezan was trying to protect it, the way a mother should.

And what had he said and done in return? He'd let his anger, hurt, and desperation bubble over, shoved her away, and threatened to deny the child its own fire. He'd been on the verge of murdering an unconscious man.

Bakr clenched his fist, letting the innocent light run over the back of his knuckles. He would help Sezan protect the baby, whatever that meant. No child deserved to suffer just because of who their father was. And he certainly would not be one of the people putting chains around its neck.

"Are you awake, lover?" Shaytana's voice cut into his thoughts. He quickly extinguished the fire to keep it from her eyes. She knew it was there, of course. She had already seen it. But suddenly he felt like he needed to hold it back from her, to keep it from being tainted by her lifeless hatred.

Bakr made himself smile as he sat up to look at her. She hadn't bothered to get dressed, her flawless gray skin shimmering with natural iridescence. Tiny, pert breasts, barely defined muscles in her stomach, one hip curving out to the side just enough to be tempting. And the temptation was enough to send him spiraling in a cascade of shame. Her intense floral sweetness nipped at his stomach like curls of smoke, at times inflaming him with insatiable hunger, and at others filling him with waves of hatred and nausea. His nightmare, his torturer. His one and only.

For years now he had cowered in her shadow, knowing in his heart there was absolutely nothing he could do to stop her or even temper her capricious wrath. All he could do to maintain his sanity was throw himself into it and convince himself that on some level, this was what he wanted. To be hurt and humiliated, used and reviled. Whatever tiny flickering of confidence Sezan's rose fire had helped to nurture in him had long ago been extinguished in Shaytana's empty pool of blackness.

But now that orange tint was burning inside of him, silently begging with its innocence. Pure, real innocence.

"Ready to go back to reality?" Shaytana asked. "Things are going to start falling apart pretty rapidly."

Bakr narrowed his eyes at her as he wrangled his mind into the present. "You mean with Qadira?"

"Not just Ahmar. Everywhere." A stack of glowing folded papers appeared in her hand, and she fanned her face with them. "Once I bring these back into Qaf, a lot of things are about to change all at once."

He pulled himself to stand, yanking on his dirty pants and doing up the buckle. His eyes scanned quickly for his shirt before he realized he didn't have one. He couldn't remember the last time he had. He was cold and he wanted one.

"Does the Seal not work in here?" he asked.

"*Here* isn't really a place, as well you know. It's a place between a place. The Seal only works in *actual* places. Like Qaf and Ard. See this is nothing, so there's nothing to work with."

"Okay." He tried to keep his eyes from crossing the way they always did when he actually thought about the nameless place. "What are you going to do?"

"I want it to be a surprise," she cooed. "I think you're really going to like it."

"Am I to assume you'll be taking over kingdoms?"

"Literally all of them," she chuckled, then she quickly flipped through the papers, pulled one out and handed it to him.

"What is it?" he asked, anticipating more jabs about how he had never learned how to read and write.

"That contract enslaves every monarch of the Nine Kingdoms and Fyre to me." She quivered with happy giggles. "I was thinking about what you said, and I realized there isn't much point in replacing any of them when I can just make them all do whatever I want. I'm thinking of starting the War of Two Worlds. Doesn't that sound exciting?"

He kept his gaze downcast, biting hard on the back of his teeth to keep from trembling. Trying to process everything she was saying was too much and the truth was he didn't care about most of it. He could count on one hand the things he actually cared about. "Does that include Jahmil?"

"Doubly so." She gave a playful growl. "I've always wondered what he would be like... you know what I mean."

"Sure," he shrugged. "Me too."

A brilliant smile filled her face, as he had expected. "Really?"

"Before we head off to send the Nine Kingdoms to war, I've got to ask you about these powers of mine..."

"What about them?"

"Well, if I'm going to be of any help, I need to know exactly what I'm capable of."

"The sky is the limit, lover. You've seen the things I can do."

The implications of that were like a dozen stones slamming into his head one by one, staggering him. "So, can I invade people's dreams and enslave them with my sexual magnetism?"

She winked. "You already do all of that, handsome."

He chuckled in frustration but forced his fingers not to clench into fists. "I'm serious, Shaytana. I mean, can I teleport? Am I going to live for three thousand years?"

"I'm not sure. You *are* part human, so I have to assume you'll eventually start to decay. It could take millennia, though."

"Can I be killed?"

"Maybe not." She pushed a finger to her chin in thought. "That guy at Karzusan practically cut your head off and look at you now." She smiled brightly, kicked up one foot like a dancer, and pinched his cheek. "Cute as a cabbage."

"Have you ever had your head cut off?"

"Just once." Shaytana groaned and rubbed her neck. "I don't recommend it."

Bakr bit his bottom lip. That was hardly encouraging. "So are there any spells or creatures that I need to look out for?"

"Baby, you are above and beyond all of that. Humans and djinn have been trying to get rid of our kind since practically the beginning of time, yet here we are."

"What about people summoning me with my name or making me tell the truth?"

"Has it ever happened?" She cocked a brow at him. "I bet if you listened for it you'd be able to hear it. But you're clearly not bound to the same rules."

"Bakr is a pretty common name."

"It's not just the name. It's the intention. Some idiot might say the syllables of my name by accident; that doesn't mean he knows my name."

Bakr ran his finger slowly over the roll of paper. "Has there never been a lilith that died?"

"Just one. And it was her own fault. Just don't go walking blindly into the most obvious trap ever laid and you should be fine." She kept her head down, gazing at him from under long lashes. "Now, come on before I start getting bored with you."

Her little dress appeared in a flash of gray light, little more than a flicker. He looked down at himself as his old Shihalan uniform materialized—tall boots, gloves studded with sharp points of steel, a long grayish green jacket made of the skin of a Narquian Hynde. His actual jacket had been torn apart by Cetus, but Shaytana's manifestation of it was perfect to the last detail, all the wear and scratches in the right place, and even the mismatched lapel buttons. It felt good on his skin.

He lifted his sword from where it lay and threaded it into the holster at his belt. "Where are we going first?"

"Ahmar, of course. Qadira still owes me a baby, and if she doesn't get it for me, then that little purple minx has bedazzled her last brassiere."

CHAPTER THIRTY-EIGHT

SEZAN

SEZAN WASN'T SURE HOW long she'd screamed for, her mind a twirling mess from being in the lilu's dreams. No, her dreams, right? She had trouble remembering anything except Bakr's wide, malicious smile flashing before her eyes. But that was not his smile, and that logical part of her brain that had always told her to run from Bakr clung to him instead. She pushed away the distorted thoughts, one blocky piece at a time until a real memory of him shone through.

His face, an inch from the temple floor, eyes round with so much worry and asking her what was wrong. She inhaled slowly, counted to ten, then released. She had blamed Bakr all this time for her bad decisions. For leaving her and not writing so she *had* to make a deal with a lilith. For making her so angry she distractedly signed a contract without reading it—a shame she would never live down—and running from him when his child deserved a father because *he* had a demon. Or a temper. Or a flighty constitution.

She pinched away the old, searing thoughts. Bakr had just as many flaws as she did, but in the end, he always protected her. Even when it meant leaving her and knowing she would hate him for it and then letting her do just that. And now she had another life inside her, and both their fires were in him because she knew no matter how he ranted and raved, he would continue to protect her child because he had once loved her.

Sezan put both feet on the carpeted floor, the time for complaining and excuses long past. She would tell Bakr about the baby. He deserved to know the life he protected was one he helped create. If he would not fight Shaytana for himself, then surely he would do it for his child. And even if he stayed only for the baby and not her, and even if his daily smile burned her heart to cinders, it would be right because the baby and Bakr would have each other. What more had she to give?

She rushed to the drawer and drew out one of Fajar's beautiful feathers, then paused and grabbed another. Then grabbed two more. She had always taken for granted her ability to pop wherever she wanted if she needed to. Bakr was right. Depending on others was infuriating. Sezan thought of the palace at Karzusan and where she needed to go first. She stood, dropped a feather, and breathed in the rush of crystal fire. For a second in the dark, her heart seized with fear. Had the lilu—Bakr's father—come for her? Would he bind her in an endless nightmare before she could see Bakr again? An audible, painful sigh escaped her lungs when light broke through the dark. She appeared on decorative tile next to an unfinished game of Mangala.

"Sezan?" Ayelet spun around, half her body out the door and into the hallway.

"I'm sorry, Ayelet."

"What is going on? I can't get two words out of Jahmil as he stomps in to kiss me and then storms back out."

"Too much." Sezan shrugged hopelessly. "But Jahmil needs to know that Qadira is planning to take over Shihala's throne by keeping my baby."

"What?" Ayelet half-laughed before falling serious. "You're having a baby?"

"Yes. It's Bakr's and part-lilu or something, I don't know. But any male offspring of mine is next in line after Jahmil. Qadira's planning on raising it and killing him off so she can take over the kingdom. And then there's a lilith who's helping her, and Bakr's father who wants the baby, too. And I just had to come here and warn you and Jahmil for Shihala before it all falls apart. Oh, Ayelet," she heaved, her shoulders collapsing in on her. "I'm so tired."

Ayelet scooped her into her arms. "That was quite a tale. And here Bakr made it out as if you were some stuffy courtesan who never did anything but harp."

Sezan pulled back and offered a weary smile. "How are you always so calm?"

"Because I trust Jahmil and know that he can fix it. And if he can't, that we can together. And because I trust Bakr and know that he'll protect whatever is important. And because I'm amazing and can rip out the throats of anyone who says otherwise with the strum of my fingers."

Sezan smiled again, but she could see the worry lines forming around Ayelet's eyes. "I'm sorry. I'm so sorry. All of this is my fault. Every piece of it."

Ayelet scoffed. "Is that why you like Bakr? You're both into martyrdom?"

"Bakr is far better than I. I deserve everything I get."

"Oh, please," Ayelet said, waving her hand.

"No, I... I sent the lilith to torture him just to keep him alive. And I accidentally signed his baby away, then lied to him about it, letting him believe Ajmal Amir was the father... and then I put my magic and the baby's magic into him and—" She groaned. "I'm worse than the lilith I made the *sakhif* deal in the first place, and—"

Ayelet's laughter cut her off. "You *are* Jahmil's sister, though you two may deny it. How seriously you two fret over little things. Yes, Qadira taking over Shihala is a big thing. Whatever a lilith and lilu are trying to take your baby is probably a big thing. Telling Bakr that the woman he loves is carrying his baby is a big thing. But a good one. But worrying whether he'll forgive you when he'd already die for you is so... Sezan, I guess. Now shut up and go fix your mess," she said, a smirk on her face and a few wisps gathering around her fingers. "And not having djinn fire inside you is not so bad."

"You really think he could forgive me after all that?" Sezan asked, scared to hope, to fill her heart full again after so many holes had been punctured through it.

"I think you should go find out," Ayelet said with a reassuring smile.

The door banged open, and Jahmil stormed into the room. "My love, my ardent, are you ready to be the queen you deserve?"

Ayelet's eyes narrowed in suspicion. "You always tell me I already am."

He laughed, a throaty, full thing that sounded hollow, and picked his wife up and swung her in a circle. "You are. But you deserve so much more. Ahmar. Eastern Elm. Zabriya. And I'm going to get them all for you."

"Why?" Ayelet asked, elongating the word.

"Is Qadira already attacking?" Sezan asked, worried she hadn't moved quickly enough to stop the war. But then, what did the other kingdoms have to do with that?

"If they are, they will meet their end. I will raze the land between our castle and theirs if that's what it takes to bring them into submission. They need a Shihalan on the throne and his beautiful wife." He scooped Ayelet into a deep hug and kissed her ardently.

Ayelet pushed him away. She turned to Sezan with wide eyes. "*This* is a big problem."

"I've held back long enough," he continued in a feverish pitch. "Wanting what I deserve is not a problem." Jahmil's eyes were sparking, wild and... covered in a dark film of evil she recognized instantly.

"I know who did this," Sezan said.

Ayelet took a step toward Jahmil, her eyes stained with worry and not leaving his face. "Who?"

"Bakr's lilith, one of the mad demons who wants my baby. She has the Seal of Sulayman, which allows her to control djinn and humans and make deals..." Then a chill ran through Sezan. "She's going to send all of Qaf to war. I need to go. Come with me?" she asked, hoping the feared savior of Qaf would help sway the battle.

Ayelet's brows creased. She flashed Sezan a quick look. "I can't leave Jahmil. I can't let him send Shihala to war when he's not in his right mind. Let me protect my family and home. I trust that you and Bakr will protect yours. He has never once failed Jahmil, and you mean far more to him."

"You will not stop me," Jahmil hashed through biting teeth. "Don't get in my way." He vied for the door, but Ayelet jumped in front, her wisps braiding themselves into a net to keep him back.

"You still have the gift I sent?" Ayelet asked, her brows furrowed in concentration and her fingers plucking invisible strings.

Sezan nodded, hands fluttering uselessly in front of her with no magic. Maybe she was a fool to try to take on Qadira, to win Bakr back. "Of course. Are you going to be okay?"

Jahmil snarled, wailing his fists against the silvery fabric. Ayelet winced. "I trust him explicitly, remember? Magic spell or not. And... if that doesn't work, I trust myself." She scrunched her nose as the net of wisps folded gently around a rabid Jahmil as a soft pita would boiling meat. A stray wisp whisked away the sweat on her brows as the torrent of white that had flooded into the room thinned to a trickle.

Sezan clenched the feather in her hands, worried for Ayelet and Jahmil, and for her baby and Bakr and all of Qaf. But she had come to Ayelet not just to warn her, but because she trusted what she had to say. And Ayelet had told her what she needed to hear. Trust Bakr. Trust herself.

"Good luck." Sezan dropped the feather, slipping back into smoke.

She reappeared slightly off target from where she had aimed and nearly fell to her death. Gusts of wind whipped past the ramparts, blowing back her hijab and threatening her balance. Fajar whistled and chirped in her deep, giant bird way.

"Sorry, girl. I didn't mean to startle you." She crouched down for better balance and slipped forward one foot at a time, her butt on the stones as she moved closer. "I know I'm not your baba. But you know me, right? I need to get to him. I need to tell him about your new sibling. And keep him from killing Qadira, though that second one's a stretch."

She found herself breathing hard as exhaustion and wind raked against her lungs. "He needs us. He needs his family. Will you help me? Maybe not burn my flesh to ash if I slip onto your back?"

Fajar bent her head nearly upside down. Then shook her feathers from head to tail. She nudged Sezan in the shoulder and laid down a wing. Sezan grinned and climbed up top, instantly warm. Then the bird took off, hurtling her into the air so fast, Sezan nearly tumbled backward, head over heels and off the bird altogether. She slung herself low, dipping her hands deep into the soft, sun-colored down. She had never noticed before how close the tips of Fajar's wings were to the color of her eyes.

They zipped through the air, so high the trees were carpet and the buildings, dust. Her eyes stung and teared at first, but a bubble of heat formed around them, cocooning her in wonder. She bit her lip and eased into a seat, raising her hands up to the sky. Sezan laughed, a bubbling joy from deep in her belly where her baby lived. She took a breath, adrenaline rushing through her veins, and stood.

Jump with me.

She bit her lip and laid a hand on her stomach. "Is it safe?"

Fajar crooned a sweet little noise.

Sezan's heart filled to the brim. "Catch me?"

Fajar trilled.

She grinned and jumped. Her hijab flew back, and air caught the torn fabric of her crimson dress. She laughed again, as loud as she could, and felt free for the first time. Then Fajar swooped gently into her fall and she landed as if on a bed of clouds. This time, she would ask Bakr to jump and drag him with her if he refused.

Ahmar's dust speck grew larger as they neared, its crystal dome reflecting the moons and stars that swirled in the sky. Fajar plummeted like a comet toward the ground.

"The courtyard," Sezan called over the torrent of wind.

Fajar looked back at her, chirping reproachfully.

Sezan chuckled. "Okay. You win. Through the dome!"

If the drakonte that rampaged through the court of Ahmar on Qadira's wedding day were already lauded on every bard's tongue throughout Qaf, she and Fajar would be legendary. The crystal shattered upon impact, falling to earth in droplets full of galaxies. Fajar landed in a ball of fire that twisted it up in a burst, then held in a simmer of flickering burnt orange.

A brain-curdling screech broke through the hard tinkle of glass hitting tile.

"How dare you? I only just got that fixed!" Qadira stormed at her from across the room, her face a deep plum with anger. "How dare you show your face in my court after what you did to my cousin?"

Fajar screeched back, and hers shook the walls. Sezan held her hand up to quell the bird, and Qadira slowed, but the wrath on her face deepened.

"This is an act of war! I will have my army burn Shihala to the ground. Already they prepare to march."

"On what grounds?" Sezan asked, pulling her shoulders back in her tattered wedding gown. Ahmaran soldiers were already streaming into the room with wary eyes that ogled Fajar.

"You think word hasn't reached my courts?" Qadira spluttered. "You killed a prince of Ahmar!"

"I did not. And neither did Shihala. A lilith gave him the beating he deserved for betraying yet another woman." She clenched her fist, glad her eyes no longer held the sun. What she had said was not untrue, even if she left out Bakr. "I should think you would be grateful, considering he planned to ruin you, too."

"Liar," Qadira hissed. "All Shihalans are."

"We can call her if you want."

"Who?" Qadira snarled, but her eyes grew wide.

"The demonic lilith who Ajmal made a deal with. You know her, she's the one you made your deal with, too."

Spit flew out of Qadira's mouth as her rage melted into pure, unintelligible fury. She waved her hands to call her troops forward, but the spasms were so erratic, her soldiers drew farther back. Their disobedience helped the rotten queen find her tongue.

"Get her, you useless pig-dogs. You wretched sacks of silver."

"I'll call her," Sezan warned, staring down Qadira's glittering lime-green eyes. The nasty queen cocked up her head with a smirk, too far gone in mindless vitriol to stop.

Sezan shrugged. She was certain with the demonic hold the lilith had on Bakr that he was with her now, a victim, a prisoner, an idiot. But her idiot. And she was no longer willing to share.

"Shaytana!" she called, grinning far too gleefully at bratty Qadira and her hoard of reluctant soldiers. "Come."

CHAPTER THIRTY-NINE

BAKR

The moment Shaytana was about to pull them both from the nameless place, her head snapped up. She growled, turning to him with a dead stare. "I almost forgot you told your little cow my name."

Without warning, she slashed her fingernails across his face and blinked out of existence. Four long, deep lines cut across his cheek and eye, blood oozing down the side of his neck. Hissing, he wiped his face on his forearm and pressed the stinging blood out of his eye with his fingertips.

Had Sezan called Shaytana? Who else? She was the only other person he knew of that knew her name. But why would she have done that?

He was about to follow down but took a step back. How did Shaytana do it? How did she and others of her kind infiltrate people's minds? Twist their nails into the deepest secrets and leave a heart bleeding, begging for more? What was their entry-point, their conduit? He'd experienced Shaytana in his mind so many times, he felt like he ought to understand the process better, but it made no sense at all. There was no ritual, no special words, no particular movements. She just did it, as easily as a breath. As light as a kiss.

It had something to do with this place, he was certain. This void between worlds. The space between Ard and Qaf. Between heaven and Jahannam. Sleep and awake. Death and life. Without time because it was only an instance, a physical representation of a fractional moment of transition, drawn out into eternity. A place that was neither this nor that; it was just nothing.

Perhaps it was also both things at once. A truth before it was spoken. Asleep and awake, alive and dead, timeless and infinite. Human and djinn and angel all at once. The lilitu drew their power from this place, themselves little more than a moment. In constant pursuit of the next...

Bakr laughed at himself. He was making things up as he went along. Like always. He didn't actually know what he was talking about. Yet, Shaytana had said that all the time she had forced him to spend in this place had been preparing him to use his powers. So perhaps making things up was part of it. Lilith and lilu were style over substance, and they had plenty of substance. Perhaps that meant it was different for everyone.

What harm could it do to try?

There was only one person he wanted to talk to, to cause to dream about him. The thought of her churned his guts like stones caught in a waterwheel, but that didn't make it any less true. He needed to tell her what he had decided about the baby. He needed to ask her...

Bakr closed his eyes and let himself fall back. As gently as a hammock of cotton, the Nothing lowered him until he was lying horizontally, or perhaps it was just his orientation that changed. He could never be sure in this place.

It could not be far to nowhere, to *his* nowhere. It should take no time at all.

He thought about Sezan, about dreaming with her. Back when things were good between them, he would sneak into her room in the harem night after night until climbing that trellis was as natural as walking. And when he arrived, she would always be waiting—smiling and joking, or playfully scolding, or simply rushing to him without saying a word. Her room would be glowing with her rose fire, her magic creating a cocoon of silence so nobody would be able to hear them together. So many nights—conversations that went on until the sun came up, mind-bending sex, and falling asleep with her wrapped in his arms. She was the only woman he had ever been able to do that with, to be comfortable enough to just hold her. His arms would go numb and his back would twitch, and it wasn't the most restful sleep he'd ever had, but he'd never wanted to let her go.

He remembered laying with her back pressed against his chest, watching her eyelids twitch and wondering what she was dreaming about. When she woke, he would often ask her, but she almost never answered. She'd just smile and nuzzle into his chest.

He let her fire rise naturally in him as he opened his eyes. The whiteness expanded out from him like always, but there on the horizon was the tiniest flicker. He narrowed his eyes, focusing on it. A bubble drifted across the flat whiteness. His instinct was to run after it, but after what happened last time, he kept his feet planted where they were. Besides, there was no space here. He was as close to the bubble now as he would be if he ran for it. Everything was an illusion.

He lifted his hand and reached for it. It didn't rush closer, nor was he pulled to it. It simply began to grow, and he realized it had been right next to him all along. He narrowed his eyes at the image in the shine—too distorted to understand.

This wasn't a portal to his father's place between worlds, it was a way out of Shaytana's. But not a path to Qaf, or Ard, or any other world teeming with beings. When he looked at the little bubble, all he could feel was himself. This was the path to his own Namelessness, the place he kept getting stuck in when he moved between worlds.

It was his birthright.

Bakr brought up his blunt, calloused finger and popped the bubble.

The world around him changed instantly, and he found himself standing in a simple room. Some panels hung on the walls with twists of golden designs. Yellow curtains billowed around long, wide windows, the shimmering light of eight moons in the background, pulsing and twisting with mythical beauty. Save a huge circular rug made of the softest white fur, there was no furniture.

Sezan was sitting near the center, her legs kicked out to one side. Red silk pants and golden boots, a bodice of golden thread with an attached skirt that spilled out behind her like a crimson ocean. Long, audacious earrings of rubies and garnet. Her hair of starlight was brushed out and hanging loose, uncovered. Her makeup was impeccable.

Her eyes, shining with all the sunflower color they always had, darted quickly around the room, filling with shock and concern before they came to rest on him.

She blinked twice as if she were looking into the sun. "You're not Shaytana."

He shook his head and took a slow step closer. "You're not either, right?"

Sezan shuddered. "Just kill me if I ever am."

"Is it really you?"

She looked down her side, lifted a leg, then the other, then shrugged. "Last I checked. I don't think Fajar would have let me ride her otherwise."

He wanted to ask but was scared of getting lost on a tangent. There was so much he wanted to say, and it was so easy for them to get lost down dark circuitous tunnels that led to nowhere. Then again, they were already nowhere.

He moved closer and sat down on the rug, a few feet away so he wouldn't startle her. "I need to talk to you."

"I need to talk to you, too," she said, her amber eyes soft. "But Qadira is about to send Jahmil to war. He's acting crazy, yelling at Ayelet, and I had just called Shaytana to keep Qadira's men back from Fajar."

Every sentence was worse than the last, but Bakr shook his head and refused to ask. He had to do this. He had to stay focused.

"Don't worry. No time is passing. It will all be waiting for us." He looked down at his knees, at the black dirt under his nails, the thick knuckles. His tongue was trying to seize up again.

"I'm sorry about Ajmal," he said finally, though the words tasted sour. "I didn't actually kill him. Shaytana did. But I let you think I had. And I'm pretty sure I would have. So, I'm sorry."

He watched in his periphery as Sezan's eyes streamed around the room, then landed back on his face. "I did not beg for his life because I wanted him to live." She ran her fingers through the soft tufts of the rug. "Is this your version of his place? Your father's, I mean?"

"How do you...?" He swallowed a hard lump in his throat. He knew the answer without having to ask, and the guilt of drawing her close crashed over him again in waves. Just as it had been all those years ago when Rahik used her as a weapon against him. Just as Shaytana had. And now his father. Every horrible thing that had ever happened to her was his fault. He itched to send her away again, to fall back into himself and pretend that everything in her life could be fixed if he wasn't in it.

But it was far too late for that.

"Are you okay?" he asked. He wanted to take her hand. Instead, he pressed his dirty fingernails into his pants.

Her red lips twisted to the side, and she glanced away. "What am I doing here? I thought... I thought I'd have to hunt you down with a flaming bird for you to ever want to see me again."

"I'm sorry about what I said about the baby. I understand why you did what you did. I was just hoping you had come back for..." He looked up at her, at her eyes that watched him with the constancy of the sun. His jaw twitched, and he looked down. "That you'd changed your mind."

Sezan crawled within arm's reach. "I never changed my mind."

He chewed on his cheek, forcing back the jealousy that flared in his heart. "I understand. I just want you to know, I won't let anybody get to the fire, yours or your baby's. I'll keep it safe. I promise."

"I know," she said simply, twisting her lips to the other side. "Which is why I never changed my mind. You're the..." She shook her head. "You're going to hate—laugh at me in a minute. And it's okay because I know you'll take care of the baby's fire anyway."

"I need to tell you something," he said quickly, frightened that if he waited much longer, the words would flee from his tongue. "I never wanted to leave you. I mean, never. Everything just fell apart so quickly. And I won't say I didn't have a choice because that's a cop-out. I messed everything up, and then I didn't have the guts to just tell you the truth. This is all my fault."

Sezan scooted forward another inch. "I mean, that's partly true. One letter would have spared us all this drama," she said, but not in the angry way she used to.

"I never learned to read and write," he said, relieved to let go of the charade no matter how she might judge him. "And I couldn't dictate a letter to you through my military envoy. Not with everything that I needed to say. They would have found out, and I... and you're a princess... and I just couldn't."

Sezan chuckled, her chest shaking in small tremors of laughter. "It's a good thing you can't die because I have half a mind to kill you."

Goosebumps rose on his flesh, and his throat tightened as if he'd swallowed a fistful of rust. He turned his face down and covered his eyes with his hand, wishing he could hide. "Please don't laugh at me."

"I'm sorry," she said, her mirth dying down to a lopsided smile. "I'm not laughing at you. I was thinking about how Ayelet was right."

He furrowed his brow. "About what?"

"About how all these things we've been worrying about and hiding from each other don't change how I feel about you or any of this." She wiped her eyes, one at a time. "The truth is, I'm not the perfect woman you dated before the war. I blame Rahik's poison. But I make terrible mistakes now. Terrible decisions." The smile vanished.

His lips parted as a tremor raced through him. "You know about the poison? How did you...?" He pressed his face into his hands. "I never wanted you to find out about that."

"Stupid man."

"I put you in danger. Rahik made me sign that contract, but I knew that wouldn't be the end of it. The only way to protect you was to leave. But now..."

"I've decided that if you should still want to stay, or... just stay after what I have to tell you, that we need to be a little more honest. Only about the big things, mind you, like terrible contracts and poison and meetings with demons. You can still tell me my eyes shine like the sun when they clearly do not."

"They do. They still do. It never had anything to do with magic." He smiled quickly, then looked down again. "If by some insane miracle we survive all of this, you'd be willing to give me another chance? I mean, you're not getting married anymore." He chuckled dryly, then groaned. "It's not the baby's fault who its father is. I don't care. I want to be with you."

She looked at him, her eyes shining brighter than ever. "The contract with Ajmal is the only reason the baby belonged to the court of Ahmar. It was stupid. I was so upset about everything, about your anger and how you wouldn't tell me how you felt after Fajar showed me, that I..." Her breath caught in a little hiccup. "I didn't even read the contract."

Bakr smirked. "You didn't read it?"

"Not a single word. My name was mostly just an X I threw on the paper."

"I can't believe you," he scoffed and shook his head. "How could you, of all people, not read a contract before signing it? That's so incredibly stupid, it sounds like something I'd do."

She smirked but worry still ringed her eyes. "I blame you entirely for distracting me like that, you know. But it's not even what I'm most sorry about. If—no, *when* I tell you this next part, do you promise to at least still smile at me sometimes? Or wait to throw a chair across the room when I'm not around to see it? I love you too much to see you angry at me every day going forward." She looked up at him through her lashes. "It's okay if you can't."

"I don't see any chairs, so I guess so," he joked, though her nervous words were tightening around his heart like a noose. "What is it?"

"I want to be with you. To jump with you. I always have. And I... You... There's not another man's baby's fire inside you." She slapped a hand to her face and downcast her eyes. "The baby is yours. And I want us to be a family. But if you hate me, that's okay. I still want you and the child to have each other, and I can just watch you two and be happy enough." Her words tumbled faster and faster. "I'm sorry. I was so scared you would leave me as you did before the war. I should have trusted you more. You're the only person I have ever trusted." She lay her forehead on the carpet before him, her hair spilling out around her shoulders.

For a moment Bakr couldn't speak or move. He was barely breathing. And there wasn't a single thought in his head, just a harsh twisting in his stomach that slowly became less and less painful and more tingly. His jaw ached for something, anything to say. All that came out was, "What?"

She sat back up and moved so their knees slipped between each other. "You're the only man I have ever loved." She placed his hand on her cheek. "And this—" She took his other hand and placed it gently on her stomach. "—is only yours."

"You're certain?" he said, eyes darting from side to side. "You're not just saying that to make me feel better?"

"Would your father be trying to steal it if it weren't part-lilu? Ajmal was sterile." She said, her eyes so serious before a giggle escaped. "He was the worst. Why did you let that happen? You've ruined other men for me forever. I hope you're ready to take responsibility for that."

A smile filled his face that started at his eyes and barely tugged at his lips. Soft and aching. He pushed a strand of hair behind her ear, leaving his other hand on her belly. "I'm going to be a father?"

"I think Fajar would resent that statement," she said, all smiles. "But yes. A fantastic one."

He laughed and heat filled his eyes. He cupped her cheeks and leaned in to kiss her when a sudden, frozen chill blasted them. His back straightened, and Sezan started, her body falling against his chest. He wrapped her protectively in his arms as the color drained from the room, leaving only shades of gray. Then one by one, the light of eight moons began to go out. The cold in his bones, black and invisible, told him who it was, standing at the edge of this reality.

His father. He'd found them. Just like he had found him before in Shaytana's Name-lessness. And it was only a matter of moments before he broke in.

Bakr leaped to his feet, pulling Sezan up beside him, and put an arm around her. Her hand clung to his jacket, dark fear threatening to eclipse her eyes. The joy that had moments ago ripped away all his thoughts was blown clear, and he was left tumbling through a new reality.

The baby was his. That was why Shaytana wanted it, why his father wanted it, why everything in the world seemed to turn on the mention of its name. Not because it would be a prince, a pawn to use in a game of mortal politics. It was a rare new lilith or lilu, one of only ten to be born in three and a half thousand years.

His father had tormented his mother for years trying to produce more offspring, thinking maybe she was something special. And perhaps she was. What would he do to Sezan if he got his claws into her? It was clear from her words and the tinge of darkness in her expression that she had already met the monster. Bakr didn't want to think about what he might have done to her. The thought of her being tortured by his father, the way Shaytana had done to him these last two years, was paralyzing. And the thought of their child being stolen and brought up by those creatures, molded to be just like them... There was no word like anger, or fear, or disgust. Any amount of death would be better.

He couldn't let that happen. But what could he do to stop it? They were so powerful, and he was so...

He gripped Sezan's hand tightly, pulling strength from her. His father's power derived from this place. They had to get out. But there was nowhere to run. The Namelessness was everywhere.

Sezan squeezed his hand back. "I trust you."

He looked down at her, at her childlike eyes that gazed at him like he had the answers. His first instinct was to call her an idiot, to crush all that misplaced confidence. He bit it back. Where had his instincts ever gotten him?

"I don't know what to do," he said. "We have to get out, but they can follow us. They're everywhere."

"What about the floating city?"

"Perhaps it could buy us some time." The wind kicked up, carrying a voice on it. Roiling tremors of cruel laughter. Bakr lifted Sezan's chin and kissed her, stealing one final moment to inhale her beauty, knowing that he may never get another chance.

When he pulled away her eyes opened softly and gazed up at his. No magic, no armor, no lies. She did trust him, he realized. And he would not let her down. Never again.

"Where is Fajar?" he asked.

She groaned. "In the middle of Qadira's court surrounded by an army. I may have been in the middle of summoning Shaytana so I could slap her."

"Great work," he snarked. "Are you ready?"

"To jump?" She grinned. "Always."

His chest swelled. He pulled her tightly to him and let them fall.

CHAPTER FORTY

Sezan

Shifting between worlds with Bakr was incomparable. No mist like djinn fire. No smoke and glass like Fajar. Just wholeness. Being. Wrapped tightly in his arms and free of literally everything else. When they emerged upon Fajar's back, she almost wished they could fall between worlds together forever.

Qadira's screaming broke the spell. Fajar screeched at the advancing soldiers who were too afraid to get near her ring of fire. The Rukh thrust out her wings, knocking out a regiment, and shook embers from her tail that tumbled along the floor setting everything afire. Sezan realized too late that Bakr had been right: no time had passed, and Shaytana had popped into the battle before them. Her little fur dress barely clung to her bony frame, and an onyx ring glinted on her finger as the amulet swung around her neck. How had Shaytana ended up with Ajmal's ring? Bakr pulled her behind him as they prepared to take flight.

"This looks fun," Shaytana said, her eyes sweeping the chaos. But when she looked up at Fajar and saw Bakr mounted on her back, Sezan clinging to him from behind, the pink in her eyes spread to an eclipse, leaving nothing but hot anger.

Sezan tightened her grip around Bakr. "She looks madder than usual. You did something, didn't you?"

The muscles in his back tightened. "I might have proposed."

She let go and slapped the side of his head. "I've been waiting for you to propose for years, and you give that demon a ring, instead?"

"I was wondering what took you so long, lover. We almost missed the party," said Shaytana, the coolness in her eyes returning as she gazed up at Bakr. But she didn't approach, keeping her distance from the massive, flaming figure of Fajar just like everyone else. "Come on down here, darling, and bring that ugly cow with you."

"Yes, Bakr," Sezan said dryly. "Bring me down."

He glanced back at Sezan. Her fire flickered in his eyes in a rainbow of emotions, all of it emblazoned on a black background; the taste of fear in his skin, in his breath. Sweat on his brow. Still, the constancy of familiar jade held through it all and held her as it always had. She almost felt bad, making him squirm as he tried to explain himself.

He grabbed her arm and said through clenched teeth. "I did give her a ring."

"How could you?" Sezan frowned so deep it bordered on comical and put a hand to her chest, tapping the finger on which she wore the stinging copper ring. She had to fight hard not to let herself smile. "I said I trusted you."

"He made his choice, honey," said Shaytana, cocking one hip. "Clearly, it wasn't very difficult."

Sezan felt Fajar's thoughts pulsing in the back of her brain, promising that she was ready to fly at any moment. And she was tempted. Oh, she was tempted. To hold Bakr back and take to the skies. To run forever and never go back, leaving a bright purple and screaming Qadira and her hoard of scattered soldiers behind. Ditching Shaytana who flicked her eyes irritatedly between Fajar's flaming embers leaving scorch marks on the floor and Qadira's occasional attempts to exact pitiful revenge by throwing something at them. But she knew he could never fully be with her, never live a life safe for himself or his child if he did not come to terms with Shaytana first.

Bakr held tight to Sezan's arm as he guided her from Fajar's back, sliding down her massive, outstretched wing until both their feet touched stone. Then keeping his eyes on the tiles, he walked her towards Shaytana. Sezan tugged and pulled, dug her heels into the ground, and kicked him in the calf, knowing she couldn't hurt him, not physically.

Halfway there, Qadira decided she had had enough. She stormed over, a flaming poker from the grand fireplace in her hand, her light green fire flicking down the sapphire stick. She swung it up behind Shaytana's head and struck. Sezan held a wishful breath, but before it landed, the lilith grinned and shot her hand up. She yanked the poker from Qadira's hand and swung around, swiping the hot tip across the queen's cheeks. Red sprung from the purple. Qadira shrieked and shot her eyes wide open. The slapped a hand to her cheek, her lips trembling, then raised her chin and refused to admit she had met her match.

"You are as empty and pointless as a sea in Jahannam. And as dull as the shine in a human's eyes," Qadira spat. "All of you are!" She swept her eyes upon Bakr and Sezan.

Shaytana *hmphed* and tossed the poker to the floor as Qadira twitched. Then, the queen, holding her hand against the blood flowing from her cheek, turned and walked away as if she had never approached in the first place. Her shrill cries broke over the chaos, allowing her men to take a step farther back from Fajar and the lilith while blocking off all the exits. A brief reprieve, surely, while the queen figured out how best not to suffer another indignity in her own court.

Bakr and Sezan arrived before Shaytana. He twisted her arm behind her back and pushed her down to her knees. It didn't hurt, the angle at which he moved the arm more awkward than anything. But she winced anyway.

"What should we do with her until the baby is born?" he asked, his hand still heavy on her shoulder. "We can't just leave her wandering around free to do as she likes."

Shaytana walked up to Bakr and wrapped her arms around his neck. Her intense floral smell assaulted Sezan's nostrils, striking her with the urge to vomit.

Shaytana kissed him, pressing her tongue into his mouth and nibbling on his bottom lip. An intense, sexual kiss that looked like it wanted to be so much more. One of her hands played in his hair as the other snuck inside his jacket to stroke his abs. Sezan really was going to lose her stomach.

Finally, Shaytana pulled back and said, "She doesn't technically need her limbs to have a baby."

Sezan gritted her teeth. If Bakr's plan was for her to draw Shaytana's sleazy powers, Sezan needed to want something from her, and she wasn't sure wanting the lilith to die a slow, painful death counted.

He laced his hand around Shaytana's waist, pulling her body flush with his. The movement was so easy and natural it sent a shiver down Sezan's spine.

"She told me that the baby was mine," said Bakr. "Is that true?"

The skin around the demon's eyes tightened, then she clapped her gaze to Sezan's face. "Why do you insist on ruining all of my surprises?"

"Because I hate you," Sezan said with a glare. "And I think you're ugly."

"Now, we all know that isn't true," she said, but a twitch in her upper lip betrayed irritation. "And why would you hate me, boo? All I've ever done is exactly what you asked me to do. Is it my fault you were drunk when we made our deal?"

"You're just lucky I was committing haram and drunk at the time, otherwise your disgusting face would have frightened me off. I don't know how Bakr stands to touch you. You have to be the most hideous lilith or lilu I have ever seen. Compared to Bakr and his father..." She sighed. "Even if I went both ways, I wouldn't touch you. That's why Bakr likes it better when you look like me, right? Isn't that what you said?"

Shaytana rubbed her canine with her tongue in a menacing look, then turned to look at Bakr. "I was joking before about cutting her limbs off. Now, I'm definitely doing it." She made a move toward Sezan, but Bakr held her back.

"There's no reason to hurt her," he said, sounding like he was in pain. Sezan's chest squeezed with memories of the lilith's power over him, but she forced them down. She trusted him. She trusted that he would protect the baby and her. That he wouldn't succumb to the demon's power. Even so, a milky sourness swam in her belly and up her throat.

"There you go again, defending her," snapped Shaytana. "You never stop defending her. No matter how much she lies to you, or tortures you, or makes you wish you were dead. You've got a real problem, you know that?" She laughed in his face. "Maybe it's worth keeping her around just to see you look so pathetic."

"You sound jealous," Sezan said, forcing a smirk. "Too bad I got to him first." But the lilith's words cut little slivers into her every pore, reminding her they were the same in so many ways, dusting her heart once more in doubt. She clenched her fists and forced herself to focus. She was getting caught up in Shaytana's games. Still, no matter what she threw on the list, she wanted nothing from the horrid creature. Not even her magic, if it would make her evil like that.

"Oh, honey," Shaytana said, pressing her lips into a sympathetic pout. She pushed off from Bakr's chest so forcefully he stumbled and walked towards Sezan. "He'd already slept with half of Qaf by the time he met you. The only reason you were ever anything remotely special is because you happen to be Jahmil's sister. Back then, Bakr was so desperate to pretend he was a real Shihalan, he would have fallen in love with the wallpaper if he thought it would secure his position." She smirked and cocked her head to the side. "You were just convenient."

A clap of anger rolled through Sezan's muscles, and she was tempted to look at Bakr, to see if it was true, but she didn't want to know. It didn't matter, right? The past? They were moving on. "At least I was a choice and not forced down his throat like your disgusting tongue."

"My lover adores my tongue like he does every part of me. Do you know how many times he has called for me in the middle of the night, begged me to come to him and make him feel the intensity of the universe like only a lilith can?" She laughed and pressed her palms into her knees as she leaned down to look at Sezan's face. "Do you know what he did immediately after your little argument in the palace?" She paused and lifted her eyebrows. "Me."

Sezan's hands shook with each thud of her heartbeat. She gave in to her weakness and flashed her eyes to Bakr. "Why?"

His eyes touched hers quickly, and she knew it was true. He turned away and pressed the bridge of his nose into his fingertips. "I just wanted to feel something... else. Anything other than anger."

"You see?" said Shaytana, settling into a superior smirk. "He plays with you, but when he really needs something, he comes to me. And do you know why that is?"

Sezan stood, taking her eyes off Bakr and his shame, and turned blades of quicksilver on Shaytana. "Why?" she muscled out through her teeth.

"Because I know everything about him. I've seen inside his soul. I've taken a tour of his heart. I know everything he loves, everything he hates, everything he's afraid of. I've experienced his memories. I am close to him in a way you never could be."

The demon's words emptied her heart of everything she believed and filled it up with a shattering white light. She pressed her fingers close together so she could feel the cool burn of copper and smiled. "Thank you, Shaytana." Then, to make sure she took every last piece of the monster's power, she threw her arms around her in a tight embrace and yearned with all her heart to have what Shaytana did. A look into Bakr's soul.

She waited for the cold lightning to strike her bones as she muttered the spell, but the copper ring was warm, buzzing through her blood like the purr of a kitten. She pressed the bony, writhing little body of Shaytana harder against her chest and closed her eyes. And much like with Fajar, she began to see Bakr. As a child begging for love from a cruel, tormented mother. As a teen, begging bread off strangers in the streets of Shihala so he wouldn't starve. As a soldier begging for the life of his men. And as Shaytana's prisoner begging for her to stop, to keep going, to feel anything but how he felt. And it broke Sezan's heart. But light began to swirl in with the dark. Of Fajar, the first one to truly love him. Of Jahmil, who took him in without exception for all that he was. And of her, who he had dreamed of every day since they had met.

As quickly as these realities and dreams and hopes and fears poured into her soul, they stopped. Shaytana screamed as she plunged dagger-sharp nails into Sezan's back, shredding her sequined bodice, her skin, and further on into her muscle. Sezan clung to her for as long as she could, never wanting to give up the gift she received. Never. But the nails grew longer, tearing through her insides as they reached towards her beating heart. Then a blanket of strange dreams chewed at her vision, threatening her sanity in the same way Bakr's father had in his dream place. She gasped and let go, falling to the earth as the copper fell silent upon her finger. The pulse of agony filled her vision.

Shaytana stumbled back, breath heaving in her chest. Then she put the finger that wore the onyx ring in her mouth and bit it off with her sharp teeth. She spat it across the room, thick black, liquid pouring from the wound. With her own blood dripping from her mouth, her eyes focused on Sezan. She marched forward, raising the claws on her uninjured hand. Sezan flinched as she brought them down, but the blow did not connect. When she looked up, she saw Bakr standing between them and holding both of Shaytana's fragile wrists in his hands.

The demon fumed and writhed in his grasp, but did not have the strength anymore to push him off. He turned his eyes to Sezan, black smoke pooling in his gaze as he took in the blood from her wounds. Then without a word, he and Shaytana disappeared.

She was alone once more, dying, as Bakr left to fight a war without saying goodbye. She lay her head back on the glass-covered tile and stared up at Ahmar's sky through the broken dome. Stars blurred in her vision. Moons passed into fading light. This time, she knew why he had left, so she let her eyes shut out the light. He would come back. He would.

CHAPTER FORTY-ONE

Bakr

A BRIGHT ARABIAN SUN struck his eyes like fire as he landed hard on the hot sand. He pushed himself up on his hands and knees. The dunes moved like the waves of an ocean, lifting and crashing and then disappearing into themselves again. The sky was pale blue. No clouds, just an expanse that went on for eternity in every direction. A fire burned low near his feet, consuming ordinary wood—smokey and human. For a moment, he couldn't remember how he had come here or why, reality as formless as the vast desert. Nothingness, and everything he had ever known.

No, not nothingness. *Namelessness.* Shaytana had brought them back to her home and made it look like his. What game was she playing this time?

Memories of Sezan's blood brought him back to himself, the way she had screamed when the silver claws cut into her. And him, standing aside and watching. Paralyzed and powerless to help. Powerless, always powerless. For all his posturing, all his authority, all the men who had looked to him for guidance over the years, starting in the woods of Vespar and ending in the hills of Orkeshi, he had never felt like he wielded any power. He saw himself as a pretender, constantly hiding behind his own bravado and praying, praying that he would never be found out.

A figure shimmered on the horizon, flickering into existence. A mirage. An illusion. Yet these things were as real to him as everything else. Dreams and lies and things unseen had dictated his life from the very beginning. He gazed at it as it moved closer, only fully coming into his sight when she was standing a few feet away.

The body concealed under a sea of dull rags. Her mouth concealed so only her eyes remained. His mother's dark brown eyes that had never looked at him with anything but hatred and fear. Not because of who he was; that had never mattered. It was *what* he was—a sack of dirty blood that should never have been born. The child of a monster. A lilu.

He knew she wasn't real, no more real than the heat bubbling on the back of his neck. No more real than the tremendous sense of longing he felt when he looked at her. She had never been able to love him. All he had wanted in his life was for her to love him. But she didn't and she never would. And so he had come to believe nobody ever could.

"I see you, Shaytana," Bakr said, keeping his eyes on the passionless face. He drew the sword from his hip. "No more games."

"You would raise a weapon to your own mother?" she said, but the voice wasn't right. It was both of their voices—Shaytana's and the memory of a voice—wrapped together into a single horrific tonic.

"I don't have a mother," he said, letting the blade rest easily against his leg. "And I don't need one."

"You will do the same to your own child as she did to you. You are not capable of loving something that looks back at you with your own eyes."

Shaytana knew what the mention of his mother did to him, how vulnerable it made him feel. But it would not work this time. Sezan loved him. Loved him in spite of everything. Knew who he was on the inside with all his broken parts and still wanted him. They were about to have a child together. And he was not going to let his child grow up the way he did. No father, and a mother who was broken by what the father did to her. Sezan was going to survive and thrive and live to forget about all of this. And he was going to be there for her and her child. *Their* child. He was going to find a way to uphold them from all the filth on the ground that worked to sully their very existence. He would give his family the safety, love, freedom, and understanding that neither he nor Sezan had ever had. And he would not bring his demon with him.

"My mother gave me life, which is as much as you ever gave me." He lifted the sword and pointed it at her chest. "I don't need either of you anymore."

Rage flashed pink in the dark eyes, and the disguise fell away piece by excruciating piece—a suit of skin and blood rotting and dropping like autumn leaves. Bakr wanted to look away, but that was what she expected. He would not turn his head from her torments.

He would not fold in on himself. He had as much power here as she did, and she didn't get to control the landscape or the conversation anymore.

The nameless world shifted as easily as sand, whipping around him in a hot, violent swirl that bit at his skin. His body should have tumbled with such harsh winds, but he stayed fixed. The world changed as always, but he refused to change his own heart to meet it.

Bakr felt his body slip beyond the confines of Shaytana's world back into the expansiveness of reality. He was on his back, gazing up at the glittering sky of Qaf. The First Moon rose in the southern sky, sending shivers of light across the waving ocean of Bahamut. He still laid in sand, but now it sparkled like shards of crystal and was cold on his bare skin.

Shaytana was on top of him, her hands pinning down his. It was exactly as it had been that night—the night she accidentally showed him too much of herself and he learned her name. She was naked—beautiful and terrible. But his guts did not twist with longing, nor did his heart retreat in fear. He looked at her plainly, perhaps for the first time seeing her as she was.

This was not an illusion. Here on the shores of the Sea of Bahamut was the place that meant more to her than any other. She'd never told him why. It didn't matter.

"I cannot believe I fell for such a transparent trick—you asking me to marry you," she scoffed, her eyes fixed on his, daring him to keep looking, daring him to turn away. He watched the pink sparkling in her eyes, but it was duller than ever before. Sezan may have only taken a portion of her power, but now it was easy to see the weakness in her. He felt the cool touch of metal at his side: his sword still tied at his hip.

"You love me," Bakr said. Not a question or an accusation. He could see it clearly now, as much as any other truth or illusion. As clear as the crystal stars flashing in the sky beyond her shoulders.

She laughed in his face, as she often did. But it was transparent. "You're a delusional fool."

"This is the place you told me that you loved me, even if you didn't mean to. Even if I didn't realize that it had happened."

"That was a stupid accident," she spat. "It's your lilu half. I underestimated it. I wasn't paying enough attention. I left myself open…"

"Exactly," he cut her off. "You opened yourself up to me. You allowed me to see inside of you, things no one is ever meant to see. You wanted me to see it. And now you've brought me back here because you want to show me more."

"You've lost your mind."

"I remember everything about that night..." he whispered. "Lying right here in this sand."

"You can try to charm me as much as you want, muffin, but it's not going to change anything." She bared her teeth in a cruel smile. "I am still going to murder your little whore. And I am going to make you pay for this. All of it."

"Do you know what I saw when I looked inside your heart, Shaytana?" He rolled her over in the sand, pushing her down under him. She struggled, but she wasn't strong enough to throw him off. Not anymore.

He leaned in close to her face, gazing uncompromisingly into her eyes. "I saw emptiness. A broken and numb soul crying out to a god that has forgotten it. Three and a half thousand years of loneliness. Disillusionment with the empty promise of immortality. And desperation for something new, different, and meaningful to come along and bring you back to life."

Shaytana furrowed her brow and opened her lips to respond. All that escaped was, "Bakr..."

"That's why you wanted me," he said, silently drawing his sword from the scabbard. "I made you feel something. Not much, because you are more dead than alive. But when you touched me, or made me cry, or scream, or laugh, or moan, and lived vicariously through me, you felt something. And you decided I was the answer, at least for a while. Being in love was something you had never done before. A novelty. And when you found out about the baby, you realized there was another experience you had never had in three and a half thousand years." He reached down and stroked her cheek. "You wanted to be a mother."

"It could still work, Bakr," she said, silently acknowledging the truth of everything he had said. "If we just get rid of that meddling, little djinn."

He shook his head slowly. "There's only one problem with your plan, Shaytana."

"What is it? Whatever it is, we can fix it. Together. Tell me."

"I despise you." He plunged his sword into her side. She gagged and struggled to get away, but he held her down with the weight of his body. Black blood oozed from her lips and her eyes bugged out. He stared at her face, tears forming in his as he twisted the blade, burrowing it through her like a drill. Her lip quivered and her face contorted, a mixture of pain and shock and anger. And, finally, something he had not expected: relief.

He held the blade in place, listening to the beat of her heart—a strange three-four rhythm that was completely inhuman and alive as everything. It sped up and then slowly began to taper off. He cupped her face in his hand, then shook his head and pulled back. She tried once again to speak but all that came out was more blood.

Bakr stood and yanked his sword out of her gut. Shaytana rolled onto her hands and knees and started to crawl, trying to get away from him. He let his foot land heavy on her back.

"Bakr!" she screamed, cracked and flaking like old cement.

"Goodbye, Shaytana." With a deep inhale, he brought up the blade and stabbed it through her heart.

Silence wrapped around him like a blanket of ice, his guts twisted in horror at what he had done. But something stronger held him upright, like a soft summer wind. He took a slow deep breath and then heaved it out.

He bent to pick up the blood-stained Seal and put it around his neck. Then he picked up the body. It was both as light as air and as cold as ice.

Bakr carried the body to the sea, which glowed pale blue with the power of the Bahamut, the Immortal One.

"Take her," he said, lifting her to the waves like a sacrifice. Then he swung the body back and forth and bunted her out into the sea. The waves caught her and swallowed her up. He couldn't say why exactly, but somehow he knew that the Great Bahamut would find her and gobble her up, a final end to her immortal torment. She deserved nothing more and nothing less than death, real death. A death that finally allowed her to become a part of the nothingness that she carried inside of her.

Bakr took a step back from the surf, then stumbled and fell to his knees. He felt like a monster who had just committed sacrilege. Or suicide. Some combination of the two. A part of himself was in that grave with her. And though it was something that deserved to die, something that had needed to die for so very long, he wept for it. For the hatred and the loneliness and the desperation. For his past and everything that had defined him for so long. His breath began to quicken, and the cries morphed into deep, throaty laughter that filled his belly.

She was gone. After all this time and everything she had put him through, he had finally done it.

He was free. Free to be whatever he wanted. And everything he wanted was back in Ahmar. He closed his eyes, thinking only of Sezan, and reached again for the power of his blood. It responded instantaneously, and he slipped back into his own empty space.

CHAPTER FORTY-TWO

SEZAN

WHEN THE BLOOD FIRST flowed from Sezan's back, she had cringed, focusing solely on the sticky warmth matting her hair and the smell of iron heavy in her nostrils that made her sick. It was her way of coping. Of not thinking about how every breath that drew her closer to death brought her baby closer with her.

The time oozing from her felt like an eternity but had probably only been seconds, like the lilu nothingness, only sharper. She closed her eyes to rest for a moment, just a moment, then felt as though she were being lifted without hands. Warmth encircled her, the prick of magic seeping into her wounds all the way through bone and ragged flesh down to where they scraped the back of her lungs. A tugging followed, like her insides were being laced together; invisible strings crossing over and cinching shut again and again until her wound was sealed.

Her body revolted against the unearthly feeling, but there was no way to resist or bolt upright. Nowhere to lean on or to fall off of. And in her exhausted, weakened mind, Sezan knew where she was, though this time it didn't seem so bad. Tricks, probably, she told herself. But the aura of safety and warmth felt so real. And just as she thought of him, he appeared. Bakr. Shining and bright and smiling at her like he hadn't seen her in years and had thought of nothing else.

He came next to her, floating or walking—it didn't matter—and slipped a hand under her head. "It's okay, now," he said, voice husky with emotion. "You are safe."

She closed her eyes, happy to press her head into his hand as they floated, floated, floated. How long had passed? She startled awake, not realizing she had closed her eyes, but he was still there, smiling.

"What happened to Shaytana?"

"Gone."

She glanced at his eyes and saw only jade.

"How?"

"You don't want to know," he said with a chuckle that filled the surrounding silence.

She caught her eyelids from slipping closed again. "So we can be a family now?"

He placed his other hand on her cheek and leaned in. "I don't see why not." Then he kissed her. Powerful, intoxicating, yes, but un-human and with none of Bakr.

She pulled away, gasping, and clawed at the darkness. This time, her hands could find no purchase, her feet no hold. She simply struggled in limbo as Bakr's eyes brightened to a splendidly vivid green.

"I'll work on my technique," he said, morphing into the hauntingly handsome face of Bakr's father. "I don't usually deign to play human, even half—it's below me—but I get hungry at the thought of you so compliant, so trusting when I pretend to be him." His eyes glittered with terrifying malice. "And now that you have so much of Shaytana's magic flowing under that silky skin of yours, you'll take a lot longer to break. Both mentally and physically." He flashed white teeth.

Fear pressed against the back of her skull like the blade of a spear, tearing, cracking, and jabbing to get into her mind, to take over her body. She gritted her teeth and held on. Pushed back. If she expected Bakr to fight, she must do the same. The lilu might have saved her life for the sake of his grandchild, but she would not ingratiate herself to him or feel as if she owed him anything.

"Let's make a deal, lilu," she said.

He sneered, his perfect lips ugly for the first time. "And why would I make a deal with you?"

"Because he is coming."

"Who, Bakr?" The lilu laughed so hard the nothingness shook. "You put a lot of faith in as shallow a lilu as ever there was, and one who's left you time and time again."

"I do," she said simply. "He will be here soon."

"You don't even know what *soon* is." The lilu's laughter stretched into a yawn. "And he has no idea where you are."

"Then make a bet. If Bakr shows up, you tell me your name."

"Ha!" He spat. "And if he fails, forever tumbling through Shaytana's dreams never thinking of you again?"

"Then I will stay with you."

"I don't want you," he scoffed, glaring at her through the sides of his eyes. "I want the baby."

"See, I can't make that deal. I already signed Bakr's baby away once, and if I do so again—when he shows up, making me the winner—he'll bring up my carelessness forever. Besides, I know you do want me. The temptation to make a child with your full blood and the half of Shaytana's magic I have is too much to pass up. You said so yourself, putting you at a disadvantage."

The lilu considered her for a moment, head cocked to the right and a finger on his chin. "The disadvantage is yours, considering I already have you."

Sezan kept up her smile, for once grateful for the poise her mother had ingrained in her for just such occasions. "But do you have Bakr?"

The lilu smirked and scoffed. "The boy's a lost cause. A real shame."

"Because of that pesky human side, right?"

"I'm listening." The demon leaned in, his green eyes shining.

"You tried to get rid of that part by killing me off last time, but that was never going to work. First, because you placed your hopes on Rahik, and second, because Bakr is, well, too human to let something like that go."

The lilu flashed his teeth. "I'm well aware of the shortcomings in that particular plan."

"So what *would* destroy Bakr?"

The lilu rolled his eyes. "I don't appreciate word games, djinn. Get on with it."

"Me loving you, instead. Now, you could pull that off with the Seal of Sulayman, but you lost that, too." She sucked breath in through her teeth and shook her head as if it were an awful shame. "Embarrassing."

"Shall I un-sew your wounds stitch by stitch?" the lilu snarled, his teeth looking more like fangs.

"You could," she replied calmly, meeting his eyes. "Or you could make this deal. If he doesn't show up because he's too busy with Shaytana, I will devote myself to only you."

His smile turned cruelly in the corners. "Tell me more."

She swallowed back the ever-present bile in her throat and tilted her chin up. It did not matter what she said. Bakr would come. "I will call your name in the night, lilu. I will tell

Bakr you are my only love and kiss you more passionately than I ever kissed him. I will sigh with pleasure as you try to break me—" The words nearly caught in her throat, but she pushed through. "—and beg for more."

"And what are the terms?" he asked, his eyes sliding up and down her frame and casting a harsher chill than the Zabriyan mountains. "Shall we bind the contract on the penalty of death?"

She kept her eyes on his, unflinching. "Can a contract even kill a lilu?"

His smile widened. "If only you had my name to find out."

"Not death." She shook her head. "Nothingness."

"This, you mean?" he cackled, spreading his arms wide. "My home? That is hardly punishment."

Sezan looked at him, through him. "Perhaps not now. Perhaps not in a century, or five. But stuck here with no dreams, no victims, no family, and no way out, I believe you'll wish we had made the terms death."

"I'm not giving him an eternity to show up," the lilu said, his voice losing its glassy charm. "He has until the rise of the First Moon."

"Fine," Sezan said, smiling. "Does that mean we're stepping into Qaf?"

"No," he snipped, brushing his fingers through his black hair. "I changed my mind. Five degrees on the mark of a timepiece." A globe appeared, stars and moons moving slowly across its surface in an inky, silver pattern.

"Fine," she said again, sighing with her own impatience. "Are you satisfied?"

A glint flashed through his eyes, cruel and dark. "I accept your terms."

"Superb. Quill please?"

The lilu smirked, and a silver quill that looked as if it could cut diamonds appeared in the air before her.

"Parchment, too."

This time a roll of the eyes accompanied parchment, a bottle of ink, wax and the magic needed for the Seal of Elm. "Happy?"

"Mhm." She set to work writing a simple contract before signing her name at the bottom. "Your turn," she said when done, pushing the paper through the nothingness toward him.

The quill vanished, reappearing in his hand. He narrowed his eyes at her suspiciously, writing his name so the Seal of Elm flashed with its binding magic.

"Fantastic," she said, wanting to pat the demon like a pup.

He growled and rolled it up so she could not see what the name he had jotted down in ink. It didn't matter. The contract stipulated she would know it soon enough.

Immediately, in fact.

She grinned as a light shimmered behind him in the dark. At first a tiny bubble, the opalescent sphere grew into all she'd ever wanted. Right on time.

"Woman," Bakr snapped, folding his arms across his chest, "are you seriously making another bet with a demon?"

"I placed my bet on you this time. That's hardly a gamble."

A wide, energetic smile overtook his face, glimmering bright white even in the darkness.

The lilu's head snapped around and a snarl escaped his lips. "All these years I've been waiting for a visit, and you choose *now* to show up?"

"And why not?" Bakr took Sezan's hands and lifted her to his side. "One time is as good as any other in this place." He looked down at her and pressed a hand against her cheek. Hidden in his grasp she caught a glimpse of the Seal of Sulayman, just as she had hoped.

"I believe you owe me a name now," she said, looking at the lilu as she leaned into Bakr. "Or imprisonment in your own darkness forever. Whichever you prefer."

The lilu clenched his fist and grated his teeth side to side, then everything fell smooth. He smiled. "A deal's a deal, gorgeous. I am Asrastar."

"Very good," Sezan said, then she turned to Bakr. "Quill? I doubt your father will let me borrow his again."

He smiled and took one out of his pocket and handed it to her along with the Seal. Then he furrowed his brow and patted himself down. "Damn it. I forgot paper."

"Can't you just..." She waved her hand about. "Magic some or something? Or shall I tattoo it into your skin next to Fajar?"

He pushed his lips forward in thought, then nodded. Ripping off his jacket, he rolled up his sleeve and put his arm out to her. "That way we'll never lose it."

Sezan looked between Asrastar's raised brow and Bakr's confidence. She shrugged. "It's an unusual medium for a contract, even by Elm's standards." She pressed the nib of the quill into his skin, worried she would hurt him. When he didn't flinch, she continued so his magic bound with the ink and imprinted upon him with a hint of rose fire.

"What are you doing?" Asrastar asked, an edge to his silky voice.

"Making sure you never come to visit, baba," said Bakr, showing him a wide, snakelike smile.

Sezan inked the Seal.

"We had a deal," Asrastar hissed. He blinked out and reappeared near them. He reached for Sezan, but Bakr snatched his hand.

She grinned and pressed the Seal into Bakr's skin.

Nothing happened. Panic gripped her. She had felt certain the Seal of Sulayman would be enough.

Then suddenly Bakr barked out a laugh. "Goodbye, baba," he said.

Asrastar snarled, his green eyes blazing with white-hot rage. He lunged at them.

Sezan flinched and clenched her eyes shut, but she was already falling through nothingness. Falling without mist or fire or any desire to ever stop.

When they landed, bright green flashed through her vision. Bakr stood before her, holding her. The impression of the Seal and the contract she'd written on his arm showed like molten gold.

They were back in Bakr's bedroom at Karzusan. She breathed the stale smell of old hashish, but forced her stomach still, determined to enjoy the moment. "It worked."

"Of course, it worked." He grinned and petted the hair back from her eyes.

"I thought you wanted to return to Ard?"

"Without saying goodbye? I wouldn't do that."

"I'm glad to see you've finally had some sense slapped into you." She wrapped her arms around his waist and breathed in his spice. "Are you sure you want to see Jahmil while he's on a rampage?"

"I sort of do. And I think you have a lot of writing to do before we take that thing back."

Sezan looked to the rusty Seal that fit in Bakr's palm as if made only for him. "I'm not sure of everything Shaytana broke, but I can try."

He shrugged. "Just write every deal Shaytana made is null and void." He wiggled his eyebrows at her. "Are you impressed? I learned some contract talk."

She bit her bottom lip and stretched up to kiss him. "I have never found you more attractive." Then she paused. "Well, maybe that one time in the hot springs."

He ran the back of his hand over her cheek, gazing down into her eyes. "Will you stay with me this time?"

"I plan to never let you out of my sight again. But I can ink it if you'd like," she smiled coyly and lifted his hand with the Seal. "I'm kind of jealous I don't have a permanent place on your body yet."

"You're inside of me." He pressed his forehead against hers. "I know you need to take your fire back, but maybe you could leave just a flicker. So if you ever have any doubts, you'll always be able to look in my eyes and know that you belong there."

She ran a finger across his jaw and tugged at the hair on the back of his neck. "It's the least I can do to return the favor."

He beamed at her. "Fajar's on her way here, I can feel it. So, we'll write all the contracts, pacify poor Jahmil, then get out of politics forever, right? I mean, who needs this? We've got a baby to worry about."

"And so many things to do before it's born. Like jump off Almawt Peak, or swim the Isles of Jasraib, or see what else lies on the path to the sun."

His impossibly wide smile somehow widened. He snatched her up and threw her down on the bed, coming down on top of her. He kissed her hard, holding her cheek with his hand and drinking her in as if she were water and he was about to die of thirst.

"Can we steal a moment before fixing all this crap?" he said through quick, hurried breaths. "Five degrees, that's all I need." He ran his hands hungrily over her hips and kissed the spot on her neck just under her ear. "Maybe ten." He rose up to look into her eyes, that eager desperate smile on his lips. "Give me twenty degrees, and then we can get back to it. You have my word."

"Come here." She giggled and yanked him closer by his collar. She kissed him, breathing him in with every part of herself. Then she pulled back, looked into his jade eyes, and said, "Words ruin everything."

GLOSSARY OF TERMS

PLACES:

Ahmar: one of the Nine Kingdoms of Qaf, ruled by Queen Qadira.

Ard: the world of humans, Earth

Ashkult: an internationally utilized, inescapable prison. Built in an area of Qaf where there is no magic.

Buhayra Ruwarin: the lake that surrounds The City of Pearls

Buhayrat Alzaybiq: the lake of quicksilver that surrounds Ashkult.

Eayima: floating island located on Ard. Legend claims it is where the Seal of Sulayman is housed.

Fyre: a small human kingdom in Ahmar, hidden in the mountains of Zabriya. Where drakonte come from.

Ghaluma: one of the Nine Kingdoms of Qaf, located on the Lower Continent. The location of Ashkult.

Izrak,: one of the Nine Kingdoms of Qaf, ruled by Queen Mapenuk

Karzusan: Capital of Shihala.

Orkeshi: mountainous borderlands between Shihala and Vespar.

Pamukkale: natural hot springs in Anatolia, the Ottoman Empire

Qaf: the world of the djinn.

Rananbar: a city at the borders of Shihala, Ahmar, and Vespar.

Shihala: one of the Nine Kingdoms of Qaf, ruled by Dowager Queen Zalika and her son, Prince Jahmil.

The City of Pearls: Capital of Ahmar.

Vespar: one of the Nine Kingdoms of Qaf, now a vassal state ruled jointly by Ahmar and Shihala.

Zabriya: one of the Nine Kingdoms of Qaf, located on the Lower Continent. A mountainous region.

QAFIAN TERMS:

Bahamut - giant, immortal, all-knowing fish that lives in the waters surrounding Qaf.

Bial'dabaye - were-hyena.

Drakonte - giant snake with feathery wings. Used as a battle mount by the Shihalan military. Originally from Fyre.

Khanaziri - a kind of Ghaluman pig-dog with a venomous bite. The milk is used to make siq'rulak, a kind of alcohol and the national drink of Ghaluma.

Makan Majhul - The Namelessness

Namur - giant cat used for riding

Qawiun - a tree that grows in Izrak. Its flowers can be used to make a powerful explosive.

Shujai root, helps with wrinkles

Tset aldhayle - six-tailed foxes, children of the stars. These swift and intelligent creatures are used to deliver mail in many parts of Qaf.

Uptka - a very fast fish

Zinbur - a kind of giant wasp

ARABIC PHRASES:

Adhhab mae Allah - go with God

Alhamdulillah - thank God/praise God

Allah yahmini - God protect me

As-salamu alaykum - Peace be upon you (hello)

Astaghfirullah - God forgive me

Bihaqi alsama' - for heaven's sake

Bismillah - in the name of God

Inshallah - hopefully, God willing

Kun hadi - be calm/calm down

La 'atamanā - I hope not?

Lā 'ilāha 'illā-llāh - there is no God but Allah

La'anaha Allah - God damn it

La' samah allah - God forbid

Sallah-llahu 'alayhi wa-salam - peace be upon him (used in reference to the Prophet Muhammad)

Takun 'alā al-salam - be at peace

Tarajae – retreat

Wallahi - I swear to God

Ya Allah - oh my god

Yalak min 'ahmaq - you fool

OTHER ARABIC WORDS/TERMS:

Abnay - my son

Akhi - my brother

Al'abalah - idiot

Alkalba - dog (f)

Amir, amiri - prince, my prince

Amira, amirti - princess, my princess

Anisa - companion, friend

Aşkım - my love (Turkish)

Eaziziun - beloved

Eben khaltee - cousin

Eimlaq - giant

Ghabi - stupid

Habibi (m) / habibati (f) - my dear/darling, also used between friends

Hinfia - spigot, sink

Jahannam - hell

Jamilati (f) - beautiful one

Jahnmi - infernal

Majnun - crazy [one]

Malikati - my queen

Marhabaan - hello

Muhbat - frustrating(ly)

Muqayada - barter, exchange

Musikh - monster

Naqli - move

Nasaar - a charm against the Evil Eye

Nikah - part of a Muslim wedding ceremony

Parasang - a Persian unit of measurement, about 6 km

Saeed - friend

Sayida(t) - lady, miss

Sheikh/sheikha - a noble man/woman of high importance, just below a prince/princess.

Tahanina - greetings

Taw'um alruwh - soulmates

Taw'um nar - fire mates

Wali - Islamic Saint [Sufism]

Ya amar - my moon

CURSE WORDS:

Al'ama - blindness (damn it)

Alqarf - excrement

Allaena

Bihaqi aljahima - what the hell?

Eaqduk allaein

Ealayk allaena

Sakhif

Sharmouta - whore/prostitute

THE FIVE DIRECTIONS:

Bahamut, Janu'ub, Sharq, Gharb, and Shamaal

GUIDE TO DJINN EYE COLORS

Black: Fear. Mist swirling in the eyes

Blue: Hope, Anticipation

Green: Jealousy, Envy

Purple: Sadness, Grief, Despair

Gold: Happiness, Joy

Pink: Anxiety, Nervousness

Red: Lust. Glows in pupils

Silver: Compassion, Commiseration

White: Shock, Surprise. Lines like lightning

Yellow: Disgust, Disdain, Loathing

Orange: Embarrassment, Humiliation

Copper: Confidence, Bravery, Pride

Brown: Malice

Gray: Awe, Amazement

Eyes are Clear: Honesty, Forthrightness

Eyes flash with bright light: Anger

Colors do not match what is being said: Deceit

THE EIGHT MOONS OF QAF

Time:

Time is measured in degrees based on the orbit of the First Moon. One degree is equal to roughly four minutes. And 15 degrees is equally to roughly one hour.

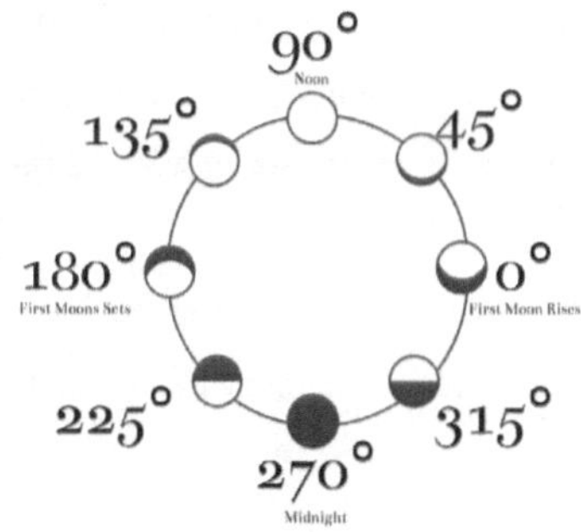

The Eight Moons of Qaf

- **The First Moon:**

A rough, rusty sphere of copper. The First Moon is the largest and brightest of the eight, taking up a full eighth of the sky when it is full. The path of the First Moon is the Qafian equivalent of 'daylight' and it is their main means of telling time. It comes up in the sharq and sets over the Bahamut Sea.

- **The Second Moon:**

Quick-moving silver moon that passes through the sky about ten and half times every 360 degrees. This moon follows the first moon, rising sharq and setting bahamut.

- **The Third Moon:**

Pale pink, this moon crosses the sky perpendicular to the first moon, bouncing back and forth as it chases the swish of the Bahamut's tail. It rises janu'ub/gharb to shamaal. It is common lore that the Bahamut's former lover lives on this celestial body, pulling and yearning for its true love and creating the Qafian tides. The position of the third moon is preferred for telling time because it is always visible except for when it dips behind each horizon.

- **The Fourth Moon (Lover's Moon):**

A dim yellow, this moon is nearly impossible to see when the First Moon is out. It only shines brightly during Qaf's *night.* It is often referred to when saying people are up to no good because only criminals, ne'er do wells, and lovers stay up late enough to see the Fourth Moon.

This moon passes twice for every single pass of the First Moon, once during Qaf's day unseen, then once through Qaf's night when visible. This moon rises sharq/shamaal to bahamut/shamaal.

- **The Fifth Moon (Witch's Moon):**

The witch's moon of soft green that passes through the sky five times, following the Five Winds and crossing the sky 45 degrees (or 3 hours in Ard equivalence) at a time (with another 45 degrees to pass over to the other side beneath Qaf).

It starts sharq and crosses to bahamut, then rises in janu'ub and sets shamaal, then rises gharb and sets sharq, then inverts and rises bahamut and sets janu'ub, then rises shamaal and sets gharb, then rises sharq and sets bahamut like it started. This follows a 405 degree (or 27 hour)/27 day pentagon cycle and is difficult to track. It is the fortune teller's moon as they track its erratic behavior through the heavens and is often associated with Saqueia and the 5 Winds.

- **The Sixth Moon:**

A soft-white moon that crosses the sky three times, 30 degrees after the rise of the First Moon, 60 degrees after midday, and at midnight. It travels from janu'ub to shamaal on each pass. It is the easiest moon to tell time by, has a medium heat, and most resembles Ard's moon.

- **The Seventh Moon (Shadow Moon):**

This moon appears in odd years as a black circle in the sky that blots out the stars but does not give off any of its own light or heat. It takes an entire year to pass over the sky, and then is gone for an entire year. The measurement of Qaf's year and the seasons are determined by the movements of this moon.

It rises sharq/shamaal and sets gharb, dividing the upper and lower continents. It separates them but also forces them to look toward each other whenever they look at it and reminds them they share Qaf. Wars take place more often in the year this moon is hidden. It is also believed by some that it gives off no heat or light because it is the servant of a celestial that is dead or away or because the celestial they serve is.

- **The Eighth Moon:**

A rare bright blue moon that only rises once every thirteen years—The Festival of the Eighth Moon. It rises janu'ub and sets bahamut/shamaal, rising directly behind Fyre. Every 130 years the appearance of the eighth moon will coincide with every other moon being visible in the sky. This is the "Festival of the Eight Moons," Qaf's most important holiday as it only comes once in most djinn's lifetimes.

It is the warmest moon, and Fyrans believe it serves the Origin, gaining its power from beneath Qaf like lava and only appearing rarely as a reminder to Qaf that the Origin is equal in power to the Bahamut, Celestials, and other minor deities.

- **The Moonless Night:**

Every fourteen cycles of the First Moon in a shadow year of the Seventh Moon comes The Moonless Night, when all of the Eight Moons of Qaf are hidden beyond the horizon. During this time, all heat is sucked from the land and the stars shine their brightest. It does not last the whole night.

ABOUT THE AUTHORS

Kyro Dean has written over 20 novels, including The Baron's Ghost, which can be found on Kindle Vella.

In addition to her works for Eight Moons Publishing, she owns and edits for the blog, Vanilla Grass Writing Resources.

She loves to speak and present and has shared her knowledge at many conferences. When not writing, she loves spending time with her delightfully curious children and talking with her plants, though they often give terrible advice.

Check out her website.Or check her out on social media (Twitter and Insta): @kyro_dean

Laya V Smith writes books because she doesn't know how not to.

Her debut novel, "The Lumbermill," won the 2021 Maxy Award for Best Thriller, was a finalist for 2021 IAN Award for Best Debut Novel, and an editor's pick on BestThril lers.com. She is the co-author of The Fires of Qaf, a series of epic fantasy romance novels by Eight Moons Publishing.

Other than reading, writing, and researching the past, Laya enjoys stand-up comedy, terrible movies, ugly dogs, red wine, stinky cheese, travel, and spending time with her friends and family.

Her website: https://layavsmith.com/

Find Laya on Twitter, Insta, and all over the internet @layavsmith